THE PAPER DOLL MUSEUM

ABIGAIL PADGETT

To Marguerite Close

"How can we know the dancer from the dance?"

(W. B. Yeats)

and

In Memoriam:

Ace Marchant

1948-2012

"One good thing about music, when it hits you,
you feel no pain."

(Bob Marley)

Chapter One

Bad Moon Rising

Creedence Clearwater Revival

The Seventeen Palms Plaza looks like every shopping mall in the world, except that it's in San Diego and so has real palm trees in the upper parking lot. That August morning was airless and brutally hot, but for a moment I heard the skittering of invisible autumn leaves blown by a chilly wind. A scent of persimmons drifted across the baking asphalt and then vanished. I headed for the underground garage and ignored the damn leaves and persimmons, which were impossible.

The ramp into the garage was abruptly dark and felt like a theatrical set. Maybe a Hall of Mirrors, only something's not right. You expect the funny metallic odor, but who's that blind old woman holding a dead fox, reflected in the mirror that makes you look like an overpacked bratwurst? And why is she pointing a gnarled finger at *you*? The Seventeen Palms was feeling like that.

Lately the whole world was feeling like that, but if I'd paid more attention I might have been prepared, or at least less *un*prepared, for the thing that appeared after lunch. Which was a grown-up version of the ghoul I thought had died inside the wallpaper of my childhood bedroom. And my first step on the White Road.

I know. Ghouls and white roads? At the time I thought the same thing. I assumed I was losing my mind.

I parked in the underground garage to protect my stash of fun-size Butterfingers from dissolving in the convection-oven California glare and sprinted up the escalator past three multiply-pierced teenagers and a woman in purple rain boots drinking an iced latte. I made note of the purple boots because by then I was obsessively taking note of everything. No one wears rain-oriented footgear in San Diego because it never rains enough to bother. The boots were incongruous and I figured anything incongruous might be significant. Not that taking note was doing any good.

The escalator beneath my feet seemed to hum the first line of "Beach Baby" over and over, filling the air with an ominous nostalgia. Southern California was the cutting-edge of oblivion back in the 60's and 70's, all surfboard cool, drawing the young to gather on beaches and ride out a looming paradigm shift that would in a single generation make strangers of their tech-savvy offspring. It was the in place to be, then, and I never got around to going anywhere else. Not that it would have mattered.

A recently-retired high school English teacher, I've been, at least to all outward appearances, a living monument to existential calm for decades. Faking existential calm isn't that difficult once you get the hang of it, and I had the usual direction from a set of disturbingly wholesome parents. Plus a single encounter with a mad grandmother who in one brief conversation told me everything I needed to know.

"Hide, sweetie!" the dying old woman grinned knowledgably when at thirteen I was driven a hundred and twenty miles to visit, only once, a grandmother I hadn't known existed. "Hide inside life for as long as you can. At some point there won't be anywhere left to hide, that's just the way it works. Hide, but get ready."

"Ready for what?" I asked, bewildered by the hospital smells and an oddly eager detachment I felt pulling at the tattered form on the railed bed. Death. The woman seemed less like a grandmother than a zany cousin you adore because she started smoking at nine and tells you what *really* happened between Uncle

Hal and Aunt Jenny before he went to prison and she joined a cult that makes hammocks out of old pantyhose. I liked my grandmother immediately, but it was obvious there wasn't going to be time to say much.

The ancient head jerked with effort as my mother's mother wrenched her gaze from some apparently delightful vision buried in the wall of her room. She chuckled at my white Keds and Pendleton skirt.

"It's coming," she said. "Just keep your eyes open."

"Grandma," I answered, one hand touching her hot, white hair and the other wrapped tight to an aluminum bed bar, "What's coming? Keep my eyes open for *what*?"

"Oh, you'll see," replied the woman for whom I had been named. And then she grinned like a kid getting a puppy, all big-eyed with instant connection, and reached both liver-spotted hands toward something invisible. Something beyond the mint green hospital wall. Aislinn Taylor did not speak again and fifteen minutes later a young doctor in a crew cut and Old Spice pronounced her dead.

By whining at my parents for months about denying me the joy of a relationship with my crazy grandmother, I neatly hid the fact that I understood *perfectly* what the strange old woman meant about hiding inside life. I'd already figured that out. Learning to conform is a developmental task of adolescence and at thirteen I was way ahead of the pack. What scared me was the suggestion that it wouldn't work forever. That someday "fitting in" would dissolve in dusty shreds like a curtain hung over an attic window in the previous century. And then what?

Fifty years later, I was about to find out.

While I'm not a thundering bore, you basically wouldn't notice me on the street. Long ago I perfected social accommodation to a high art and it's served me well. I know how to "fit." Of course there have been occasional events that I never discussed, but they were infrequent and easily ignored. But then everything changed.

It started in my dance class a couple of weeks before the day of the purple rain boots when I hurried to meet my friend Jude for a quick lunch. That class two weeks earlier was no different than a hundred others, the studio cool and dim, its mirrored wall innocent of preternatural images. Pan pipes and cellos, basic New-Agey music. We were doing an exercise in which everybody is supposed to dash around reaching for stars. A little silly, but I was used to it and dutifully stretched one arm and then the other toward the acoustic-tiled ceiling. But instead of feeling the usual draft from the air-conditioning, I felt a moment in time. The awareness coursed down my arms and filled my mind for only a few seconds, but it was there. It was a moment from my past, a fragment of a long ago summer day. I could smell hot pavement and a banana Popsicle. I was riding my bike, going to the library, warm wind pushing at my face as the Popsicle melted all over my hand.

It was as if the child I had been were still alive somewhere, and had come back, drawn by music in a dim suburban dance studio. I remained my terribly adult self while I was also another self in a forgotten world. A world in which I *knew* the pallid department store mannequins propped on metal rods at J. C. Penney's came to life at night. Or at least did things when no one was looking. In that world I could fly sometimes, although not very high and only by running really fast on rainy nights beside a particular iron fence a couple of blocks from my house. The child I had been lived with facts I'd forgotten. But they were still facts.

I wasn't alarmed and thought it was sort of pleasant, in the way a half-forgotten scent can unleash little home movies in your mind. Except something was wrong in the mirrors. Where there should have been a roomful of reflected dancers there was only a distorted screen of wallpaper, little maroon flowers, blurry now, with a ceiling border of acanthus leaves fading in and out of focus. I recognized the wallpaper. It had decorated my childhood bedroom. And I recognized the shape oozing like oily smoke from beneath the acanthus leaves, wormlike and huge, writhing down the wall to coil beneath my bed. As a child I sensed its hunger to catch me. I would be devoured, liquefied in the crush of its embrace. I would no longer exist, and my childish terror was paralyzing.

But in the dance studio I was no child. I shook my head at the ghost of a forgotten nightmare and blinked. The mirrors again reflected nothing but what was there. A bunch of women in t-shirts and yoga pants, dancing barefoot on a wooden floor. The wallpaper monster was only a memory and bore an aura of finality, like something you know you'll never see again. And yet it felt like a warning.

The experience was weird but fleeting and, as the human mind does with events that fail to fit accepted reality, I dismissed it as the effect of sweat in my eyes and oxygen deprivation. Or the antibiotic I was taking after having a root canal. Or something.

But after that, the *things* began to happen. Just little things at first. I heard Reznicek's *Donna Diana Overture* in the shower (where there is no radio, CD player, iPod – nothing). Until then I'd totally forgotten "Sergeant Preston of the Yukon" and could think of no reason to remember an obscure radio drama I loved as a kid. But the theme music brought it back. Starving shadow puppets in fedoras slid down the walls of my bedroom at 4:00 a.m., and for one whole day, everywhere I went I could smell Midnight in Paris perfume. There was a morning when twigs of light falling through a Venetian blind arranged themselves into an alphabet, trying to spell words across galaxies of swirling dust, but none of the words made any sense. And then there was the art exhibit where I saw a cat dash under the ornate tablecloth in a Rembrandt painting. I am not a cat person and don't even notice *real* cats.

Of course these things were delusions of some kind. I told myself they had to be symptoms of a transitory chemical imbalance. An illness. Something I picked up from eating mercury-infested tuna or cheddar laced with bovine growth hormones. But behind my rationalizations lay the pervasive nightmare of my age cohort – "Oh no, don't let it be an early stage of the unspeakable!" The stage just before you sauté your car keys with chanterelle mushrooms for a risotto, pack the whole mess in a freezer bag you put in the mailbox and then stand around in the driveway staring at your car as if it were a beached manatee. To say that I was scared sets a new standard for understatement. But I was committed to heroic efforts at denial and control despite secretly having a dicey track record with both. And there was the echo of my grandmother's warning.

On the day I had lunch with Jude the weird things would get way weirder, although of course I didn't know that. What I knew was that I was late for lunch. But next to the Lotus Blossom Chinese Bistro is a bookstore, and something in the window caught my attention. It was a book lying beside a butter churn holding a single huge flower with petals made of tattered lace. *Secret Addictions*, the book was called.   A sign in gothic lettering repeated the subtitle, "A guide to escaping the bondage of secrets that have died."

The book was definitely odd. It might be one of the *things*.

But it wasn't a thing. It was just a self-help program for people who can't stop collecting antique surgical equipment or vintage mayonnaise labels. There was a brief chapter on each of a hundred potential collectibles and its long-lost secret. Victorian seed catalogues, depression-era tap shoes, dinnerware from vanished hotels and sunken ships. I wasn't sure if my collection of Poe's "The Raven" in twenty-eight languages, twenty-seven of which I can't read, would count. I bought the book anyway and headed for the restaurant. I was edging toward basket case and figured anything might be helpful.

A man who looked old enough to have voted for FDR was seated at a table near the door when I dashed into the café. Tall, gangly and dressed like a silent movie cowboy complete with chaps and spurs, he smiled at me engagingly as I waved to Jude over an aquarium in which neon tetras swam in shoals around a smiling Buddha.

Oh great. A total stranger and he thinks he knows me from all those fun-filled meetings of the Lillian Gish Fan Club.

Other people attract strays, the occasional lost dog or cat. My strays tend to the unusual. Like the half-dead armadillo I found under my deck last February, probably an escapee from a nearby medical research facility. I named it Churchill and nursed it back to health on a diet of ants and hardboiled eggs. Then I drove the seven day round trip from San Diego to Walker County, Texas, in order to release it in an armadillo-rich area where it could socialize, maybe even find someone and settle down. A community newspaper did one of those heartwarming local-color stories about my trip, and for months I was inundated with funding appeals from animal rights organizations. I was used to the attentions of strays, but the old cowboy was off the chart.

Jude was reading the menu as I flung myself into a chair across from her. I was still aware of the man's intense gaze. He seemed gentle. There was nothing threatening about him. Nobody *that* old could threaten much except maybe falling on you in the middle of a heart attack. I noticed that behind round, wire-frame glasses his eyes were violet and matched his *faux* ostrich-skin cowboy boots. Basic urban weirdo, but there was an aura of business about him. He seemed to be there for a reason.

"What do you suppose 'unrobed eels' would be?" Jude asked, checking her lipstick reflected in the blade of her knife. "I'm trying to imagine a robed eel, and failing. I mean, an eel robe would just be sort of a *tube*, wouldn't it?"

I glanced at the thirteen-page handwritten menu for the thousandth time. On the cover is a suggestive watercolor of a pink lotus done in the style of Georgia O'Keefe. I am one of a group of women who've known each other since God was in Pampers. The Lotus is our hangout and for years we sifted through countless adjectives to describe the flower, finally selecting "wanton." Cute. Privately we call ourselves The Syndicate of the Wanton Menu.

Over Jude's shoulder I could see pearl snaps on the cowboy's yoked shirt flashing in the sun like little dots of light on the video maps airlines display for passengers to keep them from asking, "Where are we?" Toy plane silhouette on a yoke of lights from Boston to London, for example, suspended over a black abyss labeled "Atlantic Ocean." So no member of a tense and time-addled flight crew ever has to reveal the disturbing truth that, in fact, "We are nowhere." Nowhere was feeling about right to me.

The cowboy's hair was white, wavy and worn parted in the middle. He looked like a daguerreotype, one of the stiffly posed photos of stern-looking ancestors framed on the stairway walls of my childhood home. Except my Lutheran ancestors had all elected black serge over cowhide chaps, and this guy didn't look stern. His eyes sparkled with interest and, I sensed, urgency. Knotted about his neck was a yellow silk scarf, and on the table beside his teapot was a high-crowned white cowboy hat. When I looked at him he inclined his head slightly in courteous acknowledgement, as if we were supposed to meet. The cowboy was going to turn out to be one of the things. I fought back a by-now-familiar combination of irritation and complete panic.

"Eels, yuck!" I told Jude, trying for normalcy. "And 'unrobed' probably means skinned. Naked, their eelness exposed, every nerve hanging out..."

"Tay!" she interrupted. "Stop. I'm getting the shrimp fried rice."

"I knew that. Everyone knew that. You always get the shrimp fried rice. And don't turn around, but I want you to check out this cowboy at the table behind you."

"*Cowboy?*" Jude whispered, grinning. "Tay, I've read about this. It's a syndrome. Older woman, husband dumps her for some D-cup bimbo and she compensates by sleeping with inappropriate men. The exterminator, a guy who raises earthworms in his bathtub, her grown son's third grade soccer coach who's now a sales rep for designer wheelchairs. She doesn't even like these guys, see? The idea is, she uses herself to get even with her husband. It's deadly."

Jude is a goldmine of pop culture information gleaned from Internet chat rooms with names like "Boomer Dating" and "Sexy Sixty." I saw no point in reminding her that I've been divorced for so long I've forgotten football. Or that I don't even have an exterminator. Instead I gave my order to a waitress in a green silk cheongsam and matching garden clogs while feigning interest in the restaurant's muzak, a Chinese version of Elvis Presley's "Love Me Tender." The singer was accompanied by hammered dulcimer and what sounded like small birds pecking at discount wine glasses. Odd but relaxing.

I glanced at the cowboy again, who was reading a newspaper folded horizontally at the center. I thought I saw a headline saying, "Babe Ruth Dead, Yanks Retire Number Three Forever" but the text was upside-down so I wasn't sure. My father wore a black armband on August sixteenth every year to commemorate the baseball player's death, but the event meant nothing to me. An impossible headline now, clearly another *thing*.

The cowboy was nodding to the waitress for his check as Jude continued her lecture about women who are poisoned by unexpressed grief.

"Shhh... he's leaving," I whispered. "The cowboy. Drop your fork or something so you can turn around or you'll miss him!"

Jude knocked her fork, the menu and half an egg roll off the table.

"I just said *fork*."

"Senile dementia," she answered seconds later. "He's got to be a hundred and probably escaped from the locked wing of a ritzy retirement center. Thinks he's Hopalong Cassidy. Impressive posture and his tan's real, not a spray, but you can do better than this, Tay. It will help if you start wearing something besides t-shirts and yoga pants. I mean, that look is so... athletic. At our age men are looking for a suggestion of substance. Tasteful diamond earrings, primo bag, keys to the Mercedes on a whimsical little eighteen karat key ring."

The man was gone, but the nod he gave me as he ducked out the door was unmistakably expectant, even encouraging. A "rah-rah, go get 'em, we're counting on you" kind of nod, the sort teachers (including me) affect before passing out the culturally biased standardized tests that will determine everyone's future. The message was senseless. There is no test involved in eating lunch. The message existed only in my disintegrating brain. I wondered how long I had until friends and family noticed my derangement and began to murmur softly about "assisted living communities." With "secure" units.

I'd drag it out for as long as possible, I decided. At least a few more weeks. I was pretty sure I could fake sanity for that long.

Chapter Two

Hello Darkness, My Old Friend

Simon and Garfunkel

I rallied immediately, presenting my most sane face to Jude. "At our age men are looking for somebody with a conservative stock portfolio and good health insurance, and I *have* substance," I said after the waitress brought our food. Mine was the same eggplant with garlic and lobster sauce I've been ordering for years and I'd take most of it home since I couldn't really eat before my dance class anyway. We were all in a rut, I thought while nibbling a teaspoonful of eggplant. Me, my friends, our husbands and ex-husbands, everybody. All moving like hypnotized gophers through one wide rut in which everyone orders the same thing at Chinese restaurants, over and over. I imagined once-picturesque ponds filling with silt and cloaked in foamy green scum. The ponds were brains. We were all doomed, and I would be the first to succumb. To scum. The idea was unacceptable.

"Did I tell you my article on Poe was published last week? A university journal, small but prestigious, and..."

"Yes, several times," Jude interrupted. "You're smart. We've been knowing that. But how is this going to make your life *interesting*?"

I was tempted to reveal just how *interesting* my life was becoming, but for the twentieth time thought better of it. Jude would freak out, burst into tears and then start making calls on her cell phone to former boyfriends who were psychiatrists. I grew up in the Midwest and as a consequence am pathologically independent. Either the creepy things would stop happening or I'd call the psychiatrists myself. Until then world-class discretion was called for.

Jude cocked an eyebrow, sensing the unsaid.

"Look, Tay, I know something's going on with you. Just tell me. Behind several marriages and careers ranging from vegetarian pet food sales to my current position in aircraft housekeeping, you know I cannot be shocked. Did I tell you I found an actual chastity belt while I was cleaning a private jet yesterday? Gorgeous thing, copper filigree with black suede trim. Museum quality. The jet belongs to an Argentinean beef millionaire who obviously knows where to shop. So what's happening?"

"Nothing's happening, Jude," I lied.

Unless you mean the fact that I'm living in a horror movie.

Judith Shapiro has called herself "Jude" since 1968 when the Beatles' "Hey, Jude" hit the charts, and she considers the line, "Don't you know that it's the fool who plays it cool…" her personal creed. Jude is anti-cool. She dresses as if every day were a racetrack opening and nobody can remember what color her dramatically frosted blonde mane was originally. But everyone agrees that at least Jude can *focus*. She was focused now.

"Tay," she lectured, jabbing a shrimp on a chopstick into the air for emphasis, "you're married for centuries to the adorable, jug-eared Boy Next Door and then one day you find sex toys in his sock drawer. Overnight he moves in with an account executive for some fly-by-night company with offices in unpronounceable countries. Suddenly *they're* traveling to every fabulous place on the planet *you* always wanted to see but never did because you were raising kids and teaching high school English forever so the kids could go to Harvard. Now they're all gone and you're retired, past sixty and addicted to eggplant. Stop pretending this is how you thought it would turn out."

Jude is my best friend and it wasn't her fault she was so off the mark. But I was glad it was almost time for my dance class.

"'For all we live to know is known, And all we seek to keep hath flown?'" I quoted dramatically. "Poe. Come on, Jude. Eggplant is rich in potassium and nobody went to Harvard. Kevin went to Brown, scholarships all the way, didn't cost us a cent. And Beth, as you know, also never went to Harvard but has attended almost every university in Southern California without ever graduating or even selecting a major. I'm hoping that by her fortieth birthday…"

"And how is husband John, the Servant of Righteousness?" Jude asked, one eyebrow arching disdainfully. "Still rolling holy and making babies for the greater glory?"

After a teenage pregnancy and countless disastrous relationships, my daughter Beth finally married an annoying religious fanatic named John, who is a perennial source of concern to the Syndicate.

"I think Beth's pregnant again but she hasn't told me yet. She says she's happy, Jude. Some women are just… like that. Who are we to question?"

Outside the restaurant's front windows I thought I saw the top of a cowboy hat, its pale shape wavering in the glare.

"We are the freaking *goddess*, is who," Jude hissed with enthusiasm. "We've been around the block so many times we can do it blindfolded backward in beach thongs during a terrorist attack while singing every word of 'Lollipop' in perfect four-part harmony. We've seen it all, which is why we *are* who questions!"

You have to love her.

"Well said, Jude! Now read your fortune cookie."

"An empty shoe holds many stories," she recited. "Clearly I

am meant to seek a shoe. Or shoes. Something for the 50's dance at the club tonight. You're going, right? Do you have a date?"

"No date and of course I'm going. I have to dance to Jerry Lee Lewis doing 'Great Balls of Fire' while wearing a garter belt and a cone bra at least one more time in my life. I mean me, not Jerry Lee."

"Goodness, gracious," Jude sang. "So kinky either way! A shame you didn't hit it off with... what was his name... Al? What does your cookie say?"

"His name was Ali and he was very open about the fact that he's looking for an *additional* wife to supervise his college-age children – I think he said he has eighteen in all – children, not wives - who are studying in the U.S. His offer was quite lucrative, but I declined. Jude, I don't know where you find these guys you keep fixing me up with, but could we call a moratorium?"

"An Internet dating service," she said, glancing at her watch as if she'd just remembered she was late for life-saving surgery. "I sort of put your picture up, and a little about you..."

"You *what*? Jude!"

"Don't worry. It was just a free trial subscription, only lasts for a month. It's over now. Look at your cookie."

I smashed my sugar-paste half moon and drew out the paper strip.

"A new path emerges. Beware," I read, feeling a chill as shadows from a passing group outside draped the table like a Dali clock.

Jude sniffed in disdain.

"Too weird. Mine's better. Shoes are definitely better."

I loaded my eggplant into a takeout box, rolled my fortune into a tight ball and dropped it into a vase on the table holding a single silk rose. On the vase was a red dragon that looked more like a dachshund with scales and tiny, vestigial wings. The dragon didn't seem interested in devouring the peculiar message, but at least it was out of my hands. I thought. Erroneously.

At 12:45 the mall was a kaleidoscope of blinding sunlight reflected from car windows, framed by flowerbeds and palm trees. I jammed sunglasses over the huge green eyes I regard as my best feature and glanced at myself in the window of a card shop. Beth's teenage pregnancy, now my thirteen-year-old grandson TJ, had selected the shades because they were "awesome." Oval and darkly trendy, they make me look like an aging rock singer photographed scuttling into rehab for the fortieth time. But I thought maybe with my spiky salt and pepper hair I really could pass for some interesting has-been. The idea of being somebody else was appealing. Audrey Hepburn would be nice, except she was dead.

Even though I've been going to these dance classes for over six years, I'm not what you'd call "into" fitness. It was cheaper than therapy during the divorce and I developed a taste for it. At first I was surprised that moving strenuously for an hour and fifteen minutes *with* music could make you feel better than just sitting around and listening to it. Endorphins or something. But since the day I reached into thin air and became myself as a child, I suspect there may be more to it than that.

The health club dance studio was cool and quiet as I walked in, a windowless chamber that always felt safe, a haven. Its mirrored wall reflected fifteen barefoot women ranging in age from college students to great-grandmothers Some of the regulars are professional dancers but most are like me, women who would scream and rend their garments before going near a Stairmaster but will exercise if decent music is involved. Everyone wore black yoga pants and tops in sleeve lengths chosen on the basis of upper arm sag. Surveying the room, I thought again that a line of fashionable elastic bracelets worn to corral jiggling triceps might just catch on. Thousands of women would be happy at the chance to wear tank tops again. And I'd get rich.

"What routine are we doing today?" I asked Molly Palmer, the enviably buff fifty-something instructor who looks fourteen and sometimes sings along with the music in a husky alto. Molly's moods are mercurial and occasionally erupt in personal anecdotes that leave newcomers to the class in mild shock.

"My sniveling, manipulative sister called me this morning," Molly answered. "So we're doing something spiritual. I need to get above the need to unlist my phone."

Having heard bits of Molly's story over years of her dance classes, I had come to regard the aqua-eyed instructor as the heroine of several epic, if unwritten, novels. Molly might say anything, but it always sounds like the first line of a book club paperback. A different paperback every time. In idle moments I suspected her dramatic story lines might be a cover for something else, and wondered if she was in a witness protection program. Molly was... different.

Everyone sighed with relief at not being Molly's sister as I took my place that day after lunch with Jude, falling into the familiar trance, following the moves, letting the music take over. The patterns of the dance – front to back to side, jazz squares, Celtic stomps, relevés and martial arts punches and kicks – were hypnotic. I'd even grown accustomed to the ridiculous free dance segments in which Molly told us to be trees or jaguars or to chase our hands around the room. It was just music and exercise. Not a portal to delusion.

Molly brought me back to the moment, yelling, "Kick! Kick! Punch! Punch!" as we performed a martial arts sequence. I'd done it so many times it was second nature but was always amazed at my own image in the mirror, kicking and punching at thin air like a woman not to be messed with. The routine felt especially good now. Because something was definitely messing with me.

A visit to my doctor had been reassuring.

"I've run every test in the book and you're healthy," he told me. "Heart of a woman half your age, good bone density, excellent blood pressure and..."

"And I see cats in paintings," I interrupted. "Cats that aren't there."

"I can refer you to a specialist for a workup," he smiled, "but how do you know they're not there?"

The doctor's white lab coat smelled like my ironing board. Starch. And the sparse blond hair combed over his bald spot endowed him with qualities of a trusted uncle even though he's at least ten years younger than I am.

"Because they move," I answered. "Things in paintings do not move."

"Ah. Moving cats."

"Rembrandt," I said. *"The Prophet Jeremiah.* A cat ran under the table next to Jeremiah. It was only a split second, but..."

"Taylor," he said, "I'm an internist, not a neurologist, but I've been treating you for nearly twenty years and I know you. There's a syndrome similar to what you're describing associated with early stages of macular degeneration – sometimes people see elves and pretty landscapes that aren't there - but you don't have macular degeneration. And there's nothing to indicate the slightest cognitive problem. Everybody sees things - shadows, flashing lights, geometric shapes. They're floaters, changes in pressure on the optic nerve, reactions to infections, light sensitivity, visual exhaustion after too much reading. Imaginative people can make these optical events into all sorts of things. Like cats."

"It was a yellow tabby," I said. "And if the elves and pretty landscapes aren't there, why do people in the early stages of macular degeneration see them?"

"Just optical illusions," he said. "They go away after a while."

I wondered how everybody could have the same optical illusion, and thought it was a shame that the elves went away.

"And you're sure I'm not getting Alzheimer's or something?"

"I'm sure."

"Then I'll just have to live with these things?"

"Looks like it," my doctor said cheerfully.

Outside his office building I saw an actual cat stalking a paper cup in the burnt summer grass. "You're an optical illusion," I told it, but the cat was intent on its prey and didn't respond. "So I'll live with it," I concluded.

"You're floating through night skies, gathering stars," Molly directed in the darkened studio. "Reach, reach!"

I loved the haunting music and so tolerated yet another free dance segment in which everyone runs around the room like the chorus from *Giselle* suddenly released from any need to dance the same movements. Filmy shadows crossed the wooden floor as fifteen figures moved in erratic orbits, arms flung upward. The reaching was designed to improve muscle tone in the shoulders and back. I knew that. And the chantlike music was mesmerizing.

But not everyone was dancing. In a corner I glimpsed a solitary figure staring into the dimly-lit studio. Someone new to the class and not yet comfortable with its nonsensical aspects. An uptight corporate exec trying to lower blood pressure and stave off a nervous breakdown by exercising for the first time since her Girl Scout badge in hiking. Something like that. Except it wasn't a woman. Or a man.

The figure was of medium height and slightly stocky. It seemed oddly indistinct standing in the gloom beside a stack of yoga mats, fading in and out as the music soared and faceless dancers reached for stars only they could see. The figure appeared gnomelike one minute, vampire-elegant the next. And it was looking at me. I could feel it following my movements with malevolent interest as a scent of persimmons filled my nose. It was the smell of childhood autumns, not unlike that of peaches, but thicker and musky. The scent was strange, but worse was an uneasy sense of familiarity. The figure knew me. It had always known me.

It was one of the *things* and I was sick of it. I'd see another doctor, I decided. Okay, a psychiatrist. There must be medications…

The figure was moving. It had no feet but seemed to erupt forward like bubbling mud, leaving a trail of dirty light on the floor. It was coming toward me and suddenly I couldn't move. It was like the paralysis in dreams, where you can't run and can't scream no matter how desperately you try. The persimmon smell was so intense I could taste it and the thing wasn't going away.

It was moving toward me through the other dancers who seemed to avoid it instinctively, although of course they couldn't see it. They couldn't see it because it wasn't really there, I reminded myself through a mosquito-whine of panic in my ears. The apparition was a product of my own brain; I was definitely going crazy.

The thing was a thorny yellow shrub full of wasps that morphed into a diabolic plastic yard swan with no eyes. And then something like the undertaker with bad breath who when I was eight kept trying to get me to kiss the packed cheek of a Korean War hero in his casket before they closed the lid. The corpse had been my mother's cousin, but I'd never met him and wasn't about to kiss somebody dead. The undertaker had me by the shoulders and kept pushing me down into the face of a man in a military uniform wearing Betty Boop makeup. I could see the stitches where the soldier's painted lips were sewn shut, and I recoiled. I bit the undertaker's wrist and made everybody late getting to the graveyard while they fussed with bandages and he muttered about tetanus. The stuff of childhood nightmares. With women in yoga pants swirling around me, I figured I was finished. Time to call 911, turn myself in.

And then two things happened. The first was a crack in the studio doors. Someone was looking in, a voyeurism Molly did not tolerate. No one was allowed to observe her classes. You could participate or you could leave, but you couldn't stand around watching. But this time she didn't notice.

And the second was Molly suddenly at my side in the dark amid the moving dancers, her aqua-blue eyes rolled back and intent on the ceiling.

"Fight!" she whispered without looking at me. "You know the moves."

I am a grown woman. A *mature* woman. I exude the ineffable dignity of graying hair, of reading glasses, of experience. It is an aura that countless cultural myths insist will protect me. Grown, mature women do not fight, or need to. Grown, mature women are protected by layers of dignity. In that moment I realized what a load of crap it all was.

My sinuses were pounding with the odor of musky fruit as the source of the smell moved in sickening lurches through air grown dense with threat. The damn vaporous, bubbling thing was a depraved clown now, its ruined white face and single, painted tear a mockery of every grief I'd ever felt. My first dog, Ginger, dead in her basket. The baby I lost a year after Charlie and I got married. There were tears in my eyes, blurring my vision. I felt the thing laughing at me. It loathed me and was going to drag me to a hell beside which Dante's *Inferno* looks merely orderly.

In my hands and feet, in all the big muscles of my arms and legs I felt a wild strength I hadn't allowed since I was a child. Mindless, flailing outrage. Cold, murderous anger. A tantrum, but I could channel it now.

The thing had no right to be there! It was hideous and *wrong* in a sense I understood with primitive clarity. There were no words for what it was going to do to me.

"Get the hell OUT!" I breathed, moving toward it, kicking and punching hard. I'd done the martial arts moves a thousand times, feeling ridiculous. A bunch of mall rat women doing "Crouching Tiger" before rush hour. Please. But I'd learned. The thing might win, but I wasn't handing it over.

I stopped thinking then, felt nothing but childish fury pouring into the practiced moves, now directed at a melting clown made of garbage that came out of nowhere to destroy me. Kick side, turn, punch! Kick forward, turn, punch! Never hesitate, never look back.

I don't think anyone noticed my behavior except Molly, who moved away into the spinning dancers as the music faded to its close. The figure was in retreat now, its shape shifting and indistinct. At the corner where it first appeared, it simply vanished. My heart was pounding so hard I could feel it in my thumbs, and a sneering threat hung over the yoga mats for seconds before the studio's atmosphere slipped back to normal. Whatever it was, the sneer told me, the wretched thing was not vanquished. I would see it again.

And then the door moved quietly as the watcher departed. But just before the door clicked shut, in the sliver of light from the exercise room outside, I was certain I saw the brim of a pale ten-gallon hat.

After class I pulled on my shoes and approached Molly.

"What *was* that thing?" I asked, still shaking.

"What thing?" Molly said.

"The thing you told me to fight."

I could smell shampoo in her sweat-damp hair mixed with fresh air from the door as the others left. The air felt neutral, sane. Molly's aqua-blue eyes were blank.

"Stuff happens in here," she said, not meeting my look. "The dance, the music, it brings stuff up sometimes. I could see that you were afraid, is all. I could see that it was time for you to fight. And you did."

Then she grinned. "So who won?"

"I did, for now," I answered. "Thanks, Molly."

The late-summer shadows were long at midafternoon when I left the health club carrying a book I'd probably never read and a smelly white box of eggplant, the sky a cloudless watercolor wash. As usual I couldn't remember where I'd parked my car, but it didn't matter. I liked the dim grayness of the underground garage as I rode down the escalator. The gloom had solidity, purpose. I'd just walk around until I found my car. It wasn't far away. I could feel it nearby, waiting.

But when I saw the car, it wasn't alone. On the cement floor just in front of the left front tire was a graceful drape of color. I bent to pick it up and then looked sharply into the hundred shadows cast by empty vehicles. Nothing there but silence barely broken by the metallic wheeze and click of cooling engines. And the bright drape in my hand was the cowboy's yellow silk scarf.

Chapter Three

Bye Bye Miss American Pie

Don McLean

I wasn't sure what correct post-hallucinatory behavior was, so I just went home. The house is way too big for me now, but it possesses endearing qualities, not the least of which is being paid for. Should I fall on the proverbial hard times, I can survive by taking in ex-cons or unwed mothers or something. It's just your basic Southern California subdivision tract house. Three bedrooms, two baths. Huge kitchen where we knocked out the wall to the family room when the kids were still in grammar school. Nice deck in back I just had redone in some kind of fake-wood composite that supposedly tastes like hemlock to termites. I walked out onto the deck and watered my geraniums. Everything felt normal except for a low hum I assumed to be the aftermath of the stroke or whatever it was that just happened to me. A hallucination, clearly. And a stalker on top of it.

"All that we see or seem, is but a dream within a dream," I quoted Poe to the mass of pink *geranium maderense* edging the north side of the deck. They don't look at all like regular geraniums, but they're still geraniums. I searched for a message in that and felt like an idiot. RETIRED TEACHER DISCOVERS ENIGMATIC TRUTH IN BORDER PLANTINGS! But a couple of thoughts were beginning to take shape, slowly.

The first was that I should have driven myself straight to an emergency room and submitted to a battery of tests. I would have been admitted, asked to relinquish all belts and shoelaces and then allowed to call family and friends from the pay phone in a day room with Mylar-covered inspirational posters bolted to the walls. But I didn't, I just went home.

I didn't because the persimmon-scented thing and my response to it were real. I knew I wasn't crazy, but then I also knew that the inability to see your own departure from consensual reality is a significant hallmark of craziness. Still, I wanted to savor the experience. It was frightening and I was frightened, but also intrigued. As if I'd just seen a door in the middle of my living room wall. A door that had always been there; I'd just never *seen* it.

The thought had a precedent of sorts, a real door I never told anybody about. It was in a furnished house Charlie and I rented briefly ages ago. Just a small door on the third-floor landing, the stairs narrow and dusty. We slept on the second floor and never went up there, but one day I opened (Or did I just dream it?) that little half-door and crawled through into a large attic full of furniture and racks of old clothes. And at the end of the attic was a room - an office with a big desk, bookcases and a rug on the floor. There were ballpoint pens in a beer mug on the desk, and a pair of glasses left open atop a book, as if the occupant had just left. A man's glasses with tortoiseshell frames. And a cup of cold coffee. Not mold, not dried-out film left in the cup months before we moved in, but a cup of cold coffee. The place was currently in use!

Except that was impossible. There was no access to the attic except for the little door on the third floor landing and I was at home all day with newborn Kevin. I would have seen or heard anyone using the stairs or moving around up there, but in the six months we'd lived in that house I heard nothing and neither did Charlie, or he would have mentioned it. What I was seeing made no sense. It couldn't *be*, so I didn't exactly forget it, just shoved it aside. I never went up there again.

Thinking about that room forty years later, I reminded myself that it was obviously some kind of dream even though the memory felt real. I'd just had a baby, my hormones were in chaos, of course

I somehow conflated a dream with reality. I must have imagined that office in a nearly-inaccessible attic. Otherwise I'd have told Charlie, called the property owner, had the police up there to investigate, wouldn't I?

But I did none of those things. I did nothing and within a few days Charlie announced that his firm was sending him to Hawaii to do an emergency audit, and did I feel up to going along? I was thrilled. So we weaseled out of our lease and spent five months in a suburb of Honolulu called Makiki. Kevin likes to imagine that from his stroller at the park where we walked every day he watched the play of a toddler who would become the first black president of the United States. Little Barack Obama did live in Makiki then, but who knows whether or not he was ever in that park? Imagination is exhilarating, but scarcely reliable.

Thanks to Charlie, the CEO of the company he was auditing was indicted on charges of embezzlement and tax fraud. When the guy mentioned his inclination to put a contract out on Charlie's life, we quickly left Hawaii, returned to San Diego and rented another house in an area far from the one we'd left. I rarely thought of the impossible attic office in a half-forgotten rental, but when I did think of it, I knew it was there. It was no dream. But I never talked about it. There was no point.

What had just happened at the dance studio felt the same way.

The other thing I realized was that while the garbage-clown I'd kicked and punched into a corner belonged to me like a secret door in my own house, the cowboy didn't. The cowboy was part of the rational world. A stranger, he'd followed me to the dance studio; he knew my car; and he left his scarf as a calling card. I was being stalked by a hundred-year-old man in fake fur chaps. Weird, but I knew what to do. I had friends, police, the whole "normal" world with me on that one. I decided to run it by the Syndicate that night at the dance and come up with a plan.

I'd spent hours on my costume. A pink polished cotton sheath dress I found at a thrift store with a pink and black plaid hem-length vest made from a man's jacket. I thought the man had probably played "Smoke Gets In Your Eyes" ten thousand times in a New Jersey piano bar during the Eisenhower administration. The plaid was awful and perfect for the outfit, copied from the cover of a 1956 Lana Lobell catalogue I found on the Internet. With a half-veiled black pillbox hat and black gloves with buttons at the wrists, I'd look just like Doris Untermeyer, my high school Latin teacher.

Already middle-aged, Miss Untermeyer shocked my little Midwestern town by running off with the married Baptist minister only to return alone a year and a half later with twin baby girls the same town slavishly adored until they both grew up and left to become *Unitarian* ministers. I hated Latin and always admired Miss Untermeyer for transcending the boredom of a dead language by breaking rules I knew I'd never break. The only thing I can still say in Latin is *Ubi est insula?* ("Where is the island?"), but Miss Untermeyer taught me something more useful - that running away is a waste of time because you'll wind up back where you started anyway.

A few hours later I was ready to go and almost didn't answer the phone when it rang. But I had to go back for the wrist corsage of pink rosebuds and baby's breath I'd made to complete my costume, and the kitchen phone is next to the refrigerator.

"Grandma!" TJ howled without preamble. "John won't let me go to Palm Springs with my friend Seiji next week. His *mom's* going. She said I could go, I'm *invited* and Seiji says there's radical stuff there. They stay in a place with a swimming pool right in the middle of all these fake rocks and it has a fake waterfall. I wanna go. John's such a f..., such a waste. I *hate* him!"

Reality may be less attractive than whatever delusion you can find because it always intrudes when you least want to deal with it.

"I'm proud of you for watching your language," I began in the cloying teacher-mode I use with TJ when he's hysterical, which is often. "This is good. Now, what is John's objection to your going on this trip?"

TJ sighed dramatically. "He says it's cheap and unwholesome."

"What's cheap and unwholesome?" I asked, sighing in return. I was eager to get to the club and regale everybody with stalker tales. I didn't want to get involved in yet another of TJ's crises.

"This town, Palm Springs. I heard him tell mom movie stars used to go there with people they weren't married to."

Oh for God's sake.

"Unmarried movie stars haven't gone to Palm Springs in John's lifetime," I said. "I think they go to Los Cabos now, or someplace in Belize."

"Yeah, but he says it also has a lot of bikers and flaky old people who wear makeup, even the men, and should be in jail."

The boy's voice was wavering with frustration and choked-back tears. At thirteen he's incredibly immature. A skinny, rash-prone child with no interest in sports and few friends. So far his grades are good, but he's run away twice and has an unwholesome interest in assault weapons. I don't like to think where this may lead.

He'd latched onto Seiji, a hefty Japanese-American boy whose family moved to California three months earlier at the end of the kids' eighth grade year, as if to a life raft. Now Seiji's mother had invited TJ to go someplace fun. It was normal, it would be good for TJ. But John, as usual, saw the work of Satan.

"Wearing makeup isn't a crime," I said with a sinking feeling. I was meddling. I didn't want to; God knows I had my own problems. But I couldn't shut up.

"*I* know that," TJ whined. "Mom knows it, you know it. It's John..."

"Is your mother available?" I said, snapping my meddling rule like the stem of a wine glass in dishwater. John wasn't a bad person, I tried to convince myself for the thousandth time. And he did try to be a father to TJ. Maybe Beth could talk some sense into him.

"She can't talk, she's in the bathroom puking. I think she's going to have another baby."

I had suspected as much.

"Yes, well..." I muttered, unsure of what response to this news would be appropriate. My gut reaction – "Your mother should have had her tubes tied after the last one." – would not do.

"We already *have* two babies," TJ went on, crying now. In the background one of the referenced babies, probably two-year-old Hannah, was howling. Soon eight-month-old Benjamin would join the chorus. It was clear that TJ desperately needed a break.

"You're going on this trip with Seiji even if I have to go with you!" I blurted. "Let me speak to John."

It was madness. The daytime temperature in Palm Springs in August and September routinely hits 120. But I meant it. And John would give in. He is, refreshingly I think, somewhat afraid of me.

"I'm on my way to a dance and don't want to discuss anything about Satan," I told my son-in-law. "But I'm willing to go with TJ on this outing if it's okay with Seiji's mother. How do you feel about that?"

"I don't think he should be exposed to the sort of things that go on in that town," John began.

"Sorts," I interrupted.

"What?"

"Sorts. The plural of 'sort.' Sorts of things, sort of thing."

"Not everybody wants to be an English teacher, Taylor."

"A shame. The English-speaking world would be a better place. I think TJ will benefit from this experience, John. He'll have *fun*. Will you agree to his going if I'm there? You know how little interest I have in makeup."

"I only have the boy's welfare at heart. Young minds are

vulnerable to the snares of Satan and…"

I entertained a moment's fantasy of crushing my daughter's husband under several tons of Bibles.

"John, I was just leaving when TJ called and I don't have time to argue. Yes or no?"

In the background I could hear TJ sobbing over his half-sister's screams and apparently banging a metal object against a wall. It sounded like a toaster. Always high-strung, the kid seemed perilously close to going over the edge. It crossed my mind that he might have inherited it from me.

"Well, I suppose so," John began, "but you'll need to watch out for certain things."

"Of *course*," I replied with exaggerated conviction, not wanting to hear what I needed to watch out for. "I really do need to leave, John. Could I speak to TJ now?"

"Can I go? Did he say I could go?" the boy wept.

"Yes. You're going because I'm going, but only if Seiji's mother agrees, okay? You can call me back later and leave her number on the machine. I'll call her in the morning and talk to her."

"She's totally mellow, she won't mind," TJ said, his breath still coming in gasps. "Thanks, grandma."

"My pleasure," I answered, thinking maybe I should just sell the house and move to a nice retirement community someplace far away. Maine maybe. Except I hadn't been on snowshoes in years. I'd decide later.

The dance was in full swing by the time I parked in the club parking lot and managed to walk the two hundred yards to the door in five-inch heels without breaking an ankle. "The club" is actually what remains of an old convent built in 1908 on sandstone bluffs overlooking the Pacific. A prominent Catholic family inherited the property just after WWII and promptly sold most of it to developers. But they kept the main building, a gem of Victorian architecture. The last surviving member of that family, a spinster who lived in the grand old building and spent her time giving money to countless charities, was diagnosed with bone cancer in 1963. She spent weeks with a team of lawyers drawing up an airtight will, then delicately clamped her teeth over the barrel of a .38 Sterling silver derringer with mother-of-pearl hand grips. The house was bequeathed to the San Diego Women's Club, of which she was and I am a member. The derringer is kept in a display case in the entry hall, and practically everybody has seen her ghost hovering near it and looking sheepish.

"Tay!" Jude greeted me as I joined the Syndicate at the group's table in what had once been the convent's refectory. "That outfit's perfect!"

Jude was wearing mint green baby doll pajamas under a high school letter jacket, her wild blonde hair pulled back in a ponytail. In the dark Jude might be mistaken for Gidget. Or at least for her grandmother.

"And guess what else?" she whispered, snapping the waist of her pajama pants.

I caught a glimpse of copper filigree beneath the mint green cotton.

"You *didn't*," I said, grinning. "The chastity belt?"

"Borrowed it for the night," Jude answered happily. "It's as close as I'll come to chastity in this life and of course Joey's salivating at the whole idea. Men are so wonderfully predictable!"

"Predictable enough to grab a dance with Taylor before twenty other guys sweep her away," Jude's live-in significant other said. "How about it, Tay?"

Tab Hunter was crooning "Young Love" over the loudspeakers as a spinning mirror ball flung shavings of colored light over the dance floor. Most of the men were in James Dean gear with rolled-up jeans and leather jackets, but Jude's partner was wearing a white sport coat with a pink carnation at the lapel. I nodded my admiration for his outfit.

"Sure," I said, kicking my spike heels under the table and allowing him to sweep me onto the dance floor.

I meant to bring up the issue of the stalking cowboy right away, but everybody was dancing and milling around so I thought I'd wait until we were all seated for dinner and the talent show. I was having fun in a pleasant, low-key way that felt like home. I knew everybody, everybody knew me. No secrets anywhere, no hidden agendas, no unforeseen events.

Jill Danner, the Syndicate crafts enthusiast, would need help getting her alcoholic husband into the car eventually. Nothing new. And Penley Barrows would devote the next Syndicate luncheon to a detailed critique of the event's caterer. Pen grew up in Boston buried in money and can't abide a buffet lacking oysters on the half shell, even out of season. I observed Pen in a Ban-lon twinset eyeing the buffet table with despair. No oysters, again.

Isabel Rothman, the Syndicate's retired coloratura soprano and general music buff, would be backstage lining up acts for the dinner talent show as usual. And ex-nun social worker Maggie McFadden was on the dance floor in a poodle skirt, earnestly lecturing her partner about something probably having to do with funding for the rescue of something. I felt a swimming content. I was among friends, inside a globe of familiarity that asked nothing but my presence. Debbie Reynolds was singing "Tammy" as I drifted back to the Syndicate table. The corny lyrics made me smile.

"Fake crab thermidor, Tay," Pen Barrows stated as if announcing the death of a great idea. "But I think the Italian bread's real."

"Let's find out," I replied, wondering if I could get my shoes back on after dancing. The talent show was beginning and I was starving.

"Tay!"

It was Jude, suddenly at my side in the buffet line, eyes wide with news.

"What? Did you loose the key to the chastity belt?"

"It's sewn into my bra. But *look*!"

Jude grabbed my shoulders and turned me toward the stage.

"Oh my God."

A familiar figure in chaps, spurs and a white ten-gallon hat was lip-syncing Johnny Cash's "Ghost Riders In the Sky."

"It's the cowboy," Jude whispered. "Tay, who *is* this guy? I've never seen him at any club events and now out of the blue he turns up twice in one day."

"Their brands were still on fire and their hooves were made of steel," the cowboy sang in Cash's voice. "Their horns were black and shiny and their hot breath he could feel."

I thought I could feel that bovine breath, too. A barnyard scent of chewed hay. It cracked the globe of comfort in which I'd been floating, brought back a memory of the lumpen, changing thing I'd fought in the dance studio. The cowboy had been there, watching through the barely-open door.

"Pen believes the Italian bread is authentic," I told Jude. "And the cowboy...."

"Isabel will know," Jude interrupted. "She organized the talent show; she's backstage right now. She'll have a list of names..."

Jude vanished from the buffet line only to return in less than a minute.

"His name is Tim O'Halloran," she announced. "*Father* Tim O'Halloran, Jude. He's a *priest*! Isabel doesn't know anything about him. He signed up for the talent show online earlier today, showed up with his iPod and there he is. Oh, and she also said to watch for this new baritone she's found. Somebody named Nick Mautner. He's really going to sing, not lip-sync. He's on right after the cowboy."

I wasn't interested in the baritone.

"Yippee-yi-ay, yippe-yi-o," the cowboy pronounced into a fake mike as the eerie music filled the room, his attention focused on me now.

"Tay, he's looking at you," Jude whispered. "He knows you. What's going on? Is this weirdo stalking you? I'll have Joey break his legs. Tay? Talk to me."

Jude's current boyfriend is Joey Gisulfo, a balding, warm-hearted guy with a Brooklyn accent. He's prone to wearing monogrammed black silk shirts with white ties, giving rise to a rumor that he fled to California to avoid mob-related legal problems in New York. Jude dismisses the rumor as nonsense manufactured by people who still haven't gotten over the end of "The Sopranos," but nobody trusts Jude. I wasn't uncomfortable with the idea that Joey might be packing heat in a shoulder holster, although I hadn't noticed any guns when I was dancing with him.

"I never saw the cowboy before today at the Lotus," I told her. "I don't have any idea who he is. But I saw him peeking through the studio door during my dance class, and I think he left his scarf by my car in the underground garage. There's definitely something going on with this guy."

Jude's renown at focus was instantly in evidence.

"He's stalking you," she said, her eyes narrow as she stared at the cowboy, who was bowing to the crowd.

"It would seem so."

"He looks harmless."

"So did Ted Bundy."

Jude pondered that, nodding.

"Good point. Have you called the police?"

"I was going to discuss it with the Syndicate. He hasn't really done anything illegal, merely had tea in a restaurant, glanced into a dance studio and dropped a scarf in a parking garage. The police would assume I was yet another neurotic woman-of-a-certain-age with pathetic sex fantasies. It may all be sheer coincidence."

"There is no such thing as coincidence," Jude intoned. "But he's here. Let's just ask him! I'll get Joey."

"Excellent," I replied. Joey Gisulfo could intimidate furniture just by pronouncing his own name.

But by the time we got backstage, the cowboy was gone. I decided to quit thinking about it.

Then at the table I noticed a small envelope tucked beneath my napkin. Gray vellum, unobtrusive, just a corner visible. I swept it into my lap with the napkin and only glanced at it after Jude dashed off for another bottle of pinot grigio. On stage the new baritone, a muscular guy with a gray crewcut and the often-broken nose of a prizefighter, was singing "The Music of the Night" from *The Phantom of the Opera* with such drama the room had fallen silent to listen. I opened the envelope with trembling hands.

"Congratulations, Taylor. Today you met the final criterion," it said in Garamond type. "You showed that you have the heart to fight. Now you are cordially invited to the Paper Doll Museum. Please meet me at the organ pavilion in Balboa Park tomorrow morning at five and I will escort you. Fr. Tim O'Halloran."

"Darkness stirs and wakes imagination..." the singer's voice insisted, a resonant shadow that matched my mood.

Five a.m.? The hour was obscene, the endeavor nonsense and quite possibly dangerous.

But I'd do it. I would meet a priest in a cowboy costume before dawn in an urban park and go to something called the Paper Doll Museum. Even if Father Tim O'Halloran turned out to be a serial killer, he was real. Unlike the thing in the dance studio. At least I'd die with unblemished mental health credentials, a fate somewhat more attractive than what I feared lay ahead.

Chapter Four

Que Sera, Sera

Doris Day

The night had been foggy, and as I drove warily into Balboa Park at five a.m. a heavy mist still drifted in the twisted juniper and blue cypress trees planted by horticulturist Kate Sessions over a century ago. It's an old park by West Coast standards, and even in daylight it has an eerie, time-warped feel. You expect to see women in long, beaded dresses and marcelled hair walking with parasols amid the Spanish Colonial-style buildings.

I left the car in the empty lot by the art museum, the first time in my entire life I'd found a parking space there. The nearby organ pavilion, built in 1915 by wealthy German brothers who were crazy about organ music, was only visible in patches reflecting the ornate tastes of its time. Here a plaster laurel wreath, there a nearly-obscured head of Pan. Plaster flowers, leaves, quatrefoils, lyres, scrolls and shells comprising the pavilion's arch faded in and out of focus in the mist. It was, I acknowledged, the perfect set-up. And I was walking straight into it like the dimwit heroine of a gothic novel.

To complete the mood, someone was playing the marvelous old Austin concert symphonic organ. I recognized Bach's Toccata and Fugue in D Minor. I *would* recognize it; it's my favorite. The cascading tones seemed to fall from the dripping trees and then rise again to swirl in the mist. At the organ sat a small figure in Levi's and a pink chenille jacket. It was a woman, her white tennis shoes moving over the pedals like moths.

"Remarkable," said a deep voice rising from one of the metal mesh benches where people sit for free concerts at two o'clock every Sunday. Except it was Saturday and I was pretty sure this concert was going to carry a price.

It was the cowboy, now dressed entirely in black punctuated only by the white tab of his Roman collar. He stood, bowed slightly and then merely nodded at me in amazement, as if I'd just stepped from a flying saucer.

"Father O'Halloran," I replied formally. "I assume you're going to tell me what this is all about?"

"My wife is playing Bach," he answered, his nod now toward the diminutive figure at the keyboard. "For you. Welcome, Taylor."

"Please forgive me," I began, immediately regretting the phrase, "but I know it's Bach and welcome to what? And you're a priest when you're not being a cowboy. Priests do not marry so how can the woman at the organ be your wife?"

"Episcopalian," he explained. "We've been marrying since the sixteenth century. Of course I'm retired now, but I still help out at St. Paul's just across the street from the park, you see. We could have met there, but I thought it a bit much. And misleading. This is so much nicer, don't you think?"

The music was a fluid torrent now. My favorite Bach piece, filling my head and making my heart pound with gratitude that O'Halloran showed no interest in killing me.

"We have little time, he said. "These things can be tricky. Angie will play for as long as possible. It's the way, you see. The music carves a path to... well, what we call the White Road. And she's so very gifted, isn't she? My car is nearby, illegally parked, I might add. And our destination is not far. Shall we go now?"

"Go *where*?" I insisted. "What 'white road?' This... all of this is insane."

"Ahhh..." His voice resonated with understanding. "Yes, well, we all thought that at first. But really, we must go. Please."

I felt myself take his arm, felt my legs match his long strides, the music of Johann Sebastian Bach urging me forward from the eighteenth century as I got into his car. On the front window was a shield-shaped sticker that said, "Episcopal Clergy." The music trailed in the damp air as the priest drove at breakneck speed the short distance to one of the city's downtown neighborhoods adjacent to the park, a mixture of old frame houses and new condo developments. He stopped at a tiny, ancient cottage dwarfed between a three-story retirement community and a stuccoed condo complex with chrome exterior stair railings. The cottage was buried in shadows cast by a huge pepper tree growing in its tiny yard.

"This," he announced, "is the Paper Doll Museum. Its curator is Martine. She will have something for you, but you must hurry. I will wait for you here and then we'll have a lovely breakfast during which I'll explain as much as I can. Now, go!"

I could simply have walked back to my car in the park then, but I could see no reason to do that. Whatever this was, it didn't feel dangerous. What it felt was silly, as if I'd fallen into a children's party where there would be a magician and a scavenger hunt.

I saw a slate path beneath my feet leading to the cottage, bordered in alyssum and dwarf iris. Then five blue steps to a porch with pillars and balustrades painted as brightly as a carousel. The wooden floor was deep yellow and on the heavily paneled maroon door was a lion's head knocker of polished brass. Reaching for it, I thought I might have done well to dress in chains and clanking cash boxes, a handkerchief tying my jaw shut. The ghost of Jacob Marley materializing in the doorknocker of Ebenezer Scrooge.

"These are the chains I forged in life," I quoted Dickens to the woman who opened the door, who didn't smile. "A joke, okay? I have no idea why I'm here."

"I am Martine," the woman announced, the words lilting with a subtle accent.

Her age was indeterminate but scarcely young. Thickened midriff, webs of creases at eyes and mouth, papery skin gloving her hands. And yet she was stunning, her coffee-brown eyes sparkling with wry wisdom, her face glowing beneath elaborately coiffed red-gold hair. Perfect makeup, I noticed. A daunting accomplishment at 5:00 a.m. She wore an evocative lace blouse over a washed silk skirt the color of peach sorbet. The skirt's hem was dramatically uneven, the longest edge lace-trimmed in a WWII style that made me think of gorgeous female spies who knew how to kill with guitar strings and hatpins. So far, so good.

"Please come in," she said.

I allowed myself to be escorted to a parlor off the entry hall, then gasped. In a corner a life-sized but two-dimensional Barbara Stanwyck engaged in wordless conversation with Harry Truman, the cigarette in the movie star's jeweled holder lit but producing no smoke. A flat Japanese kabuki dancer stood near the tiny iron fireplace, and on the Persian rug three paper-thin Queen Holden babies in pastel woolen snowsuits smiled at nothing. I could see a bent paper tab on Truman's shoulder, meant to hold his pinstriped suit in place. The figures were paper dolls! Or projections of paper dolls. Lasers. Something.

Clark Gable appeared at my side in the gleaming white suit and black string tie he wore in *Gone with the Wind*. His face had no depth and his eyes looked through me to some unimaginable point of reference as the Mouse King from *The Nutcracker* danced stiffly on an overstuffed chair. Sonja Henie in a Scandinavian costume slid on paper skates toward William Holden and Kim Novak, who despite their lack of dimension exuded seething desire. *Picnic*. It was the sexiest movie I'd ever seen. Four times. And I got the paper dolls even though by then I was too old for paper dolls. They had all been mine. I had cut out their clothes and kept them in a shoe box eventually pushed to the back of a closet and forgotten. Far away but still audible I could hear the thrumming chords of

Bach's Toccata.

"... *the music carves a path.*"

"Lasers," I said to Martine. "Right?"

"*How* things happen does not matter," she answered. "What matters is *that* things happen."

"I'm afraid I don't know what you're talking about," I replied, shaken and relying on sheer attitude to get through it. The images wouldn't be that hard to create. Some technician wandering down from Disneyland could put the show together in an afternoon. But how did they know which paper dolls had been *mine*?

"I'm sorry," I went on. "Moreover, I don't know anything else, like why I'm standing around here at dawn in a room full of ... whatever they are."

"You went to great lengths to save the life of an armadillo," Martine said as if this arcane bit of information accounted for a room full of life-sized paper dolls.

"Yes, but..."

"You wrote an article about Poe. Then you found the courage to fight something terrible."

"The thing at the dance studio," I said.

"Yes."

"And...?"

"And so your travels begin."

"Travels? Does this have anything to do with a white road?"

"Yes," she said as Buster Brown and his dog Tige appeared amid the leaves of a Boston fern on a carved stand. Smaller than the other figures, no longer life-sized. And the others were beginning to waver.

The room suddenly smelled musty, like the drawers of an old chest you find at a thrift store and don't buy. I watched as the colors in the Kabuki dancer's robe swirled and froze. John Wayne, pistol in hand, shrank to a height of eight inches, scowled at the leg of a coffee table and fell flat on the Persian rug. The figures were losing whatever force gave them size.

"You are in a different world now," Martine said.

"No kidding."

"There is no return."

The woman's accent was more pronounced as she spoke urgently, holding something toward me in her hand. "And there is danger you have yet to imagine. You possess the gift, but it is accompanied by a horror that may destroy you. When the time comes, use this."

"What gift? When what time comes?" Her words reminded me of my grandmother's warning and were equally cryptic.

Martine didn't answer but pressed a small tin whistle into my hand, its red and blue paint chipped with age. An old Cracker Jack prize, I thought. I loved Cracker Jack as a kid and kept all the prizes in a Revere Ware pan with a broken handle under my bed. The little toy hung on a silver chain. Courteously I pulled the chain over my head and let the whistle fall inside my blouse. I didn't know what else to do.

"Thank you," I said.

Now can I get the hell out of here?

Martine began to pale as Truman collapsed against Barbara Stanwyck's cleavage and the three snowsuit-clad babies on the rug shrank to cardboard figures I could hold in one hand.

"I'll just see myself out," I said as the woman leaned trembling against the back of a fringed love seat upholstered in pink brocade.

"Yes, you must go," Martine answered. But her brown eyes had lost none of their sparkle as she smiled. "Don't worry. We will see each other again."

"I look forward to it," I murmured as I backed into the hall.

That and my next root canal.

"You will have questions," Tim O'Halloran said after I flung myself into his car and glared at him. "But first I must warn you never to allow what you were given out of your sight. *Never.* It is your amulet and may be used to summon help in moments of mortal danger. Go nowhere without it. Now, may I enjoy the honor of your company at breakfast? I've called Angie on my cell and she'll join us in a bit."

"Coffee," I said. "Please just get me to coffee."

At the restaurant I ordered a waffle with whipped cream and fresh strawberries and after several gulps of coffee turned my attention to Father Tim O'Halloran.

"At the organ pavilion you said 'we.' You said 'we' all thought this was insane at first. I'm afraid I continue to hold that view. Who are 'we'?"

"We are Revenants," he answered.

"What?"

"The word derives from Latin, then French – *revenir.* It means 'to come back.'"

"It means 'ghosts,'" I said. "Souls returned from the dead, vampires, that sort of thing. But unless I missed something, I haven't died and so cannot have returned from... there. I'm afraid I'm not, um, one."

I like all religions that have lots of ritual and music, but doctrinally I'm your garden-variety agnostic. I keep my cosmology to myself, as I wish everybody else would. Especially those earnest types who go door to door urging poorly-written pamphlets on people who are trying to eat lunch in peace. But Tim O'Halloran purported to be a clergyman and I had no desire to offend his calling, whatever it was. I just wanted to go home, get some sleep and relegate my recent experience to that place where you ignore things that can't have happened.

He clasped his hands thoughtfully around a saltshaker and seemed to search for words.

"You are a scholar of Poe. Think of 'nevermore' as reversible," he said. "Something irrevocably lost and now returned. You see?"

I didn't, but the waffle was fabulous. I wasn't leaving until I'd consumed the last, strawberry-drenched bite.

"You seem to be a very nice person," I told him. "I don't want to be rude, but..."

"'Revenant' is only a name," he went on, "and names do tend to obscure things, I'm afraid. But you must hear me out. Your life depends on it, Taylor. You cannot go back, you see. What was lost is now returned to you – the perception you possessed before sexual maturity - the processes necessary to the continuation of life - closed the door to that world and made you 'adult.' That door has opened again. You are an adult to whom the perception of childhood has returned, now refined by the experience of a lifetime. You are a Revenant, Taylor, and I have been sent to welcome you."

The use of the passive tense is always a red flag.

"Been sent?" I said. "By whom?"

At the first reference to flying saucers, men in black or the Templars, I was prepared to abandon my waffle and flee. But O'Halloran merely nodded and said, "There's a sort of organization. Headquarters are in Boston."

"Conveniently close to Salem," I had to quip.

"Salem?"

"Witchcraft trials, that sort of thing."

"You must take this seriously," he replied, not smiling.

"Boston *is* a sort of hub, a crossing in the White Road."

"What white road?"

He shrugged.

"We live in a culture that ignores everything but the rational and obvious, and so we're taught not to see things that are irrational and obscure. But there's another dimension, the invisible White Road that connects all things. Light and dark, past and present, life and death – all exist on the White Road. Its tributaries, side roads if you will, are all the tales in the world. One of the Boston Revenants, an anthropologist at Boston University, came up with the name. I think it's Mayan, but..."

"Mayan? I'm sorry, but this just sounds so New Agey or something. If you're really a priest shouldn't you be talking about, you know, Christian kinds of things? I'm not getting this at all."

The Mayan reference brought back another event I never talked about. My senior year in college my best friend and I were tired of getting drunk in Florida every year over Easter break and decided to do something different. She was majoring in Comparative Lit. and was writing a paper on the *Popol Vuh*, the Maya cosmology first recorded in the Seventeenth Century by a Dominican friar. She wanted to go to the Yucatan, which was fine with me. I knew I'd probably be marrying Charlie in a year or two. The trip was like a last bloom of heady irresponsibility before what lay ahead – jobs, marriage, the whole shtick.

We had a ball, snorkeling and prowling Mayan ruins every day, then fooling around with gorgeous Spanish-speaking boys at night. I was *technically* faithful to Charlie, but not terribly concerned about it. It was the 70's and while I made the dean's list every semester, I also had an alter-ego I called "Freeda Thane" (a reference to *MacBeth* I thought was hysterically funny) who loved to lip-sync "Band of Gold" while vamping on bar stools.

But in Valladolid on our last night there we were tired and pensive, regrouping for the trip home. We ate tortillas and beans at a little restaurant and went to bed early since we had to catch a plane at dawn. Students, we were sleeping on the cheap, and our "motel" had at one time been a horse barn. It was clean, but the room was actually a stall with two narrow cots against the opposite walls. At some point deep in the night I woke. I guess I had to go to the bathroom, because I slipped my feet into my sandals and stood. Except it felt like unfurling. I kept sort of folding upward until my head brushed the ceiling! It was a little strange, but exhilarating.

My friend stirred groggily on the cot across from mine and whispered, "My God, Taylor, you're ten feet tall!" before she went back to sleep.

Later we agreed that there must have been something in the beans, the tortillas and perfectly ordinary bottled Cokes we had for dinner, that caused a mutual waking dream in which I seemed to have grown nearly five feet. Because of course I couldn't have.

Except sitting in a pancake restaurant with Tim O'Halloran I could still feel the delicious stretch of my body, up and up, and the soft thump of my head against the ceiling. I was not completely ignorant of strange experiences or "other dimensions," but I could make no sense of them and so ignored them. O'Halloran was intent on his own words.

"Of course it still sounds unreal, even ridiculous and your first thought will be that you've gone mad," he said quietly. "It will take time for you to adjust. The White Road is ancient but nearly buried in the clutter of rationality now. You will have to explore it blindly. As far as religions are concerned, each has its mystics struggling to find exactly what we've fallen into. It's there, that other dimension children sense but of which adults are almost totally unaware. Oh, there's the occasional inexplicable event – the car ahead of you on a mountain road that rounds a curve and simply vanishes, figures in your peripheral vision that aren't there when you turn to look, coincidences, dreams, the list is long. The adult mind dismisses such things as senseless and forgets them, but the child mind does not. We are ourselves as children again, Taylor. We can see that other world - the White Road."

The picture of a secret office in an attic crossed my mind, then myself a stretching giant in a dark Mexican horse barn. Had those meaningless images been a glimpse onto the White Road? But they *were* meaningless, just waking dreams unrelated to real life. I couldn't think of anything to say and poured myself another cup of coffee.

"Your Salem comment wasn't entirely without merit," he went on. There is the possibility of mass hysteria, not to mentions other, more specific dangers. So far we know that each of us has unusual... *abilities*, for lack of a better word. These are peculiar to each Revenant, no two alike. Of these, it's possible that some might be of interest to governments, corporations, organized crime. We are, quite frankly, endangered and must guard against detection at all times by *never* mentioning the gift. But I'm afraid those external dangers are nothing compared to what each of us must face, alone. You saw a glimpse of it yesterday."

The violet eyes behind his wire-framed glasses were somber.

"I don't know what you're talking about," I lied. He was talking about the scent of persimmons and a thing that existed only to wound me. Horribly.

"Why the cowboy costume?" I asked, changing the subject. "Why were you watching me at the dance studio?"

"It was necessary to see whether or not you possessed the courage to fight. It was time for your enemy to appear. And I saw that you would fight."

He looked down, folding his napkin in tight triangles.

"This is all quite new," he said. "Some of the first refused or lacked the ability to fight altogether."

He looked up then, a terrible sorrow in his eyes.

"They perished, Taylor. I don't mean death in the natural sense, but something much worse. The most fortunate managed to commit suicide."

Suicide! I didn't want to hear any more.

"And the cowboy get-up?" I said, grasping for levity.

Tim O'Halloran's grin was playful.

"Tom Mix," he said.

"Who?"

"My childhood idol. A movie star in early westerns during the 20's and 30's, incredible character! Mix knew Wyatt Earp, was even a pallbearer at his funeral. As a boy I wanted to be Tom Mix. Now I can be. We can be whatever we want now, Taylor!"

"Tim," I said carefully, "how old *are* you?"

"Eighty-six."

"And the other members of this Revenant thing. Are they all, um, *seniors* too?"

"A society of geriatric nutcases?" he said, chuckling. "Everybody's first thought, of course. It is true that the youngest Revenant so far is fifty-seven, so in a way your assessment is correct."

"Old people, paper dolls, cowboy outfits on a white road," I mused aloud. "I scarcely know what to say."

"Until recently human life was at the mercy of a biology devoted entirely to reproduction. All the physical and psychological systems of which we are made worked seamlessly through the reproductive years and then suddenly began to break down. That's still happening, but now we're developing methods with which to derail the process of decay. People, especially in developed countries, live longer than ever in the history of our species," he said slowly. "Much longer. A new and unprecedented stage of life has emerged from our diet and medical advances. And something has emerged with it, something equally unprecedented. An awareness, shall we say? The intuitive reality of childhood returning, yet subject to the rational experience of many years. And with it, a grotesque and terrifying threat forgotten since childhood. When did it begin for you, Taylor? Do you remember?"

This was the tip, I realized with discomfort. The fail-safe point after which there really would be no going back. I could pretend not to understand the question, demur politely and turn away forever from whatever this was. Or I could acknowledge it and step off a cliff.

"It was in a dance class," I said. "I literally reached out and *touched* a moment of my own past. It was nothing significant, just a fragment of a day long ago. I was a girl, riding my bicycle to the library. It was summer. I was eating a banana Popsicle. That's all."

"Ah, a Popsicle," Tim O'Halloran answered softly. "How lovely. And of course, a library!"

"And then strange things began to happen. I saw a cat dash under a table in a Rembrandt painting..."

"A cat?"

He smiled with delight while waving to his wife, who had just straight-armed the restaurant's double doors and entered like a small troop of cavalry.

"Angie, please join us. This is Taylor Blake. She saw a cat in a Rembrandt!"

"Which one?" Angie O'Halloran asked as the waitress brought her a selection of tea bags and a pot of hot water.

"The Prophet Jeremiah."

"Did the cat peek from under that fabulous tablecloth?"

"No, it ran under it. Do you, um, see these things as well?"

"I'm afraid not," the older woman said wistfully, shrugging off her chenille jacket to reveal a blue chambray shirt and a lot of Navajo jewelry. "I'm *aware* of them, but I don't see them and I definitely can't do the things you and Tim..."

"Angie is one of the gifted ones," her husband interrupted. "One of the lightbearers who show the way. They're everywhere and almost always unappreciated, although always so wonderfully talented in one way or another."

"We're the flakes," Angie said. "The oddballs who never fit in."

"Because the fit is too tight," the priest said fondly, taking his wife's hand in his. "Always listen to their wise counsel, Taylor, these rare birds. They illuminate all the paths in the world!"

I saw a bird with a white ribbon in its beak, flying as the ribbon became a road, then many roads. Molly's whispered, "Fight! You know the moves." Molly's voice a bird-ribbon. Molly Palmer, health-club dance instructor with too many stories, was a lightbearer.

"But what was that thing at the dance studio?" I asked, finally bringing it up. "That was no lightbearer."

Both O'Hallorans looked straight at me.

"No," Angie said somberly, "it was not."

"It was your antithesis, a sort of ghoul," Tim pronounced. "The faces of darkness are numberless, Taylor; they accompany every life. This one has existed since your birth. It hid in shadows and terrified you as a child. Now it has returned, no longer a shadow but a thing as complex as your own life. It will destroy you now if you let it. Beware."

A new path emerges. Beware.

"My fortune cookie yesterday at the Lotus...," I began as a cell phone chirped the opening bars of Beethoven's Ninth, "and something my grandmother said just before she died..."

"Of course," Tim said into the little device. "Right away."

"I'm afraid we must go," he said. "Hospital call. I'd planned to explain much more, but a parishioner is near death, you see. We'll speak again soon, my dear. And don't worry. You're relatively safe for the time being."

When they were gone I found my own cell phone in my purse.

"Tay?" Jude Shapiro gasped. "It's five-thirty in the morning! Have you lost your mind?"

"I'm not sure," I answered. "Can you meet me at the pancake place by the park in twenty minutes?"

"You *have* lost your mind. I'll be there in fifteen with a bag over my head because I won't have time for makeup. This had better be good, Tay."

"Definitely," I told her. "It's definitely good."

Chapter Five

It's Only Make Believe

Conway Twitty

"You got me up at dawn to tell me *what*?" Jude demanded. She'd arrived barefoot in jeans and a striped pajama shirt of Joey's, her hair a mess.

"I've been invited. No, welcomed," I explained as we stood on the sidewalk outside the restaurant. "As I said, the cowboy welcomed me to some group called Revenants who do something on a white road and I have an enemy who will destroy me, except I can blow a whistle and somehow that will help. A woman named Martine gave it to me at the Paper Doll Museum."

Jude's look gave new depth to the term, "askance."

"Tay, it's five-something in the morning. The damn birds aren't even up yet and you're telling me there's a museum that's open? And there is no 'Paper Doll Museum,' anyway. If I didn't know you so well I'd assume you're on drugs."

I pretended to be outraged but didn't really blame Jude. I'd have thought exactly the same thing. Only weeks ago our Syndicate do-gooder, Maggie McFadden, had lectured us through an entire lunch about the prevalence of methamphetamine abuse among housewives in economically depressed farming communities.

"Oh God, you're not, are you?" Jude went on, escalating. "You've been acting strange lately. Don't worry. We'll get you into Betty Ford, or is that just for alcohol? Whatever. We'll get you someplace. Maggie will know where. Wasn't she just trying to get everybody to go to a fundraiser for a new drug treatment program? Give me your cell; I'll call her right now."

I sighed. I wasn't used to getting up at 4:00 in the morning and felt like going back to bed. For the week.

"Maggie is always trying to get everybody to attend fundraisers, Jude, and no, I'm not on drugs for crying out loud and you can't have my cell phone. Calm down."

Jude rolled her eyes at something apparently hovering just above her hair.

"Okay, sure. I don't know what came over me. This happens every day. I mean, *daily* my best friend calls at dawn from a pancake shop to tell me she's been inducted into a secret society of geriatric leprechauns who do sound and light shows with paper dolls. This is so ordinary, Tay. I am so calm."

"Well, it beats the alternative."

"Which is…?"

I made a face. "Oh, the usual. Dementia, a tangled brain talking to people who've been dead for fifty years. I was getting worried, Jude. I thought I was losing it."

"Everybody worries about that," she acknowledged brightly. "Joey has promised to step on my oxygen tube if it happens to me, although I know perfectly well he won't do it. But Tay, there's nothing wrong with your mind!"

"No, I don't think so," I mused as the bells of St. Paul's announced the hour. "You know, the cowboy said he's retired but volunteers at that church."

Jude grinned. "Good idea. Let's check it out. If he's really what he says he is then there will be some evidence, somebody will know him, right?"

The gothic interior of St. Paul's Cathedral still held the night, its air scented with cold candle wax.

"I always feel like I've walked into another world in these places," Jude said uneasily.

I grabbed a church bulletin from a massive oak table just inside the door and nodded.

"I think that's the point. And look, Jude."

"Look at what? How can you see anything? It's dark in here, Tay."

"The Reverend Doctor Timothy S. O'Halloran, Retired, Parish Associate," I read from a list of names on the back of the bulletin. "The guy's legitimate, Jude."

"So what about this Martine, the woman with the paper dolls? Let's check her out, too," Jude said.

I couldn't argue with Jude's logic but also couldn't shake a sense that Martine and the museum weren't quite the same thing as The Reverend Doctor Timothy O'Halloran, AKA Tom Mix. O'Halloran, for all his eccentricities, was real. Martine and the paper dolls weren't, exactly.

How *things happen does not matter. What matters is* that *things happen.*

"Sure," I answered. "It's close. We can walk there from here."

The city was waking up, beginning its day. As we walked I noticed a girl in a school uniform throwing ad fliers from the back of a pickup truck. Outside a coffee shop a woman in a business suit and tennis shoes walked a Boston terrier who smiled and wiggled his docked tail as we passed. The mist was burning off. It was going to be hot, again.

"It's right up here," I said, turning into the street with the three-story retirement community. Except even from a distance the little cottage didn't look the same. It looked shabby, the yard a patchwork of bare dirt, anemic weeds and trash. A chill filmed my teeth as we approached a neglected porch sagging under the weight of a mildewed couch and five plastic milk crates full of empty beer bottles.

"Where?" Jude asked.

"Umm, here," I said, gesturing to what was obviously an urban rooming house only months shy of demolition. It was the same place only different, as if the house I'd seen was itself in the past. Now it stood feverish and ruined. Beside the door was a list of names in a foggy plastic sleeve. "Jack Ripper, Apt. 1," had been scrawled in blue crayon over another name now scratched out. Three other names were faded beyond legibility.

"Tay, this is a flophouse," Jude said. "This is not a museum. It'll be full of winos and a guy who killed his wife in Ohio thirty years ago because she accidentally bought plain aerosol cheese spread instead of pimento. Let's get out of here!"

"I just have to see," I replied, skirting an empty half-pint Jim Beam bottle standing capless on the top step. My hands were shaking and I felt sick.

"Is Martine here?" I asked a man who came to the door only after I'd knocked for five minutes. He was wrapped in a grimy sheet and so thin I couldn't help but think of Gandhi.

"What? Ain't no Martine here. You a social worker? I ain't get no food stamps last month, y'know? Damn near starve in here. You gimme a little sumpin', right?"

I could see the hall and a slice of the parlor over his shoulder. I could see the pink love seat Martine had leaned against as the paper dolls shrank and faded. Except now the love seat was in shreds and weathered to the color of raspberry tea, both its arms wrapped in strips of duct tape. But it was the same love seat, I was certain. Somehow the love seat was reassuring.

57

"Thank you," I said, stuffing a ten-dollar bill through a tear in the screen and turning to retreat. "You've been very helpful."

"Whaddaya mean 'helpful'?" the man bellowed in a voice surprisingly deep for someone so lacking in body mass. "Fuckin' lousy ten?"

A teenage boy doing Tai-Chi moves on a balcony of the chrome-railed condo building looked down briefly, then resumed his exercise.

"Tay!" Jude whispered as if speaking in a normal voice might prompt the man in the sheet to chase us up the street brandishing a meat cleaver. "This is dangerous."

"I was there," I said. "I was in that house this morning. I'm not imagining it. In a parlor... there's a pink love seat with fringe..."

"I know, I know. And Clark Gable. We're leaving now, Tay. I'm parked around the corner. We're going to my car. Now!"

Jude's determined barefoot stomp away from the crumbling house kept her several paces ahead of me, dragging us both forward by sheer force of will. She didn't notice the homeless woman in a brown coat asleep against a spidery tree in the sidewalk median. But I did.

The woman's eyes opened and her face broke into an enigmatic grin as she looked at me. The sparkle in those coffee-colored eyes was familiar.

"Martine?" I whispered. But the woman merely shook her head and allowed her eyes to close again. Beneath a sailor's knit cap pulled low over her ears a few curls of red-gold hair were visible. I sprinted to catch up with Jude but said nothing, and when I turned to look back, the woman in the brown coat was gone.

"You know what I think?" Jude began minutes later as she drove me to my car parked near the organ pavilion.

"What, Jude? What do you think?"

"I think whatever this is, it's interesting. And I think we'll just keep it to ourselves, not lay it out to the Syndicate. Agreed?"

"Why?" I asked. "Because they'll think I'm nuts?"

I am nuts!

Jude jammed a bare foot on the brake to avoid hitting a pigeon strutting down the white center stripe of the street.

"No," she said. "Because some things just need quiet. Some things need to stay quiet or they get twisted. They get wrecked."

Quiet? This was not like Jude, who once admitted that during those rare times in which her bed is unshared, she falls asleep listening to Meatloaf.

"What do you mean?"

Jude eased her car into a parking space next to mine and I watched as a maintenance man in a white uniform swept the steps of the art museum. I'd never seen white uniforms in the park before, but then I'd never been there at dawn either.

"I've never told anybody this," she began, "but there was this guy, the love of my life, Tay. It was years ago, in the South where I grew up. I was a just a kid, a flight attendant. I worked a now-defunct airline that ran little propeller planes between Texas and Louisiana, mostly for oil business types. But the guy I'm talking about - his name was Luke, Lucien technically, Lucien Salnier, a Cajun - wasn't an oilman. He was a journalist, a few years older than me with these molasses-colored eyes and curly black hair. I was head-over-heels for him before we finished dinner on our first date."

"And so...?" I said, glad for a conversational topic that made sense. "What happened?"

Jude was staring into the steering wheel, her front teeth leaving pale depressions in her lower lip. "I blew it, Tay," she said. "He was.... odd. He wrote for a bunch of southern papers and traveled all over doing research and interviewing people, but that's not what I'm talking about. That's not what I mean."

"So what *do* you mean?" Jude's saga of yet another bad love affair was like a tonic, its familiarity solid ground. She could, if asked, recite decades of them. But even in my shaky condition I sensed a difference.

Jude turned toward me. She looked like The Little Match Girl just as the last match goes out.

"This 'Revenant' thing? He was like that."

Her tone suggested unfathomable tragedy.

"You're going to have to be more specific," I said.

"He had about a million books – folklore from all over the world, science books about time and black holes. He collected ghost stories, stories about haunted shrimp boats and extinct woodpeckers that live in wild places."

"Woodpeckers? Jude, I'm not tracking this. What do woodpeckers have to do with anything, and if they're extinct how can they be living?" Every word brought me back to something like "normal." I guess paying attention to other people can do that.

"That's what I mean," she said. "Luke kept telling me nothing is what it looks like on the surface; nothing is a hundred percent true. That everything we're told is just a story and the interesting stories are the ones that are doorways to other realities, things we don't understand."

"I still don't get the woodpeckers," I admitted, happy to say 'woodpeckers'."

A woman who can show interest in woodpeckers isn't crazy.

"Even now people see these huge, extinct woodpeckers in the Tunica Hills in Louisiana, Tay. Ivory billed woodpeckers. But nobody believes the people who see them because the birds are supposed to be extinct, except maybe they're not."

"And your point is?"

I don't care what your point is because this story is saving my life!

"I didn't believe Luke. He embarrassed me with this stuff. I was afraid he was crazy and dumped him. I never saw him again, but one day I got a package in the mail. It was one of those little girls' music boxes with a ballerina inside, only he'd replaced the ballerina with a carved woodpecker, an ivory bill."

I shook my head slowly "And...?".

"So forty years ago I dumped the man who was probably my soulmate," Jude concluded, "and all I have left is a music box with a woodpecker that dances to 'Swan Lake.' I'm afraid something terrible will happen to you if you go around talking about Revenants and Paper Doll Museums. I mean, you'll just wind up weird and lost like that, extinct and dancing all alone to music meant for swans, see?"

The logic was challenging, but I got the message anyway.

"You're probably right," I told her. "And Tim said basically the same thing, that I shouldn't discuss it with anybody. People might freak out; there could be witch hunts. Let's just go on as if it never happened, okay?"

"That's what I think," Jude said as I got out of her car. "It never happened."

I waved as she drove away, trying not to yell, "But it did!"

The park was still deserted and seemed fake, like painted scenery left behind by a troupe of actors who won't be back. In greenish-white sunlight burning through the mist, trees and buildings and empty black pavement shimmered and exhaled silence.

The maintenance man who'd been sweeping the art museum steps was closer now, seeming to check the bolts on a "Two Hour Limit" parking sign near my car. It should have occurred to me that nobody checks bolts on parking signs. His back was to me as I fumbled for my keys, and then he turned. I was beside my car when something about his gait made me look at him. Only it wasn't a "him" anymore. I wasn't sure what it was, but the mint-green air suddenly smelled like persimmons. It flopped toward me as if trying to ice skate for the first time and there was a scraping sound as its feet dragged across the pavement. And the face staring at me was not flesh, but something hard and gray in the filtered, tinny light.

Plaster! The face was the almond-eyed face of Pan repeated in plaster across the ornate façade of the organ pavilion. And the hands weren't hands but plaster scallop shells from the same frieze, moving on lumpy arms beneath the white sleeves of the uniform. Arms arching above the Pan-head as if to split wood with an ax. The thing was going to smash my windshield, or my head!

Too much, this is just too much, I really am out of my mind, why didn't I just stay in bed?

But I remembered Tim O'Halloran's words. I had to fight. Revenants who didn't fight perished horribly. I wasn't up for perishing horribly. I just wanted to go home, get some sleep and forget all of it.

I'd left the car unlocked with all the windows down, so I was able to slip in and start the engine quickly. Throwing the car in reverse, I backed away from the thing. The curb weight of my Volvo is about a ton and a half. More than enough to obliterate a plaster statue the size of an average man. There would be some damage to my car. Well, there was going to be damage to my car anyway. But as I revved the engine in neutral and then slammed it into drive, laying forty dollars worth of rubber on the asphalt, I had second thoughts.

The mist was burning off but my vision was still unclear. The thing was shuffling forward; I could hear the thump-scratch of its feet. But what if I just imagined the Pan face, the scallop-shell hands? What if I murdered a park maintenance employee in broad daylight while normal people drank coffee and walked Boston terriers? The media coverage would be mortifying. DERANGED LOCAL TEACHER KILLS INNOCENT PARK EMPLOYEE. At the last split-second I swerved. There was a soft crunch as the car brushed the thing, but it was still standing and I didn't stop. From behind I heard a chalky roar, like the crowd in an old movie newsreel.

Perra loca! it yelled once and then the roar just stopped, as if a plug had been pulled. In my rearview mirror the parking lot was empty.

My Spanish isn't great, but everybody knows what "loco" means, and the Spanish word for dog is *perro*. Spanish is gendered, the feminine endings usually "a" rather than the masculine "o." *Perra loca*? Crazy female dog. Crazy bitch.

Maybe. Maybe the maintenance guy was just a regular maintenance guy, swearing at me in Spanish because he was Mexican. Maybe he had a temporary green card and was up at dawn trying to support a family. Maybe I was a public menace.

At home I tried to sleep and then gave up, drank more coffee and paced a rhomboid pattern on the deck until the park offices opened at nine.

"Maintenance workers in white uniforms at six a.m.? No, ma'am. Maintenance crews begin work at nine and wear green. There are no official services in the park from midnight to nine a.m. except security patrols by San Diego Police. Was there something else I could help you with?"

Probably, but where to begin?

"No, but thank you," I said and hung up.

When the phone rang a few minutes later I jumped a foot.

"Mrs. Blake?"

I haven't used "Mrs." since the divorce, but neither did I change my name, so I guessed I should say yes.

"Yes?"

"This is Miyoko Foxwell."

The voice seemed direct, lacking that forced warmth that lets you know it's a total stranger trying to sell you a half-price week at a failing time share in Utah.

"Yes?"

"Seiji's mother?"

"Ah," I said, scrambling to remember why somebody named Miyoko, mother of Seiji, would be calling. It came back in pieces. TJ. A trip to Palm Springs. My crackpot son-in-law John and satanic influences. I'd volunteered to chaperone my grandson on a trip with his pal.

"It was so good of you to invite TJ on this trip with Seiji," I began. "I'm sure my son-in-law's concerns must seem very odd, but..."

"TJ has told us about his stepfather," the woman interrupted, almost whispering. "My husband and I understand that he's..."

"A fanatic," I finished, sighing. "I can't begin to account for my daughter's judgment in marrying him, but there it is. He thinks Palm Springs is demonic and so I agreed to accompany TJ as a buffer against... whatever it is his stepfather thinks. I do apologize, Mrs. Foxwell, this is so intrusive and pointless. I thought I'd just drive over and take a hotel room, be around to placate John but not intrude on you and the boys."

"Oh no, I'd be pleased if you could come with us, no problem. I'll make the arrangements at the hotel," Miyoko Foxwell said with audible relief. "I do interior design and this is a business trip for me. Client wants me to 'Feng Shui' his house. I told him I was Japanese and Feng Shui is Chinese, plus I was born and raised in Colorado Springs anyway. The closest I've ever been to China is reading Amy Tan novels. Not to mention that the Feng Shui craze peaked ten years ago. I don't know anything about it and had to look it up on Google, but he doesn't care. I wasn't sure what I'd do with the kids during my interview with him, figured I'd just drop them off at a movie. I'd love your help. You don't happen to have a magnetic compass, do you?"

"I think they're all magnetic," I said, again grateful for normal words like "compass." "And I'm pretty sure there's one buried in the garage with my son's old Boy Scout stuff. Do you mind if I ask why you need a compass?"

"You're a lifesaver!" Miyoko Foxwell said happily. "Feng Shui has something to do with directions so I need a compass. We'll pick TJ up at around 6:00 next Saturday morning and be at your place by 6:15. I look forward to getting to know you!"

6:00? I was going to become psychotic from sleep deprivation if I wasn't already.

"Wonderful," I said. "See you then."

An hour later I decided to feel righteous about not running down the maintenance man even though he wasn't a regular park employee. Whatever he was, he couldn't have been a plaster Pan with seashell hands. I was stressed, I told myself. Who wouldn't be, after getting up at 4:00 a.m. to hallucinate life-sized paper dolls in a flophouse? Of course I imagined the pan-faced maintenance man.

It worked until later when I reached into the back seat of my car to stash a bottle of water for my dance class. There was something on the floor. An ornate plaster scallop shell lying on the mat. Chunks of plaster and pale dust crumbled from its broken edge.

"Oh shit," I said, feeling ice cloak my rib cage. I'd caught the thing's "hand" with the side of an open window when I swerved to miss it. I hadn't imagined anything. And I had no idea what to do with it. Throwing it in the trash seemed quixotic, like pulling out white hairs as a defense against aging. There is no defense. Creative acceptance is the way to go, according to advice Jude often shares from her website research. I tried to think of something creative to do with a plaster scallop shell that was really a souvenir from an encounter with my ghoul, the dark side of Revenance.

By itself it was really sort of pretty. Even so, I wasn't going to take it into the house, where I imagined it hunching along my hall floor in the middle of the night, leaving a pallid trail of plaster dust as it moved toward me in the dark.

In the end I drilled a hole in it and nailed it to the fence where it showed through a gap in the wisteria. It looked nice there, and I could keep an eye on it. At least until I had time to move somewhere under an assumed name and vanish before it was too late.

Chapter Six

The Wayward Wind

Gogi Grant

The following week was so ordinary the whole Paper Doll Museum thing began to feel like a movie you see while traveling. You remember the plot of the movie, but everything else is vague, as if it didn't really happen. A cineplex in a shopping mall across the highway from the motel, wasn't it? Or that art theater next to a wine bar with baseball posters? Was it in St. Louis during the conference or on that trip to Phoenix for somebody's niece's wedding? The specific thing, the movie, remains. But the memory is unmoored and hard to pin down. Nor did I want to pin this one down. Either I was going crazy or I was a Revenant with special powers and a threatening ghoul whose nastiness makes open heart surgery look like fun. Neither option was remotely attractive and the ordinary business of my life took on a luminous quality I savored like an exquisite coffee.

I cleaned closets and filled five lawn and leaf bags with clothes Maggie McFadden picked up for distribution to a women's shelter, a Tijuana project involving orphans and something about Somali refugees. The whistle on its chain was still around my neck, but I told myself I might have found it while cleaning out closets. Maybe

I wore it so I'd know where it was and could give it to TJ. The Paper Doll Museum, Tim, all of it had been a peculiar dream I shouldn't have shared with Jude, but it didn't matter because she wouldn't say anything.

A professor at one of the community colleges read my article on Poe and called, asking me to give a talk to one of his classes. "Of course you'll be sure to include Poe's influence on Dostoyevsky?" he said. I had no idea what Poe's influence on Dostoyevsky was, but agreed. I'd look it up. I was back to normal.

At the Syndicate's weekly lunch, our Bostonian Pen Barrows talked about her five-year-old granddaughter who writes poetry but still hasn't gotten over an intense fear of ceramic cookie jars. Jude, as usual, wore chiffon and a picture hat and made a huge point of telling everybody how sane and level-headed I am. Fortunately nobody takes anything Jude says seriously, or it would have been a dead giveaway to my no-longer sane and level-headed condition. Jill Danner mentioned a quilt exhibit she'd like to see the following week and Maggie and I agreed to go with her. Maybe I'd buy a quilt. Isabel Rothman raved about Nick Mautner, the gifted baritone she'd found for her little theater group's revival of "The Fantasticks." In October they were staging the show in Commedia dell'arte costumes, a touch Isabel insisted had never been done.

"I'm still not sure if Mautner's an ex-cop or an ex-con, but my God, that voice!"

"And he's hot," Jude noted, glancing in my direction. "Did you see those biceps?"

Everyone praised Isabel's luck in finding a baritone and agreed that we should volunteer to work on the production. Except Maggie, who first demanded that at least ten per cent of the box office be donated to a legal defense fund for Tamils fleeing political oppression in Sri Lanka. Pen wrote Maggie a fifty dollar check for the Tamils and said, "For Pete's sake, Mag, give it a rest!" Everybody laughed. Nice, normal day. Uneventful week. Calm before another storm.

By 9:30 the following Saturday morning I was in full grandmother jacket slathering sunscreen on TJ at a water park in Palm Springs. We'd decided that I'd supervise the kids at the water park while Miyoko met with her Feng Shui client. Then we'd have a late lunch and take the kids to a museum to get them out of the heat. I was enjoying myself as much as possible at 108 degrees amid screaming kids sliding down a four story corkscrew of water. Over and over and over.

I am not one of those women who get all misty-eyed over babies and run around introducing ridiculous laws every time somebody under eighteen trips on a rug. I'm basically neutral about children. Some are interesting and some are not. But after raising two and teaching high school for most of my life, I understand them. And while I already knew that my grandson was what is euphemistically deemed "troubled," something happened that made me more concerned about Seiji than about TJ. One of the *things*.

During the two and a half hour drive from San Diego to Palm Springs, TJ explained at length that his career goal was to become a superhero named Deathworm. He would obliterate evil "control freaks" like his stepfather with the Russian AEK-919K Kashtan lightweight submachine gun (including laser aim feature) he hoped to get for Christmas.

"Shoots nine hundred rounds per minute, dude," he told Seiji.

"So? It only holds twenty or thirty rounds," Seiji replied, shifting heavily against his seatbelt. "You'll have to reload all the time. My choice, I'd go with the Shipka 9X18. Only shoots seven hundred but *way* easy to reload those clips."

"A *Bulgarian* gun?"

It was apparent that TJ regarded Bulgarian weaponry as kin to the common marshmallow.

"Secret police use it, dude," Seiji replied with authority.

"Dude!" TJ gave in, trumped.

I was sitting in the front passenger's seat and turned to introduce some upbeat topic not involving mass slaughter, when it happened. Seiji glanced guiltily at the back of his mother's head.

"Good thing about the Kashtan, though, is it comes with a silencer," he said softly. "You might need that ... sometimes."

Miyoko had put a Barber cello concerto in the car's CD player, and inside layers of sound I saw six coins floating near Seiji, who was still talking to TJ although I could hear nothing but the gentle cello descant that seemed to be breaking my heart. The coins swept and turned in the music, and then one by one fell into Seiji and vanished. My chest ached with sorrow as I watched, not wanting to see, not knowing what it meant and terrified that I knew anyway.

Thirteen can be total hell for some kids, the transition from childhood to adolescence a perilous journey most adults don't even remember. Or want to. But I was seeing it. Or seeing *something.*

Minutes later I pulled myself together and made up a reason to ask about coins. Another English teacher, a friend from the school where I taught, had sent me his recently-published collection of poetry, I told Miyoko. The Barber reminded me; one of the poems was about a cello heard in an icy park. So lovely. But the poem I liked best was puzzling. It was a long poem, strangely sad, each of six stanzas ending with a reference to a coin.

I thought it sounded plausible.

Miyoko frowned. "Is your friend Japanese?"

"No. Why?"

"Then the poem must be *about* something Japanese," she went on. "Six coins? Those are the coins placed in the pockets of the dead at Japanese Buddhist wakes, before the body is cremated. They are to pay the soul's way at the River of Three Crossings. Your friend's poem was about death."

I felt sick. Six coins. My grandson's thirteen-year-old pal. Was

I seeing something about a future that could still be changed? Was this part of the Revenant "gift" Tim O'Halloran told me I had? I didn't want to remember that. I wanted it not to have happened. I was scared.

After the water park we had lunch at a Mexican place where the kids consumed impossible quantities of food. TJ eats like an Olympic athlete and still looks like Howdy Doody after a three-week prison fast. Beth has always claimed she doesn't know who his father was, and I have to admit I've scoured her old high school yearbooks looking at photos of boys she dated in the summer after her senior year. None of them has TJ's disturbingly intelligent blue eyes, hay-like reddish blond hair or whole-body freckles.

Seiji, on the other hand, could do with a junior membership in Weight Watchers. He towers over TJ but is also three times as wide. Privately Miyoko explained that she has a brother who went through exactly the same stage and then trimmed down once he stopped growing. The brother is now six-two, 185 pounds and owns a trendy spa in Colorado. Miyoko and Seiji's dad expect the boy to follow in his uncle's genetic footprints and so don't hassle him about eating, she said. He's having a hard time as it is. The move was difficult, they're having financial problems, Seiji's a little prone to depression.

She also said the Feng Shui client was impressed when she figured out which way was south using my son Kevin's old Boy Scout compass. The client was so enthusiastic about his decorating project that he wanted to do something immediately and decided to start with Fu dogs to guard his front door. Except there's no place in Palm Springs to get Fu dog statues and his wife thinks they're hideous. Miyoko had her laptop open on the restaurant table and found a pair of granite Fu dogs she thought the wife could handle. They looked like corgis with big teeth, but were sort of cute. Four cell phone calls confirmed that a Chinese import warehouse in New Jersey had them in stock and could ship them on Monday. But Miyoko had to show the clients the photos and make payment arrangements if they wanted the dogs, which she was sure they would.

"This is cruel, but could you possibly take the boys to dinner while I run back to see them again tonight?" she asked. "I know I'm taking advantage and I'll make it up. I just don't want to lose this account. They're so jazzed about redoing their place and they seem to have limitless money. My husband's an engineer but he lost his job and is grabbing temp gigs right now. We need the extra income this will bring and you're really helping. How would you like it if I came by and gave you a free consult for your house? Do you have a room you're thinking of fixing up?"

"It's really no problem about dinner with the kids," I said. "You don't have to repay me."

She seemed thoughtful. "What color are your walls?"

"Walls?" In my lifetime, no one has ever asked me what color my walls are. Most of them are covered in bookcases and posters from art museums.

"Yes. You know, those flat, perpendicular surfaces that enclose living room, kitchen, bath...?"

"White," I admitted. "Sort of off-white. My ex-husband, TJ's grandfather, got a deal on a drum of off-white paint and sprayed all the rooms. It must have been fifteen years ago."

"Ex-husband and fifteen-year-old paint?" She grinned. "You need me!"

"Well, maybe you could just come by for coffee and give me some ideas," I said. "But no Fu dogs."

"Deal."

The museum was mercifully air-conditioned and I wandered around learning more than I ever wanted to know about the local Cahuilla Indians, whose language belonged to the Uto-Aztecan group. They could have chatted in Old High German for all I cared, but I was happy to read about it in cool, dim air while the boys watched a video on Native American puberty rituals five times. Miyoko and I watched it once and were not unaware that their interest was specific to some 1894 photos of bare-breasted Cahuilla girls included in the footage.

"Beats *Playboy*," Miyoko noted with resignation. "At least they'll get some idea of what real breasts look like."

I would have to remind TJ not to mention these antique breast photos to his stepfather. John insists that his two-year-old daughter Hannah wear the bra-top to her swimsuit at the community pool.

Later we went back to the motel, Miyoko's client picked her up to go order Fu dogs and I let the boys select our dinner destination. They chose a road house casino at the edge of town from a tourist brochure. The place boasted a "killer" mechanical bull said to have thrown even "champion rodeo cowboys."

The food was actually not bad and the bull was surrounded by piles of inflatable mattresses, so the boys didn't break any bones. A guy in camo gear showed them how to fall and they would have stayed there all night if I hadn't dragged them out around nine. That was when an influx of heavily made up young women in tiny Spandex skirts and push-up bras arrived, inciting the camo guys to drink more beer and monopolize the bull, showing off. John would have a coronary at the amount of jiggling mammary flesh on display.

TJ said he wanted to go to the bathroom before we left, so Seiji and I waited for him by a display of barbed wire near the door.

"What do you think it's like when you're dead?" Seiji asked, studying a row of Dodge Six-Point Star wire.

Kids will often talk to strangers about their problems. I should have known this was coming.

"There's a line from *Hamlet* that says it all," I answered, wishing I could think of something other than Shakespeare. "'The undiscovered country from whose bourne no traveler returns.'"

"Bourne?"

Why do I always have to sound like I just swallowed the complete works of somebody when I'm in tight situations?

"It means 'boundary, edge,'" I said. "Death is a place from which nobody comes back to tell about it, and so we just don't know. What do you think?"

"Oh," he said somberly, "I think maybe it's nice. Nicer than here, y'know? Kids don't like me here. I'm not American. They call me Cunt Eyes and Sumo Butt. I hate it!"

"Seiji," I said, giving him a quick hug, "you've got to believe me on this. *Everybody* goes through little patches of time when people are rotten to you and the whole world sucks. Even adults. But the little patches of time don't last. They get better. That's just how life works, okay?"

"It does?"

"Yeah."

At least I'd gotten away from Shakespeare, but it was weak. And thousands of Asian people immigrated to California in the 1800's. Despite epic discrimination and a couple of massacres in the old days, they've been here ever since. Asian kids are nothing unusual in California schools or anywhere else. Seiji was just the fat new kid on the block and subject to the usual fat-new-kid cruelties. But he was taking the ethnic slurs seriously.

TJ showed up and Seiji kicked the cigarette machine as we walked out. TJ seemed to admire the action and walked back to kick it himself. Solidarity of some kind. It was still hot and the kids were restless.

"I could use a Coke or something," Seiji announced as we drove past a miniature golf course with a sort of game pavilion behind it. The golf course was dimly lit and seemed to be closed, but I could see that it had an Indian theme. Lots of cement wigwams and resin statues holding tomahawks in the sweltering gloom. But the pavilion was ablaze with light.

"Okay, but only for a little while," I said. It was still early, Miyoko wouldn't be back yet. A few pinball games would be fun.

Except there were no pinballs.

"Oh my God," I gasped when we walked in.

A sequined Dolly Parton who needed a shave was lip-syncing "Silver Threads and Golden Needles" on a low stage as a crowd in jeans sang along. There were couples of all ages and several kids around; it felt pretty wholesome. But it was still a drag show and John would have me arrested.

"We've got to get out of here," I told TJ urgently.

"No way! This is fun!"

Both boys joined the song, yelling, "You can't buy my love with money, for I never was that kind," then dissolving in giggles.

"I can't believe you know the words," I said.

"We had a substitute teacher last spring; he played the banjo and taught us these lame old songs," Seiji explained while TJ got Cokes from a machine. "He was fun."

"Okay, but let's go."

A Cher with astonishing biceps launched into "If I Could Turn Back Time."

"After this guy finishes his song, okay grandma?" TJ threw a kernel of popcorn he found on the floor at a girl in pink fringed boots.

"Jerk!" she said, tossing her hair in a gesture that reminded me of Jude.

TJ searched for another kernel of popcorn. Seiji was watching the guy doing the sound board. I gave up and got myself an Orange Crush.

The kids weren't remotely fazed by the fact that we'd wandered into a nest of female impersonators. If I made a big deal of it, I'd just poison their minds and ruin the end of the evening. I felt like a dinosaur, though, in college before I even knew what a drag show was.

The air outside was still in the 90's when we left, but the sky was clean and breathless, the stars eerily close. A beefy Indian with a long braid was either asleep or drunk in the back of a pickup truck beside Miyoko's car. I got in, turned on the fan and rolled down the windows, then stood beside the car waiting for it to cool. The kids got in and turned on a CD Miyoko bought at the museum. Indian flute. Then they got back out because I was just standing there, watching the Indian in the pickup. I felt odd the way you do as an anesthesiologist opens the stopcock valve on a needle stuck in your arm and says, "Count backward from ten." You're hyperaware and determined to make it at least to five, but by eight it seems like too much work.

"Dude!" TJ said, his blue eyes wide.

The Indian was standing now, dressed in animal skins. His dark eyes beneath epicanthic folds identical to Seiji's turned to me and I thought I should say something. I thought I should *teach*, actually. The old wiring. I had no idea what was going on.

"Thousands of years ago people came here in boats paddled across the Pacific Ocean," I said for no apparent reason. "Others may have crossed a land bridge that once connected what is now Russia to what is now Alaska, and these people were the first Americans." I sounded mechanical, although it wasn't quite my voice and felt more like thinking. It was my voice in a dream, alto and husky. Also pedantic.

I wasn't sure I'd really said anything at all, but the Indian nodded and began a guttural chant that somehow melded with the flute music coming from the car. He pointed to the miniature golf course and the kids and I grew wide-eyed as one of the Indian figures in a breechclout turned his head stiffly to look at the sky.

"Jeez, look!" TJ yelled. "It's a sound and light show! Somebody must have turned it on. This place is totally cool!"

The cement teepees were made of skins now, and smoke from many small fires drifted upward. The Indian figures were all moving in slight, abrupt jerks as if they were unused to mobility, but their eyes were alive. A woman who looked like Miyoko smiled at a chubby baby in a cradleboard and beyond the San Bernardino Mountains I saw a procession of millions, climbing down the sky. Dark-haired people with Asian eyes walking through centuries, splitting into threads across the North American continent. Their footsteps seemed to be drums within the earth, vibrating the gravel parking lot beneath our feet.

"A sound and light show," Seiji said, shaking his head. "Who ever heard of a miniature golf course with a sound and light show?"

"Well, this one *has* a sound and light, show, dude," TJ insisted. "It's right there!"

"Chumash," the Indian in the truck chanted, pronouncing each word slowly, as if it were a prayer. "Haida, Tlingit, Kwakiutl. Nipmuc, Wampanoag, Choctaw, Tunica, Apache, Shoshone…"

Names of Indian tribes. I knew them; the names were in my head but I couldn't think of any more. I panicked.

"Dream of Blue Frog!" the Indian suddenly bellowed, pointing dramatically at Seiji. Then he collapsed in the shadows of the truck bed as breathy flute notes fell around us in the hot dark. The figures in the miniature golf course were still, the fires nothing but orange paint in the moonlight.

"Shit, dude, all those people look like you!" TJ whispered. "The First Nations, like in school, y'know? You came later but you were an American before anybody else!"

Seiji looked at me, shaking a little. "What's 'Dream of Blue Frog'?"

I'd glanced at an old flier at the museum for an art exhibit named "The Dream of the Blue Frog." The exhibit was years ago, but I read the flier anyway. I read everything.

"The Blue Frog is a *nutakem*," I recited from the text. "A spiritual being who lives deep inside the earth, under the springs that gave this place its name. He is strong and wise and taught the Cahuilla shamans magic."

I couldn't remember anything else but TJ saved the moment.

"And you're the Dream of the Blue Frog," he yelled. "That's so incredible, dude!"

"Oh," Seiji said, but I saw him straighten his shoulders a little as we got in the car.

It took me a while to piece it together, but I was sure it had something to do with the Revenant business. I could apparently conjure scenes out of my mind. Because for sure that's where this came from. Blue Frogs, ancient migrations, it was all a mishmash of information throbbing on electrical synapses in my brain. But two children had seen it as well. It happened. And I was exhausted.

Back at the motel Miyoko was repeatedly grateful for my help and the kids fell asleep in seconds. I lay awake for a while thinking about the Indian. How had I done it? And would it help?

In a corner by the window the heavy drapery moved slightly and a faint scent of persimmons billowed in the blast from the air conditioner.

"Go to hell," I told it, and fell asleep.

Chapter Seven

Through the Valley of Fear

Billy Joel

The following Tuesday Miyoko came by in the morning with paint chips and a twenty-pound illustrated book on decorating.

"I guess I was thinking of you as maybe Country French," she said over coffee in my kitchen, which is completely lacking in cobbled floors, shutters, rough-hewn cabinetry and copper pots hanging on chains over an open hearth. There is a hearth, just no copper.

"But now I'm leaning toward Arts and Crafts," she concluded, opening the book to a page showing a Frank Lloyd Wright floor lamp with a mica shade. I choked. The lamp cost almost nine hundred dollars before shipping.

"To be honest," I said, "until you mentioned it I hadn't given any thought to doing anything with the house. But then I came home and looked at the kitchen and it's so... 70's."

"Probably when the house was built," she noted briskly,

pulling a three-ring binder from her bag and pushing it toward me. It had multi-colored slots and folders and a lot of graph paper.

"First, just collect ideas," she said. "Make notes, take photos, tear pages out of magazines at the dentist. Keep it all in here. Colors you like, cabinet hardware, somebody's drapery fabric. Then we'll come up with a *plan*."

"Plan?"

"We'll start with the kitchen, but co-ordinate the whole house. Not all at once, but you want the theme to flow throughout. Don't worry, I'm madly building my contact list here and can get you some good deals."

Good deals on a theme? I was lost.

"Miyoko, you're being a dear, but I'm afraid this is all out of my league. My friend Penley Barrows has a place in La Jolla overlooking the ocean, though. Why don't I give her your number? She's been talking about redoing an atrium."

She pulled herself staunchly upright, although at 5'2' in a sitting position the gesture lacked gravitas.

"I wouldn't *charge* you, Taylor," she said, softly outraged. "I want to repay your kindness to Seiji."

"The kindness was yours to TJ," I countered, feeling a sweep of drawing-room courtesy that made me think of Jane Austen. "You have no idea how good it was for him to get away and have a good time."

I wanted to conclude with something like, "If there is debt, it is mine," while turning pale with modesty, but restrained myself.

"Can we stop this any time soon?" she said, grinning. "Come on. Seiji told us about the sound and light show at a miniature golf course, an Indian who told him he was the dream of a blue frog and how you explained that Native Americans are the descendants of Asians and all that. He's decided he's an Indian shaman or something. He and TJ are designing t-shirts with blue frogs to wear to school. He's… a tiny bit better, Taylor. Whatever you said out there, whatever happened, it made a difference for him. So, was there really an Indian?"

"Sort of," I said. "He was asleep in the back of a truck."

"Kids have such imagination, don't they? A shame we lose it when we grow up."

"Yes," I answered, not mentioning that it may not be "imagination" and it doesn't always stay lost. I wondered if Miyoko Foxwell would wake up one day at sixty, the child she had been alive again in her mind. Why some people and not others? Did it really happen to me and what did it mean? And what happened to those Revenants who didn't fight, but allowed a childhood ghoul now grown deadly, to destroy them? I'd call Tim O'Halloran. He hadn't told me enough, by far.

It was all so weird I couldn't get my mind around it, but my house felt safe. It held the story of my adult life before everything changed in a dance studio when I reached up, touched my own childhood and became something I didn't understand. Redecorating my house would honor that adult life, wouldn't it? And help me hold on to it. I was definitely warming to the idea as a defense against what was happening to me. Besides, it would be fun.

After Miyoko left around 1:00 I skipped lunch and drove to meet Jill Danner and Maggie McFadden at the quilt show. It was at a community center in an older neighborhood of parched tract houses and apartment buildings in discolored stucco. It's a mixed neighborhood, Bondoed cars on cement blocks in driveways, multiethnic kids dressed like Pilgrims and Indians for school Thanksgiving pageants. But there are no bars, and locals congregate at a diner that serves the best liver and onions this side of the Mississippi. The diner reminds me of home, even though San Diego is a sprawling city rife with problems my little town would have taken out in the woods and shot. You can never go home again, but occasionally there's a diner that's close. I liked the neighborhood.

"Taylor, you've got to see the work on this nine patch and star!" Jill Danner called across the registration table as I walked in. "It's in the corner next to the Chess Club Exhibit. Maggie's there. Come on back as soon as you register."

At seventy-six Jill is the oldest member of the Syndicate and probably the most well-adjusted. She genuinely loves life, an enthusiasm that seems to make her flyaway white hair leap from her head like Medusa's snakes. Or else it's the chlorine from the pool where she does laps every morning. Her richly lined skin is the color of pink cotton candy, a fact she says prohibits her ever wearing red. We used to tell her she should think of herself as an artist, but it would only irritate her. If Jill could spend an hour with any person living or dead, it would be William Morris. She believes in Crafts with a capital C and volunteers two days a week teaching hospitalized kids to make elaborate picture frames and birdfeeders out of Popsicle sticks. To Jill, a quilt show is a religious experience.

"I can't believe the way she used the feather stitch in this border," she noted reverently when I joined her and Maggie. "The juxtaposition of feathery curves with the crisp lines of the nine patch and star. It's stunning!"

"Yes," I said, trying to look stunned by tiny stitches, millions of them, in some fabric. My only sewing project, an apron made in a junior high home ec. class, was unrecognizable and fell apart before my mother could donate it to the church rummage sale.

All the quilts had three by five cards in plastic sleeves with information about the quilter. This one had been made and quilted by "Mrs. Arthur Steininger, 83, a resident of St. Luke's Assisted Living Facility." It was queen-size and cost $498. A round red dot on the plastic sleeve indicated that somebody had already bought it and Jill was distraught.

"The butter yellow is a perfect match for the walls in my guest room," she sighed. "And you just don't see perfect hand stitching like that. It's practically a lost art. Everybody uses quilting machines now. She should have charged twice as much."

"There are lots more," Maggie McFadden suggested, stating

the obvious. "Let's keep looking."

Maggie was a Sacred Heart of Mary nun until, she says, "One day the whole nun thing just seemed pointless." There was nothing dramatic, no doomed love affair with a priest or doctrinal dark night of the soul. She left the order cordially twenty years ago at forty-five, went to work as a social worker for an Interfaith Consortium and moved into a two-bedroom apartment with a retired gay rabbi named Shlomo she met at work. He was in a wheelchair and invited her to move in with him because he needed live-in help. But over time they developed a deep platonic friendship that lasted until he died five years ago and left her the whole apartment building. Maggie's philosophy is eclectic and several standard deviations to the left of Karl Marx, and she looks like an Irish Bella Abzug. But at fifty yards you'd still peg her as a nun. I guess once it's there, it never wears off.

We wandered around admiring Baltimores, Log Cabins, fat squares and picture quilts, all with running commentary from Jill. Maggie was quite taken by an indigo blue and white queen-size in the Drunkard's Path pattern, and kept going back to look at it.

"It's a reproduction pattern; blue and white quilts were all the rage in the late 19th century," Jill explained, "because the indigo dyes didn't fade in the wash. Also because blue and white were the colors of the Women's Christian Temperance Union, so Drunkard's Path was a popular pattern. This one's machine-quilted but the top is well-pieced. I'd get it for Steve, but he's trying AA again."

Maggie and I nodded supportively, not for the first time. Steve Danner is a functional alcoholic who never missed a day when he was working and isn't much different now that he's retired. He plays golf and maintains a year-round vegetable garden until five o'clock every day, when he opens the Glenfiddich and doesn't stop until he falls over. Jill adores him and long ago gave up on getting him to change. She goes to Al-Anon meetings and has learned to live around Steve's drinking. The only rule she has is that he can't drink while they're traveling. Steve toes that line, and as a result Jill travels more than anybody in the Syndicate. They go someplace nearby one weekend a month and plan to spend

Christmas in Austria. So far it works for them.

"I'm going to buy it," Maggie said, and rummaged for her check book.

Jill and I went to watch an appliqué-cutting demonstration while Maggie negotiated, but I wasn't really interested. A quilted wall hanging barely visible beneath several others arranged on a table caught my eye and I absentmindedly went to look at it.

"It's really ugly," Jill said, following me. "You can't be thinking of buying that thing!"

I didn't want to buy it, but for some reason I was drawn to it in the way you can't keep yourself from slowing to look at wrecks on the freeway. It made me dizzy. Rows of ragged four-point stars on black and blue squares surrounded a center square in black velvet. The big dipper was outlined against the velvet in glued-on silver sequins. The points of the stars were done in a welter of fabric — old dishtowels, denim from blue jeans, a striped rayon probably from a blouse that had once been purple. There was no continuity and the thing definitely wasn't pretty, but it contained a story, I thought.

"Antonio Maxwell," Jill read from the three by five card. "From the Phoenix Project. The quilter is a man. Unusual."

"What's the Phoenix Project?"

"I don't have the slightest idea, but Maggie might know. A lot of the quilts are by people involved with senior centers, various social service programs. A way for them to make some money. It's probably something like that. Hey, how about grabbing a bite here when Maggie gets done? I'm starving and they're setting up a fried chicken thing."

I had skipped lunch. I could smell the chicken.

"Good idea."

Maggie kept her brown-paper-wrapped quilt on the floor by her feet to avoid getting grease on it as we sat on folding chairs and wolfed down fried chicken and mashed potatoes made from a box. The salad was orange Jell-O with crushed pineapple and mini-marshmallows in it, a concoction I hadn't seen in at least forty years. I was content. Some kids were trying to dance to the background music on the loudspeaker system and kept yelling, "Turn it up!" Somebody did. Billy Joel doing "River of Dreams." The sound rang in my head.

"So Taylor, you didn't see one you liked?" Maggie asked.

"There's one... it's a wall hanging. I don't 'like' it, but there's something about it. Do you know what the Phoenix Project is?"

"I've heard of it," Maggie said. "A program for people with disabilities. Major disabilities. Training, that sort of thing."

Joel's honky-tonk gospel piano pulled at me, the pounding notes like sharp little tugs. "Through the valley of fear," he sang. "To a river so deep." I had to look at that quilt again.

"I'll be right back, "I said.

It was still there, but glowing now, the sequined Big Dipper blinding. Real stars throbbing in the fried-chicken-scented shadows of a rundown community center. I knew no one could see the stars but me. Or the blood running from a triangle of red bandana that made up half a star point, or the bruised flesh behind it. The thing was screaming inside Billy Joel's voice, inside the gospel choir backing him, inside the thumping piano.

"The music makes a path, you see," Tim O'Halloran had said.

This was a path to anguish, cruelty, pain. I was shaking.

"Taylor, are you all right?"

Jill and Maggie were close behind me.

"There's something wrong with this quilt," I whispered, staring at what I knew they couldn't see as the music roared in my head. The thing was bleeding from its ragged seams, its black and blue squares were bruises throbbing with pain. And in the center, the

Big Dipper, blazing.

"It's the drinking gourd," Jill said. "The few slaves who made it north, illiterate and hunted, following the North Star that's always visible near the tip of the Dipper's handle."

The symbol might be a desperate echo from a brutal time or just a constellation. But whatever it was, it burned my eyes.

"I've heard that sympathetic people would hang quilts on fences to guide the escaping slaves," Maggie said. "That the quilts held coded maps in their designs."

Jill shook her head. "It's a charming idea and a book about it is actually used in schools, but the story's wholly fictional, I'm afraid. And there were no slaves in San Diego unless you count the local Indians under the heel of the Spanish padres. Taylor, you don't look good. I think we should go. Fried food, I imagine."

Maggie was watching me.

"It doesn't matter that stories are fictional," she said. "Everything is fictional. What matters is which stories you believe."

I remembered Martine. "*How* things are done does not matter. What matters is *that* they are done." Something had been done here, and only I could see it. But what was I supposed to do? I turned to Maggie, wild-eyed.

"Please, will you just check on something for me? This Phoenix Project. Can you find out who Antonio Maxwell is?"

"Sure," she said.

At home I called Tim O'Halloran and left a message. Then I watched TV for a while. Three back-to-back segments of a crime series in which there were no bleeding quilts and police invariably caught the perps while engaging in clever repartee. I wished anything were that simple. In bed, the tin whistle on its silver chain was sharp against my chest.

At eleven-thirty the phone rang.

"Tim?" I said groggily.

"Who's Tim?" Maggie McFadden asked. "And I don't know what happened to you at the quilt show, but you were on to something."

"What? What do you mean?"

"I'm not blind, Taylor. You were so upset about that ugly little quilt, and when you asked me to check on the quilter it felt serious. So I made a few calls." Her voice was edgy.

"And...?"

"Antonio Maxwell is a twenty-three-year-old paraplegic. Fell into an empty swimming pool when he was five and broke his back. Single mom's been in prison since he was ten, no other family. Thirteen years in foster care and group homes, Taylor. Rotten life for a kid who can *walk*, but he managed to grow up. Now he's missing."

"Missing?"

"He's supposed to be living in a board and care, except I got the address and went there after we left the quilt show. The place is abandoned. Woman next door said she hasn't seen anybody go in or out for three days. I called the police, they're investigating, so far they haven't found anything. What did you see, Taylor?"

I could have pretended not to know what she meant.

"Pain," I said. "Can you come by tomorrow, Mag? I have to tell you something." I really wanted her to come immediately, but I didn't know why. It was late. But something was terribly wrong.

"I'll be there," she said.

Chapter Eight

Hearts Made of Stone

The Fontane Sisters

"Tim, I don't think I can do this," I whined when O'Halloran returned my call early the next morning. I was still in my bathrobe, waiting for the coffee maker to cease gurgling. A throbbing afterimage of that quilt appeared every time I blinked.

"I'm crazy, I see things, I seem to be able to make other people, at least children, see things that somehow get created out of my mind, except some of them *don't* come from my mind but are just there. Everywhere I go, it's like I'm in two worlds. The real one and some other one that's *extreme*, Tim. Everything's overdone, dramatic, scary."

I told him about plaster man, Seiji, the Indian and the damn bleeding quilt.

He sighed. "And you wish the scary world would go away. It's difficult in the beginning, I know. But you're a Revenant, Taylor. You have to live in both worlds now. You have no choice."

I didn't believe that. "There are always choices, Tim."

"Yes and no," he answered. "Did you choose to be born, grow old, die?"

I sensed deep philosophy winging its way. I didn't want winged philosophy, I wanted *out*.

"No, but…"

"Well, Revenance is now a stage in the life cycle, for some. We can no more escape it than we could escape puberty. It does get easier, Taylor, as the ways in which you will function as a Revenant become clear. From what you've experienced so far, my guess is that your gift may involve intercession in situations of threat, that sort of thing. We assumed as much from your behavior with the armadillo."

"Churchill," I said, remembering the plated little animal with its piglike ears, standing on its hind legs to eat crumbled hardboiled eggs from my hand. "But Tim, anybody would have wanted to save the poor thing. It doesn't mean…"

"No, Taylor, many would have simply ignored the creature and left it to die. Others would have killed it. You did neither; you assumed the inconvenience and personal expense of nursing it back to health and then transporting it to a locale where it could live. It's too soon to tell, but the gifts we enjoy as Revenants seem to be only intensified aspects of the personalities we've had all along. We'll know more later, and there's some talk of a manual or website…"

"Oh dear God, a manual? Come on!"

I didn't want there to be a manual. A manual would give solidity to something I didn't want to acknowledge was there. At the same time my real inclination was to race to my computer and order one. Were they on Amazon?

"It's just an idea at the moment," he continued as if we were discussing a dubious business opportunity. Soy-based dèsigner wine or something.

"As I explained, there's a fledgling headquarters in Boston, just getting underway. It's all so new that nobody's sure how to proceed, but there is unanimous agreement about secrecy, Taylor."

His voice was that of a newscaster announcing the assassination of a world leader.

"We have peculiar powers even we don't understand yet. They seem to be idiosyncratic, different in every Revenant. As I've said, governments could take an unwholesome interest, religious extremists could go berserk. We could be impounded, used, even slaughtered. The creation of a written document, however helpful, could fall into the wrong hands. It would be dangerous."

"It could be written in code," I suggested, warming to the idea. "In some terribly esoteric journal article like 'The Heron as Symbol of Commerce in Fourteenth Century Norwegian Woodcarving,' except if you only read every third word of the text it's something else entirely. A how-to guide for Revenants."

"A code is under consideration," Tim said. "And with your permission I'll notify headquarters that you might be interested."

I love codes, symbols, the whole literary game. "Sure."

"Meanwhile, perhaps I may be of immediate help," he said hopefully.

"I'm listening."

"Humor," he said. "Imagination. Of course you knew there was something terrible hiding in your closet at night when you were a child, correct?"

"It wasn't in the closet, it was in the wallpaper," I answered. "Like Charlotte Perkins Gilman's 'The Yellow Wallpaper.' Except I hadn't read 'The Yellow Wallpaper' yet and it wasn't a creeping woman. It was something writhing around inside the design, like a huge snake made of smoke. In the dark it could get out of the wallpaper and come down the wall. Sometimes it would hide under my bed in loops and might wrap around my leg if I had to get up and go to the bathroom."

There was a silence in which I sensed that he hadn't anticipated so much detail.

"Good heavens. Well, what I mean to say is that while childhood horrors are no longer hidden from us by the blinders of adult life, neither are childhood delights. I've found that a return to childhood enthusiasms, paths once imagined but now long-forgotten, create a buffer against... against the darker things."

"Your Tom Mix costume," I said.

"Exactly!"

Right away I knew Tim's method wouldn't work for me. I hadn't wanted to be a movie star as a child. I wanted a space ship to land in my back yard, just beyond my bedroom window. I'd crawl through the window and tell curious, antennaed extraterrestrials about Abraham Lincoln and Clark Bars, and they'd tell me where dogs go when they die. It would be a beautiful place with fields and forests, and Ginger would be there, waiting for me when I died, too.

"I'll have to think about this," I told Tim. "Thanks. And by the way, I'd like to know more about what happened to the Revenants you talked about. The ones who wouldn't fight."

"I'll email you some information. You'll need to delete the links immediately upon reading them." There was reluctance in his voice. "Although it's best not to dwell on these things."

"I won't dwell. I just want to know. Thanks, Tim"

It was well into September and murderously hot. I pulled on baggy Bermudas and a tee shirt and watered everything until Maggie showed up around 8:30, gripping a manila folder. She was wearing red sandals, bright green cropped pants and a pink Hawaiian shirt with macaws on it, and still looked like a nun.

"How do you do it?" I asked her.

"The benign, otherworldly look? Years of practice. Helps to spend some time in a Guatemalan prison for organizing indigenous farm laborers, too."

"Mag! I didn't know you'd been in prison!"

Her benign, otherworldly green eyes twinkled behind silver aviator frames that have been out of style since Gloria Steinem wore them. But they're perfect on Maggie.

"I didn't say I had. In fact, I haven't. What I said was that it helps with the look. But enough about me, Taylor. I think we've got a job on our hands. Mind if I have my coffee iced?"

Over years of southern California Septembers, which are frequently comparable to Septembers in the baking Hoggar Region of Algeria, I have perfected a life-saving iced coffee that can be made in seconds from instant. Maggie likes hers sweet, so I put a couple of spoons of powdered sugar and a dash of nutmeg in with the instant crystals. You stir a little boiling water in, just enough to dissolve the crystals, cool the syrup with an ice cube, and then add cold water and more ice cubes. No waiting for hot coffee to cool.

"Mmm," she murmured, sipping appreciatively. "Now, we need to talk about Antonio Maxwell. It was his quilt in which you saw pain."

She was matter-of-fact about it, as if seeing pain in quilts were nothing unusual. I didn't know what to say and probably looked like the proverbial deer-in-headlights. Tim had just reminded me that secrecy was essential. I couldn't tell Maggie I was a Revenant. I shouldn't have told Jude, but figured she was safe.

Maggie regarded me evenly. "Taylor, I don't know why you saw something in that quilt. These things happen. Remember, I grew up in Catholic schools where stories about visions are part of the curriculum. Then I spent twenty-five years in a religious order founded by a French widow and her deceased husband's best friend, a priest, for the care of prostitutes and abandoned children. It's always a good idea not to judge, and there's absolutely no point in getting all clinical about this stuff unless somebody's running a scam, which you're not. The point is, something's wrong and you got a glimpse of it. How you got the glimpse doesn't matter."

I remembered Martine's words again. *How* things happen doesn't matter. Well, okay.

"I don't know what I'm supposed to do," I said.

"Neither do I, but let's start with what we've got."

Maggie is the director of the Interfaith Consortium now and widely respected in the social services community, both left and right-wing. She knows everybody, can get whatever information she wants, and did. A copy of Antonio Maxwell's case file lay open on my kitchen table.

A photo stapled to the folder showed a sickly young man of mixed race, probably African-American/Hispanic, with gorgeous eyes and acne scars. His mother was African-American and doing twenty years as an habitual criminal after sequential convictions for possession, prostitution, assault with a deadly weapon and attempted robbery. After aging out of the foster care system at eighteen, Antonio lived in state-funded board and cares, private homes in which people receive money for the care of the disabled. The last of these was an address in Linda Vista, a "transitional" central San Diego neighborhood that's home to waves of immigrants. Antonio had lived there for three months.

Much of Linda Vista's real estate is WWII military housing, now amended in a haphazard array of additions, covered patios and semi-detached garages that may function as chicken coops, drug labs or small restaurants. At one end is a wealthy private university, and there are large homes with breathtaking views from which the area took its Spanish name, "pretty view." But there are parts of Linda Vista where you wouldn't want to go at night.

"The police have been to the address, of course," Maggie said. "Place is empty. The property was rented to a couple, Denise and Bradford Holland, who've lived there for nearly a year. Antonio was the only tenant."

"These people have to be licensed, right?" I said. "Just anybody can't sign up to take care of…"

"The system is overburdened," she interrupted. "Underfunded, understaffed. Everything runs months, even years behind schedule. The Hollands filled out the paperwork and a social worker did a home visit before Antonio was placed there, but…"

"But what?"

"But nobody had run the checks on them yet. As it turns out, 'Bradford Holland's' Social Security number belongs to a Kentucky tobacco farmer who died eight years ago. Holland's wife showed a Canadian birth certificate that turned out to be bogus. Denise and Bradford Holland do not exist."

I felt a chill run through the muscles beneath my skin. What had these people *done*?

"Exactly," Maggie replied as if she'd read my mind. "Either Antonio is dead and what you saw in the quilt is a message received too late, or he's still alive and we have to find him."

Her directness was reassuring.

"But the police…"

"…are doing everything they can," she finished my sentence. 'What we, what *you* can do is different from what they can do. I went back and bought Antonio's quilt after you and Jill left, Taylor. It's in the car. Shall I get it?"

I didn't want to see it again.

"Yes," I said.

But once Maggie had it spread out on my kitchen table, it was just an ugly jumble of fabric. No blood at the seams, no injured flesh in the black and blue background. The kitchen was quiet. A plastic sequin from the big dipper design came loose and fell on my bare foot. I leaned to pick it up, then put it back where it had been.

"He put the dipper in as a sign," I said. "The Drinking Gourd story, slaves following the North Star to freedom, maps hidden in quilts on fences. He must have read the book Jill mentioned when he was in school, remembered it and made the quilt as a map so somebody could find him!"

"Antonio would have been sent a flier about the quilt exhibit by the Phoenix Project," Maggie said, thinking aloud. "The exhibit was planned a year ago and invitations mailed to all the social services agencies shortly after that. They in turn would have sent the announcement to individuals connected to their agencies or projects, their clients, later but still in time for work to be completed. Somewhere in the last three months Antonio found out about the quilt exhibit and made his quilt.

"But how did he get it to the exhibit? If he could deliver the quilt, why didn't he tell somebody he needed help?"

Maggie looked at her notes.

"It came to the exhibit with two other quilts made by clients at the Linda Vista Settlement House. That's a big place, serves mostly the Vietnamese, Laotian and Filipino communities.
"Antonio's not Vietnamese, Laotian or Filipino," I pointed out.

"No, but the Settlement House is near the address where he was living. I talked to the director there last night and she said Antonio's quilt was delivered one morning about a week ago by a little girl who said she found it in the alley behind the house where Antonio was living. It was in a white plastic bag with a note saying, "Take to Settlement House," taped to the bag. The letter from the Phoenix Project announcing the exhibit was inside. The people at the Settlement House never saw Antonio, have no idea who he is."

"But what about the Phoenix Project? Surely somebody there...?"

"Checked that out," Maggie went on. "Antonio's case worker at Phoenix, young guy named Scott, did the intake interview with Antonio over the phone. The Phoenix Project does training programs – computer stuff mostly, medical coding, web site development, jobs handicapped people can do from home. Phoenix provides pc's and Internet service once training's completed, and helps clients get work. Antonio was scheduled to start a year-long training program in two weeks. Scott would have met him in person then. Right now he doesn't know any more about Antonio than we do."

"Damn!"

"Look at the quilt, Taylor. If it's a map, maybe we can follow it."

I looked hard, eager for my Revenant craziness to surface with bizarre messages. I saw four-point stars on black and blue background squares, each star point made of two fabrics. Dish towels, denim, rags. In the center a patch of balding black velvet, the big dipper outlined in glued-on plastic sequins. But I didn't see any map. I didn't see anything except what was there. The loose sequin at the end of the dipper's handle throbbed a little in the sunlight. Or else I was imagining it.

"Something about the dipper," I said.

The silence buzzed in my ears as we sat there staring at the quilt. My kitchen was too quiet.

"Music!" I yelped, remembering. "Music helps."

I leaped up to turn on the radio I keep in the kitchen so I can listen to NPR on the rare occasions that I cook, and wrenched the dial to a classical station. A Debussy arabesque. We stared at the quilt. Nothing.

Except I felt sweat running in rivulets down my back and my breath was shallow. A tsunami of oblivion, hot and colorless, was gathering. Somewhere.

"Maggie, we can't just sit here," I decided. "We have to... go there, to the house."

It made no sense, the police had already been there, interviewed neighbors, the whole drill. But I was suffocating in my kitchen with that ugly, silent quilt.

"Roger," she said, grabbing her keys.

The house was a run-down rental, once painted blue but now faded to splotches of grayish lavender. Half-dead palms drooped over knee-high weeds growing through the rusted frame of an overturned grocery cart in the yard. A new wooden wheelchair ramp led to a cracked cement porch. The door was locked and the place exuded emptiness. I pushed through the weeds to the back of the house and noticed a pile of rocks in a corner by the fence, barely visible beneath an overgrown bottlebrush tree. The rocks made me shiver in the heat.

"Oh, no," Maggie said, watching me stare at the rock pile. "You don't think...?"

"No."

I didn't think Antonio Maxwell was buried under the rocks; they'd been there long enough for weeds to grow through them in the spring and then turn brown in the late summer heat. I just thought the rocks shouldn't have been there at all. They were ordinary rocks, round and stained with iron.

San Diego was once a shallow sea, and as the surrounding mountains fell apart and rose again with the shifting of continents, the broken fragments broke further and were slowly rounded by warm salt tides. Everybody is familiar with these rocks. They underlie the entire city just beneath a thin layer of soil, a foot deep at best. The rocks are why San Diego houses do not have basements. The ground is all concretized rock, prohibitively expensive to excavate. Planting a small tree here requires a crowbar and days of work prying up densely-packed rocks. But nobody had planted a tree in the yard where Antonio lived. Nobody had planted anything, or intended to. There was no hole or spindly new tree anywhere in the yard. So where had the rocks come from?

Maggie was bent over, tearing up weeds.

"Taylor, look at this!"

Near the back porch was a dipper made of rocks, nearly lost in the weeds.

"He made that! Antonio must have made that," I said. "But there's no wheelchair ramp from the back porch and no way to get back here through the weeds from the front."

"He dragged himself down those steps on his arms to make this thing some time ago," Maggie stated, watching the porch as if seeing a video. "Taylor, what does it mean?"

I would have killed for a plaster statue and an Indian, but all I saw was dust swarming in the bright, quiet air. I might be a Revenant, but it wasn't going to help. I had no special power. No power at all. And then it hit me.

"There are no basements in San Diego!" I yelled, surveying the foundation of the shabby little structure. The housing code has required cement slab foundations here for years, but this house predated that law. It sat on cement blocks only inches above the ground.

"Maggie, somebody dug those rocks out from under the house!"

"Oh, God."

She was up the steps in seconds, rattling the knob on the back door. I grabbed a twenty-pound rock from the pile before joining her.

"Look out," I said and smashed the rock down hard on the doorknob, which fell with the faceplates and lock at my feet. The door was eaten by termites, held together only by countless coats of paint. I pulled what was left of it open.

"Antonio!" we both yelled in the small kitchen. Silence.

The place wasn't filthy or particularly clean. It was just old. And deserted except for a few flies lazily bumping against the dusty window. We stomped on the floor, tried to peel the worn linoleum back but it had been installed with that black asphalt goo that over time turns to stone. An area rug in the living room was easy to move, but the floor there was also intact. We flew to the airless hall, bathroom, two bedrooms.

In one was a wheelchair, a poster of a rock group on the wall, a twin bed with dirty sheets and against the wall, a sagging bookcase. I quickly glanced at the titles and grabbed a well-worn book with a photograph of a quilt on the cover.

"Maggie, look! This is that book Jill was talking about. She said it's used in schools even though the story isn't true. Antonio must have read it years ago and kept it."

"Taylor!"

She'd opened the closet door and a stench of excrement and coppery dried blood billowed into the room.

I dropped the book and ran to kick a pile of rags off the closet floor. Hacked-up blue jeans, shreds of dish towels, a torn red bandana, the remains of a purple rayon blouse. The fabric of Antonio's quilt. On the floor was a large square of new plywood.

"Maggie!" I think I screamed, gagging on the smell as I pulled up the plywood and a nebula of flies rose in a buzzing arc.

The hole was about three feet deep and four feet wide, nothing but bare dirt and rocks. And crumpled within it was a naked figure with wasted legs. He looked gray in the dim light from the window, covered in flies.

"Is he dead?" I said, shaking all over.

Maggie was on her knees, then flat on her stomach at the edge of the hole, leaning down. I saw her fingers touch the side of his neck.

"I think I feel a pulse!" She sat up, reached in a pocket and threw her car keys at me.

I was on my feet and running even as I heard Maggie vomiting. In the car I grabbed my cell and dialed 911. Then we soaked a rag I found in the kitchen in cool water and folded it over his head while we waited. He didn't move and there was no visible rise and fall beneath his ribs. No sound but flies buzzing at crusted wounds, sliced flesh. We didn't say anything. There was nothing to say.

Then a siren, the pounding of boots and a young male voice.

"Jesus fucking Christ! What the hell happened to him?"

We stayed until the paramedics got him out of the hole and into an ambulance. He wasn't dead, but barely alive, they said. Maggie gave her name, phone numbers, made official noises. Then she drove me home.

"I'd rather you didn't say anything to the Syndicate," I began.

"I never say anything to the Syndicate," she answered softly. "This isn't that world."

Chapter Nine

You Ain't Nothin' but a Hound Dog

Elvis Presley

When Maggie called the next morning I was at my computer researching Poe's influence on Dostoyevsky for my talk at the community college class. I've never developed a taste for Russian writers despite their melancholic brilliance. You'd think the style would appeal to me, but I come to a dead stop with every unpronounceable name. My flaw, unquestionably, but insurmountable. I was stuck at "Svidrigailov" in an essay on *Crime and Punishment* when the phone rang.

"Antonio will live," Maggie said. "I was sure you'd want to know right away."

I did want to know, but I wasn't sure about anything else.

"Good," I said. "That's good, Mag."

There was a silence in which the sickness and rage of the previous day crashed against a papery intellectual wall I was constructing out of Dostoyevsky. The wall dissolved in insubstantial flakes. Maggie waited.

"Tell me the police found those people, Mag!" I blurted, tears coming from nowhere. "How in God's name could anybody... it was monstrous, hideous... that pathetic boy in that hole... the *flies* for God's sake!"

I was sobbing.

"You saved his life, Taylor," she said. "He's going to have a life."

"I want those people *dead*," I choked. "I want them beaten bloody and cut with knives and buried alive in a hole in ninety-degree heat and left there to rot! What kind of monsters..."

"Maybe I should come by?" Her voice was calm.

"Maggie, have you seen anything like this before? The work you do... you deal with things... things that are never in the news. This has got to be the worst..."

"No," she said quietly. "They're all the worst."

"But this was depraved, sadistic, insane!"

"Depravity lies at one end of the human continuum, Taylor. It's there. We want to call it 'insane' to set it apart, but unfortunately it's not apart. Children pull the wings off moths. Teenage boys throw cats from rooftops. The inclination is extinguished with age in most. But not all. So are you going to be okay?"

"Yeah," I answered. "I've got a talk to give, some research to do."

"Go to your dance class, too. Work off the shock."

"Are the police going to find those people?"

I wanted the police to find those people. I wanted those people to experience police *brutality*. Me, your typical liberal, opposed to the death penalty and all that. Suddenly I understood the other side. It was visceral.

"They'll be identified and caught, someday, somewhere, Taylor. You won't know when it happens; you'll have gone on with your life. And so will Antonio. That's what matters. Understand?"

"Can we see him?" I asked. "Is there anything we can do for him?"

I'd take up a collection I thought. Provide something that would help. I wasn't expecting her answer.

"No."

"Why not?"

"Your part is over, Taylor. It's finished. Anything more will only obstruct the course of your life, and Antonio's. I've made arrangements for his care with an excellent agency. He'll be out of the hospital in time to start his training course with the Phoenix Project, if he wants to, and he'll have professional counseling. It would not be kind to interfere; it would only confuse both of you and ultimately go nowhere."

I saw his photograph in my mind, a stranger with long-lashed eyes. And I saw him curled and broken at the very threshold of death.

"I just want to do something..."

"You've already done something," Maggie said with finality. "It is enough."

After I hung up I thought about the word "enough." From an ancient English word that meant, "It suffices." I would probably understand the word if I were dropped amid grimy 8th century Anglo-Saxon peasants with names like "Aethelthryth" and "Scowyrtha" that I wouldn't be able to pronounce. But I could pronounce their word "enough" now, and wondered how I could have known Maggie McFadden for nearly twenty years and never seen her as *wise*.

I gave up on Poe and Dostoyevsky and went to my dance class. Molly Palmer was engrossed with an iPod connection to the sound system. No startling stories that day, just Molly doing what she does. And yet Molly's gift for dance, like Angie O'Halloran's for

Bach cantatas, had carved a path in my life. A path that would lead to a pile of rocks in a weedy yard, a sweltering hole beneath a closet and the abhorrent reality of sadism. But the path was there for me to follow, dragging with me Maggie and all the baggage of a shared conviction that the torture and killing of anything, human or animal, is an abomination. The path that had begun where I now stood, in a shopping mall dance studio. Apparently I really was a Revenant and could see what others could not. But without lightbearers like Molly and Angie and the thousand others I'd never noticed, the gift would simply spin on itself inside my mind, trapped. I would simply be mad. I wondered if Molly knew what she was, and if she did, what else she might know. And I wondered how many others I'd failed to see.

We did a routine I love, an old one that's mostly a girl singer belting out adolescent sexual-identity angst with terrific orchestration. I put everything I had into the music and was pouring sweat by the time we got to the martial arts section.

"Uppercut!" Molly yelled as we spun to the music, "punch forward! Look at what you're hitting. Mean it!"

I had no problem meaning it. In the empty air before me the blank faces of Denise and Bradford Holland ruptured like rotting pumpkins with every punch. It felt good. Violence solves nothing; I know that. But a bit of violent *fantasy* is sometimes effective.

At home I took a shower and threw my sweaty dance clothes in the washer. The anger and nausea were gone; I was crisp and clean, and unclear about my next move. Dostoyevsky, I decided, is best studied after sunset when Russian names may be blurred by shadows. And it was only 1:30. The rest of my life stretched ahead like a field of wildflowers. A *mined* field of wildflowers. I was a Revenant and I had no idea what to do.

But Tim had said that childhood delights could buffer the childish horrors I now realized were only too real. There *are* monsters, and not all of them exist in forgotten closets. But what "delights" could I dredge from over a half-century in the past? I made iced coffee, grabbed a fun-size Butterfinger from the fridge and sat on the deck, realizing what a bore I must have been as a child.

I had no siblings, and although I spent my days in school or playing with friends, my deeper life was lived in books. Nobody had a TV until the time of Queen Elizabeth's coronation, for which we were allowed to leave school at noon and go to the homes of kids with TV's so we could watch it. No one questioned the point in American schoolchildren sent to watch the coronation of a British monarch. We still thought we were sort of British, I guess. The bond is close.

I remembered a bunch of kids sitting in my living room as the test pattern jumped and jittered and finally fell off the tiny screen to reveal a young Elizabeth surrounded by thousands of people in ermine capes and costumes we associated with *The Tales of King Arthur*. My mother served lemonade in paper cups as Handel's *Coronation Anthem #1* quivered the glass over her botanical prints on the wall. I loved the music, still do. But the crown looked like it weighed as much as the single-volume *Columbia Encyclopedia* kept open for years on the buffet in the dining room until I was strong enough to lift it out of a bookcase. I thought the crown must be hurting Elizabeth's neck. Tim had Tom Mix, but I wasn't finding inspiration in Queen Elizabeth.

I paced around the patio. Books, then. Maybe there was a character I could use from one of my childhood favorites. There were those orange-bound biographies in the school library and I read every one of them. Thomas Jefferson, Clara Barton, George Washington Carver. Yawn.

The Wind in the Willows, *The Bobbsey Twins at Mystery Mansion*, Nancy Drew and *The Secret of the Old Clock*. I debated over Nancy Drew for a while, but then remembered my disappointment at discovering that there wasn't really a Carolyn Keene. At ten I was bitter about that, feeling duped until much later when I discovered that the first twenty-three books in the series were written by an obviously clever woman in Ohio named Mildred Wirt Benson. I wore black on the day I learned of Benson's death in 2002. Maybe I should create a Mildred Wirt Benson costume, I thought. Except she dressed just like my mother and I look gawky in shoulder pads.

My childhood had apparently been devoid of figures I could revitalize in the interest of happiness as a Revenant. But I *had* been happy as a child. I remembered playgrounds, Brownies, walks with my dog Ginger in the woods at the edge of town. Ginger was a big fox terrier with a few black spots on a field of shedding white fur my mother was constantly brushing off the furniture. My father said it was a good thing there were no foxes left in the woods, because Ginger wouldn't know what to do with one. She was most content snuggled beside me in bed, her short ear flaps occasionally twitching to indicate interest in whatever I was reading to her.

It hit me then. I didn't need a costume. It wasn't a costume I needed.

The animal shelter was open until 5:00. It was just a trial run, I told myself. I wasn't sure a dog was the answer, or that I really wanted a dog. The kids had dogs – a beagle named Moonwalk, called "Moonie," and later a Chihuahua named Kitsch. I took them to vet appointments and helped the kids deal with their deaths. But they weren't *my* dogs. They were my children's dogs and I was in that parental role behind which, it occurred to me, it's easy to miss practically everything.

A chunky young woman with spiked blonde hair and seven earrings in one ear was happy to show me the dogs available for adoption.

"Matt here is a pit bull/lab mix and really a super guy," she said, indicating a stocky black dog with a wide pink nose. Matt wagged his tail and looked at me with unabashed longing through the chain-link of his cage. I had not prepared myself for this and my heart, as they say, melted.

I didn't necessarily want Matt, whose musculature suggested rowdy play, damage to furniture and exuberant walks in which I could barely hold the leash. I just wanted Matt to have a home, be happy.

Jenny, a golden/shepherd mix, and Conan, a "senior" basset hound, evoked the same response. They all did. The place was a symphony of swishing tails in which I was drowning.

"Who's this one?" I asked, noticing white fur with big brown spots in a bottom cage at the end of the row.

"Oh, we haven't given her a name, um, yet," the young woman said while handing kibble treats through the chain-link. "She's probably a senior, looks like some kind of terrier mix, maybe a bit of dachshund in there, hound, anyway. The ears are definitely hound."

The young woman was not enthusiastic about the brown and white dog.

"Were you looking for a small dog, apartment size? We have a litter of Chihuahua pups just brought in. Adorable. The mother died and they're still needing to be fed every two hours, but if you're up for that we can throw in some bottles and a couple cans of formula."

I sat on the floor to look at the brown and white dog.

"Hey," I said.

"That one's technically not adoptable," the young woman explained. "She was picked up in a park a couple of days ago. We wormed her, did the flea and tick patch, but it'll be a while before we can do all the shots and everything. She's still under observation. She may be, you know, a little old for adoption."

The dog stood up in her cage and was watching me, her brown eyes distant and resigned. She didn't expect anyone to want her, and held herself apart with an aloof dignity I recognized. I'd done that look myself. In my head the chords of Handel's Coronation Anthem echoed.

"Queen Elizabeth is 'a little old,' too," I said. "But she's still Queen."

"Huh?"

In her cage the dog wagged a brown-spotted white tail, only once. She got the joke. She liked me. But I still had work to do.

"I live alone," I began softly. "The house is okay, just a regular ranch-type although I'm getting ready to do some decorating. And you'd have a yard. My grandson TJ is in and out and can be something of a pain, but he'd be good if you wanted to play ball or something."

I realized I didn't even own a ball.

The dog cocked her head, one side milk-chocolate brown and the other white. Both her hound ears were brown. She seemed unsure about what I was saying, but I thought I saw a little sliver of hope in her eyes.

"It's complicated, though," I whispered.

The young woman was doing something with a clipboard and seemed not to be listening.

"I'm a Revenant. You'd have to put up with some weird stuff."

In the dog's eyes I saw a realization that had nothing to do with the details I was giving her. She saw that somebody was interested, somebody might want her, and suddenly she was all wags and astonished posture. I felt like wagging myself, a child again with no need for pretense.

"Can you get her out of the cage?" I asked the young woman.

"Okay, but…"

Those first white-paw steps were tentative. She wasn't sure she could trust me. Maybe I'd change my mind, turn my back and leave her there. There is no greater betrayal.

"Never!" I told her, holding my arms open, and it was all over. I was crying for the second time in one day, but this time it was all good. A warm white dog with big brown spots was in my lap, licking my face, her tail lashing the air with joy. In my head the slow progression of Handel's prelude drew to its close, where the chorus erupts in an anthem called "Zadok the Priest." I've loved the music since I first heard it at the coronation of a queen.

"Got a name for her?" the shelter attendant asked, seeing that no matter what she said I was taking my dog home.

"Zadok," I answered, still in the music, the scent of dog like a perfume of childhood. But of course that ancient name doesn't resonate in English, doesn't sound right, gets translated. It didn't matter.

"Sadie," the young woman said. "Cute name. She looks like a Sadie. You'll have to sign some forms saying you know she hasn't had her shots here and all that. You'll have to take her to a vet, get her shots up to date. And you knew we have a fee, right?"

I would have signed over everything I own.

Sadie watched the passing scenery from the passenger's seat as we drove home, from time to time turning to lay a tentative paw on my leg. In the house I realized I needed dog food, toys, a harness and leash. We'd go to a pet place later. Right then I put Handel's *Coronation Anthem #1* in the CD player and turned it up. Gently holding Sadie in my arms, I danced in my kitchen to the prelude. My life had changed and I could never go back. But I wasn't alone any more.

Chapter Ten

Just What the Truth Is, I Can't Say Anymore

The Moody Blues

We never made it to the pet store, just played in the yard and shared a large omelet for dinner. Sadie loved the omelet, although dogs will basically eat anything so I didn't take it as a tribute to my culinary skill. I wondered how her cholesterol was, or if dogs even had cholesterol issues. Maybe I should have used Eggbeaters. I'd go out for dog food first thing in the morning.

When it was time for bed I lined a laundry basket with old towels, lifted Sadie into it and then read for a while. As I turned the light out I could hear her snoring softly on the floor. Five minutes later I heard rustling as the basket overturned and then felt a gentle thump as thirteen pounds of dog jumped onto the bed. People who sleep with their dogs regard them as family members. Apparently she had slept with her previous owner, and I wondered what had happened and how Sadie had come to be found half-starved in a park.

"Okay," I told her and then watched as she turned in a circle two or three times the way dogs do. It's an inherited memory of wolf ancestors getting comfortable in tall grass, I've read. She settled next to me with her head on a throw pillow I only use while I'm reading. I'd get another pillow for her, I decided. For reading. Tim O'Halloran had been right. I was myself, rational, making plans. Dog equipment, a trip to the vet. But I was also a much younger self in another life made of moments unbroken by adult responsibility and fear. This particular moment, falling asleep beside my dog, thrummed with a sense of security I had completely forgotten.

Hours later I woke abruptly. The room was completely still, an interior gloom muting slabs of moonlight on the carpet near the windows. And the feeling of security had morphed into that state in which you don't trust the fact that you're afraid because there's nothing to be afraid of. Except Sadie was standing at the end of the bed, staring into the darkest corner, the fur down the middle of her back standing up in a ruff. Universal dog-language for *something is there.*

"What is it?" I asked, knowing perfectly well what it was. On one hand, nothing. Just a kink in the darkness, one of those black hole densities that simply occur in 3:00 a.m. shadows and pull sleep away like a robe. They appear and vanish occasionally and mean nothing. Or so we tell ourselves. On the other hand, it was the unspeakable threat it had always been, invisible in darkness but palpably *there.* When I was a child it threatened obliteration – "I will pull you away. You will not exist." The threat now was worse – "I will tell you the one thing you cannot bear to know. That there is no point in existing. You are meaningless." Its presence was a cold, persimmon-scented film on my skin.

I felt it name me a pathetic fool in a game I couldn't win, a game that can't be won. Seiji was none of my business, Antonio a worthless waste of time better left to die, my friends vacuous buffoons. The man who fathered my children was gone to the bed of another woman and the children themselves were inhabitants of an alien world. My dog would die like the others before her and fill my heart with a grief I could never escape. My life was a tedious, repetitive shuffle toward an equally tedious oblivion. And all the gift of Revenance had brought me was an end to the blindness that renders life endurable.

From the darkness I sensed that bland, condescending attitude common to people who are sure they're right and you're wrong and they're doing you an immense favor by telling you so. Only this one was in my bedroom, which really pissed me off.

"Just bag it!" I yelled, on my knees now behind Sadie. My fists were tight, both arms pulled back and ready for a block-and-punch. I was entirely sensible of the fact that I looked ridiculous and didn't care. "You're a *ghoul*, for God's sake! Bizarre career choice. How many times do I have to tell you I don't want the crap you're selling?"

Sadie wasn't growling, which would have indicated the presence of scent or movement. She merely stood rigid, staring into shadows.

"It's my, um, ghoul," I told her, sitting back on my heels and snapping on the bedside light, dispelling the darkness. Of course there was nothing there, but my heart was pounding anyway. Adrenalin rush, the primitive fight-or-flight reaction to danger. I felt a bit of chagrin and then quickly dumped the thought. *It* wanted me to feel stupid, crazy, terrified of imagined threats no one else could see. Except Sadie had seen it, too.

"Would you like some warm milk?" I asked, heading for the kitchen. I was going to have cocoa but remembered reading somewhere that chocolate isn't good for dogs. She was thrilled.

Jude called in the morning and I told her about Sadie.

"A dog?" she said as if the meaning of the word were unclear.

"Yes, she's right here so don't say anything disparaging."

"You mean she can hear me? I know their hearing is better than ours, but..."

Jude isn't stupid; it's just that she takes everything seriously.

"It was a joke," I said.

"A joke meaning you don't want me to say anything *disparaging* because this dog is so important to *you*, right? Tay, this doesn't have anything to do with... with what happened that morning, does it? The paper dolls and all that?"

Not only is Jude not stupid, but she misses nothing.

"I had a dog growing up," I began, "and now..."

"Okay, I think it's wonderful," she interrupted. "What's her name? What color? How big is she?"

"About thirteen pounds, white with brown markings, and Sadie," I answered.

"Sadie? Oh, that's fabulous, Tay! I have to see her. Will you be home later? How about I come by around noon?"

"Sure," I said. "I'll make a salad or something."

Then I called a neighbor who has two schnauzers for a recommendation to a nearby vet and made a run to a pet store. I got a case of the locally manufactured dog food the vet recommended when I called her, and Sadie seemed pleased with the cocoa brown harness and leash I selected at the pet store. It had a design of acorns and leaves woven in and reminded me of fall. I thought she looked very chic in it, and caught her checking herself out in the mirror on the hall closet.

"It's you," I told her, and then saw myself standing behind her in the mirror. Baggy t-shirt, dance pants, no makeup. I looked like the "before" photo in an ad for one of the image-improvement workshops Jude is always talking about. She's never gone to one because, she says, she doesn't need to. But she thinks everyone else should. I was beginning to see her point.

In my computer was a brief email from Tim O'Halloran.

My Dearest Taylor,

See links for some answers to your question. Such sad events occur in normal life, but these are known to have been significant. The St. Louis incident is the first to be documented. Please note that we are careful never to use specific terminology in writing.

I hope you are settling in and that your day is pleasant.

Yrs.

Fr. Tim O'Halloran

There were four blue links and I clicked on the first eagerly. I wanted to know what happens to Revenants who do not fight. Given my way, I'd want to know everything knowable, a proclivity not always consistent with common sense.

The first was dated two years in the past, an article in the *St. Louis Post-Dispatch*. It told of a sixty-two-year-old violinist with the St. Louis Symphony, a virtuoso "...said in his best moments to rival Jascha Heifetz." In what must have been his worst moment, the violinist died of an apparent heart attack during an episode in which he burned both the score for Elgar's *Violin Concerto in B Minor* and his priceless 18th century Pietro Guarneri violin. The violinist had no history of illness, but was said by friends to have been troubled by unknown personal problems in the months leading to his death.

The story was disturbing. Surely this man had been a gentle soul, ferocious only in his passion for the sound of gut strings, tuned to perfect fifths and bowed to vibrate over an exquisitely wrought wooden sound box. The violin. But something had warped that sensitivity, turned it on itself and made him destroy what he most loved. A ghoul that had threatened a boy now returned to destroy a man.

I sensibly told myself not to investigate the Elgar concerto the man had burned, and then immediately typed it into Google, bringing up enough download clips to form an impression. The music was not ponderous, not tragic. More like an orchestral sound track for a movie in which everything turns out all right. And woven through it, now below and now above like a swooping bird, were the delicate, complicated notes of a violin. Had it been his favorite work? The one that fell closest to his spirit? If so, he had not been an intemperate man. Even when a bit of well-placed temper might have saved him.

I clicked on the next link, dated a year later than the newspaper article about the violinist. It was several copied pages from a medical report. A seventy-year old retired nurse, whose hobbies included trying to hybridize a rare orange iris and running a small appliance repair business from her garage, had been found wandering barefoot in an icy DeKalb, IL, cemetery several miles from her home. Family members reported that the woman had begun "seeing things" several months earlier and insisted that "a creature with the feet of a bird" was stalking her. After several months, when all medications failed to produce improvement, she was diagnosed with catatonic schizophrenia. At the time of the last medical report she was still mute and largely immobile, although staff occasionally found her hiding under her bed, at which times she was put in restraints.

That was it. I wasn't going to read the other two. But of course I did.

A man who owned a chain of laundromats in Oregon hanged himself in a room papered with pictures of Mount Fuji. And the woman proprietor of an antiques shop in North Carolina went to an estate sale and bought a set of six Steubenville soup bowls with matching tureen. She wasn't seen again until her body was found in a remote cave seven weeks later by some college kids on a geology field trip. In both cases individuals close to these people reported that "something had been wrong," but they couldn't describe what it was.

I phoned Tim O'Halloran.

"Tim, this is horrible," I began. "These people were frightened witless! They didn't know where to turn, didn't have a chance. I was lucky. I had you to explain it. If you hadn't been there I would have gone insane or died or vanished, too."

"No, you wouldn't," he said quietly. "Remember, I didn't contact you until you had shown that you would fight. Not every Revenant is invited into the organization, Taylor."

An unpleasant picture was taking shape in my mind.

"Are you saying that if I hadn't gone after that thing in the dance studio you wouldn't have taken me to the Paper Doll

Museum, that you wouldn't have told me what was happening to me?"

"Martine would have found you and given you your amulet in any event," he said. "But without your instinct to fight, the amulet would have been useless to you and you would have been useless to us. What we know so far, and we know tragically little, is that every Revenant must battle what we for lack of a better word call a ghoul. A thing that devours the soul and leaves something ruined and abhorrent where once there was a person. Some are simply not capable of the battle. We had to see that you were capable."

"But if people knew about this, they'd be ready, Tim. They'd be armed. It's not right to keep it a secret. I don't understand how you could…"

"You *are* armed, Taylor, first by your own personality and now by your amulet, although you must use it only in that moment when you can no longer fight. To survive, you must be willing to stand up for yourself, for your right to enjoy the fact that you exist." His voice became a dramatic sneer. "Now, when your biological function to the species is over. Now, when you can no longer work long hours in support of whatever social system surrounds you. Now, when you're just…taking…up…space."

"Tim!" I was shocked. "You'd better believe I have a right! I absolutely have a right to take up whatever space I damn well choose. What's the matter with you? I can't believe this!"

His laugh was warm.

"Precisely, Taylor. You'll even fight me! It's wonderful. And if the time comes when you can't, remember the weapon on a silver chain around your neck."

"Martine's gift," I said.

"Yes."

"Tim, who *is* Martine? *What* is she?"

"A remnant of childhood, perhaps," he answered. "All

Revenants see her in the beginning, and she appears randomly at odd times. Taylor, when you were a child and the wallpaper snake came down your wall and hid under your bed, what did you do when you had to get up in the dark? When you had to put your feet on the floor where it could grab you?"

"I'd yell for my parents and my dad would come and turn on the light. When I got older I figured out how far the snake could reach, and I'd jump way beyond that. Jumped back in, too. Later I had a reading light and I'd turn that on. Then I just sort of forgot about it; it wasn't there any more. Why? What does it have to do with Martine?"

"She may be what's left of that process, the protection by adults we gradually internalize as we mature out of childhood and learn to care for ourselves. Now our monsters are back and so is a new sort of protection, but because we are adults it must be earned. Martine's gift will protect you in extremis, Taylor. You earned it."

I didn't want anything to happen to Tim O'Halloran, another Revenant who had answers.

"Do you have a weapon, Tim? Did you go to the Paper Doll Museum?"

"Yes and no," he laughed. "Martine gives each of us what we need to defeat the horror when our own resources are exhausted, but each event is different. The Paper Doll Museum was created from inside you. It could be experienced only by you, and only once."

"I figured that out," I said, remembering the derelict Victorian cottage, the pink love seat now stained and rotting. "I went back."

He laughed again.

"Everyone does. So tell me, Taylor, have you found some happy corridor from long ago you may again traverse as a Revenant?"

"Her name is Sadie," I answered, grinning. "She's a

terrier/hound mix."

"Ah, a dog!" I could feel him beaming through the phone. "I never had a dog as a child, but Angie's brought home a succession of bassets we've both adored. We lost our last one about a year ago."

"Is Angie there?" I asked, humming a bit of "Matchmaker" from *Fiddler on the Roof*. "I'd like to tell both of you something."

"There's a senior basset named Conan at the animal shelter," I announced minutes later. "He's available for adoption."

"Conan!" Angie yelped happily. "Oh, Tim...?"

"Let's go see this fellow," Tim agreed and I smiled all the way into the kitchen to make a salad for Jude, who arrived carrying a fleece-lined dog bed with microfiber sides. It looked like a giant donut.

"I got the taupe because, you know, you said she's white with brown and I thought it would match. But it comes in five colors for the sides including celadon and terra cotta, so I can exchange it..."

"Jude, it's perfect," I said, hugging her. "I can decorate the whole house around it!"

"I can't imagine a whole house done in taupe," she said, sitting on the floor to greet Sadie, who pulled her new bed into the breeze from the deck doors and jumped in. "Look, she likes it!"

Over lunch Jude noticed the big decorating book Miyoko had left. It was still on the kitchen table and Jude raised an interested eyebrow.

"You weren't kidding about decorating?"

"Maybe paint," I admitted. "Nothing major."

"Major is not a bad idea," she said, obviously measuring my kitchen for a bulldozer. "Just be careful about granite."

Jude's web surfing had apparently turned up something about

granite. There's a lot of it around here. Whole mountains. I hoped it was nothing serious.

"What?" I said.

"You mean you didn't know?"

"Didn't know what?"

"Tay, you've got to get out more. The whole world knows about granite countertops for crying out loud. Most of them are perfectly okay, but watch out for exotic imports. Some have radon in them and the ones with uranium can emit a lot more radiation than you normally get. I can't believe you don't know this."

Jude never ceases to amaze me.

"I didn't know," I said humbly, "but it doesn't matter because I was just thinking about paint."

We both stared at the little sparkly flecks in my faded gold countertop. I hadn't actually looked at it in years. It was clean, serviceable and might as well have had "1973" gouged into its surface with a Philips-head screwdriver.

"On the other hand..."

"Absolutely," Jude agreed. "We should go to one of those home stores and look. I'm sure there's something fabulous that's affordable and won't be radioactive."

"Actually, I was going to look for, I don't know, something different to wear. I was thinking you might be right about the t-shirts."

I knew Jude would be vindicated, even pleased. But she grabbed the phone in something resembling ecstasy.

"I'm canceling my hair appointment," she explained while punching numbers. "This is going to take *hours*, but you're in luck. I don't have to be at work until five!"

Chapter Eleven

Donna, Donna, the Prima Donna

Dion and the Belmonts

There is a difference between roaming around a shopping mall checking things out like an investigative reporter (Hideous Floral Prints Are In!), looking for something specific (I must have black sandals by Friday.) and that moment when shopping is necessary to document change. A few months after Charlie moved out - the divorce wasn't final yet but that was the day I realized I was just me again, free-falling through a world in which the terms "wife" and "mother" would no longer provide definition – I bought purple towels. I don't like purple, the towels are so bulky I have to use them for rugs and the face cloth is too thick for anything except washing the car, but at the moment those towels shimmered with promise. They were unlike anything ever before, and they were entirely mine. I told Jude my purple towel story as we navigated the department store's dizzying perfume section, heading for the escalator.

"Purple towels can hold it all together when it's all falling apart," she agreed. "Of course for me it's hair, but the idea's the same."

A group of adolescent mannequins in trendy outfits sat casually out of reach in the escalator well. I could have sworn that one of them, a sultry boy in low-slung jeans and at least three

119

layered shirts, was looking straight at me.

"Hair?" I asked Jude as we reached the second floor and three more mannequins staged at the top of the escalator. They were women this time, dressed to leave for a pre-symphony cocktail party where they would pretend to know a lot about Bartok. This time I was sure. They did see me. Their eyes moved.

"I told you about Luke," Jude answered, steering me toward a section devoted to a designer I can't afford. "After I realized what I'd done, when I realized I was going to spend the rest of my freaking *life* without him, I just went to my hair guy and said, 'Do something, anything, make me look like somebody else!' He did me up in Farrah Fawcett blonde. I always go back to it, y'know? Hey, how about this?"

She was checking the inside seams on a cropped tweed jacket draped over the shoulders of one of the mannequins. The jacket was tan with flecks of pumpkin, pistachio, various browns. The stores always show fall clothes starting in August despite the fact that if Southern California may be said to have a fall, you won't see it until December. That's when the temperature sometimes drops below fifty at night and the liquidambar trees finally change color, although nobody notices because by then there are Christmas lights everywhere. I wasn't crazy about the tweed jacket due to the orange flecks and my tendency to look like Daisy Duck in cropped tops. But I kept staring at it because the mannequin wearing it was staring at me.

"Jude," I said, trying not to make a scene, "there's something weird about this dummy. It's looking at me."

Jude glanced upward at the long-lashed brown eyes, so carefully painted they seemed alive. "They're modeled on real people, the faces anyway," she said. "Imagine somebody making a thousand fiberglass copies of your head. But that's how it's done — fiberglass painted in different skin tones. The bodies are another story. I mean, how many six-foot tall women do you know who wear a size two?"

I hadn't even known there *was* a size two. The dummy

nodded as if to confirm Jude's remarks, and tilted its head toward a rack of slacks. I could see the line where her head had been attached to her torso.

"I think that one's called Natalie," Jude went on, holding an olive green crocheted tank top next to my face. The top looked a little like the covers for toilet tissue rolls an aunt of my mother's used to give everybody for Christmas, except those were usually pink.

"Natalie! What are you saying? That the dummies have names? Jude, you're crazier than I am!"

"No, seriously, they do. Or at least these do, the ones with real faces. The manufacturers sell them by name."

She pointed to a row of armless, headless torsos wearing the same tee shirt in different colors against an illuminated wall. The torsos were made of a semi-transparent material that allowed light to shine through.

"Those are much cheaper, no names," she went on. "You only see the gorgeous ones with painted faces and wigs like Natalie in big corporate stores that have the budget for them, but they're really sort of passé. They're fragile; kids are always knocking them over and breaking them; they don't last long. This is one of the last stores to use them. In a few more years they'll be history."

I could have burst into tears. Department store dummies fascinated me as a child. When Jude wasn't looking I impulsively gripped "Natalie's" chipped hand. "I'm sorry," I whispered. "It won't ever be the same without you."

I did not imagine the iridescent smile unfolding on the painted lips, revealing a creepy absence of teeth, or the rough squeeze of the painted hand in mine. And no one but I saw the head of every mannequin on the floor nod regally, like a room full of royalty acknowledging my presence. I could have been in the grand salon of the Titanic. That sense of doomed elegance.

Jude was intent on a low-cut cocktail dress in a silky black and white geometric print that would make a skeleton look fat.

"There are pregnant dummies, too," she went on, grinning. "And you should see the torsos they use for men's underwear. Talk about anatomically correct!"

"The connection is obvious. Jude, how do you know all this?"

She stuffed the black and white dress back on the rack. "Taylor, I've had more jobs than the Teamsters," she said. "At least five of them have been in department stores. I love the employee discount. Now, we're going to find something devastating for you!"

A roomful of impossibly thin six-foot-tall fiberglass women with identically arrogant expressions turned to regard me. Appraisingly, but with a certain warmth. And then they moved. Locked in place by the chrome stands that held them upright, they nonetheless leaned, pointed, and shook their heads in despair every time I picked an article of clothing. At Jude's choices they actually chuckled, but Jude didn't notice. This was a Revenant thing, I concluded. A dream of my childhood that had come back. I loved it.

A foot with melded toes nudged me toward some belted slacks with complicated pleats in front and braid at the hem. I tried them on.

"Tay, those are fabulous on you!" Jude gushed. "How did you find them?"

An arm crosshatched with scratches pointed to a feather-light sweater in a green Jude said perfectly matched my eyes, and in an empty dressing room a wigless half-woman held out a densely ruffled scarf in the same green with a sort of mummy-tan and black design. But the *coup de grâce* was a short black trench coat with multiple capes that literally fell into my hands as I passed a blonde mannequin over whose arm it had carelessly hung. She looked like a bored aristocrat who'd just murdered her third husband and found even *that* boring. She winked as I slid my arms into the sleeves.

"Why do they all have that weird, aloof look?" I asked Jude, winking back. I had to have that coat.

"The manufacturers use high-fashion models for the heads," she answered. "Ever seen a high-fashion show?"

I wanted to have seen a high-fashion show. It was on my list of pointless things it might be fun to do someday.

"No."

"That's the look. The models all live on amphetamines and watercress and develop a contempt for people who eat real food, plus I think starvation does something to their brains. On the runway they glare at the crowd as if they're on their way to be guillotined and don't care. It's tradition. Go pay for your stuff. We need to look at shoes."

To get to the down escalator we had to go through the children's department where a plastic toddler in yellow overalls snagged my pants leg on a toy bucket in its hand. Turning to detach my cuff, I leaned straight into the face of a boy mannequin with molded red hair and freckles. The young Huck Finn in a school backpack and chinos, his eyes were eager and I watched as his plastic mouth formed a wide "O" of excitement. He was pointing to a chalkboard sign with "Back To School!" in lopsided whitewash letters. The chalkboard was held by a cardboard wizard in curling beard and pointed hat decorated with stars and quarter-moons. The cartoon figure was intriguing if only for its hint at an original Merlin now sanitized in a Disneyesque wash. The wizard shifted slightly; the boy mannequin pointed. And I felt the way I did as a child when confronted with arithmetic problems. The way to the answer was right there; I just couldn't see it.

"I think low-cut boots will look great with those pants," Jude said as the plastic boy's mouth locked again in its plastic smile. I could feel the wizard vanishing behind me as we moved downward on murmuring, metal treads.

In the shoe department I found exactly what I wanted.

"Tay, those shoes look like something witches would wear," Jude pointed out. "The toes curl up."

"Yes," I said happily and pulled out my credit card. A bit of the old uniform, then. I wondered if the millions slaughtered as "witches" over the ages might have been Revenants. But Tim had said Revenance was new. The slaughtered witches had merely been different from whatever group was dominant in their context. As I would be in mine now. The tin whistle moved gently against my chest as a handsome male mannequin in ski gear near the door raised one hand in farewell.

At home I put Mussorgsky's "Pictures at an Exhibition" (the orchestral version, musically incorrect but much more dramatic) on the CD player and modeled my new outfit for Sadie, who was happy shredding tissue paper out of the department store bags. In the hall mirror I seemed an apparition, a Doppelgänger, another self familiar yet not well known, like an advertising image. I might have been Betty Crocker, except there really is no Betty Crocker and she never wears black trench coats with caped shoulders. Or shoes with back-curling toes on which little bells would not be completely misplaced. Whoever I was, I thought I looked at least more interesting than usual. Taylor Blake, witch fashionista. Hell, why not?

Through the patio doors I could see dusk evolving the way it does in September, little more than a feverish dimness that seems to rise from the long shadows cast by shrubs, trees, houses. Along the beaches at this hour people stare out to sea, watching the horizon for a flat oval flash of green light just as the sun sinks from view. There is no story connected to this occasional burst of refracted light. Seeing a green flash brings neither good nor bad luck, has never been said to be the eye of Neptune or a low-flying Martian saucer. Green flashes are purely a natural phenomenon devoid of imaginative interpretation. Nonetheless, at sunset 365 days a year, surfers, tourists shopkeepers and beachwalkers grow still and gaze dreamily toward the edge of the planet for this glimpse of green. Inland, it is not possible to see a green flash. But at the back of my yard, just above the wall of Japanese barberry, a wavering, flat green oval appeared and as quickly vanished.

With a Bic pen I was pretending to conduct the ninth movement of Mussorgsky's work, and continued as I pushed open the patio doors. It couldn't have been a green flash. Maybe a transformer blowing out on a utility pole in the alley behind the barberry. Something like that. But it wasn't.

Beneath the unremarkable shrub where a green coin blazed for only a second stood a wooden hut held several feet above the ground on the legs of a chicken! The thing had come from another culture and a distant century, but I recognized it and waved my pen in delight. The Russian music had brought it, the house on fowl's legs. And the mind of a little, forgotten Taylor insisted that if I "conducted" with sufficient energy, its occupant would show herself at last. Baba Yaga, favorite among my childhood repertory of folk tales. She lived in a hut on fowl's legs and rode across the forest floor or the night sky in a mortar, oaring the air with a pestle in her right hand and sweeping away the path behind with a broom in her left. No one could follow Baba Yaga in her travels. No one could find her.

At seven I cut her picture from a magazine to which my mother subscribed for me called *Highlights for Children*, and taped the picture to the door of my room. There were skulls on her fenceposts and her servants were three horses, white, red and black. Inside her hut lived disembodied hands, "friends" about whom no one could ask, and live. As a child I was sure Baba Yaga would protect me, from anything. And here she was over a half century later in my yard. The mantle of my adult self had fallen away with my usual clothes. I didn't feel the need to explain or interpret. I just stood on the deck in fashionable black and fairy tale shoes, conducting Mussorgsky with a ballpoint pen, waiting.

And from the chimney of the doorless hut she emerged, her bony knees at her chin as she sculled the suburban California dusk in a mortar. It would have been ludicrous had she not been stunningly, irredeemably numinous - the awe-inspiring, epic hag of universal legend. A witch. Sentry at the portals of all unknown worlds. Sentry at the door of death, and, I realized, at the door of whatever world I'd fallen into. I watched, mesmerized, as a figure born on some prehistoric Eastern European night plied the warm air above my head.

On that ancient night, I thought, everything living starved and froze until only one was left breathing amid the icy bones and gnawed flesh. That one saw Baba Yaga in a paroxysm of lonely terror, drew her countenance in blood on a stone, and fell through the door she held open. Nothing remained but an image on a stone then, and after centuries it has not changed. Baba Yaga is the guardian of all mystery, universally feared and barely tamed in Halloween silhouettes swooping over full moons.

In her face and streaming gray hair I saw the brushstrokes. Her appearance was a painting, a shell constructed by centuries of human awe. But her eyes were not painted. This was no fragile mannequin built to mirror all that is superficial. She existed before the builders. Her eyes were alive and in them blazed a staggering intelligence that while eerily remote was tinged with mischief. I was dying to talk to her.

But she swooped close and said something that sounded like "dobro proshlo" in a voice like the creak of frozen trees, and then she was gone. She was gone, the hut was gone, the music ended, and I was standing on my deck holding a Bic pen aloft, my mouth gaping in amazement. I was a Revenant and from my child-self had come an archetype to fly around my yard. This after a collection of department store dummies had picked out my clothes. All wonderful fun but what did it mean? Or did it have to mean anything?

In the house I called an acquaintance whose husband teaches Slavic languages at a university here.

"Hi, Gloria. Yes, I'm loving retirement. Listen, is George there? I've run into a little snag in some research I'm doing, just a phrase. I'm not sure about the language but it's likely to be Russian. It sounds like 'dobro proshlo.'"

I heard her pronounce the curious words over the rattle of tableware in the background. "It is Russian," her husband said, "but it doesn't make any sense. It means something like 'welcome past' or 'hello past.'"

"Wow. Thanks," I said and hung up.

So Baba Yaga had swept by with a comment, but what did it mean?

I put my witch shoes carefully back in their box and changed into my usual garb to walk Sadie, but inside I felt the way saints who've just had apocalyptic visions must feel. I had been in the presence of the most ancient guardian of my kind, and was inspired, although it was all so vague. "Hello past, welcome past?" Had I missed a welcome that was now past, or was I supposed to welcome the past? What past? I hated not knowing.

Sadie and I walked for over an hour, stopping frequently so she could sniff information about the neighborhood. I wondered if animals had archetypes like Baba Yaga to frame their big issues, whatever those were. I asked her, but she was busy digging in a pile of twigs and didn't answer. But when we got home she stopped dead at the front door and barked. Dog archetypes probably involve guarding. The minute I walked in I knew somebody had been in my house.

As soon as I unclipped the leash Sadie ran all over, nose down, alternately sniffing and casting concerned looks over her shoulder. She wasn't sure I got it, but I did. Something is left by the most careful intruder, if only an unfamiliar bend in the air. A sense of recent movement, molecules still swirling, unseen but felt, from the passage of a mass that shouldn't have been there.

I had left the deck door open. It's left open all summer, only the sliding screen door is closed, and I never bother with the flimsy little lock. On the worn floor just inside the door was a shred of dried grass. It might have stuck to my shoe. I might have brought it in. Except I hadn't stepped in the grass as I watched Baba Yaga. I'd stayed on the deck. I hadn't been down the steps from the deck into the grass all day. But somebody had, and had entered my house while I was out.

Sadie was whining in the living room, scratching at a shelf in a bookcase. Her hound nose at work.

Nothing seemed out of place except a framed etching of an apple in the Durer style. It was postcard-sized in a black frame that

I'd propped on a shelf next to my desk. One of my students had given it to me at a farewell party the kids threw when I retired. The rest of the stuff they gave me – coffee cups and ballpoint pens I didn't want but couldn't discard - was still in the trunk of my car. But I'd brought the little etching in with the idea of hanging it on the wall next to my computer, except I never got around to it. The etched apple was in the same place I'd stashed it months ago, only now it was about two inches off, its edge abutting the spine of *Larousse French Dictionary* instead of *Langenscheidt's German Dictionary*. An insignificant difference only I would notice, and then only because Sadie had smelled an alien hand on the little gift. But why would anybody sneak into my house in order to move an amateurish etching done in a high school art class two inches along a shelf?

I went through the rest of the house, my bedroom, the rarely-used guest room that's actually a dump, and the room I have for TJ when he stays with me. Nothing was different, nothing was stolen, and after the sense of invasion settled to a faint memory, I called my daughter Beth.

"Did TJ pop by here?" I asked. "I was out walking the dog and thought maybe..."

"Mom, you didn't tell us you got a dog!" Beth replied. "You need something like that. That's cool. And TJ's at Seiji's, has been since they got out of school. I'll tell him about the dog, though. That's just so cool!"

Beth is well over thirty and still tends to sound like she did at fourteen. But then I'm afraid I still sound like I did at twenty, so it's probably genetic.

Next I called Miyoko Foxwell. "I'm ready to get started on the kitchen," I told her. "And the first thing I want to do is to get a decent lock for the patio screens."

"Don't bother," she explained cheerfully. "Anybody who wants in has only to put a fist through the screen. I suggest an alarm system, although they can be more trouble than they're worth. Has something happened?"

"I'm not sure," I said. "Maybe."

"How about I come by tomorrow morning and we'll make some plans, check out some paint, flooring, countertops, everything? I'll bring samples."

"Great," I said while spooning dog food into Sadie's bowl.

I wasn't alarmed, just baffled. Helpful mannequins and a Russian witch were wonderful; a mysterious intruder was not. I was beginning to feel an edge of delight with the gifts of my Revenant state. But the real world was still present, its complexities more specific than shifting world of Revenance. Yet there was an interface.

The paper doll museum wasn't quite "real," but the tin whistle on its silver chain around my neck was. The stars and blood and bruises I saw in Antonio's quilt weren't real, but he was. The little mannequin had pointed to a back-to-school display. The etching of an apple someone moved on a shelf of my bookcase was meant to be a fond "school" symbol, an apple for the teacher. The student who'd given it to me was a freshman at UC Berkeley now, long gone. I couldn't quite remember her name. But I sensed a vague connection. The Huck Finn mannequin's excitement had something to do with "school." A little broad, since I've spent my entire adult life in schools. But the idea was there. I closed and locked the deck doors before turning my back on the dark outside and heading for my desk and Poe's influence on Dostoyevsky.

But the apple in its black frame was unsettling. Somebody had been in my house for no discernible reason. The senselessness of it was unnerving.

Chapter Twelve

Material Girl

Madonna

I was glad I'd stayed up late accumulating a stack of notes on a Russian and an American writer in the heyday of spiritualism. It was good stuff and as usual, I was proud of Poe. *Crime and Punishment*, I learned, wouldn't be the same without him. But the day was going to unfold in complexity surpassing even that of Russian novels, and I wouldn't remember Poe until I saw Pen's dollhouse later that night. Then I would *definitely* remember Poe.

The day began in a blaze of activity destined to be forgotten by dinner, but it was productive. Miyoko Foxwell arrived at nine with about eight hundred pounds of sample books.

"You won't believe the change in Seiji," she said as we had coffee amid piles of flooring samples. "He's become an Indian, Taylor! Whatever happened in Palm Springs – the sound and light show at a miniature golf course or whatever it was? – really made an impression on him. He found a youth group online associated with the local tribe, the Kuumeyaay, and they seem to have accepted him. Yesterday we spent hours driving the kids - TJ goes along with all this - out to 'the rez,' where the youth group dug a septic tank pit for an elderly tribe member."

"TJ?" I said. "His mother can't get him to empty a wastebasket. He's not exactly prone to manual labor, to put it mildly."

"Well, they did it," Miyoko said. "I think TJ's just sort of hanging around the edges. But Seiji's really into it, says he wants to be an anthropologist and preserve indigenous cultures. He's letting his hair grow so he can wear it in a braid, but we figure this will have passed way before his hair's that long. Meanwhile, it seems to be good for him. Overnight he's got new friends, these Indian kids, and they text each other on their cell phones all the time. What can it hurt? His dad says he went through a Dungeons and Dragons phase at that age when he thought he was a magician, and frankly I've never gotten over my Imogene Cunningham period. Seiji being an Indian is fine with us."

"You're a photographer?"

She looked rueful. "I wish. Afraid I don't have Cunningham's talent, but I love to fool around with it now that everything's digital. Black and white, mostly. So shall we start with countertops or floors?"

I tried to remember that I only wanted to paint the walls, but it was hopeless. The floor lay there disloyally, faded vinyl tile in a grayish pattern that must once have looked like bamboo or something. There was a worn path from the hall to the deck doors. It looked as if somebody had skated across the room on sandpaper every day for the last ten years.

"Floor," I said, opening a Pandora's Box. Once begun, fixing up an old house is an avalanche. The minute one thing looks new, everything else looks like an artifact out of the Old Testament. But I didn't know that yet.

After perusal of at least two hundred samples, Miyoko was not enthusiastic about the one I loved. It was called "Plank" and consisted of limestone cut to look like eight-inch wide boards in a variety of buttery neutrals ranging from the palest tan to a sort of maple syrup color.

"Stone floors are hard on the back," she said. "And that one's discontinued anyway."

"I'm sure I can find it somewhere on the Internet."

"You know they dye the limestone to get those gradations in color."

"I have nothing against dye."

"I thought you wanted to do the walls in sage. It won't work."

"I'm rethinking the walls."

"Stone floors are cold in the winter."

"What winter? Miyoko, it gets chilly here for about three months and I've got a big area rug for the family room I put down then. It's in the garage. The rest of the time a plank stone floor will be fabulous!"

"At least it won't show scratches from Sadie's nails."

I didn't point out that Sadie's nails are and will be carefully clipped.

"Yes," I said. "There's that."

Miyoko sighed. "Actually, since it's discontinued I'm pretty sure I can get it for you at a big discount. If anybody's got enough left."

After three calls on her cell phone she smiled. "You're in luck! Half-price, they're glad to get rid of it and will deliver this afternoon."

I had imagined this would take months. Everybody in the Syndicate has redecorated something and complained that it took forever. "This afternoon!"

"They'll stack the pallets in the garage."

"Pallets! As in with a forklift?"

She was trying not to laugh. "Stone's heavy, Taylor. You've never done this before, have you?"

I'd never even *thought* of doing this before. I picked drapes, rugs and bedspreads, and Charlie painted walls and fixed plumbing. I only had the deck redone last February because the original redwood was twenty years old and had turned gray. And rotten. The cement base that holds the umbrella over the table out there fell through, which was how I found the armadillo.

"Not exactly," I admitted. "So what happens after they forklift the pallets into the garage?"

"You know, it's a little dark in here, don't you think?" She was looking at my cabinets as if they had spoken to her. As if they had an *idea*.

"What? I'll turn on the light. How do I get the stone planks out of the garage and onto the floor, Miyoko? Somebody will have to take up the old floor, glue down the new one, all that."

Her dark eyes were sparkling as she stood and turned 360 degrees, nodding at whatever the cabinets had said. She literally beamed.

"You were right about the plank stone, Taylor. Those colors are perfect! I just couldn't see it."

"See what?"

"The whole picture, the theme. It's just... you."

Miyoko Foxwell and I had known each other for mere weeks. Scarcely adequate to the impression she was creating. And at that point even I was deeply unclear about who "I" was.

"What picture? What theme?" I asked.

"Light, change," she said softly. "And music. You've got a million CD's; obviously you love music. The acoustic effect of the stone... but visually softened by warm desert tones. I don't know, it just feels like you're expanding somehow, changing. You need more space, more light, more resonance. But you have to have solid rock beneath your feet, curiously disguised as wood. Listen, there's a laminate countertop, a neutral that looks like granite with flecks of warm beiges and grays that will blend the floor to the decking, indoors to out. Here…"

She'd been pawing through another sample book and showed me the picture. It looked great, but I was still a little bent at being characterized by a person who hadn't known me for thirty years. Still, "light and change" felt right. My old life held the enchantment of familiarity, but it was like a little watercolor landscape, treasured and pale. I needed harder edges now, reams of light. Miyoko had me nailed.

"I really like it, the countertop," I said. "I see what you mean about picking up the deck color, but how about the cost? And really, it's not fair, your doing all this for me gratis. I could never even have found the flooring, much less gotten it immediately at half price. I insist on paying you like any other client."

"You're not 'any other client,' laminate is the least expensive countertop stuff around and a morning of my time is no big deal," she said. "But I do have a huge favor to ask." At "huge" she bent her arms behind her head like a statue of Atlas straining to hold the earth on his shoulders.

"Wow," I said. "That huge."

"Yeah. And it's really okay if you can't do it, but Dave, that's my husband, is in Phoenix for a week. Big project, something about irrigation in Mexico, and we're hoping it'll mean a full-time job for him. But I really need to run up to Palm Springs. You know, the Feng Shui client? When TJ heard all this, he invited Seiji to stay here with him. With you. I said we'd discuss it. Taylor, believe me, helping you with floors and countertops is nothing compared to this! I'll be back as soon as I can make it on Sunday."

"No problem," I answered, thinking there might be a problem. I have Kevin's old bunk bed in TJ's room. The thing is thirty years old and falling apart from a decade of TJ jumping on it, and he has to sleep on the bottom bunk because he still falls out of bed occasionally. But 150-pound Seiji on the top bunk would be a recipe for disaster. "I'd be happy for Seiji to sleep over with TJ. It's just..."

"Of course you have plans," Miyoko said.

"It's not that. It's... come and look at TJ's bed."

"Oh, Taylor, you're wonderful," Miyoko said as she eyed the wreck of bunk bed against a wall. "You thought I'd be hurt if you mentioned Seiji's weight, right? But is this really the only thing?"

"That's it," I said. "I don't want to hurt Seiji's feelings, but..."

"Easy to fix, Taylor. Do you have a wrench, pliers, screwdriver?"

Miyoko is inspiring. She looks like a tiny geisha who might recite haiku in white makeup over a formal tea ceremony while barely moving. But she had Kevin's old bunk bed broken down and reconstructed as two beds against opposite walls in a half hour. I dragged mattresses and held boards for her to fasten, but she did all the work.

"There," she said. "If one of these beds collapses under Seiji, he won't fall far and we'll replace it. Now, your cabinets. I have a great idea!"

"The floor will be enough. I can't afford..." I began.

"True," she agreed, "which is why I have this idea. Replacing the cabinets is out of the question and even refacing them would be pricey."

"But they're going to look horrible with the new countertop. They look horrible now." I was whining.

"Not for long!" she said. "What do you think about an ivory? Eggshell enamel, washable. And for the walls a deep, muted yellow that picks up the lightest shade in the floor? Clean out the cabinets, sand them down and the boys can do the painting on

Sunday."

I could see the ivory cabinets and burnt-butter walls. I could also see two thirteen-year-olds covered in paint, plus the floor and the dog.

"Just gut the room," Miyoko said cheerfully. "They'll get paint all over but it won't matter. After the cabinets and walls are done I'll get a crew in here to install the counters and lay the floor. It's going to be wonderful. I'll bring the boys on my way out of town."

I was helping her carry sample books to her car when the phone rang.

"Taylor, Angie and I are in your neighborhood and I have news," Tim O'Halloran said after I ran in to grab the phone. "You sound breathless."

"I'm redoing my kitchen."

"Ah," he said. "Everyone does that."

"Are you saying all Revenants redecorate their kitchens? We should buy stock in a home store chain now, ahead of the wave."

"New kitchen, new car, cosmetic surgery, it's different with each person, but we do go through a phase at the beginning."

"What did you do, Tim?" I asked. "In that phase?"

"I bought a winery. Just a small one near here, Mourvedre grapes exclusively, but I think you'll find our modest little red interesting. Angie designed the label. It's a basset hound wearing a burgundy beret. We've a bottle for you, which brings me to one of the reasons for my call. We adopted Conan and thought we'd stop by for a minute. Angie wants to thank you for suggesting him."

"Of course. I'd love to see you," I said, wondering what happened to my quiet, orderly life. A ton of dyed limestone would arrive any minute, I hadn't had lunch and the living room, which has been my office for years, was buried in books and papers. Tim was a kindred Revenant and becoming a friend, but I still felt like a character in a nineteenth century British novel who's just learned the vicar is dropping by. I was cramming books into bookcases when the phone rang again. It was Pen Barrows.

"Taylor, can you make it for dinner tonight? The most interesting thing arrived on my doorstep today and I'm having the Syndicate over to see it."

"Dinner would be great, Pen," I said, thinking I'd wear my new outfit. "But what 'arrived on your doorstep?'"

"A dollhouse."

Pen has a five-year-old granddaughter, which would cast the arrival of a dollhouse well within the boundaries of the unexceptional. But Pen was throwing a dinner so we could all see it, which *was* exceptional. Who gets dressed for dinner and drives clear across town to look at a dollhouse?

"I'll explain when you all get here," she said. "It's not just *any* dollhouse. You're going to love this, Taylor, since you're into American history and everything."

I am not into American history but rather American literature, although unless you're a postmodernist there's a significant overlap. I saw no reason to draw the distinction for Pen, who was just being gracious. Pen is gracious to a fault, and the rest of us are always trying to get her to loosen up, be thoughtless and rude occasionally. It never works.

"Sounds intriguing," I said.

"Great. Drinks at six-thirty and by the way, Jude's told everyone you have a new dog. I hope you'll bring her. I got dog biscuits and I'll put a box with some old sheets in it behind your chair at the table so she won't feel left out."

"Pen, you're marvelous," I said. "We'll be there."

The Syndicate stopped bringing hostess gifts every time we go to each other's houses years ago, but it wouldn't do for Sadie to show up without one her first time at Pen's. I didn't have time to go shopping for a canine hostess gift and was feeling frazzled when the doorbell rang.

"Tim, Angie, how nice to see you. And oh my God, Conan!"

The basset wagged courteously as I petted him. Then he went to do the sniffing ritual with Sadie, who seemed to remember him from the shelter. Angie hugged me and Tim handed me a bottle of wine, both exclaiming their happiness over having a dog again.

"I thought our last one was, well, our last one," Angie said. "I don't know how I could have been so stupid, but thanks to you *that's* over! So how are you doing, Taylor?"

This was the woman who played a Bach toccata in a park at five a.m., making my path to a museum of paper dolls. She knew everything. There was no point in dissembling with Angie O'Halloran.

"I don't know," I said. "I feel like I'm inside a kaleidoscope. One minute mannequins are helping me select clothes, the next I'm buying limestone. A plaster Pan that was trying to demolish my windshield broke off one of its seashell hands when I almost smashed into it with my car. The shell's nailed to my fence because I couldn't think of anything else to do with it. I saw a message in a quilt and found a boy left to die in a hole. One of my oldest friends is having a dinner party about a dollhouse, and while I was walking Sadie somebody sneaked into my house and moved an etching of an apple two inches on a bookcase. Everything's different now. I guess I understand about the Revenant thing, but it happens too fast. I feel myself slipping away too fast, Angie. I don't know who I am now, except I just bought this great new outfit and the cabinets are going to be ivory. Do you think ivory will work?"

I don't usually babble; it was embarrassing.

"Tim," she said while wrapping a wiry arm around me, "I'll bet the dogs would like to play in the yard, don't you?"

"Splendid," he replied and vanished through the kitchen and

onto the deck, Sadie and Conan following.

"Honey," Angie said, "let's sit down in here with all your books and let me tell you this isn't easy and you're doing great!"

I threw books on the floor to make room on a couch.

"Tim must have had a hard time at first, too. Did he?"

"You have no idea," she said, laughing. "Tim's never been rigid about religious stuff, but he's a priest and loves his work. For a while it was pretty scary. After he got through the stage where you think you're nuts, he feared somebody would find out and he'd be defrocked, lose his retirement benefits, everything. The Judaeo-Christian tradition doesn't exactly welcome new ideas, y'know. It was hard for him."

"So what did he do? Did he tell... whoever priests tell things?"

"No. He told me, Taylor. And we just figured it out together. Then when he found that there were others, well, we felt a lot better. And the lightbearers are invaluable, people you might have dismissed as 'odd' before all this happened, like me. They don't really know about Revenants, but they're intuitive and sense that something's going on. Let them share their talents with you."

"Like you playing Bach for me," I said. "Tim is so lucky."

"Yes, he is," she agreed. "So, do you have somebody to help you?"

"Oh yeah," I said. "I have terrific friends. One of them was with me when we found... the young guy. She understood when I saw things in his quilt that nobody else could see, and didn't ask any questions."

"How wonderful! We'd like to meet her. But that's not what I meant. I meant someone close, who'll go the distance with you."

"Sadie," I answered. "I'm so glad to have Sadie."

Her blue eyes were direct. "Taylor..."

"Okay, I've been divorced for over six years," I said. "My friend Jude is forever fixing me up with men, but it always feels... silly."

She grinned. "I can't imagine having to go through that again. It must be awful! Just don't be blind if the right one turns up, okay? Tim insists it's easier when there's somebody close who understands and can help."

"A lightbearer."

"Yes, Taylor. You will do well to find many, but it would be great if you find somebody special, an oddball outsider whose peculiar gift will be exactly what you need."

"That's so romantic," I said for lack of anything else to say.

"Not at all," Angie replied. "It's practical. Now, I think Tim has a bit of news for you and then we must go. Hang in there, Taylor. You really are doing well, you know."

"Angie, I'm so glad you're here," I said. "It's good to hear I'm doing okay."

"That's really why we came," she admitted, grinning again. "You already knew we'd brought our new basset home."

I grinned back. "I figured."

As if on cue Tim returned from the yard and clipped Conan's leash to his harness. The priest was wearing jeans and his violet cowboy boots with a clerical shirt and I had to smile, wishing I were as comfortable with my crazy new self.

"I've been in touch with headquarters," he mentioned.

"Revenant headquarters, in Boston," I replied. "What did headquarters say?"

"That you've been invited to spend a few days there working on a guide for Revenants. All expenses covered, of course, and a lovely apartment on Beacon Hill. You leave on Monday."

"Tim! I can't just run off to Boston!"

"Why not?"

I couldn't think why not. "I can't leave Sadie," I said. "I just got her. It would be cruel."

"But Sadie would accompany you! And I'm told there's a lively gathering of dogs and their people on the Common every afternoon. Just walk down Charles and you're there."

I could see where this was going. As in *I* was going.

"Could I think about this and call you later?" I said, mentally packing.

"Tomorrow would be fine," he replied happily as the sound of a truck backing into my driveway set the dogs barking and provided escape. "I'll have details for you then."

"That's my limestone," I said as they left. Angie just smiled and did a thumbs-up.

"Remember, you're doing fine!" she yelled.

Chapter Thirteen

Where Have All the Flowers Gone

Kingston Trio

Pen Barrows' house, a Spanish colonial revival on a cliff overlooking the Pacific, has an old plaque beside its wrought iron gate indicating that it's an historic landmark. Pen thinks the plaque is ostentatious and has trained bougainvillea over it, but the place reeks of history anyway. People have lived in Southern California since the last ice age thirteen thousand years ago, but Pen's house was built in the late 1800's, which in terms of European presence is seriously old for California. She and her husband, Greg, bought it eight years ago when the last of their three kids left home and they needed less space. A Bostonian to the bone, Pen had to take a class called "Spanish Colonial Style" before she could trust herself to select a single stick of furniture. As a result, the place is beautifully done in rustic armoires, terra cotta pots and colorful woven hangings beside which Pen, with her flaming red hair and porcelain complexion, says she feels like Deborah Kerr in "Night of the Iguana."

Jude and I arrived at the same time and hurried with Sadie along the tiled and illuminated walkway to the courtyard at the front of Pen's house.

"I don't know what I'm supposed to say about a dollhouse," Jude whispered, glancing at Tim's bottle of wine tucked under my arm. "And why are you bringing wine?"

"Hostess gift from Sadie," I explained. "There's a basset on the label."

"Of course," Jude said, shaking her head as Pen opened the wrought iron gate and beamed at our feet.

"And this will be Sadie!"

"She thought you might enjoy this," I said, offering Tim's wine.

Pen sat on the ground, staying in perfect hostess character as she let Sadie sniff her hand. "How lovely, and look at this handsome fellow on the label!" she told my dog, who wagged happily in response. "Thank you, Sadie."

Pen's graciousness would probably extend to life forms all the way down to the amoebic, but I appreciated her attention to Sadie. Little is more endearing than kindness shown to your dog. I determined to gush over Pen's dollhouse in return despite never having gushed over anything in my life. Things were different now.

"Taylor, I love your outfit," Pen went on as Jude and I helped her up from her courtyard tiles. "It's new, isn't it?"

I felt terrific.

The rest of the Syndicate were already there, having drinks on the enclosed, cantilevered deck Pen and Greg built by knocking out an entire wall and defying the constraints of the house's architecture.

"Spanish colonial is supposed to be about thick walls enclosing the family from heat and bandits and all that," Pen said at the time. "But we're not going to cook in the courtyard, which is what it was originally for, the 'family' is grown and gone and what's the point in having an ocean view if you can't see it? For the bandits we have a security system. The architectural heritage people would have us tarred and feathered if they knew, so if they ever come to the door I plan to hide."

Pen may be the exemplar of social elegance; let's face it, she leaves thank-you notes for the trash collectors. But that endearing quality is accompanied by an alarming inability to deal with messy situations.

Maggie and Isabel came to meet Sadie and make much of my new clothes, resulting in a fond smile from Jude that stopped just short of *Didn't I tell you?* Pen opened Tim's wine and everyone toasted Sadie. I was back in that warm vale of the known, amid friends who knew (almost) everything about me and loved me anyway. I didn't want anything else. Not a ghoul forgotten since I dumped my training wheels. Not terrifying visions. Baba Yaga and the mannequins were great, but I still didn't want to go to Boston to help draft a guide for other people who were perfectly content in their lives before some brain-glitch made them freaks. Like me. I wanted to be right where I was. I didn't want to be a freak.

"It's time for you to see my 'acquisition,' and then we'll have dinner," Pen announced. "It's in the living room."

We all trooped inside and settled on Mission furniture to stare at a sheet-draped form in front of the fireplace. The room glowed in amber light from table lamps with carved wooden bases and tantalizing scents wafted from the kitchen. Tim's wine was heady. And then Pen pulled the sheet off. A familiar eeriness washed across my brain like a drug. It was a dollhouse. But it was something else as well.

Shit, here we go!

Pen stood facing us in a shawled knit blouse and matching slacks the color of old vellum. Her hair, saved from pumpkin orange only by subtle golden highlights, was swept back in a loose chignon held in place by a scrimshaw clip supposedly carved at sea by a whaling ancestor. Spanish house in California or not, Penley Warren Barrows looked as if she were on her way to a matinee performance by the Boston Symphony. Sixth row center.

"This was my family's house on Beacon Hill," she announced. "Although I don't remember it. Or my father. He died in a fire that completely gutted the building before I was three months old. My mother had taken me to a doctor for inoculations when it happened, or we wouldn't be sitting here right now. At least I wouldn't."

Amid a chorus of interested questions I stared at what appeared to be a miniature brick row house in the Federal style, stark in its detachment, like a single domino. It had four stories, each with two windows flanked by black shutters. Behind a fourth-floor window something tiny moved, sending little shocks of foreboding I knew meant trouble.

"One of the many Boston historical societies closed or merged with another one, I'm not sure about the details," Pen explained, "but the letter said they've had this model for ages, couldn't store it any longer and didn't want to just throw it out, so they tracked me down and sent it. It was signed 'George A. Hibbard,' but there was no return address so I can't even send a thank you."

I imagined a bespectacled historical society gentleman alone with the dollhouse on a snowy Boston night, wind moaning in a chimney as tiny things moved about in the tiny rooms. *Of course they sent it to you, Pen! They wanted to get it as far out of Massachusetts as possible!*

"The letter said that Louisa May Alcott, who lived nearby in Louisville Square, actually came to the house to visit friends in the late 1800's," she went on. "Beacon Hill was quite the literary mecca then. It's even possible that Frederick Douglas accompanied Alcott there on at least one occasion! Taylor, I know you'll want all the history and I'll tell you at dinner, but look..."

She leaned to move little clips on the sides and the entire front wall fell away, revealing the interior. Sadie, who was curled at my feet, growled softly but nobody noticed. Jude had flung herself to her knees, as had Isabel, to look inside. Maggie stood behind them, chatting about Federal architecture with Pen. I didn't want to go near the thing.

"Tay," Jude called from the floor, "you've got to see this. There are little bitty *books!*"

Of course everyone assumed I would want to crawl around on the floor in my new slacks in order to see little bitty books. I am the syndicate's big reader, book maven, general literary geek. A failure to show interest in dollhouse books would seem peevish. I remembered my vow to repay Pen's warmth toward Sadie by gushing, and gamely dropped to the Kelim carpet in front of the fireplace.

The miniature interior was indeed marvelous. Every room was fitted with exquisitely rendered furniture done to perfect scale. On the first floor was an entry hall tiled in microscopic marble, a small parlor, dining room and kitchen. The whole second floor was a large living room lined in bookcases and featuring a grand piano, with the third and fourth floors given to bedrooms.

"The piano is a music box," Pen explained to Isabel, who was entranced by it. "Go ahead, pick it up. If you touch the pedals it will play."

Isabel is an opera singer and carries the traditional heft, which she dresses in long, soft tunics and fabulous shawls. Sprawled on the floor she looked like Desdemona in the last act of Verdi's "Otello," a part she's sung more than once. No stranger to stage gestures, she drew the piano out of the dollhouse in her large hands, softly pressed the minuscule brass pedals beneath the lyre and then did an impressive swoon as the room was filled with strains of Beethoven's "Moonlight Sonata." The sound was so radiant that no one breathed and even Sadie cocked her head to listen. Isabel was actually in tears.

"Pen, this is simply exquisite!" she said as the music stopped and everyone sighed.

"I knew you'd love it," Pen said. "It's yours. I want you to have it."

"What? No, Pen," Isabel replied, setting the piano carefully back where it had been. "I couldn't."

Pen was beaming. "Of course you could. You all could. This is a replica of my home, although of course I have no memory of it.

What was left of the building was sold to developers after the fire and my mother bought a house in Wellesley with the insurance money. Then she tried to enroll in business courses at Babson College so she could learn how to invest what was left. The bloody sexist pigs didn't admit women, so she bought textbooks for the classes she wanted and taught herself! Invested in blue chips like General Electric and made a fortune. I want to give the dollhouse to my granddaughter so she'll have some sense of the past, well, *my* past. But first I want each of you to choose something from it for yourselves. You all mean so much to me. Please."

I watched as Maggie selected a framed miniature of Rembrandt's "Saskia as Flora" from the wall of the living room.

"I've always loved this one," she said. "It feels like an alter ego, a life I didn't choose. Thank you, Pen. It's perfect."

The painting is of a young woman elegantly dressed in shades of green, her head dressed in flowers as she holds a flowered staff. She looks somberly over the left shoulder of the viewer, as if into her own puzzling future. Of course Maggie had once been such a flowered creature, before she chose a life of less ephemeral imagery. But she remembered.

Jude chose a shiny golden birdcage that looked like a pagoda.

"But Jude, the bird's missing," Pen said. "It's just an empty cage. Why don't you pick something else?"

Jude glanced meaningfully in my direction. "No, it's exactly right for me," she insisted. "I already have the bird. A woodpecker. I'll keep this on my nightstand. Thanks so much, Pen."

Jill Danner was completely entranced with the dollhouse as a whole and took photos of it from every angle with her cell phone, saying she might do a picture of it in needlepoint for Pen. She took great care in selecting her treasure and finally pulled a four-inch rug from one of the bedrooms.

"This is a tobacco felt!" she exclaimed as we all looked blank. The little rug had a Moorish design in plum, teal, pink and brown, with black fringe.

"Early twentieth century," she explained. "These used to be packaged with tobacco and cigarettes as giveaways. They're collector's items now. I'm going to frame it. Pen, I've wanted one of these for years!"

It was my turn and my hands were shaking. Something *had* moved behind a window in the dollhouse, but nothing was moving now and I didn't want to spoil the mood. In the miniature kitchen was a group of dolls with plastic heads, a man and three women seated tightly against a table. The women wore identical flowered housedresses and aprons, the man a plaid suit.

"Who are these?" I asked Pen.

"Just dolls," she said. "Whoever made this must have put them there. I guess they're supposed to look like characters from Alcott's time. So what would you like, Taylor?"

The dolls glared at me.

"Ah, this!" I took a tiny raven on a tiny classical bust inside a glass dome from a low table in the living room. "Look, Pen, it's Poe's raven 'perched upon a bust of Pallas'! I love it. Thank you."

Pen was pleased. "Do you suppose Poe ever visited the house?" she asked.

"Not with Alcott," I answered, forgetting, as usual, to stop lecturing. "She was only seventeen when he died and although he was born in Boston and lived there briefly as an adult, Alcott wouldn't live there until long after his death. I doubt that their paths ever crossed."

Pen seemed disappointed.

Taylor, you are such a buzz-kill!

"But I'm sure he walked past these windows," I amended quickly. "He would have gone to Beacon Hill when he was in Boston, to visit literary friends. His very footsteps would have passed right there," I said, pointing to a little patch of cobbles at the house's base.

"Ah, yes," Pen sighed, and I was redeemed.

Over oysters baked in their shells with sorrel purée and braised Brussels sprouts Pen told us that her mother, Beverly Warren, never remarried after the death of Pen's father, Garret Warren, in that fire.

Pen, who has no siblings, said she was born in England. After many childless years, her mother had happily announced that she was expecting and then been called to the country home of a sister in Kent to help settle the complicated estate of the sister's husband, a casualty at the end of WWII. But Pen's mother became ill, and doctors in England feared that the exhausting trip back to Boston would jeopardize her pregnancy. So she stayed and Pen was born there. It was all in the society pages of the *Boston Globe*, Pen said, including an article with posed pictures of the family's happy reunion after Pen's mother returned with the newest member of the family. She passed around a faded newspaper clipping in a carved ebony frame. In it were a handsome man with Pen's long nose and a woman in a pompadour hair style and square-shouldered suit holding a baby.

"That's me, that baby," Pen went on. "My mother kept the clipping on the mantel in our house in Wellesley and never tired of telling the story. I knew it by heart by the time I was three, what a wonderful man my father was and how thrilled they were to learn they were going to have a baby at last. I look like him, don't you think?"

"Definitely the nose," Maggie noted. "Did he have red hair, too? In the photo it looks darker than yours."

"No, he was a brunette and so was my mother, but she said half her English cousins were 'ginger.' That's what they call redheads in England. I got the red hair from her side."

I was intrigued at the idea of Pen having been born in the country of Byron, Blake, the Brontës, the Brownings, and that was only the B's. "Wow, Pen, that means you have dual citizenship. I'd love to see your British passport!"

Pen looked surprised. "I don't have a British passport," she said. "I don't think my birth was even recorded over there, not that I've ever checked. It was right after the war, you know. Things were in turmoil and I was born at my aunt's farm in Kent, not in a hospital. Mother said my dad pulled strings to arrange a birth certificate in Boston. Why would I want a British passport?"

"Oh, in case the United States government collapses or something," I joked. "You know, you'd be welcome in England as a citizen."

"While the rest of us stay here in anarchy!" Maggie said, holding up her empty wine glass. "I'll drink to that as soon as possible."

Maggie and Isabel carried dishes to the kitchen as Pen opened another bottle, and Jude wandered out on the deck to admire the view. Sadie was asleep in the box Pen had tucked against the wall behind my chair. I walked back into the living room to look more closely at the dollhouse, unsure why I was uneasy about Pen giving it to a poetry-writing little granddaughter who's afraid of cookie jars.

It was just an elaborately furnished model, I told myself. Some history buff with a lot of disposable income had probably spent years choosing the painted pewter grandfather clock, the fabulous piano, the monitor-top refrigerator in the kitchen.

Refrigerator?

It was then that I noticed the console radio in the living room, the tiny telephone on a desk. And the bathrooms on the upper floors, each with a toilet, sink and shiny white tub. There were no refrigerators, telephones, radios or modern indoor plumbing when Louisa May Alcott had visited this house. It hadn't been created to commemorate the 19th century, but rather the 20th! The house was created to reflect the era in which Pen's parents had lived in it. But why? Beacon Hill was long past its prime by WWII and wouldn't be returned to its former glory by massive renovation projects until the 1960's. At the time the model was meant to reflect, the area would have been little more than a genteel slum.

And so what? Pen was delighted with it, would give it to a granddaughter along with an illustrated copy of *Little Women*, I was sure. They would talk about Alcott and Frederick Douglas and Thoreau on his pond not far away. No one would care about the refrigerator. I was a nit-picking pain in the ass. Yet I couldn't shake the sense that Pen's dollhouse was dangerous.

I stared into the narrow little model. The dolls were no longer seated in the kitchen, but were in the upstairs bedrooms. Someone must have moved them, I assumed. Someone playing dolls for a few minutes. Maybe Jude.

The man in his plaid suit stood over a fourth floor bed on which lay one of the women, while the other two women sat alone in separate bedrooms on the third floor. The figures seemed deliberately frozen, like children playing statues. I had a sense that they'd resume whatever they were doing the minute I turned away.

"No more wine for me!" I called into the dining room where everybody was settling in for desert. I'd have to ask Tim about the effects of alcohol on Revenants. It was just a dollhouse. All dollhouses are creepy in subdued light. I'd have coffee and not look at it again.

But of course I did, and felt a vaporous cold move under my skin. The doll on the fourth floor bed was screaming, a thready sound like a mouse crushed in a trap but not yet dead and wild with terror. I saw a miniature river of red spill from under the doll and pool at the feet of the man in the plaid suit, who did not move. Nothing moved but the steady, tiny drip of red soaking the bed, the floor, the cardboard shoes of a plastic doll.

I looked away into the dining room where Pen was pouring coffee as Isabel served tarts on crystal desert plates. There was music on the stereo, a Mozart piano concerto Isabel had chosen to honor Pen's gift of the little music box. I've heard the piece countless times and it always makes me think of summer afternoons in which elegantly-dressed people picnic in balletic movements beside a rippling lake. But this time a threnody loomed from inside the music, a somber lament mocking the innocence of the piece's tone. When I looked back at Pen's dollhouse, the doll in the plaid suit was rooted halfway down the stairs from the fourth floor to the third, tiny red footprints like exclamation points on the floor behind him. On the bed now soaked in blood, the face of the woman doll beneath her little wig of red plastic hair, was gray and sallow. I told myself that dolls cannot die, and nonetheless knew she was dead.

Shaken, I called to the group that I'd join them after at quick trip to the loo, where I splashed water on my face and felt crazy. Except I knew I wasn't crazy and also didn't know what to do. But I knew Pen Barrows, my gentle, courteous friend of many years. I was sure whatever that dollhouse was, it meant harm to Pen and her granddaughter.

On the way back I glanced at the dolls and noticed that they were all in the kitchen again, sitting in exactly the same positions they'd held when Pen first revealed them. The dead doll was "alive," the fourth floor bed bloodless. Deliberately I turned to adjust a cushion on the couch, then looked again. Now all four were on the stairs. They were going up, I realized. They were going to enact the death scene again. It occurred to me that they would never stop; they would play the scene over and over forever.

"Pen," I announced over my pear tart, "I'm doing a bit of fixing up at my place, and I love the color scheme in the dollhouse parlor. Would you mind if I borrowed it to show my decorator? She's so good with ideas, you know? If she could see it..."

"But I thought you were just doing the kitchen," Jude interrupted.

"I was, but Miyoko, my decorator, keeps talking about a theme for the whole house – colors and everything – and I kind of like the parlor wallpaper in the dollhouse..."

"Of course," Pen said. "Borrow it for as long as you like, and do let us know about the colors!"

After dinner Pen and I loaded the thing into my car, draped in a couple of old beach towels she brought from her rag bin. Covered, it looked merely awkward and harmless belted to my back seat, but I thought I could hear tiny footsteps inside.

Jude had contributed substantially to our demise of three bottles of wine, so I gave her a ride home. Joey would drive her back to Pen's in the morning to pick up her car. The little golden birdcage resting atop Sadie's back in Jude's lap caught the pinkish-gold of sodium street lights as we drove in companionable silence.

"Nice evening," I said as a footnote.

"Tay, did your... I mean, when you were little...you weren't *abused* or anything, were you?"

"*What?*"

Jude was slightly loaded and isn't known for subtlety even when stone sober, but this was out of the blue.

"I just thought maybe, you know, this thing that happened to you? The paper doll thing? Maybe it's a sort of repressed memory about some terrible abuse when you were a kid. Pen's dollhouse made me think of it. Her nice history that's made her the way she is. I mean, there's a ton of stuff, websites and everything, for women who still have all kinds of strange symptoms because..."

"Jude," I interrupted, "knowing your father was burned alive before you could even sit up doesn't exactly constitute a 'nice' history, and Pen is the way she is because that's just who she is. Some people are *born* nice. And I can't believe you'd suggest...but then I guess I should, huh? Your old boyfriend, Luke. You thought he was crazy, too."

That remark was way below the belt and I felt like shooting myself. Jude sniffled and I saw a tear fall into Sadie's fur.

"Oh, God, I'm sorry, Jude," I apologized. "I shouldn't have said that; it was stupid and cruel. It's just that my father didn't rape me and would have killed anybody who did. Literally. Nobody raped me; nothing terrible happened to me. My parents weren't perfect, but they loved me and took care of me. They *protected* me. I feel as protective of them, of their memory now, as they did of me then. I just lost it when you suggested..."

"You're lucky," Jude said quietly. "A lot of little girls aren't."

"I know," I said. "I know I'm lucky. And I've never given you any reason to think otherwise about my childhood, so what's this about? Did something happen to *you*?"

"No. That's not why... well, one of my mother's boyfriends sneaked into my bedroom one night when I was twelve or thirteen, but he didn't do anything to me."

"Good," I said.

"Because my mother was watching from the door and when he put his hand over my mouth and got on top of me, she grabbed my bedside lamp and broke it over his head. But that's not..."

"Good for her!" I yelled. "So did she kill him?"

"Nah, but he had to have eighteen stitches before they threw him in jail. Mom bought me new sheets and swore off boyfriends. A year later she married a nice guy who taught me to drive and helped me with algebra. His name was Ben. They both died in an automobile accident ten years later."

As is so often the case with Jude, I had no idea where this was going and merely waited.

"I'm just worried about you, Tay," she went on. "You're my best friend and I want you to be all right."

"I am all right, Jude," I reassured her.

"Every book I pick up has a story about a woman having nightmares and not knowing why she throws up at the smell of cigar smoke or something. She can't feel close to men and compensates by ruthlessly taking over small corporations or collecting thousands of Pez dispensers until one day they fall on her in an earthquake and kill her. And all because her sicko father or some nasty uncle..."

"Jude! Stop. I'm not entirely sure what a corporation actually is and don't own a single Pez dispenser. I've never been abused by anybody. It's not that, really. It's something else. And have you thought of going back and reading the classics? There's something to be said for the old heroines who went into service in order to save the family farm, fought off the syphilitic advances of the baron and found a way to thwart black rot in cabbages on the side."

Jude laughed. "Like Pen's mom," she said. "Raising Pen alone after her husband died."

"Sure," I said. "Like that." But I wasn't at all sure what 'that' was. The story inside Pen's dollhouse wasn't exactly one of the classics.

Chapter Fourteen

Ball of Confusion

The Temptations

I'd planned to put the dollhouse in my garage, but when I got home I noticed a light inside my house. I didn't remember leaving a light on, although in my rush to get to Pen's I might have. I couldn't park in the garage because the garage was full of limestone, so I parked in the driveway and approached the house from the front. The porch light was on, but from the street I'd seen another light deep inside, just a glimmer visible through the sidelight windows flanking the door. It made me uneasy. Sadie was barking maniacally before I got the key in the lock, and I heard myself bellow, "What the hell!" seconds after I pushed the door open.

My house had been invaded. Books were pulled from the bookcases in the living room, my desk drawers lay upturned on the floor, papers everywhere. Even the kitchen showed evidence of scrutiny, with canned goods removed from cabinets and stacked on the counter. Chunks of thick, broken glass from the deck door sparkled on the floor.

I scooped up Sadie, stumbled back outside into the yard and dialed 911 on my cell. I'd left the door open and I saw no movement, but what if the intruder were still in there? I got into my car, locked it, and turned on the engine. If I saw anything move in the house, I'd just back down the driveway to the street and head for the police station. Then I realized I had no idea where the police station was, a fact that could leave me careening aimlessly through late-night suburban streets like a pinball.

Charlie's car was stolen from a downtown parking lot years ago, and once a pickpocket relieved me of my wallet and passport in the Paris metro. But neither event was more than an annoyance. Neither felt personal; this did. My home had been invaded by a stranger, my things torn out of place. It made no sense. The police arrived five minutes later, red and blue lights flashing. The neighbors came outside and stood around in their yards, each group dispatching a courier to approach me and ask what was going on.

"Somebody broke into my house," I told them and the police. "No, I wasn't here. I just got home. I'm fine."

More police came, more flashing lights. One of them, a detective in khakis and a polo shirt, had been in school with my kids.

"You're Kevin Blake's mom," he told me. "And Beth. He had a younger sister named Beth. Kev and I ran track together. I used to come over here, eat dinner with Kev sometimes. I'm Chris Delgado, Mrs. Blake. Remember me?"

I didn't remember Chris Delgado. Between Beth and Kevin there'd been scores of kids around, devouring food like locusts and playing Bon Jovi at top volume. More than two decades in the past. And the beefy detective in my yard wasn't a skinny teenager in track shorts anymore.

"Of course I do, Chris," I answered. "I'm so glad you're here."

"I recognized the address when the call came in," he said. "Didn't know if Kev's family still lived here, but I wanted to see. Normally there'd just be patrols, not a detective. But hey, you're Kev's mom. So tell me what happened here."

"I came home from dinner with friends and found my house... well, you can see."

I kept my arms wrapped around Sadie. In the strobing glare of the police lightbars the interior of my house looked like a scene from a crime movie, yet the exterior (tan siding, little fake shutters in black) insisted that it was, indeed, a perfectly normal place. A nice place. *Mine.*

"Have any idea who did this? Or why?"

"No," I said. "It makes no sense."

"Where's your husband? He out of town?"

"Kevin's father and I have been divorced for some years," I said. "I live here alone."

Something about that statement didn't sound right. I'd never thought of myself as living "alone," just as living *here.* "Alone" is a state of mind, I guess. But not my state of mind.

Chris Delgado looked uncomfortably past me toward the street.

"Um, is there any chance Mr. Blake was angry, came here to take something or, you know, get even? In a divorce situation people can do some pretty stupid things."

I vaguely remembered that Charlie was doing a riverboat cruise on the Danube about now. I also couldn't remember the last time I'd seen Charlie, although it would have been cordial, whenever it was. Charlie and I pretty much wrote the book on polite divorce, and after the first year or two we eased into an amiable distance that permits friendly family gatherings and the occasional meeting over coffee, usually to discuss TJ's problems. The idea of Charlie demolishing my house was ludicrous.

"No," I told Delgado. "Charlie's out of town, but he could have had nothing to do with this in any event. That's not a possibility."

"How about one of your students? Maybe some kid you flunked, and he didn't graduate? That sort of thing? Maybe a kid on drugs?"

"I've just retired from teaching, and for the last ten years I taught only advanced English classes," I said. "Nobody flunks those advanced-placement classes. The kids are all devastated over B's. Nobody flunked and if any of my students had drug abuse problems, I wasn't aware of it."

He seemed to be running out of likely suspects.

"Still, maybe some kid who hated you, hated Shakespeare, who knows? And, um, how about your personal life. You know, men friends? Some guy with his shorts in a twist because you wouldn't..."

He trailed off miserably.

"Sleep with him?" I completed the thought, smiling for the first time since I opened my front door.

"I was going to say 'marry him,'" he said to his feet.

He was being so beamish and deferential I started to relax.

"Of course you were, but I'm afraid there's nobody like that on the horizon, Chris. Really. I'd tell you if there were, but there's not. I can think of nobody who would do this to me. It wouldn't be so frightening if I could put a story around it, some reason for it no matter how far-fetched, but I can't. There's nothing of any real value in my house, nothing worth stealing. But I think somebody was here before. I'm pretty sure somebody broke in once before."

"Tell me about that," he said, gesturing for a uniformed patrolman to take notes.

"It was yesterday. Early evening. I walked the dog for quite a while and when I got back – it would have been around eight-thirty – she, the dog, just went crazy running around and barking. There was a bit of grass on the kitchen floor. I think whoever it was came in from the deck. The deck doors had been left open and the screen wasn't locked. Anyone could have just walked in."

"And that's it?"

"What do you mean?"

"Was anything taken? What made you think somebody broke in?"

I saw a look pass between Delgado and the uniform. There's no word for that look in English, but it's a sequence - arrogant pity morphing into noble intent. The old folks can be a bit dotty but by God, it's our job to protect them!

"Nothing was taken yesterday," I stated evenly, choosing not to mention the two-inch displacement of an apple etching on a bookcase shelf. No point in providing further evidence of eccentric silliness. "However, it can't have escaped your attention that something has happened tonight. My guess would be that someone has been watching my house and breaking in when he sees me leave. Tonight I left at six dressed for dinner. One would not have to be a trained statistician to predict that I'd be gone for at least two hours. As it was, I was gone for over four."

"What about the dog?" the uniform asked. "The dog woulda barked if somebody broke in. Dog woulda raised hell, the neighbors would come to see what was going on. But nobody heard no dog."

"*Any* dog or *a* dog," I said. "She was with me."

Chris Delgado knit a tanned brow. "You take your dog out to dinner with you?"

That look again. The pity replaced now by a shadow of distaste. I was obviously a whack job who dines with pets.

"Listen, does your daughter Beth still live in San Diego?" he asked, glancing at his watch. "Probably a good idea if she could come over, if she's here. Be good for you to have somebody here."

I didn't feel the need to have "somebody" hovering solicitously, especially my prone-to-overreaction daughter.

"Detective Delgado, I did not attack the interior of my own home before dashing out to dinner at an ocean-view restaurant with a dog," I said, biting off every word. "And what I need to have here is not my daughter but *the damn police!* Now I would appreciate it if you'd go into the house, assess damage, see if the perpetrator is by any chance still in there, and do something about fingerprints."

The schoolmarm persona proved effective.

Delgado made a whuffling noise, sort of like Basset hounds do, and called for a crime scene unit on his cell. I called my insurance agent on mine and left a message. Then I called Miyoko Foxwell, who'd said she was into photography. The first thing the insurance agent would ask for would be photos. Miyoko said she'd be there in fifteen minutes with an extra memory card.

"Taylor, this may turn out to be a blessing in disguise," she said after reassurances that Sadie and I were fine.

"Blessing! Miyoko, it will take me the rest of my life to re-catalog my books!"

"Think about color for the living room," she suggested brightly. "I'll be right there."

Sadie and I sat in my car until the crime scene techs came and dusted for fingerprints, after which Delgado asked me to do a walk-through in order to determine what had been stolen. I left Sadie in the car and went with him. What was immediately apparent was that if anything had been stolen, it wasn't immediately apparent. Delgado noted that popular items such as the TV and sound system hadn't been touched. The few "nice" pieces of jewelry I own were on the floor of my bedroom beside my overturned jewelry box, which played a few bars of "Lara's Theme" from *Doctor Zhivago* when Delgado picked it up in his gloved hand. Charlie had given me the jewelry box on our second date. For a second I felt like bursting into tears.

"This isn't looking like a burglary," Delgado said. "This is looking like a shakedown. Somebody looking for something. Looking *real hard.* Got any idea what?"

His look indicated that I was no longer the pitiful eccentric of his earlier suspicions. Now I was quite possibly muling drugs for a Mexican cartel or something equally nefarious. The image was oddly flattering, so I didn't point out that employees of Mexican drug cartels do not wait courteously for you to leave for dinner before ransacking your house. They just blow off the door and shoot you in the knees until you tell them where the drugs are. In Spanish. Then they kill you and some of the neighbors, if they have time.

"You can't actually think…," I began, laughing.

"Nah." A grin revealed big white teeth I thought I remembered, in braces. "You used to make these terrific potato pancakes with applesauce on top for dinner and we'd have to recite verses from 'To An Athlete Dying Young' to get second helpings," he said. "'Runners whom renown outran, and the name died before the man.' See? I never forgot. You were sort of weird as a mom, but in a neat way."

"Housman," I said. "Thank you. I tried."

We were standing in the guest room, which although ransacked didn't look much different than it had before. Delgado pulled a nylon rectangle featuring four white snakes extending forked tongues against a blue background from the mess.

"What's this?" he asked.

"The flag of Martinique," I explained. "Kevin and his significant other, Suzanna, vacationed there a while back. They always send such… unusual gifts. He's in Stockholm with the Foreign Service, and they travel a lot."

"Wow," Delgado said. "I haven't talked to Kev in years. Sounds like the dude did all right for himself. Is Suzanna the Mrs.?"

It was the middle of the night and my house was a crime scene. Delgado's bulky warmth and connection to my previous life had dissolved my fear, which felt good, but I still didn't feel like explaining my son's love life right then. He's in a seemingly permanent relationship with an attractive, intelligent woman who regards marriage as a distasteful anachronism the sole purpose of which is to ensure that men control all the world's assets and property. Unmarried, she and Kevin are nonetheless devoted to each other and while they don't want children, they plan to foster teenagers from war-torn countries when they retire. In the meantime they live all over the world and send me quaint ethnic gifts I have no idea what to do with, although I appreciate the thought.

"Not married, but they've been together for years," I abridged the hopelessly complicated narrative.

"So Kev sent you this snake flag," he said, grinning as he tickled the outstretched tongue of a white, coiled fer-de-lance viper. "Say, I've got a daughter, she's nine and a handful, says she wants to be a herpetologist. Of course a few months ago it was rodeo clown and before that something about doll fashions. She changes her mind all the time, but right now it's snakes. She'd love this thing!"

"It's yours," I said with unfeigned enthusiasm. "I'll email Kevin, tell him you were here and how much your daughter will enjoy the flag. He'll get a kick..."

"Something wrong?"

Email. A small shower of paranoia rattled in my ears. Had somebody read my correspondence with Tim O'Halloran? Was somebody tracking Revenants? *Attacking* Revenants? There was nothing to suggest that, no message scrawled in blood on a wall, no message at all.

"My computer," I told Delgado. "Some notes for a talk I'm giving. I'll be a blithering idiot without those notes!"

In the living room he checked the plugs on my computer, which was intact atop my desk. A slide show of standard-issue scenery flipped across the screen. Meadow, forest, ocean. I was going to have to do something more creative about screensavers.

"Check it out, see if your notes are there," he suggested as Seiji and Miyoko arrived carrying brooms, buckets and mops.

I quickly pulled up my notes on Poe and exuded fake relief. "Still there," I told Delgado. "And I'd like you to meet my friends the Foxwells, Miyoko and Seiji. This is Detective Chris Delgado."

"You're going to catch the guys that did this," Seiji told Delgado confidently. "It was probably drugs and they went to the wrong house, don't you think?"

"Good man," the detective growled and punched Seiji on the arm, causing everybody to smile. I almost offered coffee and then remembered the kitchen was a mess.

Seiji was wearing a baggy t-shirt with a carefully painted blue frog on the front. The design was attractive except for the crossed machine guns beneath the frog, which was holding aloft a quarter-moon *a la* Hamlet with Yorick's skull. "Blue Frog Dream" was printed backward in shaded letters over the figure.

"Great shirt," I said.

Seiji nodded. "TJ did it. It's reversed so you can only read it in a mirror."

"TJ did that?"

"Yeah. You know, he's always drawing stuff."

No one in my family or Charlie's can draw a recognizable stick figure, yet our grandson had been drawing pictures since he was four. I wondered again who his father was.

"I'll do what I can in here," Miyoko said from the kitchen door where she was snapping photos. "Seiji, I don't want you in this broken glass, so how about you start picking up books in the living room. Taylor, you can't stay here tonight so after we straighten up a little, you can come home with us, okay?"

It hadn't occurred to me that I would have to move out of my house. I wasn't *going* to move out of my house.

"You're wonderful to offer, but I'll be just fine," I said. "My bedroom's okay, just a few drawers pulled out of the dresser. And everything out of the closet. Easy to clean up. Sadie and I will be fine and the boys can get to work on the kitchen tomorrow. I had to empty the cabinets anyway and it's already half-done."

"Deck door's smashed," Delgado noted. "They broke the glass to get in. If you're going to stay here tonight we gotta secure that. Any old boards in the garage?"

"No, just some limestone," I answered. "A bunch of pallets…"

One of the uniforms shot Delgado an upbeat look about pallets.

"Should work," he told the detective. "Wanna help me unload some limestone?"

"Roger," Delgado replied.

Within forty-five minutes they'd hammered together a covering made of a pallet boards for the shattered door and Miyoko and I had cleaned, swept and mopped the floor and moved everything from the cabinets to the living room. Seiji was asleep in my car with Sadie and I was exhausted.

"I can't thank you enough," I told Miyoko. "But it's after midnight. I'll deal with the rest of this tomorrow."

"I've got photos of every room," Miyoko assured me as she pulled Seiji from my car and Sadie blinked at me sleepily. "Call me tomorrow."

"And I'll have a patrol cruising by every twenty minutes all night," Delgado said, handing me his business card. "Call this number if you need me."

"Thanks so much, Chris," I said, sincerely. "Your being here really helped."

When Sadie and I were alone, I looked around carefully. Nothing was broken except the glass deck door. Sadie's bed had been moved away from the broken glass and left in the hall. All the lamps were intact, all the electronic equipment untouched. What had been touched was every enclosed space in which you'd keep something – drawers, bookcases, cabinets, medicine chests. Yet nothing was missing. The intruder had not found what he was looking for. But what could it be? I honestly didn't own anything worth stealing. Except apparently I did.

The cops had put the box springs and mattress back on my bed, and I forced myself to change the sheets. A stranger's hands had touched my bed, but I felt nothing like the revulsion that should have prompted me to throw everything down to the mattress pad in the washer, on hot, and drench the frame in disinfectant. Whoever broke into my house had been trying to find something, not to defile anything. What remained was an aura of failure. It didn't make any sense.

I thought I'd have trouble getting to sleep, but Sadie's soft snores were hypnotic. They muffled the incessant brain-chatter that usually reminds me, just at the point of slipping off, that I'm out of stamps and really should be able to remember the formula for an isosceles right triangle. I curled close to Sadie and was asleep in minutes.

Chapter Fifteen

The Lion Sleeps Tonight

The Tokens

The insurance agent called at eight, waking me up. I promised to email pictures and then made sure the answering machine was still working. I didn't want to talk to anybody. I just wanted to wander around the wreckage of my house. Everything was limned with that nostalgic shock you feel when finding something lost long ago. *Wow, those are the shoes I wore on that trip to Alaska!* But the moment passes and you shrug as you throw whatever it was in the trash. Except I couldn't throw everything I owned in the trash. I had to sort through it, a journey derailed by my usual proclivity to distraction.

I decided to tackle the living room first, since I actually live in there. The cops had moved the bookcases around, and there were scratches and pale patches on the walls. The carpet was many shades of what once was beige, with bright rectangles of the original color where the bookcases kept it from fading. But it was Sadie's tail-wagging discovery of a mummified mouse flattened against the baseboard that pushed me over the edge. The place was dingy, dated and a possible source of plague. I called Miyoko.

"There's a mouse-mummy in the living room," I told her.

"Be a miracle if there's only one. Have you decided on paint yet, and what's the news about whoever broke in?"

"No news, I haven't talked with the police yet, and I just

realized my house isn't exactly stunning. I mean not just the kitchen. The living room looks like one of those small town museums where they display the 1937 set of World Book Encyclopedias, a cracked Haviland tea service and somebody's WWI uniform, Miyoko. It's amazing that I never noticed."

"Which is why I keep repeating the word, 'paint,'" she replied. "Give me your insurance agent's email and I'll send the photos. With the photos and a police report your homeowner's policy will cover most of this. While your agent is assessing the damage, box up your books and pick... a... color, okay? An earth shade – something muted. And then maybe one dramatic wall in a deep tone? We'll need something big there – vivid ethnic painting, a sculpture, let me think about this."

"Okay," I said, overwhelmed.

"I got the paint for the kitchen cabinets; it's called "Celtic Linen" and everything's here for the kids to use - plastic drop cloths, rollers, trays, the works. I'll drop it off with the kids. Meanwhile, go to liquor stores for boxes," she added. "The size they ship wine in is just right for books. See you when I get back from Palm Springs!"

When I went out to the car I remembered Pen's dollhouse, sitting shrouded on the back seat. I carried it, still covered in beach towels, into the garage and tucked it against the wall behind a set of wooden TV trays I hadn't used in years but were too nice to discard. Then Sadie and I hit three liquor stores before finding a windfall. Twenty wine boxes the owner was just about to cut up and bundle for the dumpster. Back home I stacked them in the hall and then picked up the book I'd bought on my way to lunch with Jude. It was on the hall floor beside the catch-all table where I'd tossed it. *Secret Addictions*. Sadie stretched out in her bed and I sat on the floor beside her to glance through the book for a few minutes before getting to work.

The introduction quoted a bunch of psychologists talking about "collection addictions," which apparently involve the collector getting an endorphin rush by finding more and more items. The most common collections involve coins, stamps, shoes, purses, guns, sports and military memorabilia and replicas of angels and various animals. I was surprised to see "snakes" and "dice" on the list. Why would anybody collect *snakes*? The dice seemed doable, if uninteresting. All dice are pretty much the same.

But the book was about historical collections, hence the subtitle, *Escaping the Bondage of Secrets That Have Died."* The author suggested that obsessions with artifacts of the past might mean the collector is afraid of change and feels out of control in a world now changing at warp speed. I'm no fan of pop psychology and so didn't read the section about curing such addictions, but the chapter on patent medicine labels was fascinating. One urging, "Get Fat on Loring's FAT-TEN-U and Corpula Foods," featuring a big-busted woman in a ruffly white outfit was my favorite. Women in 1895 bought pills to get fat much as my contemporaries buy equally ineffective pills to get thin. I wondered why the Victorian ladies didn't just eat more ice cream, and then had to get up and Google the dates for ice cream production, learning that there was plenty of ice cream around in 1895 and that the original ice cream churn had been invented in 1843 by a New England woman named Nancy Johnson. I don't know what I did before the Internet. When the phone rang I'd forgotten why it was buried under mounds of books and that I didn't want to talk on the phone anyway.

"Sorry, I couldn't find the phone," I said breathlessly over my answering machine's recorded message.

Tim O'Halloran's voice betrayed concern. "You couldn't find your phone?"

"Um, no," I said, snapping back to reality. "Someone broke in last night and went through my house while I was at dinner. My books are all over the floor with the phone under them. Somebody was looking for something, Tim. The police used the term 'shakedown.' Do you think this could have anything to do with...?"

"Is Sadie all right?"

"I'm sorry, I should have told you she was with me. She wasn't here. We're both fine. But do you think...?"

"Thank goodness! And you say the intruder was looking for something?"

"Yes. Every cupboard, drawer, closet, and shelf was searched. And yet as far as I can see nothing was taken. Were they looking for Martine's gift, Tim? It's on a chain around my neck, always with me like you said."

"As it must be," he answered. "However, in any hands but yours it possesses no power. It's worthless. Even if someone knew of these amulets, and only *we* do, they have no value except to us."

My mind was creating scenarios.

"But what if some power-hungry loser with bad tattoos and one arm heard about Revenants and thought he could grab a little magic?"

"You're describing Captain Hook, Taylor," he observed drily. "And if information has leaked, headquarters would know. There's a computer set-up monitoring the Internet 24/7. Your intruder is much more likely to have been looking for something else, something unconnected to your being a Revenant."

"But what? Nothing was taken."

"Then he didn't find it. Nonetheless, such an event must be disturbing. Would you like to come and stay with us for a few nights, just until things are more settled at home, and then of course you'll be in Boston..."

I'd forgotten about that, but it was suddenly appealing. Getting out of town felt like a reprieve. "My grandson and his friend will be staying with me tonight and tomorrow, but thank you, Tim. And yes, I think Boston will be just the thing."

"Excellent. I'll arrange for your tickets now, on an airline that will permit Sadie in the cabin. We have a wheeled dog carrier you may borrow. You'll leave for a week, but the ticket will be open so you may stay longer or return at any time if need arises. Perhaps we could meet prior to your departure? I'd like to provide a little information about the agenda and that sort of thing."

"Of course," I said. "Except the kids will be here later today, and I won't have a free minute after that until Sunday night, when I'll be packing."

"Well then, how about right now? I can bring Sadie's carrier and help you straighten things a bit while we chat."

Forty-five minutes later he was at the door holding a carry-on size black nylon wheeled dog carrier, a cardboard tray of coffees and a giant turkey submarine sandwich with balsamic dressing that smelled like an Italian restaurant. We sat on the deck and I wolfed my half of the sandwich while he told me about Boston.

"The organization is headed by an extremely competent woman named Hallett Gardner," he began. "It all started in Boston, you see, and Martine sometimes appears to the Boston Revenants, providing clues to the identities of others."

"Clues? Is that how you found me, how you knew about the Paper Doll Museum? What clues?"

He was thoughtful. "The process cannot be explained and appears to be random, but from time to time Martine shows up in Boston, always unexpectedly in incongruous places. She communicates to the Boston Revenants in odd ways, but they've become adept at reading her clues. She doesn't seem to know about all new Revenants, only some. In your case she appeared onstage in the costume of an eighteenth century Oxford don at a production of *Peter and the Wolf.* Of course only a Revenant could see her, and one was in the audience – an MIT professor named Harry Laufer, who'd taken his grandchildren to see the show. She jumped down from the stage, walked up the aisle to Harry and handed him a package wrapped in brown paper. Then she vanished!"

I was dying to hear what this had to do with me. "And…?"

Tim held up a hand, begging my patience. "Laufer tucked the package in a pocket and later opened it alone. It was a pen and ink drawing of a lavish Victorian hotel, lots of gingerbread woodwork and turrets. On the back was written, "English teacher saves armadillo, Paper Doll Museum," and an address.

"That's all? There are thousands of Victorian buildings, English teachers and armadillos, Tim. And what address? Mine?"

"No, the address was your destination. The Paper Doll Museum. But first the Boston Revenants had to figure out where you were. The drawing was by an artist named Peter Anderson and called 'The Del Looking South,' so..."

"So it was the Hotel Del Coronado!"

"Yes, Martine favors old places, old things. They were able to ascertain that the English teacher and the armadillo were in San Diego because the hotel is. Martine never gives names; she communicates in puzzles, but they're simple."

"Children's games," I mused. "So what happened next?"

"I had been identified earlier, was contacted and given the charge of locating and watching you. When I saw that you would fight the ghoul, I was honored to escort you to the address Martine provided. You know the rest."

"Revenant headquarters are in Hallet's home," he went on, "one of the historic Louisburg Square mansions on Beacon Hill. Your apartment is within walking distance."

I remembered Pen's dollhouse, Pen mentioning that Louisa May Alcott had lived on Louisburg Square. I would be near Pen's first home, now a miniature replica in which tiny figures enacted a bloody story, over and over. And something about the name "Hallett" was familiar, but I couldn't remember what.

"You will be one of four Revenants hand-picked for particular talents that Hallett and the Boston group feel are useful at this juncture. You'll meet every day and..."

"Talents? Tim, I don't have any 'talent.' I'm a high school English teacher."

"Precisely," he replied, watching Sadie repeatedly chase a

mourning dove who seemed to enjoy the game. "You're very well-read, and an expert on stories is needed."

"There must be thousands of college professors like this guy from MIT, a few Revenants among them, who're more well-read, more 'expert' than I am."

"Not at all, Taylor. Such people are specialists – 'Researching Authorship in the Anonymous 16th Century Morality Play,' 'The Influence of Symbolist Art on the Genesis of the Anti-Hero,' that sort of thing. A broader, if shallower reach is necessary."

I wasn't getting it. "A broader reach toward what? What am I supposed to *do*?"

He stood then, leaned toward me across my deck table and managed to look grim even though he was wearing his cowboy shirt.

"I'm sure that will become clear once you're there. But please try not to lose sight of the fact that to some extent our future may depend on this effort. So far there is no public awareness of Revenance, but as our numbers increase and there are more 'incidents,' well... some method for protecting ourselves from exploitation by the media and researchers, at the very least, must be created. This guide, if indeed there is to be one, will be a first step. You must not underestimate the role you are about to play, Taylor."

He was watching me closely, almost *inspecting* me the way you'd look at complex painting.

"I'm not underestimating the role," I told him. "But I think somebody's *over*estimating me! This Hallett Gardner... why did she pick me? Why not *you*? You know so much about all this and I..."

"You may know more than you think, Taylor," he replied softly. "And you're one hell of a fighter!"

Flattered, I did a couple of Tae Kwon Do moves as we went back inside, but something was still bothering me about that name – "Hallett." I knew the name. Something about Early American folklore. Cape Cod. Then it hit me.

"Goody!" I yelled at Tim O'Halloran, causing his violet eyes to widen behind his glasses.

"Goody? Am I to interpret this as enthusiasm for the task ahead?"

"No. Well, of course, but that's not it. The name – Hallett. Goody Hallett lived on the Cape during colonial times. She was accused of witchcraft because she singlehandedly cared for the local Wampanoag Indians during an outbreak of smallpox and didn't get sick, or at least that's the story. When the bigwigs in Wellfleet or Eastham – I forget where she lived – tried to oust her from her home as punishment, she wore red shoes to the hearing! I'll bet this Hallett Gardner is Goody's descendant."

"Red shoes?" Tim said.

"The shoes of a witch back then. Only witches would wear red shoes. She did it to taunt them. And she got to keep her house because they were afraid of her! Tim, I keep wondering if there's some connection between us and 'witches' even though you said there weren't any Revenants until recently. If Goody is an ancestor of this Hallett…"

"This is why you're needed, Taylor," he said, grinning. "Your thinking is, shall we say, all over the place. And while historically, 'witchcraft' is a function of ignorance and greed, that isn't to say there have not been people possessed of unique abilities since there have been people. It's possible that we are only the latest version, genetically programmed with certain proclivities that have somehow been activated. Who knows?"

We were in my living room packing books into wine boxes. I stared into a box with a line drawing of a unicorn on the side. "Genetically" had triggered a memory.

"I had a grandmother I never met until an hour before she died," I told Tim. "She was crazy, mentally ill, or that's what I was told. But my parents took me to see her on her deathbed and she didn't seem crazy then. She told me to hide inside life for as long as I could, but then to be ready because something would happen. I'd say something *has* happened. I think she knew, or sensed… something. Or am I just imagining she did?"

He'd already packed eight boxes and brushed dust from his hands on his jeans as he leaned against my faded wall.

"Good question," he said, "and one I, too, have entertained. There is danger in romanticizing psychiatric illnesses, which cause unimaginable torment in those who suffer them. Yet I sometimes wonder if there might be more to psychosis than we understand. Your grandmother certainly *seems* to have predicted what has happened to you, and warned you. Moreover, she was at the very edge of death at the time. Her remarks may reflect less her psychiatric condition than her proximity to death. As a priest I've seen, and hospital personnel have as well, people do and say curious, inexplicable things while making that transition."

"Could she have been a Revenant, Tim? Maybe that's why she seemed crazy."

He shrugged.

"It's possible. There may be many throughout history who began to manifest little bits of it as it developed, and were regarded as mentally ill because of it. There's no way to know, Taylor."

"But what about you?" I asked. "Was there anybody in your family…?"

"I'm quite old, Taylor," he mused. "My grandparents lived at the end of the Victorian Era, a world almost unimaginable now. Of course they said strange things, but that strangeness is only a reflection of their time."

"You're not answering my question."

"Well, my mother's father was a clergyman, Anglican. I followed in his footsteps. And as I recall, his wife, my grandmother, was a pious clergy wife. I don't remember her saying anything at all."

"Sad," I noted politely. "So what about the other grandparents?"

"Ah," he sighed, a sparkle flashing in his eyes. "That would be Angie's favorite story. They were spiritualists, you see. They followed the Theosophist Madame Tingley to her compound here in San Diego, bought property, never left. When they grew old, my parents came to care for them and then *they* never left, accounting for my eventual arrival here. I'd inherited the house, you see. But I don't remember anyone saying anything to me that could be construed as a warning."

"Still, *spiritualists*," I insisted.

"It was a craze back then, like diets are now. Everybody was doing it. Which doesn't mean your idea lacks merit. It may be that as Revenants we are something long-encoded in human DNA, something waiting over the centuries to emerge when the right confluence of events occurred. Interest in realities other than the obvious seems hard-wired in the human brain, and erupts regularly in such movements as spiritualism."

He nodded somberly. "But whatever we are, our task at the moment is protect ourselves. What was done to your grandmother can be done to us, and worse."

I glanced at my watch. It was almost time for Miyoko to drop off the kids. Tim handed me a packet of plane tickets, a map of Beacon Hill and a key to the apartment where I'd be staying.

"Why don't you leave your car at our place and then I'll drive you to the airport?"

"Good idea. Thank you."

The rest of the weekend was busy, but TJ had researched methods for cabinet painting on his computer and directed the work with a seriousness I'd never seen him exhibit.

"We're going to do this *properly*," he said a hundred times as we scrubbed and sanded the doors in the yard to diminish the ammonia fumes and dust. "These cabinets are going to be works of art!"

And they were. By Sunday morning it was done. My cabinets were dry and gleaming, and I taught the kids to sing *The Marines' Hymn* while we screwed the new hardware TJ had selected at Home Depot back on doors and drawers. Seiji had a crème brûlée streak in his black hair that made him look like a skunk groupie, so TJ used a salad fork to paint in his own streak but seemed unsatisfied with it.

"It doesn't show up," he said angrily. "My hair's *stupid*. Why do I have this shitty hair? Nobody else..."

I was tired, but fought my way back to being an officious pain.

"The Anglo-Saxon vocabulary is so retro," I said for the thousandth time. "Can you think of a better way to describe your hair?"

"Yeah," he answered, his voice cracking. "Why do I have this fucking lousy orange hair that looks like puked-up carrots?"

Seiji was trying not to laugh, but I did so he'd know it was okay.

"Good work," I told my grandson. "Except for 'fucking' I'd give that an A!"

"How many points off for 'fucking'?"

"All points. You're back to zero. Remember that next time."

TJ affected a worldly posture. "I know all about 'fucking' anyway," he said.

"Everybody knows all about it. That's why it's so boring. But I loved the carrot-puke."

"Everybody knows what *what* means?"

It was Miyoko, who'd come in the front door we left open to dissipate the last of the paint odor.

"FUCK-ING!" the boys yelled, giggling.

"Why don't I go out and come in again?" she said. "I didn't hear that."

I explained my method for dealing with banal obscenities to Miyoko while she beamed at my cabinets and the boys raced off to load Seiji's stuff in her car.

"I'm flying to Boston for a week tomorrow," I told her. "It just came up, sort of a job thing, some research."

The Syndicate would have grilled me for details, but Miyoko just said, "Super. I'll schedule the tile, carpet cleaning and the rest of the painting while you're gone. So how about color for the living room?"

I hadn't picked color for the living room. "Oh, God. I have no idea. Could you just, you know, do that?"

She wasn't surprised. "Sure. I think I've got a handle on your new style. But we need to think about security. I know it's a little more financial drain, but given what's happened, I'd feel better if the house were not left empty at night. I can probably find a security guard to sleep here for a couple hundred. Delgado will know of somebody. Can you swing that?"

It made sense.

"Yes," I agreed.

After they left I realized I had to inform my daughter and the Syndicate that I'd be gone. It was sudden, but not totally out of character. Hey, only months earlier I'd driven to Texas to drop off an armadillo, hadn't I? I sent an email to everybody mentioning a research project that I'd forgotten to mention, and told them all I'd email. Then I checked the weather in Boston (mid-60's to mid-50's – lovely!), unplugged my computer and packed, wondering if Sadie would need a jacket for walks on cool east coast evenings. Surely I could find one there.

Then I spent a couple of hours on the Internet reading up on

Boston, discovering that Poe's "The Cask of Amontillado" may have had its origins in the murder of a brutish soldier by his peers at a fort on an island off the coast of South Boston. The body was supposedly bricked into a wall, and indeed a human skeleton was supposedly discovered in a wall of the fort many years later. The murder took place in 1817 and Poe, stationed there ten years later, would have heard the story. I hoped I'd have time to go there, and to check out the Beacon Hill address immortalized in Pen's dollhouse. There was something horrific about that dollhouse.

Chapter Sixteen

Hooked on a Feelin'

Blue Suede

Sadie spent the six-hour flight to Boston in her carrier on my lap. I unzipped it so she could brace her front paws on the armrest and look out the window, which she did with rapt attention to cloud formations except when I opened the packaged meal I'd bought at the airport. I ate the ice-cold cookie and gave her a few bites of processed chicken culled from the limp sandwich on my plastic plate. Dogs will eat anything.

It was 11:00 p.m. when we landed, but only 8:00 in my Pacific Time Zone mind, so I was alert to every nuance, none of them ominous, then. I didn't miss the fact that even over the hot-metal-and-diesel-fuel scent that characterizes every airport, Boston smelled good. It smelled like fall. I lowered the cab window a little just to bask in it on the way to the apartment.

"You got a fever, lady?" the cabbie groused, turning on the heater in retaliation.

"Malaria," I answered, trying for a Dutch accent. "Tsetse fly iss bahd in Brokopondo, voot? But I thenk iss noot contagion."

From hundreds, possibly thousands, of strange research papers submitted by my students over the years, I am a junkyard of arcane and generally useless information. My remarks to the cabby derived from conflation of a long-ago sophomore paper on tsetse fly fossils found in Colorado (Miocene Era; live ones only found now in Africa) and a more recent senior paper on a tribe called the Maroon in the rain forest of Brokopondo, a district of Dutch-speaking Suriname. The Maroon are descendants of Africans who escaped slave ships docked in Suriname and hid in the rainforests, where the indigenous Amerindians taught them herbal treatments for malaria, according to my student. Thus I was perfectly aware that Malaria is carried by mosquitoes, not tsetse flies, which don't live in Suriname to begin with, and really isn't contagious. But it sounded horrible and was effective in shaving off those extra miles cab drivers love to tour with out-of-town passengers. We climbed Beacon Hill as if pursued by demons and he didn't even sneer at the tip.

After I stashed my bag in the two-floor apartment, one just above street level and one half below, Sadie and I walked gaslit brick sidewalks for an hour or so, checking out the neighborhood. Leaves tumbled from trees and skittered at my heels as she explored a little, iron-fenced park. When the skittering became whole swirls of leaves swept up and flung above the streetlamps, I was inspired, but remembered what it meant. Clipping Sadie's leash to her harness, I dragged her from the park and back to the apartment just as the dark slipped gears and the first drop fell. Rain!

I hadn't seen real rain in years, much less a storm. I hung my clothes in a closet, grabbed pajamas from my suitcase and snuggled with Sadie on the queen-sized bed beside the two street-facing windows. They opened directly onto the sidewalk, so the bottom halves were shuttered on the interior to prevent passersby from looking in, but the top halves were bare. I watched through rain pounding on glass as lightening illuminated the wind-lashed little street trees, and felt that druglike contentment that attends being safe and warm while outside danger howls. I was a child again.

The feeling was still there in the morning as I surveyed the apartment. The street level floor was a combination bedroom/office, with living room, tiny kitchen and bath downstairs. I drank coffee from the well-stocked (including dog food) cabinets downstairs while watching the feet of pedestrians barely visible above the two window wells. The place was like a nicely decorated cave, magical and provident in that it offered an unusual perspective. I figured I was going to need that.

Hallett Gardner had left a folder of maps and tourist brochures on the desk, including a schedule of meetings. I was to be at her Louisburg Square residence at 9:00 for a continental breakfast and introductions. There would be breaks for lunch and dinner, and a dogwalker had been arranged for Sadie. Hallett had thoughtfully also left a box of ziplock baggies for Sadie's "personal needs," as was de rigueur for Beacon Hill's dog owners. I couldn't wait to meet this woman, obviously a world-class hostess as well as a Revenant.

Louisburg Square, between Pinckney and Mt. Vernon Streets, was only a short walk from my apartment on Revere, and Sadie and I enjoyed every inch. Many of the old federal-style buildings boasted gorgeous window boxes on the street level – coleus, asters, mums and gerbera daisies adorned streets now awash in autumnal sunshine. I'd brought the smartphone the kids gave me last Christmas, and snapped shots of my favorites. Maybe I'd use them for screensavers on my computer when I got home.

I wasn't really surprised when a butler in swallowtail coat and black cravat opened the door of Hallett Gardner's Greek Revival mansion. He was bent with osteoporosis and leaning on a walker, but his smile was contagious.

"Please join Miz Gahdnah on the pahtio," he pronounced in that East Coast Kennedy accent, humming the opening bars of Beethoven's Ninth as he escorted me through enormous doorways marking the boundaries of a living room and a library. We emerged in a brick-enclosed patio bordered in white geraniums.

"Thank you, Spalding," a tall woman in a white silk blouse and pearls smiled beside a silver coffee urn and a pile of croissants. Her white hair was long and worn in a simple chignon. The style accentuated both the aristocratic planes of her face and a rascal smile suggesting that she didn't take being aristocratic too seriously. "And welcome, Taylor! I should explain that Spalding has been with my family since the Hindenburg Disaster and is a bit old-fashioned. That outfit is his idea, not mine! "

We both smiled. "Mrs. Gardner," I began formally, "please accept my thanks for everything you've done. The apartment is delightful and you were so kind to think of Sadie…"

"Yes, yes," she replied. "I'm afraid you may find me strange, but what has happened to us has become my life, Taylor. I've inherited enormous, embarrassing wealth, and devote every penny of it to 'the cause,' if you will. The social niceties can be a bit time-consuming, so I tend to dispense with them. Please call me Hallett, and have a croissant."

"What, exactly, are we going to do?" I asked, eyeing the array of sliced meats and imported condiments beside the croissants. Sadie was sitting politely at my feet, but her nose kept angling toward the table.

Hallett gave her a slice of warm ham before regarding me with the palest blue eyes I've ever seen. "We're going to establish a preliminary network for Revenants. Martine is, if you'll pardon a disrespectful comparison, like a faulty wire. Occasionally she lets us know when new Revenants emerge, but more often she doesn't. We've only begun to organize and we're learning quickly how to survive and function. But there will be more of us, Taylor. They need our help. Do eat something because we need to start soon. Oh dear, here are the others."

Spalding had escorted two men and a woman through the French doors opening onto the flagstone patio. One of the men looked like Jean-Paul Belmondo only shy and balding, while the other could have been a blond, sunburned Paul Bunyan in a baseball cap with "Beetle Bank" embroidered above the bill. The woman wore her mid-length blonde hair in a carefully windblown style and had chosen a long flowered skirt and pink scoop-necked top for the occasion. She wore no jewelry and betrayed no feeling beyond an amused half-smile. Paul Bunyan quickly doffed his baseball cap and nodded toward Hallett.

"This is awfully nice of you, ma'am," he began as the woman in the long skirt beamed appropriately and the other man inhaled as if preparing to give a speech.

"Please," Hallett Gardner interrupted. "We have so much work to do. Let's assume we're all grateful for each other's presence, have a quick bite and then get on with it. Taylor Blake, Marlow Helland, François Loreau and Anne Greenleigh, please introduce yourselves as you enjoy a bit of breakfast and coffee. Spalding will bring you to the conference room at nine-thirty sharp."

We all stared at each other as Hallett left, closing French doors behind her. The enclosed patio was warm in the morning sun, but a communal chill hovered between us - strangers linked only by a common, incomprehensible experience. Prey to sickening apparitions and able to see things invisible to the rest of the world, we might be gifted, but we were also lepers. I tried to imagine a meeting of real lepers and figured it might feel pretty much like this – an awkward, distasteful gravity. Sadie broke the suffocating moment by gently sniffing Paul Bunyan's pants cuff. He immediately dropped to one knee, scratched behind her ears and then scooped her into his arms.

Standing with my dog, who was wagging her tail in joy at being closer to the food, he said, "Well, I'm Marlow Helland and I grow soybeans in Minnesota, but who's this nice lady banging her tail into my ribs?"

"That's Sadie," I answered, "and I'm Taylor Blake, San Diego."

The guy who looked like Belmondo held a pale hand to Sadie's nose and said, "I am François Loreau, from Paris. *Je suis enchanté,* Sadie."

My dog licked his hand and then inclined her head toward the ham, but he missed the message and merely bowed slightly from the waist.

"We'd be lost without that dog," said the woman in the long skirt. "And I'm Anne Greenleigh, Louisiana. Let's eat while we can."

I was starving and sat apart eating at a tiny table with Sadie as the others milled around the food, talking about how nice the weather was. François seemed miserable, Anne close to laughing and Marlow completely lost. When Spalding came for me twenty minutes later I was glad to go outside to meet the dogwalker, although not glad to relinquish Sadie to a stranger. Or to relinquish Sadie at all. We'd never been apart since I took her from the shelter.

The walker was a young woman in jeans and an MIT sweatshirt, no doubt a student. She was holding the leashes of a miniature poodle and two fox terriers. Sadie joined them in the sniffing ritual and seemed fine about leaving me for a romp with peers, which I told myself was great while I fought an urge to grab my dog and run. Except, I realized, there was nowhere to run.

"I'll take her to the Common where they can run free in the dog area, then I'll bring her back in about an hour," the young woman explained. "Then this afternoon my roommate will come and do the same thing. Don't worry, she'll be fine."

"She will be with you for the remainder of her visit," Spalding said. "I will bring her to you, mahm."

"Thank you," I said, and went inside to find out who I was now, among total strangers whom I guessed were my own kind in the same way a poodle and two fox terriers were Sadie's.

The "conference room" was the entire third floor of the house, recently redone with an impersonal, officelike feel, but Hallett's touches were nonetheless in evidence. Lithographs of the Common and the Swan Boats in the Public Garden, a muted abstract in shades of gold and gray, and above the mantel of the small fireplace and dominating the room, a curious painting of a woman's long-skirted legs, her feet *in red shoes!*

Hallett watched me admire the painting, and when I silently mouthed "Goody?" she answered with an almost imperceptible nod. So I was right. There was some connection between Hallett and a woman who over three hundred years in the past had trounced the Colonial witch hunters at their own game. It was reassuring.

"You have been chosen for this task on a basis of several criteria," she began once we were settled in comfortable chairs around a pine plank table so old it might have been used in Goody's time. "One of those criteria is trust, which you cannot possibly feel for each other at this point, although you must bond despite that. We are all vulnerable, not least from the loneliness that we now feel because we are no longer like others. We must establish connections, and quickly. Toward that end, I ask each of you to describe your meeting with Martine and display the amulet you were given. Anne, would you start?"

The woman named Anne Greenleigh blinked her eyes slowly in a gesture I would later understand to be the mark of retreat into consideration. Anne was not quick to answer and spoke in short sentences.

"Cemetery," she said. "It was a nice afternoon. I went to drop some bullet casings on my husband's grave. Fourth husband. Ex. Six casings. He shot me six times."

Six little brass cylinders materialized in the air above the table, tumbled downward and bounced against the pine. As each bounced, it vanished.

"Looks like he shot you with a .22," Marlow observed.

"He did," Anne agreed. "The d.a. brought the shells to me after the trial as a memento. I was tired of looking at them, figured I'd return them. There was a funeral not far away, people singing 'Rock of Ages' loud enough to hear clear over in Mississippi. Martine was there, standing under a tree. I could barely see her for the Spanish moss and assumed she was another grieving widow. Not that I was grieving. So I politely ignored her. We're very polite in the South. Well, usually."

Marlow Helland smiled with admiration while François Loreau paled and crossed his gangly arms over his chest. I wasn't sure I believed the story, but then noticed scar tissue only partially hidden by Anne's three-quarter-length sweater sleeves. At least one of those bullets must have gone through her arm.

"Strange things had been happening to me," she went on, "but by then strange things were nothing new. Months of surgery, drugs, y'all know what I mean?"

We all nodded.

"When Martine told me a ghoul was out to destroy me, I told her she was about four years too late. Because the ghoul was good and dead right under our feet. She said no, there was another one, and gave me this."

From the waist of her skirt Anne Greenleigh pulled a green silk tassel attached to a delicate mesh belt.

"My great-great grandmother ran a two thousand acre plantation *alone* after her husband died," she said. "I think this must be from her drapes."

Everybody looked around as the theme from *Gone with the Wind* filled the room and then faded.

"François?" Hallett was moving along, but her smile let us know she was responsible for the special effects. "You can all do this as well," she said. "One of the perks."

"Ziss," François said softly, his French accent making everybody try to look decorous and sophisticated. Except for Hallett, who was already decorous and sophisticated. From his baggy shirt he shakily pulled a small scallop shell worn on a soft white cord around his neck.

"A shell," Marlow pronounced in an attempt to diminish the Frenchman's obvious discomfort as we all awkwardly conjured shells that floated into each other like bumper cars before evaporating.

"It is... it *was* a confection in my childhood, "François struggled to go on.

I was sure everybody wanted to say, "French children eat *seashells*?" but would have died first. A sort of bratty humor disguising our mutual discomfort, momentarily.

"...name is *Roudoudou*. There is a soft sweet inside, bright colors, that is licked. Like a lollipop, but in this shell. As a boy it is my favorite."

"And Martine?" Hallett prodded.

François had given up on the past tense and seemed to relax.

"Ah," he said, "she is in the Luxembourg Garden where I am a boy I bury my *billes*. A girl is practicing on a flute, Telemann I think."

"Bee-yuh?" Marlow asked, cocking his head.

Music from a single flute drifted above our heads. It was Mozart, not Telemann, but I didn't say anything.

"*Oui.* I am very good but my parents do not allow me to keep the *billes* I win." François made a marble-shooting gesture with knuckles and thumb on the table and we all nodded as colored glass spheres caromed across the table, then disappeared. The guy buried marbles in a park. "I bury them there long ago and where I bury them is Martine. I am happy to see her because I think... I was to think... I am mad."

"You're not alone, we all thought that, or I sure as hell did," Marlow boomed supportively. "I was scared shitless...oh, sorry... scared out of my mind until this thousand-year-old guy named Gus, he lives in town now, works as a greeter at Walmart in these faded bib overalls and a dress shirt buttoned clear up to his neck — till he left a note in my tractor inviting me to an old movie house that closed forty years ago. It's falling down now, full of rats, nobody's been inside for years. But I went, figured why not, I was going crazy anyway. And the place was like it was when I was a kid! Gus took me there but didn't go inside. When I went in, Martine was there and we had popcorn and watched *13 Rue Madeleine* with James Cagney. That was my favorite movie and..."

"And your amulet?" Hallett, again.

"Oh, yeah."

From under his shirt cuff he tugged a black and white bracelet, woven of flat plastic cords. A short lanyard. Every American kid makes lanyards at camp, and the mixed scents of lake water, campfires and mildewed swimsuits came and left.

"I made these at camp when I was a kid," he explained to François.

"So did I," said everyone else, including Hallett.

François' brown eyes were aglow.

"In France they are called *scoubidou*," he informed us. "And never the bracelet like Marlow. Only keychain in France, and most French children do not go to camp. We make *scoubi* at home, for fun."

"I still remember how," Anne said, tearing strips from one of the notepads Hallett had placed in front of each of us. "You make the square by taking four cords and..."

"I also remember," François joined in, leaning to see how Anne was folding her strips. "But you must have three pieces, not four."

Hallett grinned.

"I could have Spalding go out for some plastic cord, or shall we forego that? Remember that while the joys of childhood are again ours, the wisdom of our years has not entirely fled. We have an enormous amount of work to do, and little time. Taylor, it's your turn."

I told the story of the Paper Doll Museum and showed my whistle. A paper Buster Brown and his dog Tige scampered across the table and dissolved into my hands.

"I had those Queen Holden baby paper dolls, too," Anne whispered. "And you were right about 'Picnic.' Sexiest movie ever made!"

"Has anyone ever had to, you know, use the amulet?" Marlow asked uneasily. "What happens? How does it work?"

Hallett looked grim. "Of course we must discuss that, but first, more coffee?"

The interruption felt apprehensive, and the only sound was the occasional clink of cups on saucers until we reconvened ten minutes later.

Chapter Seventeen

Dead Man's Curve

Jan and Dean

"We aren't sure how the amulet functions," Hallett addressed Marlow's question. "In these circumstances what actually happens may be lost in a tsunami of cultural debris – religions, folklore, witchcraft, sorcery, shamanism, even drugs. But we have identified one event we feel may answer your question. It took place in Paris only a few months ago. François?"

"I have a small shop in the Marais," he said. "There are many small shops, hundreds, each selling a particular thing that some people want to have... to collect. In my shop are postcards, very old French postcards that show the Eiffel Tower when it is being built, people in Provençal costumes and others that are... not so nice."

Everyone smiled knowledgeably.

"Near to my shop is another that sells old games. It is called *Le Jeu*, that means 'The Game,' and the owner, Frederic, is very fat. He sit high at a desk on a platform above the shop and look down, all day smoking cigarettes and organizing thousands of little cardboard houses. They are called *Jeu de Construction* and while new ones are plastic like Legos, these are old ones of hard paper that are in books to cut out, very fancy houses, whole towns a child makes of paper. These are this man's favorite thing, these old paper houses cut by children now dead for a century. And this Frederic is one of us, a Revenant.

In his accent the word bore a misty echo.

"How do you know?" I asked. "Did you and he talk about...it?"

"No, I do not know Frederic," he answered. "I wave at him when I walk by his shop, and he know mine is the postcards because he send customer to me, but we do not speak."

"So what happened?" Marlow pushed.

Hallett passed out copies of a French newspaper article with attached English translations. We all read in silence that Frederic Langelin had died of a massive stroke late at night in his shop. The merchandise was in disarray, but since nothing appeared to be missing, foul play was not suspected. Langelin was single, seventy-two and had no relatives but a sister who died in childhood. It was a small article.

"But he died," Anne said. "Frederic Langelin died. So how did the amulet protect him?"

"I am there," François explained. "I go to my shop very late because I forget a phone number. I write it for my wife and leave it in my shop. So I pass Frederic's shop and I see the floor is red. It move, the floor, like it is alive! Some of it begin to climb the stairs to Frederic there above. I see his mouth, he is screaming but I cannot hear. In his hand is a little girl's rosary, tiny and white, like a girl would have for her first holy communion. I can see the mark where he tear it from a leather cord around his neck. He is holding this thing and screaming."

"But that doesn't prove..." Marlow began.

"Wait. I see that the red carpet is *mice*. The whole floor covered in mice that are not normal. They are red and stumble, fall, keep moving. They are horrible, something wrong with them, each a monster. I pound on the door, try to open it, but it is locked."

"I see Frederic call for help with his amulet when these mice come that night, creeping and stumbling up the stairs to his balcony like a moving carpet. Then all his paper houses… they move down through the air from the balcony and stand silent on the floor of his shop. The mice turn back, go inside the houses, each door close. Then nothing."

Nobody was breathing.

"What did you do next?" Hallett asked.

"I hurry to my shop, call police. When they come, Frederic is on the floor of the balcony. The police take him to hospital. They trust me, leave with me the key to lock after I guard Frederic's shop. So I can go to my own shop if they do not return quickly, you see? I am in Frederic's shop and all his paper houses stand on the floor like a town. All the little doors shut."

Anne Greenleigh pushed her hands into her sweater sleeves.

"So I get down and look into one house, then another. In each is a thing I never see in my life, like a terrible blood-red mouse only… monster! One has eight legs, all different length, and a single, curved white tooth like a carpet needle. Another with one blind eye and tiny, human hands. All have sores, tumors, horrible tails, always something wrong with the body. The red fur, like blood."

Marlow grimaced. "Oh, man…!"

"These are not real mice; these are disease, freak, not normal. They can be only in the mind, except they are there. In each little house. Dead. These mice go into Frederic's houses. That is what mice do, go in houses. And I know then that Frederic's houses kill them."

"I'm liking this," Anne said, trying for a game smile.

"When the police return, the mice are gone, only the paper

houses are there on the floor. I alone see these mice. I alone guess what happened."

"We think Frederic Langelin died of natural causes during or after the event," Hallett said quietly. "What matters to us is that his ghoul didn't win. Frederic Langelin's houses protected him from that. Nothing can protect us from natural death when the time comes, but the amulet *does* protect Revenants too exhausted to fight."

I felt the chill I'd tried to bury since stepping off the plane.

"And if the ghoul *had* won?" I said. "What would have happened to Frederic Langelin then?"

Every head turned toward Hallett. She stood and walked to a window, then turned, backlit by a polished autumn sky.

"Something worse than death," she said quietly, light from the window casting tiny flares against her hair while her face remained in shadow. "That is why you must understand Frederic Langelin's story. You must understand that he was rescued from a nearly indescribable horror by the power of his amulet."

"What horror is worse than death?" Francois said. "While we live it is the great fear, to be *néant*, nothing."

"Frederic Langelin is *gone*," Anne said. "He's dead. What could the mice have done that would be worse? His little houses didn't save him, Hallett. The mice, the city of paper houses, that's all an illusion. We have them. We know what they're like. But they're not real. Langelin's death is real."

"I saw the houses. I saw the dead mice," Francois insisted.

"And you saw them take Langelin out in a body bag," Marlow countered. "That's what's real."

Hallett pressed her palms together, then straightened her shoulders.

"My husband was a gentle man," she said as if beginning a

story, but there was a terrible vibrato in her voice. "And my husband was a Revenant."

"What happened?" I asked, aware of what "was" suggested. We had not been introduced to a husband and that sense of mutually inhabited space common to homes of the married was entirely absent from Hallett Gardner's house.

"We doubt that it occurs often, that both husband and wife... But we were second cousins, Philip and I. There may be a genetic component."

No one said anything, waiting.

"What happened is very difficult for me to tell you, but I will speak of it only once so that you will understand the meaning of what François saw in that little shop."

Everyone stiffened as if expecting a blow. Hallett looked past us, her eyes like pale blue glass.

"Philip could not fight," she whispered. "He had seen Martine; he had an amulet. It was just a bit of driftwood and he didn't really believe in it, not that it would have mattered if he had. Philip never fought. He was so gentle, so incapable of aggression. But I'll get to the point."

There were tears in her eyes now, and the men looked at their hands while Anne and I reached ours toward Hallett.

"I only saw his ghoul once, but I learned what it can do. It ate his soul," she went on, shaking her head at us, needing no support. "He lived only a short while, which is the single mercy. He lived in terror, attempting to hide from it in strange places about the house. I once found him inside the old coal-burning furnace in the basement. He wouldn't eat or drink, then he'd go into the kitchen in the middle of the night and consume strange things – a bottle of ketchup, egg shells, bits of newspaper, moaning, 'Stop, please stop,' over and over. The thing controlled him, made him its puppet."

"When he could speak to me, on the few occasions he

recognized me, he begged me to kill him."

"He was sick, mentally sick," Marlow said gently. "Surely there were doctors…"

"Of course," Hallett answered. "The best. Philip was hospitalized, heavily medicated, nothing helped. He screamed until his throat bled and no sound came out. He vomited, was incontinent. He ate his own excrement."

I felt a bone-deep nausea made of fear. The thing could do this to me.

"But however horrible, this was not the worst. This was not the hell our ghouls bring, but only symptoms. I saw the hell in his eyes and you all must understand this, – it is an emptiness with no end. Once in the hospital he tried to tell me what it was like, that everything was empty of meaning. He pointed to a chair and said, 'chair,' then told me in a flat, mechanical voice, as if he were a machine, 'The word holds nothing, Hallett. It's just a sound. There really is no such thing as 'chair'. There's no such thing as *you*, Hallett. There's no such thing as *anything*. It's all a LIE!'"

I knew Hallett's story was true, felt the truth of it throbbing at the base of my brain. The thing that threatened me, the thing we called "ghoul," played sometimes like an evil child. But it was no child and its nature was the antithesis of life – which is not death, but the annihilation of meaning.

"Philip lost fifty pounds," Hallet went on. "He pulled out his teeth; but not before he bit the thumbs off both his hands and spit them on the floor of his hospital room. At the end his eyes were black, all color gone. No one could look at him. And yet the thing tortured him. I had to help Philip, so I brought him home."

The room was suddenly ice-cold. No one moved.

"I brought him home in a straitjacket," Hallet said, her hands knotted to quivering fists at her sides. "His doctor knew; he gave me the syringe and the morphine, carefully explained the precise milligram level beyond which the dose would be fatal. Morphine suppresses breathing, you see. I was told where to stop. But I was given a sufficient amount to surpass that level by far."

I listened for birds, the sound of traffic outside, but there was only a high-pitched silence.

"Philip and I loved each other," Hallett said. "A deep love, like music that ran in our veins. We could not hurt each other. We never had. I would not hurt him, but I would end his suffering. There was no other way."

My breathing was so shallow I felt dizzy. Everyone remained motionless, as if suspended in time, as Hallett went on.

"But when the moment came, for only a split second, those swirling eyes cleared and he screamed, 'No, Hallett!' He ran from me then, stumbling and falling, the straitjacket binding his arms across his chest, its stiff edge cutting the flesh of his throat. There was blood in his mouth, bubbling out. I'd had him brought here, to this room, which was our bedroom then, the whole third floor our private realm. He threw his head and shoulders against the window behind me, again and again. This window you see now. I didn't try to stop him. I didn't move. Finally the window shattered. He leaned over and pushed himself across the broken glass without a sound. It was two years ago in November, just after Thanksgiving. Snow on the ground. I stood looking down at what lay below for hours, until it was too dark to see."

She drew a deep breath, looking at each of us, taking our measure.

"But that's not all," she continued. "Philip was dead, his body no more than a broken shadow on the snow. I was aware of nothing else, only that shadow far below. But at some point I felt a presence in the room behind me. A sound, as if the carpet were being crushed under a heavy weight. When I turned, I saw something. It was the size of a piano, emerging from the fireplace, swelling and stretching toward me and filling the room with the stink of death. It was a sort of slug, and I knew it was Philip's ghoul. He'd told me of his childhood terror of the creatures, learned during a visit to Texas when his older brother hid them by the dozens in his clothes, his bed. Philip was only four, and..."

"What did you do?" Marlow interrupted, ashen, his fists clenched.

"I don't remember clearly," Hallett answered. "I knew that it had eaten Philip alive, and the knowledge was like a storm. Later I saw smashed lamps, broken furniture, silver slime on my hands and clothes. I realized that I had beaten it with every object I could find, slashed it with broken light bulbs, torn it to shreds with my bare hands. I killed it. It died in this room. It shriveled to a gnarled, dark thing like a petrified twig, and then it vanished. But before it vanished I saw something in its dark surface, like a carved face. It was Philip's face, only a half-finished likeness, distorted and ill-defined. As if the ghoul had fed on him, consumed something from him that left only this barely recognizable image. It fed on Philip's fear, his bewilderment, his inability to fight."

"Why could you kill Philip's ghoul when we can't kill our own?" Anne asked.

Hallett was pale from the exertion of telling her tale, but went on. "The ghoul is a darkness with which we are born," she said. "We believe that it also dies when we do. But death is a long and mysterious process. It only begins with the cessation of brain function, which is the acceptable definition of death in our time. But there is no culture, including our predominantly Christian one, in which aspects of the dead are not said to manifest in various ways, for a certain period of time after death. Philip's ghoul simply wasn't yet gone, although it would have died in time. I only shortened the process, but I'm glad I did."

Marlow's look was gentle.

"Hallett, this was hell for you," he said. "I'm so sorry; we all are. We're grateful that you fought, that you killed Philip's ghoul. But what did you do then, all alone here with the wreckage of the battle and Philip's body still lying down there?"

"I straightened the room and then called the mortuary," she said. "But I still see his shadow in the snow down there. I will always see it."

François was the first to stand and silently bow with grave formality toward Hallett. Then the rest of us did the same.

"Now we'll have lunch and begin our work," she said.

Chapter Eighteen

Remember What the Dormouse Said

Jefferson Airplane

Lunch was catered by a restaurant on Charles – plates of grilled apple and blue cheese salad with toasted walnuts, hot bread and coffee. We were subdued after hearing Hallett's story and ate quietly, lost in private thoughts. Hallett, however, was businesslike and explained that dinner would be more "comprehensive," but a light lunch was essential to remaining alert for the afternoon's work. Which, as it turned out, was completely over my head.

When we reassembled in the conference room, Harry Laufer, the professor at MIT who'd been given the clues that led to me, arrived with a tablet and palpable enthusiasm for the task at hand. He looked as if he'd slept in the rumpled suit he wore over a Red Sox tee shirt, and the wild gray curls springing from his head hadn't seen a comb in days. In his pierced left earlobe was a plain silver earring, a barely noticeable loop that made me think of gypsies.

"Hello, Revenants from the hinterlands!" he began in a New York accent. "I'm Harry Laufer and what can I say? If Martine hadn't turned up to wreck my perfectly ordinary life – and let me mention she was standing outside a men's room off the Infinite Corridor dressed like a seventies hippie – I thought she was a hologram! - you wouldn't be seeing me now."

"Um, 'Infinite Corridor'?" I had to ask.

"It's a hallway," Harry said. "At MIT. Famous."

He seemed puzzled, as if MIT's hallways should be at least as familiar as, say, the Washington Monument. I wasn't sure whether Harry Laufer harbored secret dreams involving stand-up comedy or was just strange. Hallett settled the issue.

"Professor Laufer holds three doctorates and is fluent in seven languages," she said. "His IQ is too high to measure, and while I don't begin to understand his work, it's safe to say he knows more about computers than all but about twenty other people on the planet and even that's open to debate. He may know *more* than the other twenty."

"At a certain point 'knowing' ceases to mean anything," Harry replied. "For example…"

"Harry is the core of our operation," Hallett interrupted, smiling, "and is here to provide us with *basic* information that is germane to our task."

"Yes. Well. I've organized some data," he said as the red shoe painting vanished into the wall, revealing a screen on which was projected the same newspaper photo of Frederic Langelin we'd seen earlier.

"I was able to access Langelin's medical records and autopsy report, and can state with roughly 97% certainty that his death at the time it occurred was inevitable. He had three coronary stents and was or should have been – who knows? - taking seven different medications the purposes of which were… well, he was circling the drain, to put it gently. We may take some encouragement from the fact that his ghoul – the red mice – could not prevail and that his death, while of course sad, was natural."

François grimaced at the floor as if lost in an unpleasant memory. Marlow cocked his head.

"Are you saying you hacked into both an official police document and a private physician's records, in *France*?"

Harry Laufer shrugged. "It's nothing," he said. "The salient fact is that we seem to have evidence pointing to the efficacy of the amulet each of us wears."

He tugged at his earring and grinned.

"And because François, another Revenant, was able to see Langelin's ghoul, we may tentatively hypothesize that all Revenants can see them, although there's so far nothing to suggest that anyone else can."

Anne Greenleigh shuddered.

"Damn thing only shows up when I'm alone," she whispered.

Everyone murmured agreement.

"Except for the first time, when it sometimes appears in a public context so that the new Revenant will think he or she is insane because nobody else sees it; that's the pattern," Harry said. "Langelin was alone. We have to assume he'd fought, God only knows how many times before, but this time he was at the end of his rope. He invoked the amulet, and at that point François, who wouldn't have been there at all under normal circumstances, looked through the window. What're the odds of *another* Revenant appearing at that precise moment?"

The scene framed itself in my mind. A sick, lonely, obese old man in a tiny Parisian shop late at night. The creeping tide of misshapen red mice. The silent little paper houses he loved, making a last, protective city for Frederic Langelin. He was a Parisian, citizen of a place many regard as the model for the word, "city." Nice.

"The odds would depend on the number of Revenants in existence, then the number in Paris on that date, etcetera," Anne said. "Do you know... any of that?"

"No," Harry said. "To date I can only verify forty-seven living, functional Revenants in the United States and less than half that in Western Europe. But we're just getting started. I've got six psychology and sociology grad students at universities all over

Boston on payroll tracking world media online for markers. Of course they've been told it's a study involving medical and social demographics in a particular age cohort, but…"

"Ages fifty and up," Hallett interjected, anticipating the question. "Assuming we are able to create some sort of guide at all."

"Or should create it," Harry went on. "It is impossible to overstate the problems that will accrue to public awareness. But public awareness is inevitable. The issue you all must address is how to provide essential information to new Revenants as they appear, while protecting ourselves and them. We've got a sociologist in Chicago working on organizational structure. She's using a non-parametric statistical analysis, which makes sense, although I wonder if the old Wolfowitz model might not eventually prove more effective."

"Harry, we don't know what you're talking about," Hallett said. "And please don't explain. Just help us get to work."

"Right," Harry said and then spent the next two hours giving a PowerPoint presentation about ciphers and codes. I learned that I'd been walking around inside a maze of codes since birth and never knew. Perhaps the most famous one, "Code Adam," Harry informed us, is popularly assumed to have been created by Walmart in 1994, and means "missing child." The code was named for six-year-old Adam Walsh, abducted from a Sears store in 1981 and later found murdered. If you hear "Code Adam" on the public address system in a Walmart, expect staff to flock to the exits, stopping anybody with a child in tow. Hospitals, groceries, department stores, banks, all public transportation and even movie theaters employ codes. Also government agencies, police and the military. Everybody uses codes, including families and groups of two or more friends. The basic idea is to present information in a condensed form not readily comprehensible to anyone outside the context generating the code.

"Problem is," Marlow offered, "any code can be broken. I was career military until retirement – encryption profiling. There's software that can sort codes electronically in seconds."

"And who's going to be able to read these codes, anyway?" Anne asked. "If we create a guide in a code so complicated it takes a computer to break it, our people will be eaten alive by ghouls before they can figure out a word! This isn't going to work."

"Yes and no," Harry said. "See, we already have a proto-code. Anybody here *not* understand what I mean if I say 'Martine, ghoul, Langelin'?"

"Okay, Martine means the initiation, the gift of the amulet," I said. "Ghoul is the shape-shifting nightmare of our childhoods, now back with a vengeance. And Langelin is the first instance in which a Revenant saw another's ghoul *and* saw it vanquished."

"My English is not good," François said, "but in any language what is clear in these words is that two are names that can mean nothing to anybody and one, 'ghoul,' is different. This word is the same in France, something like the evil spirit that haunted the town of Evreux in the 12th century, the *gobbelin*. But French people do not talk about such things."

"The French Revolution obliterated magic in France," Harry mentioned. "Nobody knows *anything* anymore over there. A tragedy."

Hallett glanced at her watch.

"You're digressing, Harry."

"What I say is that names are good for code because they are just names," François went on. 'Ghoul' is..."

"Too obvious," I finished the thought.

"Excellent," Harry boomed. "We now have 'The Langelin Effect,' denoting cross-Revenant ability. So far it involves Revenants seeing the ghouls of other Revenants, but perhaps there is more. Now what do we do with 'Martine'?"

Everybody was taking notes and Hallett seemed pleased, but I still had no idea what we were doing.

After a break Harry provided more slides and a long overview of current occult organizations, the search confined to the United States, Canada and Western Europe. Rosicrucians, Freemasons, Knights Templar and Malta. Kabbalists, Gnostics, Wiccans, Adepts, Magis and Druids. Every main group had countless spurs with different names, the list numbering in the thousands. I felt a sudden absence in my life: I'd never belonged to an occult organization. Well, until now.

Anne was skeptical.

"Look," she said, "all these folks are *choosing* to run around talking in hieroglyphs or whatever it is they do, dressing up and doing ceremonies and all. They get a big ole kick out of it, makes 'em feel special. Nothin' wrong with that; I like to dress up myself sometimes. But we don't dress up and we didn't choose this. I don't think we're an occult organization."

"Correct," Harry said. "Except that we have to be."

The afternoon had been long, the information overload dizzying, and I was hungry. Yet an idea was hatching in my mind. I could feel its little struggles to become coherent, then that first stretching of wings.

"Uh," I began, "Maybe that's the answer."

"What's the answer?" Anne.

"What's the *question*?" Marlow.

Everybody was tired and dying for dinner.

"To celebrate our meeting, I bring champagne," François mentioned happily, pronouncing the word "shom-paing."

"Wait!" I insisted. "There are thousands of occult organizations, each with elaborate rituals and symbols and secret codes. Harry said they're all over the Internet. All we have to do is make up another one that *looks* just like them, only imbed our own code in it so that any Revenant, but nobody else, will catch the code words like 'Martine,' and see the ruse. Anybody else will just see yet another cult."

Hallett had stopped in the doorway.

"Tim was right," she said directly to me. "You have a remarkable mind."

"Ah," said François. "The first toast is for Taylor!"

Over dinner and French champagne we decided to divide all existing occult organizations into four broad categories alphabetically. We'd spend the next day researching our individual categories on the Internet, and reconvene on Wednesday to patch together a trumped-up occult organization complete with Chaldean symbols, levels of enlightenment and a protocol for contacting headquarters. I got the end of the alphabet and was looking forward to researching "shamanism, sorcery, tarot, thaumaturgy, theosophy, vampirism, were-animals, witchcraft and wizardry."

Harry issued a warning before we left.

"We have tablets for all of you and your quarters are all wired for wi-fi," he said. "You may do this research alone in your quarters if you choose, but I advise against it. Better to do it here. You'll be swimming in dangerous waters, exposed to an avalanche of complex ideas that have been around for thousands of years. Most of this stuff is bogus, just trappings. But not all of it is. For example, some of the Kabbalistic mathematical formulae... Anyway, don't be sidetracked, fascinated, drawn in. You need to stay on task and remaining in company will help. Understand?"

I didn't think anybody did, but we all nodded.

Anne and I agreed to go to a movie later, and after two major walks during the day, Sadie made it clear that all she wanted was to go back to the apartment and curl up on the bed. Once there, I sent upbeat emails to the Syndicate rhapsodizing about autumn leaves, and one to Tim saying things were going well. When it was time to meet Anne for the movie I left the radio on a classical station for Sadie and was happy to be out in the crisp evening air.

The streets on Beacon Hill are paved, but the sidewalks are

uneven brick and murder on shoes. Nonetheless I wore my witch boots because the only other shoes I brought were white trainers with reflective patches on the back. It had taken me a single day to realize that California casual would not do in Boston, where everybody not wearing tasteful tweed is wearing even more tasteful black. With tasteful shoes.

I met Anne at her place only a block from mine and we immediately agreed to take a couple of hours the next afternoon for shopping.

"I'm going to freeze to death if I don't get a coat," she said.

"In black," I pointed out, nodding at a trio of women in the window of a restaurant, all in impeccable black.

"That seems to be the rule. I love your coat. Maybe I can find one like it."

"I have mannequin shopping aides," I explained, grinning. "They chose it for me."

Anne laughed and nodded.

"I have a cookbook that talks," she said. "It was my grandmother's, stained pages, binding's falling apart and it has a biscuit recipe the New Orleans Junior League would kill for. All my husbands complained that I was a lousy cook, but no more! I just pick a recipe from the book and this voice that sounds like Basil Rathbone playing Sherlock Holmes tells me what to do. My fig pie in a bourbon crust keeps winning prizes."

"This Revenant thing has certain benefits," I agreed.

"And one big ole downside," Anne noted somberly.

"Yeah," I said.

The movie theater was on Tremont Street so we walked down Charles and through Boston Common past the Frog Pond, an expansive, paved pool about a foot deep. The tourist information Hallett had left for us explained that the pool was used in July and

August for wading and then as an ice-skating rink from November to April. In fall and spring it was a reflecting pool, romantically lit and attractive to artists, poets and lovers. The lovers were in evidence, holding hands and gazing at each other on benches as leaves tumbled in the night wind and fell to float on the water.

"What those kids don't know about love and marriage would fill a library," Anne said, shaking her head.

"They're not supposed to know," I replied. "The continuation of the human race depends on their not knowing."

"I take it you're divorced?"

Somehow it didn't bother me; the story of my marriage felt like the plot from a novel read long ago.

"The usual," I said. "He met a pair of D-cups and couldn't say no, or that's what my friend Jude would say. Really, I think it was just... time."

"At least he didn't shoot you."

"There's that," I answered.

The movie was a typical girl-meets-boy, but saved by great location shots. You don't see that many movies set in Iowa.

"Makes you want to open a small rooming house in the middle of nowhere and wait for the star-crossed lovers to show up," Anne noted. "Although now that I think of it, I run a B&B in the middle of nowhere and they show up *all* the time! You wouldn't believe the stuff they leave behind. I have a collection. Best item is a black lace bustier with those miniature bottles of Johnny Walker you get on airplanes built into the bra."

"You have *got* to meet my friend, Jude," I said as we started to walk back across the Common and suddenly I realized I'd lost my scarf.

"Rats!" I said. "It must have blown off. It goes with my new outfit the mannequins picked for me. I'm going to run back to see if I can find it."

"I'll wait here by the pond," Anne said, heading for a bench. "I like this place."

It was late and the Frog Pond was deserted, although there were still people walking on the many paths crisscrossing the Common. It felt safe enough, and I'd only be gone a few minutes.

I hurried back through showers of leaves and found my scarf blown across the face of Neptune at the base of a fountain at the corner of Tremont and Park. I had to climb into the fountain, which luckily had been drained, to retrieve it. I must have looked absurd but I didn't care. I loved that scarf.

I could see Anne in the distance, sitting on a bench at the end of the Frog Pond. The Common was enchanting and the dance of leaves fanciful, but there was something ominous in the scene as well. Something that hadn't been there earlier. I looked around for nefarious characters on the paths and saw only several couples in long black trench coats, a family of shivering tourists in Bermuda shorts carrying shopping bags, and a woman walking a Jack Russell terrier while reading a book by the light of an LED headlamp. Nothing ominous, yet the feeling wasn't going away.

Anne saw me coming, stood and turned away from the pond as I noticed an odd scent on the wind. Sassafras. When I was a kid the old people used to make a tea from it that smelled like hot root beer.

There was a dark shape in the water just behind Anne. A shadow, I thought. Except there was nothing to cast a shadow. The lights were at the water's edge, not high above. And the shadow was moving. It was creeping out of the pond in furtive, jerky movements that made me think of Frederic Langelin's mice. Except this was no mouse. It was at least five feet long and darkening under the water as it grew dense, no longer shadow but not yet definable.

Trying to run in my witch boots. I waved my scarf at Anne in warning, then pointed to the thing behind her. It was morphing into a shape now, long snout, thick tail, dark reptilian skin.

No. It can't be. It's impossible. There are none of these here, they've never been here, this is wrong.

Anne made that prize-fighter's gesture, hands clasped over her head, glad I'd found the damn scarf.

"Look out, look behind you!" I yelled, but my voice was lost in a rush of sassafras scented wind. A lone man in a business suit hurried past. Two women talking to a teenage girl. Nobody looked at the pond.

"Anne! Look out!" I screamed, waving my arms. But the sound of my voice merely echoed as if I were inside a glass bubble as I tried to run and somehow didn't move.

The thing was pulling itself out of the shallow water. Only feet from Anne, it opened a nightmare mouth, revealing pointed teeth and a cavernous, yellow-pink throat that gleamed in the moonlight. I was still running in that dream-paralysis as Anne sensed the thing and turned.

It was an alligator. An alligator on the Boston Common, water from an autumnal pool dripping from its head and the five-fingered hands scratching against the pond's edge. The muscular tail moved under the water, making silent ripples across the moonlit surface. I was close enough to hear it breathing, a sound like rice spilling on stone as the scent of sassafras stung my eyes.

For a second Anne seemed frozen, then she screamed, "Bastard!" and kicked at one of its eyes. The thing made a gravelly hiss and lunged at her, its antediluvian mouth stretched wide, but she sidestepped and kicked at its teeth, hard. I could see bits of pointed ivory splash against the shallow water and sink. Dragon's teeth in a New England park, incongruous and deadly.

The alligator was backing away, retreating into the water, but Anne was after it.

"Go back to hell where you belong!" she yelled, up to her knees in water and kicking viciously as the tiny black eyes and reptile skin dissolved, shadow in sparkling splash, like smoke. Then it was gone.

I could move again, and did, helping her from the pond. She was shaking.

"Damn thing is SO not supposed to be here!" she said, her shoes dripping on the path.

"Is it always an alligator?" I asked, my heart still pounding.

"No. Usually it's worse," she said. "A *lot* worse. This was just weird. A gator, *here*?"

"A first," I agreed, telling myself to calm down, get used to weird. "And your shoes are wrecked. Definitely a reason to go shopping tomorrow." I was trying to make light of those god-awful teeth, my helplessness, the reality of Anne's ghoul. It didn't work.

She cast an uneasy look back at the pond, now still as a painting in autumn moonlight.

"But you saw it, right? This really happened?"

"Oh, yeah, Anne. It happened, smelled like sassafras."

"You could smell it, too?"

"Yeah. Like root beer."

"It always does," she said softly.

We walked back up Charles Street in silence, arms linked over the squishing of her shoes. I touched the silver chain at my neck. She laid a hand over the green brocade tassel at her waist.

"Hallett's husband, Philip..." she began.

"But you fought it, Anne," I said. "Philip wouldn't fight."

"What happened to him... it makes death look good. I'm so scared, Taylor. Are you?"

"Yes," I said. "I'm scared."

Chapter Nineteen

Could This Be Magic

The Dubs

Wednesday was overcast and chilly. Everyone showed up at Hallett's early and settled by the fireplace in the conference room, where Anne and I recounted our experience with her ghoul to a rapt audience. Hallett taped the story, explaining that Harry had created a system with which to cross-reference details in Revenant experience.

"Sassafras," she repeated. "Taylor, you also smelled sassafras even though you couldn't move and couldn't make yourself heard, couldn't warn Anne?"

"That's right," I said.

She nodded. "With mine it's vitamins. That moldy chemical smell from a bottle of vitamins."

Marlow grinned. "I always know the damn thing's around if I smell Easter lilies. Used to make me sick when I was a little kid, bored out of my mind in church with that gaggy smell in the air. All I wanted was to get outside and hunt for eggs!"

"Mine's persimmons," I offered, "although I don't know why."

"I know why mine is cloves," François said, rubbing his jaw. "I am a boy at the dentist and there is that smell, the clove oil he put on my teeth to stop pain. Except it does not stop. I hate the clove smell!"

The exchange was comfortable, as if we were just sharing personal stories. "I've never seen Mt. Rushmore, but somehow it doesn't matter." "My wife and I honeymooned in Oshkosh, of all places." That sort of thing. And yet we were talking about the scent of a horror that drove Philip Gardner to fling himself through a third-story window to protect his wife from the consequences of murder.

After chatting for a while we bent to the task of researching occult organizations. There was no sound but the soft clacking of keyboards for hours, punctuated by an occasional chuckle or murmur of admiration. Lunch was again catered, thick mushroom soup and spinach quiche with elegant little fruit tarts for desert. Anne was the first to comment on our proposed organization and website.

"I just spent the entire morning reading about 'Rosicrucians' and it's all this Egyptian malarkey," she began. "Amenhotep, a whole slew of Ramses, cuneiform writing and tomb paintings. There must be a hundred organizations right now, and I'm not including the ones that were around since the fourteenth century and died out, all saying the Egyptians knew the secrets of the universe, except they didn't have it quite right until Christianity came along. Or something like that."

Forks hung in midair as we waited for the conclusion. Anne knit her brow.

"There are all kinds of 'rites' that people have to learn to get from one level to the next, and some of the costumes are to die for, but I have to be honest. If I were out there looking for information about what's happened to *me*, I would not be reading up on Rosicrucians or anything like that, y'all know what I mean? All this mysterious folderol just doesn't have anything to do with me. I never heard of these groups until yesterday and even if I saw 'Martine" in a website full of Egyptian names it still wouldn't get through to me because the rest of it puts me off. I think I'd want something familiar, something I can relate to, y'know?"

"I also do not hear of the 'Hermetic Order of the Golden Dawn' until reading of it today," François said. "But I am interested and there is a group in Paris. Maybe I go to a meeting. But I agree this is not same as us."

"Golden Dawn has something to do with the Rosicrucians," Anne mentioned. "The first level or something."

Hallett was restive.

"Harry wisely warned us not to get sidetracked," she said. "These organizations can be interesting, *have been* interesting for centuries. But at the moment their only use to us is the model they may provide. Marlow, what are your thoughts?"

The soybean farmer was wearing a plaid flannel shirt and shrugged as he ran both hands through his graying blond crewcut. "Well," he began, "I just read a lot about the Kabbalah; it seems real interesting. I guess I'm like François; I wouldn't mind listening to somebody talk about it, except I think you're supposed to be Jewish. But like Anne said, if I were looking to find out about Martine and the damn ghoul, I wouldn't go into anything like this stuff. I wouldn't understand it, at least not right off, and I'd give up."

I felt bad. This had been my idea and it wasn't working, yet something about it still felt right. My own research into occult organizations at the end of the alphabet had revealed a labyrinth in which anybody could wander for years. And yet would I look to tomes describing the role of magic in pre-industrialized societies for information about the creature in my dance studio? No. Neither did I feel more than occasional interest in solstices, megaliths and herbal remedies. So much for shamanism, witchcraft et al.

"I've always been interested in Tarot cards," I began, "and there's a connection between the writing of Aleister Crowley, who created a famous Tarot deck, and the Golden Dawn thing, which is connected to the Rosicrucian thing, all of which employ aspects of Kabbalah. What I think we've discovered is that all these mystical schools of thought are and always have been interconnected. But so what? They're not connected to *our* experience and so Revenants, who will presumably be like us, won't be drawn to anything that looks like them. We need to figure out what the connection between us actually is, other than Martine, ghouls and the threat of a hell from which suicide is the only escape, and use that as our starting point. I guess."

I had that sense of something stuck at the edge of consciousness, like a familiar name you can't remember fluttering just out of reach. Two minutes later it breaks through the filmy wall that held it trapped, and you yell, "Dean Martin! It was Dean Martin who sang "'Standin' on a Corner Watchin' All the Girls Go By,' right?" Except even after two minutes passed I still couldn't pin down whatever I was trying to think. Some accessible commonality behind which to hide information. I could feel it, just couldn't give it a name.

"Let's take an hour to consider this individually and then meet again in the conference room at two," Hallett suggested as Spalding cleared the table.

"And please," François said as if he'd just remembered something, "I invite you all to go to Hull."

Marlow guffawed. "Go to *Hull*?"

"Yes. This evening. I rent the van to take us there. To photograph the horses."

Anne was trying not to laugh. "The horses of Hull? I thought it was hounds. François, what on earth are y'all talkin' about?"

He was, as ever, dead serious. "You do not know of these horses?"

"No," Anne, Marlow and I said in unison as Sadie cocked her head, looking curious.

"Or Hull," Anne added. "What's Hull?"

Hallett smiled at François. "The others are not as familiar with local landmarks as you are," she said. "Perhaps you will explain."

With his slender hands François grasped an imaginary pole and made horselike movements with his head. "In the Marais are many shops, as I say. Things to collect. I have the postcards, Frederic has...had... the paper houses. But my friend Suzanne, she is very old but so smart and funny, she has the carousel animals. Little statues, tiny carousels with the music box inside, many books and pictures, diagrams, CDs and one real carousel animal she never sell. An ostrich carved in Germany, real gold leaf on the saddle and eyes of black quartz from Saxony. People say the eyes move, watch you. Suzanne know more about carousel animals than anybody in the world, and when I say I go to Boston, she ask me to photograph famous Dentzel horses in town of Hull nearby. So I invite you to come!"

"Hull is about twenty miles south of Boston on a peninsula," Hallett contributed, "a beach community that once boasted an extraordinary amusement attraction called Paragon Park. The park long ago vanished under condominium developments and nothing of it remains but the Paragon Carousel. Among its horses are a few carved by Gustav Dentzel in Philadelphia. These are the collector's gold standard among carousel animals, so you will understand Suzanne's eagerness for photos of them."

Everybody smiled weakly. I was interested, but thought the beach would be cold and what would I do with Sadie? Anne was looking for something in her purse and Marlow pulled a violin case from behind our coats in a closet. There was not measurable enthusiasm for François' horses until Hallett spoke.

"Hull is also known for its remarkable seafood restaurants," she mentioned. "All offer the local specialty, baked haddock, but there's a new place that specializes in escoveitch, jerk fish, and a tantalizing curry shrimp."

"Escoveitch?" I asked.

"I think it's Jamaican ceviche," Hallett said, "and I'd love for you all to be my guests for dinner."

Marlow grinned. "How about you're *our* guest?"

"That would be lovely," Hallett answered, and so we were going.

Sadie, Anne and I seized the open hour to dash down Beacon Hill and across the Common to a department store at Downtown Crossing. We went straight to the coat department, and while Sadie enjoyed being petted by the clerks and other shoppers, I watched the mannequins. A blonde in a bright red puffy jacket smiled with chipped lips at Sadie but made no move to help Anne select outerwear. When a svelte dummy in a floor-length white velvet evening coat touched my arm and then pointed to a forest green pea jacket with bone toggles, Anne noticed.

"Tell her I need *black*," she whispered, "maybe something with a zip-out lining?"

The pea jacket was more my style than Anne's.

"It's not for me but for my friend," I told the mannequin and was surprised when the elegant head turned slowly from side to side. The message was clearly, "No."

"Damn," Anne said. "They'll only shop for you!"

"Oh, come on," I urged the six-foot-tall doll dressed for an embassy dinner during a blizzard. "She's one of *us*," I insisted. "She can see you."

The painted eyes blinked slowly and Anne seized the moment.

"I could never wear floor-length velvet," she whispered admiringly. "But I'll bet you know just the thing to knock the socks off my friends back home. Something *you'd* wear, if you lived in Louisiana."

I should have known flattery would work, given the nature and purpose of mannequins. This one nodded, smiled that toothless smile and inclined her head toward a wall of fashion photos. We walked in that direction just as a young woman pushed a stroller holding a howling toddler too close to the chrome post supporting another mannequin, a sultry brunette wearing several fake fur scarves over a tight yellow riding coat. The toddler stood up in his stroller, grabbed the shiny metal stand and pulled the mannequin over.

Anne and I grabbed her before she hit the floor and the toddler, dislodging only a single painted hand that slid beneath a rack of coats and broke. I was still holding the dummy with one arm and Sadie's leash in the other hand as store personnel hurried to help and the toddler's mother carried on as if somebody had sprayed napalm on her ear-splitting offspring. But Anne was looking at a broken finger on the floor, pointing up at a coat.

"Taylor, look," she said, tugging the coat from its hanger and trying it on. It was perfect. Black wool with flared sleeves and six big silver buttons decorating the front, very chic but still roomy and comfortable. "And there's a zip-out lining!"

"Thanks so much," I told the brunette mannequin as I released her to a cute guy with an earring who said, "I'll get her another hand, no problem."

"Let's get out of here," I told Anne, who paid for her coat and wore it as we scuttled away. On the street level we stopped in the shoe department and bought identical black suede ankle boots, sheepskin-lined with thick, bouncy soles to buffer the bricks of Beacon Hill. At home I figured I could wear mine for walks with Sadie, and Anne said she'd use hers for house slippers.

Back at Hallett's, Marlow was sitting alone on the chilly patio, playing an odd little violin and singing. The sound was haunting and the words were muted by the closed French doors, but I recognized the melody – "In the Still of the Night." The Five Satins. I'd danced to it in high school, certain that I was deeply in love with a basketball player named Jimmy Steve Oberon, when what I was in love with was the music.

"Brings it all back, doesn't it?" Anne said. "The music."

"Yeah," I answered, wandering out to listen. Marlow's violin had eight pegs instead of the usual four, and the ebony fingerplate was elaborately set with a flowered design in mother-of-pearl. The scroll was a dragon's head with mother-of-pearl eyes. He stopped playing and grinned.

"Never seen a hardanger fiddle before?"

"No," I said. "What's a hardanger fiddle?"

"Norwegian. This one was my grandfather's. He used to play it out in the fields sometimes. I remember the music drifting on the wind. Now I do it."

"It's beautiful," I said, still worried about what we were going to do next, how we could construct a way to reach out to our own kind. My idea had failed and I felt responsible.

But the afternoon proved unproductive, filled with rambling thoughts and desultory conversation. We finally decided to take a break and reconvene at Hallett's for the trip to Hull at six. As we were leaving, Marlow put on his baseball cap and François asked, "Marlow, what is 'Beetle Bank' you have on your hat?"

"Ah," Marlow said, pleased that somebody was interested, "I farm organically. No toxic insecticides, none of that. So we, that is, really organic farmers, make beetle banks, among other things, to control pests naturally."

We were all standing around in Hallett's Georgian hall, struggling to pay attention despite the unlikelihood that any of us would ever grow soybeans.

"A beetle bank," Marlow went on, "is just a row of grass and other stuff – fava beans, bachelor's button, coriander, borage and buckwheat - we plant at intervals between the rows. It's something new, an idea only created in the 90's and not really used until a couple of years ago. Beetle banks provide a home for ground beetles that control other insects, the pests. Birds, too. Ground-nesting birds love the beetle banks, make homes there and also eat the bad bugs. And the bachelor's button is pretty out there, when you're alone in a tractor driving up and down, like a painting. I dunno, the beetle banks are *nice*, not just scientific."

"Maybe we are like that," François said softly. "We are also new idea and not scientific. Maybe we fight the pests, the ghouls, and help things grow. Maybe this is what we are for. We are beetle banks."

"Wow," Anne said. "I like this. It feels right, like there's some *point* to what's happened to us."

Marlow grinned. "How about I get baseball caps for everybody?"

"Absolutely," Hallet said. "I'll wear mine to the symphony!"

At the apartment I fed Sadie, changed into warm clothes for the evening and checked my email. Miyoko wrote that she'd hired Chris Delgado's retired-cop father, Carlos, to guard my house every night, and that the renovations were progressing nicely. She said Carlos heard someone on the deck at about midnight the previous morning, but the prowler fled when Carlos crashed through the half-painted kitchen in pajamas, wielding a flashlight and a Smith and Wesson .44 Special. He said the fleeing figure was long-legged and thin, sufficiently athletic to scale my fence.

I stretched and stared out the windows at Boston's trees, fading orange in late afternoon light. Across a continent, somebody was relentless in a desire to invade my house. To find something in my house even though I knew there was nothing in my house worth finding. The intruder had ignored the usual, saleable objects – jewelry, electronic equipment – and so was desperately searching for something else. Something that either wasn't there or of which I knew nothing. It was unnerving, and the contrasting safety of autumn and my snug urban apartment was as palpable as a warm touch.

I liked Boston, Sadie seemed happy. Maybe I should just stay, find a place of my own and start a new life. The thought was engaging. I like having options, alternate lives unlived but always possible. Still, I would go home and put an end to whatever threat this shadowy intruder represented. The Midwestern ethic precludes running from anything.

But my Boston fantasy had nothing to do with the intruder or with running. It was about being a new me. A Revenant Taylor, born in the middle of a sprawling country, my life lived at its western edge until that life ended in a dance studio and a new one began. That its final chapters might be acted out on the East Coast had a geographical completion I liked. I might never actually do it, but in my mind it was already done. I was a creature of trees and seasons, brick sidewalks and black clothes, who would fight a pestilential ghoul and use my gift to help life thrive when I could. I was a Bostonian Revenant!

The identity was fun but also reminded me that I had some research to do. Boston was mine now, its streets another, if imaginary, home. But it had once been my friend Pen's home as well. And her legacy, a dollhouse, hid ghosts Pen's little granddaughter should never see. I'd stay a few extra days, I decided. Once we finished our work with Hallett, I'd find out what I could about that house.

Sadie wasn't tired and seemed eager to go, so I took her along to meet the crew at Hallett's and drive to Hull. She could sleep in the van while we were in the restaurant, and might enjoy riding on a carousel. I mean, how many dogs get to do that?

Marlow played his fiddle and we sang several choruses of "Michael, Row the Boat Ashore," "Jacob's Ladder" and "Amazing Grace" as we drove through New England dusk, acting like kids while house lights flickered on as if triggered by our passing.

And then we were there. François and Hallett had made arrangements for a private showing of the Paragon Carousel, which glowed with its thousand lights in the dark beside an ocean most of our ancestors must have crossed at various points in time. Even Sadie was fascinated by the glittering platform and strained at her leash as we got out of the van. A man in a dark blue captain's uniform with brass buttons approached and said, *Monsieur Loreau?*

Je suis François Loreau, Francois answered, stepping forward to clasp the man's hand, then introducing all of us.

In François' French accent our names were sonorous in the salty air, the syllables a litany honoring our strange privilege and its demon threat. The man in blue spoke to François in French for a few minutes, after which François reverently climbed aboard the carousel and began to take pictures. Our host stayed with us and explained in English that he spoke French because he was from Quebec.

"Carousels may be the descendants of ancient equestrian training grounds in which horses were tethered so they galloped in a circle," he said. "Their riders practiced throwing spears through a suspended ring, hence the traditional brass ring."

Marlow nodded with interest. I didn't buy it. The sparkling circle with its rococo carving and fanciful horses had nothing to do with anything as mundane as target practice.

"Why do men have to make everything be about fighting or sex?" Anne whispered. "They get everything *wrong*. I think carousels must have started with people just spinning around, getting dizzy. Kids always do that, it's part of some religions. The horses came later."

"I think you're right," I whispered back. Spinning is the easiest way to escape reality, if only for a few minutes, assuming you don't vomit or run into a wall. Primitive but effective.

"The Paragon is what is called a 'grand' carousel," our host went on proudly, "as its horses march four abreast. Only four are actual Dentzels, but all were carved of bass wood by German and Italian immigrant craftsmen in the early twentieth century. It has two horse-drawn chariots, really just benches secured to the floor and meant for the aged and ladies too modest to straddle a horse. No one ever sits in the chariots anymore, but they're traditional. All carousels have them and the carving on ours is museum quality."

François was taking hundreds of photos of the Dentzel horses from every angle. The rest of us waited patiently, adults pretending to listen to a lecture until what we knew would happen next. I had already selected my horse, a prancing black Friesian with laughing eyes and a scalloped saddle blanket painted in Moorish designs.

"The red Arabian is mine," Hallett whispered as the man in blue documented the artwork on the carousel's boards and shields. "The one with the silver hood and jeweled breast harness."

Anne was staring at a beautiful white horse with wide blue eyes, bedecked with garlands of carved and painted flowers. "She's mine," Anne said. "Her name is Gelsey."

"What kind of name is that?" I asked.

"I don't know," Anne answered. "It's just her name."

Marlow had wandered to one side of the carousel and was eyeing a spotted horse in Indian trappings when our host said, "Of course you'll all want a ride?"

"Why, yes," Hallett answered. "That would be charming."

We walked up the ramp and Hallett held Sadie as I grabbed the Friesian's chrome barley-twist pole and pulled myself into the saddle. Sadie was twitching with excitement as Hallett settled her in my arms.

"I think this will be interesting," she said, then headed for the red Arabian as the Wurlitzer band organ groaned to life and the platform began to move.

At first I felt a little silly but quickly fell into the curious sensation of going up and down and around in a broad circle at the same time. The chill air made my eyes water and blurred my vision, but I noticed François in a silk top hat, moving about on the platform, grinning and taking pictures of us. I thought he must have borrowed the top hat from our host, because I hadn't seen it before. Anne on her white horse two rows in front of me turned to wave and stars seemed to arc from her hand and stick blinking against the navy blue sky. When I turned to wave at Hallett behind me, I noticed that her long hair had come loose and her shoes were glowing red. Marlow on his Indian paint wore a Crusader's cloak that flew behind him in the wind, and François in his magician's hat now wore a red satin cape as he climbed on one of the Dentzel horses.

Illusion, I told myself. *You're a Revenant. Get used to it.*

Then from her perch against my stomach Sadie extended a paw to brace herself against my arm holding the silver pole. The sleeve beneath her white foot was not that of my black coat, but a rough green material richly embroidered in Slavic designs. And the barley-twist pole wasn't a pole but a broom. I was Baba Yaga!

The carousel spun faster and the Wurlitzer band organ filled the sky with music I remembered. My grandmother played the song on a cumbersome old Victrola in her living room – "After the Ball Is Over." I knew the song, and apparently so did everybody else. Hallett was the first to sing, her voice a clear soprano. Anne and I joined singing alto, then Marlow's tenor and François' surprisingly deep bass, his lyrics in French.

We were a choir as the carousel spun faster, seeming to rise higher and higher with each note until nothing surrounded us but inky blue-blackness and throbbing specks of light. Stars. We were flying in the music on a platform of magic created from deep inside the human soul. And in that moment I understood what we would do, how we would reach frightened Revenants hatching all over the world.

The answer had been there from the beginning. Tim's words at dawn in a park, "The music makes a path, you see," as Angie played a Bach fugue on which I would ride to a museum of paper dolls. Anne's words only that day as Marlow played his fiddle, "Brings it all back, doesn't it? The music." Languageless music that operates in a part of our brain used for nothing else. An *ancient* part of our brain, mysterious and incomprehensible even now. Perhaps a part hoarding the awareness that has opened to us, waiting over millennia for the right confluence of factors before it would emerge.

"After the dancers' leaving," I sang the final chorus at the top of my lungs while Sadie howled along, "After the stars are gone."

The carousel floated slowly to a stop and we dismounted in silence. Marlow, his Crusader's cloak now vanished, hurried to help me with Sadie.

"Music," I whispered over Sadie's one brown ear, then said it again and again.

In the van everyone was silent until Hallett spoke. "This is the reason you came," she said. "Music is the one code understood by all people. It can be used to attract Revenants to a source of information. Thanks to all of you, and especially to Taylor."

As we drove away the thousand lights on the carousel went out, but I could still see its afterimage like a negative photograph floating in the dark.

Chapter Twenty

Leader of the Pack

The Shangri-Las

At Hallett's's suggestion we all shared platters of sweet brown stew fish, jerk lobster and pepper shrimp, ideas flying.

"We need music that can attract people all over the world, at least the western world," Anne said. "Not just American pop songs only we know."

"American pop songs are everywhere," François answered. "I hear them same as you. Good for dancing and practicing English. But not all people like that kind of music. We must have classical as well."

"And music from movies," Marlow said. "Like 'Oklahoma' and 'The Bridge on the River Kwai'." He whistled the River Kwai theme as we all started writing lists on our placemats.

"Barber's 'Adagio,'" Hallett said quietly, her words like a gloved hand, silencing the table. "I'd like it if we included some of Barber's 'Adagio.' There was a string quartet for Steven's funeral and I asked them to play that."

I knew the music. The BBC Orchestra, in a performance broadcast worldwide, played it on September 15, 2001, in honor of the thousands of Americans who died on 9/11. The delicate, eerily mournful piece has been described as the perfect metaphor for grief.

"Of course," I agreed, followed by murmurs of assent. The music would serve as a warning to Revenants that some among us have, and without question will, perish. For a time I heard in my mind the haunting chromatic ascent of Barber's violins, then violas, then cellos – a breathless sadness rising, then falling and rising again like something lost below an unknown ocean that has no surface. I was glad that Philip's suffering had ended, but angry and terrified at the cause. What *was* this thing we called "ghoul," that could leave a man so broken that no choice remained but to be killed by his beloved wife, or by his own hand?

"Taylor," Hallett's voice intruded softly, "don't think about it. Only think about fighting it."

I got the message, and threw myself into a discussion regarding the relative merits of the harmonica theme to "Midnight Cowboy" as opposed to the same song with lyrics, "Everybody's Talkin' at Me." By the time we finished dinner and headed back to Boston there was general agreement that a mix of classical, pop and folk themes plus movie soundtracks would have the widest appeal to our age category. We sang every song we suggested. We were acting like kids on a field trip, I thought, then realized we *were* kids again, sporadically. And from our childish perceptions we would build that most rational and adult of artifacts – a map – for others to follow. But how?

"Um, I'm not getting what we're going to *do* with this music," I said.

"Let's let it percolate overnight," Hallett suggested. "Harry will look into the legalities, copyrights and all that, which will take some time. Let's meet again tomorrow afternoon, then work through dinner."

That meant I'd have the morning free. I was eager to investigate the history of Pen Barrows' infant home on Beacon Hill, now a dollhouse hiding behind its balsawood walls a repetitive and bloody, drama. But a single morning would be inadequate to the task. I'd barely get to the Boston Public Library and arrange for a card in order to access its collections when I'd have to return to Hallett's. Then I remembered another project on my agenda – easily accomplished in a morning.

"Do you know whether Fort Independence is open now?" I asked Hallett.

"Castle Island is always open," she answered, "but the fort is closed to tours except during summer months. May I ask why you want to go there?"

"A story of Poe's, 'The Cask of Amontillado,' is said to have been inspired by the murder of a vicious soldier by his mates at the fort in 1817. Supposedly they got him drunk, bricked him into the corner of the fort's dungeon and left him to die. Poe was stationed at Fort Independence ten years later, presumably heard the story and used it in his own. There are persistent rumors of a skeleton found in the walls of the fort many years later, probably apocryphal but still intriguing. I'm giving a talk on Poe to a community college class when I get home, and thought I'd take some pictures."

"Ah!" interrupted François. "I read all of Edgar Allen Poe, all the stories, and learn 'The Raven' when I am in school. *'Le Corbeau dit: Jamais plus.'* 'The raven say, Nevermore.'"

His delivery was dramatic and everyone clapped.

"I'd love for you to go along," I said, "although since we can't go inside there won't be much to see."

"But you will tell me the story and I will walk where Poe walked!"

No one else was interested, so François and I made plans to meet at my place and take a cab to the island, connected by a causeway to mainland Boston since the 1930's.

The next morning was overcast, and sharp winds blowing down from Canada threatened a freak, early snow. I would happily have foregone the trip, but François arrived in a down jacket and earmuffs, bearing coffee and croissants. He recited "The Raven" in its entirety, in French, to Sadie as I sipped coffee and pulled on three pairs of socks and my fleece-lined suede shoes. I loved hearing the poem, strange in a language that does not stress syllables, so the familiar beat of Poe's words was lost in a curious, dreamlike detachment. Then we walked Sadie and talked about poetic meter until it was time for the cab I'd called. On the way to Castle Island François leaned forward eagerly, watching the landscape as if his long-dead idol might be glimpsed ducking into a Starbuck's.

"Do you think this story is true?" he asked after we exited the warm cab and were nearly blown over by the wind on Castle Island. "This story that Edgar heard, of the soldier left to die in these walls?"

I looked out at whitecaps churning on the Atlantic, my teeth going into shock from cold. But I'd researched the story and was determined to tell it.

"This much is true," I began. "On Christmas Day in 1817 there was a duel between two soldiers stationed at Fort Independence. The offense inciting the duel is not known, but the bad guy, named Drane, killed the good guy, Massie. Subsequent events have not been documented and fall under the rubric of folklore, but are nonetheless well-known to this day. In revenge the other soldiers supposedly chained Drane in a corner of the fort's dungeon, bricked him in and left him there to die. Ten years later Poe was assigned to Fort Independence and it's fair to conjecture that he heard the story, which may have figured in his later creation of 'The Cask of Amontillado.'"

"But is it *true?*" François insisted, his lips turning blue from the cold.

I thought the answer to that lay curled inside Martine's remark. What matters is *that* things are, not *how*. Gustavus Drane really did kill Robert Massie in that duel two centuries in the past. And the story of Drane's living entombment really does exist, as does Poe's variant of it, transported to Italy. The fact and the story both *are*, although the fact owes the debt of awareness to the fiction. What is, what has survived, is the story, a kind of truth.

Unable to explain my reasoning, I just said, "Sort of."

We were walking on the path around the five-sided fort, which looked dismal and uninteresting in the oyster-colored air. I was freezing and noticed that with the exception of some sleazy-looking young thugs trying to build a fire in a trash can in the picnic area, there was nobody else around.

"It's likely that Poe heard the story," I yelled at François over the wind. "Almost certainly, he did."

The granite-block fort wasn't particularly interesting from the exterior, and after we'd walked the length of one side I was ready to view the excursion as a wash.

"Why don't I call another cab on my cell and let's get out of here," I suggested.

But François had spotted a small door in the wall of the fort and sprinted up the embankment toward it. I followed, admiring his enthusiasm while wondering at what wind-chill factor frostbite occurs. I told myself it wasn't really that cold, I just wasn't used to it. François was tugging at the iron handle on the little door set in the base of the fort when suddenly he was sitting in the brown grass, the door flat over his legs.

"It is open!" he said unnecessarily. "We go in!"

"I don't think..." I began, but he'd already propped the door against the fort's granite wall and vanished inside. I scrambled after him into a sort of tunnel that led from the exterior of the earthwork foundation to the parade ground inside. At least it was warmer, the five thick walls of the pentagon-shaped fort holding the wind at bay.

"We're trespassing," I told François more out of some half-felt sense of myself as the responsible host than any real concern. The worst that could happen was that we'd be told to leave, and so what?

He merely shrugged and loped away, clearly looking for something. The dungeon no doubt. I was struggling with the

Velcro on my smartphone when he gestured and yelled, "Here! I think it is here!"

The dead grass crunched under my feet as I tramped across the parade field toward a gloomy corner that looked like a cloister, arched doorways one after another, shadowless now beneath the cloudy sky. In a doorway was a tumble of granite, bricks and loose mortar lying in chunks on the stone floor. The area couldn't possibly be the undisturbed site in which a chained skeleton was or wasn't found over a century ago, but François was ecstatic and slipped a bit of New England granite into the pocket of his jacket.

"I know I break the law," he said, "but I will never be here again and to have a souvenir... I will be happy to go to jail for this!"

I grinned and then pulled on my best teacher-face. "I think there's a French Consulate in Boston," I said. "Do you happen to have the number?"

He was snapping photos of the gloomy arched doorways, the pile of rubble.

"No. Why do you want the number of the French Consulate?"

"We'll need them to get you *out* of jail," I said.

He laughed and I turned to walk back toward the tunnel entrance, briskly crossing the wide parade ground while no doubt exuding that embarrassed righteousness you feel when a companion insists on committing some insignificant crime that in the wrong hands could become a front-page scandal. "French Tourist Arrested for Vandalizing U.S. Monument," typed itself across my mind. Never a fan of politics, I couldn't remember if the current administration was pro or anti-French at the moment, and when I looked over my shoulder to see if François were following me, he'd vanished. I took a few snapshots and waited in a corner near the tunnel and out of the wind, imagining a Christmas Day duel nearly two centuries in the past, a man sealed alive in a freezing tomb, and the young Poe hearing the story a decade later.

It was then that I noticed the thuggy teenagers who'd been trying to set a fire in a trash can. They'd apparently seen the open tunnel into the old fort and were approaching quickly. Approaching *me.* Four emaciated teenage boys and a slightly older, fatter one with bad teeth and a snarl copied from heavy metal bands in vampire costumes. Trouble.

"Whatchu doin' out here all alone, granny? Where's grandpa? He off takin' a piss somewheres?" the fat one pronounced as he lit a cigarette and the others chortled mirthlessly.

I thought it must be a clove cigarette because suddenly the air was saturated with that pomander ball scent. Spicy, it made me think of winter holidays, mulled wine and clove cookies. In the middle of a cold, deserted fort where it seemed likely that I was about to be attacked by a gang of pathetic losers on their way to fates I didn't want to think about. The scent was out of place and I wished I were anywhere but where I was. Panic.

I've spent most of my adult life in high schools; I knew these kids. Not too bright, half-literate and wretchedly unhappy, yet too lazy and unmotivated to do anything but fail, they were the ones who'd drop out at fourteen, do time in juvy and wind up in prison within a few years. In the meantime they'd drink, do drugs and mindlessly follow some older sociopath who gave them a false and very temporary identity as tough dudes. The pattern repeats itself endlessly and is unchangeable. There will always be such creatures and while as individuals they're weak and apathetic, in packs they become ugly. I'd confronted them year after year in schools. But I'd never been alone inside a windswept granite fort with a pack of feral adolescents.

"Is there something we can help you with?" I said, faking bravado. My heart was pounding, but years of experience taught me never to show fear or even ambivalence in their presence.

The fat one dropped the cigarette he'd just lit and ground it into the grass with the heel of his motorcycle boot, which did nothing to diminish the dense clove odor pulsing in the air. They were all wearing fake leather jackets that were really plastic and crackled in the cold as they moved. One of the skinny ones, a pale boy with bloodshot eyes and visible scalp sores, giggled and pointed a crackly arm at something across the field.

"Look, the old man's goin' batshit!" he announced. "You that *scared*, grandpa?" he yelled across the dead grass. "You sure fuckin' oughtta be, 'cause you about to get *hurt*!"

They all snickered in agreement, but they were looking behind me at François with an edge of unease. When I turned to look, my heart sank.

Oh, shit.

Something was emerging from one of the arched doorways far across the empty field where François had been taking pictures. It was lunging at François. Or the head was lunging. A distorted lion head moved snakelike from a huge, spiked turtle shell. The creature had six thick legs ending in bear's feet but couldn't seem to coordinate its legs and fell to one side, then the other, as its scorpion tail lashed against the rubble, sending up clouds of dust. François' face was white with terror but he stood his ground, hurling bricks at the thing. It was his ghoul, I realized, at a particularly bad time. And François was *singing*.

The parade ground was huge, but his voice bounced off the five granite walls in a repetitive, and familiar, echo. *Alouette, gentille Alouette*, he bellowed, his voice growing louder as the lion head dodged bricks and snapped its teeth. Human teeth beneath a feline nose and human eyes desperate and blue against tawny fur. The thing was a hybrid, a hodgepodge of human and animal parts both aquatic and terrestrial, like a clumsy, discarded myth. *Alouette, je te plumerai*, François roared, and the ghoul seemed confused, its bulging eyes rapt as it cocked its head, listening.

"Look at 'im," one of the boys yelled. "Old fart's havin' a fit or something. Throwin' bricks and singin' some shit. He's loony!"

Of course they couldn't see the ghoul: they weren't Revenants. And François was too distracted to take note of them or me. They were only feet from me now.

"Stop right there!" I barked. "What you'll get from us is two cheap cell phones, under fifty dollars in cash and enough prison time to destroy what's left of your lives. Turn around and get out of here before you make a really stupid mistake."

"Wanna know what's stupid?" the fat one said, sneering. "What's stupid is some ugly old bitch and her in-sane boyfriend suckin' up air, know what I mean? You just suckin'up too much *air*."

They stood close to each other, their shoulders touching. An unpleasant odor drifted from them, layered over the fading scent of cloves. Testosterone, sweat, and something like the smell of burnt vinyl on their breath. I vaguely remembered a drug workshop given by the police for the faculty at my school.

"Think of holding a match to a brand-new shower curtain just out of the package," the drug officer told us. "That's the smell of crystal meth. It can make people violent, homicidal, suicidal. Bad stuff. Don't mess with anybody on meth. Just get away and call the police."

I invariably remember life-saving bits of advice like this slightly beyond the point at which their usefulness has expired.

"Time to dance," the fat one whispered. "Then we do grandpa."

The pale boy with scalp sores came at me, giggling, and I stopped thinking. My mind went blank, shrunk to a single, muted thread behind the fierce thudding of my heart. But my body remembered Molly Palmer in a shopping mall dance studio teaching martial arts moves choreographed to music. I could hear François's voice bouncing in surges across the empty space. I'd never danced to "Alouette," but the meter was pronounced, palpable in the cold air. I'd sung the song in grade school.

I should explain here that I didn't think I could fight off a gang of drugged-up male predators forty years my junior whose combined weight exceeded mine by at least seven hundred pounds. Scared witless, I didn't think *anything*. I just caught the rhythm of François' song, crouched, and on *la tête* of the third line, *Je te plumerai la tête*, I sprang up and landed my right foot hard between Scalp Sore's legs. Then I pulled back in a practiced move and on the second *tête* I smashed the heel of my right hand into his nose as he bent over clutching his crotch and gagging. I felt his nose break under the heel of my hand. It was like a wet popsicle stick that bends farther than you expect and then suddenly snaps, except that it happened much faster. The sensation was not pleasant and I drew back.

The others were on me a second later. After that my kicks and punches were wild, random and ineffective and I found myself on the ground with my arms over my head as they pounded on me. I wished I'd remembered the whistle, but I didn't, so I kept kicking hard in time to the song, thinking this was really a lousy way to die.

Then they were screaming, "Jesus fuck! What the fuck *is* that? Go, go, we're outta here!"

I saw them running toward the tunnel door, a spray of blood flying behind the one holding his nose and howling. Fatso was limping so badly he was hopping, and I enjoyed thinking that maybe one of my kicks had managed to tear a ligament in his knee.

Then I looked behind me. *Right* behind me, only inches away stood a figure from a horror comic. A dun-colored human skeleton in rotting blue rags, it held a rusty flintlock pistol at arm's length in one hand at eye level, the other bony hand at its side. The traditional dueling stance I'd seen in countless movies. Blackened chains hung from its wrists and ankles, creaking faintly in the wind. I rolled out of range, barely breathing, and struggled to stand.

In a far corner across the parade ground François was still singing and the ghoul was quiet, watching François now with something like adoration, its six legs folded beneath its shell. The lion head swayed to the sound of François' singing. But even from a distance deep inside its bulging eyes I sensed that speck of dense *absence* that is the only gift of our demons. A vacuum into which every meaning may vanish forever. The thing was playing with him, acting a part designed to mislead.

"Don't fall for it!" I tried to yell, but of course he couldn't hear me. Nor did he need to. I could tell that he'd seen what lay behind those eyes.

Retourne, he screamed, no longer singing, throwing bricks at its head with furious power. *Retourne, va-t-en!*

I didn't have to speak French to understand *retourne*. "Return, go back!"

The skeleton at my side was fading, collapsing, losing substance. I heard the flintlock pistol clatter and break apart, saw the empty skull sink on the collapsing ribs as François' ghoul became a transparent mist and then was gone.

"Wait," I said to the cracking bones in front of me. "You must be Drane, the one they sealed in the wall. Are you Drane? Did it really happen?"

But the thing just crumpled in a heap, became vapor and vanished. Where it had been, a flat bit of metal like those little brackets that hold shelves in bookcases, clinked against the stone floor. When I picked it up, it was ice cold.

François looked around, saw me and ran to join me. He was panting, exhausted. "Did you see it?" he asked.

"I saw it," I said, feeling dizzy as the adrenalin wore off. "Lion head with human eyes, six legs, turtle shell with spikes. But there was something else inside, much worse. Did you see the boys, the skeleton?"

"I see nothing but the Tarasque, Taylor. I do not see boys. And what skeleton? Are you all right?"

"You saw nothing but the *what*?"

He sat on the stone floor against the fort's interior wall and I collapsed beside him. "The Tarasque," he explained, looking at me strangely. "An old French tale of a monster, a strange dragon that ate people of a village in Provence long, long time in the past. I visit my grandparents in Arles every summer and there is a parade of the Tarasque. She is charmed by the singing, in the story. A woman, some say St. Martha, sing to the creature and she is tamed. Then the villagers beat her, the Tarasque, to death. That is the story. Taylor, you look bad. What is wrong?"

"She?" I said. I felt light-headed and nauseous. Something wet was running down my neck and a pain in my ribs and left thigh kept ramping up. "This French dragon thing was female?"

"Blood!" François said after touching the back of my head, then glancing at his red-stained fingers. "Where is your cell phone?"

"Bag," I answered, suddenly weak, as if some low electrical charge always humming in my bones had been unplugged. "Dial 9-1-1 and tell them to send medical help." Oddly conscious but too tired to speak, I heard François make the call and tell them where we were. Then I heard him talking to Hallett. But my thoughts were interior and his words were just background noise, like the explanatory voiceover in a movie you've already seen three times.

The feral boys were real and might have killed both of us for no reason except opportunity. Yet they were hollow cartoons, meaningless shapes compared to that darkness I'd felt inside François' ghoul. And the ghost of a story had appeared to save my life.

Paramedics came, wrapped my neck in a brace and gently fastened me to a board. In the ambulance I told François, "It was Drane. He was a skeleton in rags with a dueling pistol. He came and scared them and they ran."

"Ah," François answered his eyes uncomprehending as he anxiously watched me, then the traffic. "The hospital is not far."

"No, really," I insisted. "He was there, Drane, the guy they sealed into a wall. At least *something* was there. Look. This came out of his gun when he fell apart."

I handed François the bit of metal still clutched in my right hand.

"What is this?" he said.

"I don't know," I answered. "But it's real."

Then through the ambulance window I saw a sign on a pole. It said, "Massachusetts General Hospital Emergency." When the paramedics snapped the wheels of the gurney down and pushed me into bustling, antiseptic warmth, I noticed a navy blue sleeve with patches saying, "Boston Police, A.D. 1630." I suppose I was in shock, but the "1630" part was intriguing.

"Five adolescent males in plastic motorcycle jackets," I told them. "One fat older one and four skinny ones. Check hospitals for somebody with scalp sores and a broken nose. Did the original Boston Colony really have a police department?"

Nobody answered and then I was whisked behind a white canvas curtain where a young Asian woman named Dr. Fang looked at my head and said, "Ouch! You're going to need stitches. We'll try not to shave more hair than we have to." I wasn't thrilled about the head-shaving or the stitches, but some inner gyro told me I was okay. After a while I heard Hallett's voice talking to François outside my curtain, then Harry Laufer's.

"Holy shit," Harry said, "I know what this is. It's a frizzen."

"A what?" François said.

"It's from an antique flintlock gun, the piece of steel the flint would strike to make a spark. You say Taylor found this at the fort?"

"Yes," François answered, his eyes widening in comprehension. "It is from... a story."

"Keep it," I told him. "It's a real souvenir."

Later I heard Hallett on her cell with Anne Greenleigh.

"I'm having a cot delivered to Taylor's," she said. "I hope you won't mind coming right over to stay with her and sleeping there tonight. She's injured, may have a concussion and is too weak to fight. She can't be alone at any time."

I hadn't thought of that.

Chapter Twenty-One

Blues in the Night

Frank Sinatra

I had eleven stitches in my scalp, bruised ribs, a black eye, contusions on my arms, legs and back, and enough painkillers to stupefy a herd of rhinos. Dr. Fang wanted to admit me to the hospital for observation, but after I pointed out that my apartment on Revere was only two blocks away, she agreed to let me go. François was distraught, feeling that his impulsive behavior in breaking into the fort had been responsible for my injuries. He felt even worse for having not been at my side during the attack and emerging unscathed while I looked like a poster for a battered women's shelter. Hallett and Harry Laufer reassured him but I could tell it wasn't doing any good.

Anne Greenleigh was waiting outside my apartment when we pulled up in a cab from the hospital at one o'clock. She'd brought a carton of pine nut soup from one of the restaurants on Charles and made sure I ate before drawing a warm bath and shooing Harry and François out. Hallett left as soon as I collapsed in bed to sleep off the painkillers, and I barely heard Anne coming in and out with Sadie for the rest of the afternoon. But by five-thirty I was undrugged, awake and appalled at my visage in the bathroom mirror.

"My God, I look like Grandma Moses!" I told Anne. "I've aged twenty years!"

"The black eye doesn't help," she replied. "But I've had the same problem. Some days I start out looking like *me* and then I glance in a mirror and see my momma's Aunt Lacey just the way she looked at my first wedding. I hate that, since she died three days later, bless her heart, but that's why we have makeup. You'll need a good foundation and..."

"I keep thinking," I interrupted. "Those boys were scared off by a moldy skeleton holding a flintlock dueling pistol. I'm sure the skeleton was created out of my mind. I've done this before; it's got something to do with being a Revenant. I created Drane because I'd been thinking about him. Nobody knows if there really *was* a Drane, but when he dissolved, a piece of a flintlock gun fell on the ground and I picked it up. Harry said it's called a frizzen. Do you think pieces of stories can sort of solidify like that?"

"There are probably pieces of old guns all over that place," Anne said, trying gently to train my short hair over the shaved stripe on my scalp. "You're going to need a hat."

"Marlow said he'd send us all baseball caps with 'beetle bank' on them. I can wear that," I said. "Although maybe mine should say 'director'."

"You need a hat right now, Taylor. You look like Frankenstein's monster, and what do you mean, 'director'?"

She was rummaging through my makeup bag and smiled when she found a little tub of flesh-colored concealer I'd bought on a shopping spree with Jude and never used.

"My point," I said, submitting to being made up, "is that sometimes I can see stories, or parts of them, other people can't see that are really there. And then sometimes I can make them seem to be there when they really aren't, but only for a little while. Then they go away."

"We all do that with little things, but you're an English teacher," Anne said. "It's not surprising that you'd do stories. I do it, too, only they're more like scenes from history, things that are lost. There's a plantation in ruins off a little dirt road not far from my place, and sometimes I can bring it back, make it the way it was in 1830. I can even see the people, but it doesn't last very long. I think I'm going to write a book about the place."

"What a great idea! You can just go there and watch the story write itself, which will be fun. But I think conjuring up Drane may have saved my life," I said.

Anne's cell rang and she answered it.

"Hallet," she mouthed at me, then said yes, it looked like I'd be able to make it for dinner.

I ached everywhere, but insisted on walking the two blocks to Hallett's, still thinking about my ability to make whole vignettes out of nothing. When we arrived, François followed me to the dining room in a torrent of apology I found excessive. Maybe it's my Midwestern thing, but while you have to accept responsibility for whatever you do, one acceptance is enough.

"It really wasn't your fault," I said firmly. "It was just a fluke, one of those things…"

"Fluke?"

"An anomalous event that couldn't have been foreseen," I said. "They happen all the time."

Un hasard, he muttered. "Not the same in French and we do see those criminals, Taylor; to go into the fort where they could see us is stupid. *I* am stupid."

"Okay," I agreed. "It was all your fault and you owe me. How about a tour of Paris next time I'm there? I want to see all the places tourists never see. And dinner. A fabulous dinner, at least eight courses, in some cellar restaurant where the chef cowers in sullen disgrace if you don't like the *sauce beurre blanc.*"

I had no idea what "white butter sauce" might be, since butter tends to be yellow, but remembered the term from a recipe printed on a bag of overpriced shrimp. When François' face brightened I knew I'd hit pay dirt.

"Ah," he sighed. "When will you come? I will be delighted to be host!"

"I have no idea," I answered, but I *will* show up eventually and I expect a grand time in honor of being attacked by thugs while you fought for your life against a dragon in a turtle shell."

"It will be my honor," he said, and stopped apologizing.

Over dinner I learned that much had been accomplished. There would be a website, Marlow explained, based on the musical theme we'd chosen. I didn't get most of the discussion, but everybody seemed enthusiastic and Hallett congratulated us on a job well done. Harry and the MIT students would take over from here. We'd have a celebratory brunch the next day, in time for everyone but me to catch planes. I still had work to do in Boston.

"I guess a website's a great idea," I said, "but how is this going to educate Revenants? How are they going to know the website is a front for an organization of people like them who have to remain in hiding? How will they see through the façade, and how is this going to help them?"

Marlow was grinning. "Every page a different game, recipe, quiz, each with a cartoon figure called Martine insisting that participants *must* fight the ghouls," he said. "Even the recipe and quiz pages will be set up in an adversarial mode that demands aggression against a monster in order to get the desired result. Revenants will get the message. Different music for each page and terrifying cultural images any Revenant will recognize as stand-ins for our personal ghouls. The dated music will repel kids who might otherwise be attracted to the monsters, but even if that fails, there's an email registration form that can automatically weed out respondents under, say, fifty. There's no real point in registering anyway, unless you *are* a Revenant, recognize the codes and register in order to make contact. There will be a text box for comments."

Everybody was nodding triumphantly, as if this all made sense.

"And then what?" I said. "Suppose I manage to find this website and fight my way to a recipe for hazelnut pudding or something. What happens?"

"You get the recipe," Harry said, laughing. "Brought to you by a *buruburu*."

"A what?"

"Japanese ghost that haunts graveyards and forests," Marlow explained. "It's an ancient, one-eyed figure that seeps into your vertebrae and causes you to shiver. Or else die of fright. We thought we should include a few eastern ghouls."

Hallett was beaming and Marlow was so flushed with enthusiasm that his graying crewcut seemed to crackle.

"Monsters from every culture," he went on. "Solitaire games, for example, with cultural ghouls worked into the suit designs. I found some great woodcuts online, pictures from stories I heard as a kid – Hel, Jormungand and Fenrir."

"I do not know these," François said, followed by murmurs of interest from the rest of us as forks settled on plates and we looked to Marlow like children anticipating a story.

"I'll tell you what my grandmother told me," Marlow began. "These three are the children of Loki, the trickster and Father of Lies, and his mistress, a monster. Their daughter Hel is a beautiful woman from head to waist, but below the waist she is a rotting cadaver."

"Yuck!" Anne said.

"She rules in the land of the dead," Marlow went on. "Jormungand is a terrible serpent so immense that his body encircles the world, his tail clenched between his teeth until the day he emerges from the sea. But the most fearful of these siblings is the eldest, Fenrir, a wolf so powerful that no chain made by the gods could hold him. So the gods appealed to the dwarves, who made a ribbon of six things that cannot be seen – the sound a cat makes when it moves, the beard of a woman, a bear's sinews, the roots of a mountain, a fish's breath and the spit of a bird. Fenrir is bound by this fetter until the day he is unleashed and calls to his brother and sister. When this happens, there is a terrible battle in which the world may end."

Like a child, I felt shivers of delight at the story and would have clapped my hands, but Harry Laufer's voice, solid and contemporary, brought back the cloak of adulthood.

"It would seem that Fenrir is unbound and has called to his siblings," Harry said. "*All* his siblings, who are all these tales, the thousand tributaries of the White Road upon which we have no choice but to stand. We have become characters in the story that is that road. I'm afraid what we do now, how we play our parts, may be more important than mere individual survival. Marlow's Norse tale is mirrored in countless others that involve terrible forces chained for centuries, forgotten but waiting to emerge and bring destruction. Seems like it's happened. The chains have broken; something terrible is loose, and our website is for the moment the only way to rally those who can fight."

With her fork Anne pushed a bit of scalloped potato toward the edge of her plate, staring at it as if it might speak.

"So we're supposed to save the world?" she said more to the shred of potato than to Harry.

"Possibly," he answered jovially. "Something like that."

"From what, Harry?" Hallett asked. "A Norse wolf, a snake and a woman who's half corpse?"

"Oh, not unless you're Marlow. These symbols are his heritage. Mine," Harry continued happily, "is called Amalek, once an ancient race of Anti-Semites, now the name of a monster whose nature is irrational doubt, who just says, 'So what?' to everything. Amalek is the nightmare of the Jewish people. François sees a Tarasque because the Tarasque tales he heard as a child live in his mind. But these are only a few images from the many stories that feed the White Road; they both illustrate and mask something for which we have no words. That something is what we fight."

244

"I still don't get it," Marlow said. "Why us? Why now?"

"Who knows?" Harry replied. "Age of Aquarius? The Mayan Prophecy? Big cosmic shift cracking a code buried in our DNA when we were still little arboreal primates swinging in trees above lumbering dinosaurs? All we know is that it *is* us and the thing that attacks us wishes to, and can, destroy what is essentially human – the capacity to attach meaning to experience. We are the first, and only, line of defense."

"I saw Philip's humanity destroyed, his ability to experience meaning," Hallett said. "And why us? Let's face it. We're the outpost, the first defense, as Harry said. We're no longer slaves to the reproductive process, no longer animals programmed to mate incessantly and then bring food to a nest of hungry mouths. That's over, we're free of it and can *think* again for the first time since puberty. If this thing can get through us, those behind us are lost."

Hallett's words made sense to me, but Anne had scraped her potato back to the center of her plate and was hitting it with the back of her fork.

"So we're superheroes?" she said, abandoning the potato to scowl at the group. "Look, y'all. I'm sixty-three, fifteen pounds overweight and very attached to my hair colorist, who charges a fortune. I have a business to run and three kids to help, one still in college. I don't want to think how I'd look in mesh tights and patent leather boots with strapless swimsuit made out of a flag. If this Amalek is the Jewish nightmare, Harry, what I've just described is the nightmare of every woman over forty. I *refuse* to be a superhero!"

Hallett and I applauded and the guys laughed.

"Forget Wonder Woman," Harry said. "Remember that one of the elements in the dwarves' binding of the wolf Fenrir was the 'beard' of a woman. It means that hidden strength that can't be seen, far surpassing the posturing of men, that emerges in women when something they love is threatened. There's a reason women are traditionally excluded from combat; they're too ferocious, don't play by the rules. Once engaged, which admittedly takes some doing, women are savage killers. You don't need a costume,

Anne. You and Taylor and Hallett already have all you need."

"Well, maybe a red, white and blue *scarf* or something," Anne said, grinning. "But no swimsuit."

"Harry is selecting a few MIT students to design the website and the games," Hallett explained. "In particular a game that mirrors our experience, explains what we know so far and explains that no 'player' is alone. This is apparently quite simple and can be accomplished in a matter of weeks. I'm pretending not to understand that the site will appear to originate from Ethiopia in order to dodge certain copyright issues involved in the use of the music."

"Ethiopia is not a signatory to the Berne Copyright Protection Treaty, Hallett," Harry explained as if everyone else already knew this. "We don't have time to play copyright chicken with music corporations."

"It's still not right. It's breaking a law."

"What's not right is failing to help others, to do what we have to do," he said. "American copyright laws are irrelevant at this point. I can't believe you're taking this... position." His voice faltered when he, and everyone sitting at the table, realized the implication of the remark. Hallett Gardner had been willing to kill a man to end his suffering.

"You're right," she said. "I'm being prudish. Ethiopia it is."

I'd missed the afternoon's discussion and still wasn't clear about anything.

"How will Revenants find this website?" I asked. "I don't spend much time playing games online, except sometimes the ones that are supposed to improve your memory. I wouldn't go looking for games *or* music if..."

"What *would* you type into Google, Taylor, if you were searching for information about being a Revenant?" Harry interrupted.

I thought about it, thought about what I might have done if Tim O'Halloran hadn't been there to help.

"Martine," I said. "I'd type 'Martine'."

Harry beamed. "She's the common denominator. All Revenants see her. She's our best bet as an attractor and her name will be on every page. While you and François were out touring forts and hospitals we decided to name the site 'Martine' and decorate the home page with enough ghouls that any Revenant will make the connection, with a page-by-page soundtrack of all the music we've selected. Music that reminds them of their lives, that their lives and all human life are worth fighting for."

"Martine dot com," Marlow said. "That should work."

But François was smiling and shaking his head. "I should have been here this afternoon," he said. "What you will see if you type 'Martine' is a cute little girl. It is books for small children, very sweet and happy, made in Belgium for many years. If somebody has a tablet, I will show you."

Harry dug his out of a briefcase and we all gathered around François as he brought up picture after picture of book covers featuring an angelic little girl.

"This one is *Martine at the Farm* and this is *Martine at the Sea*," he translated. "These are old ones, from 1954."

"Like the Bobbsey Twins," Hallett said.

But as François scrolled through more than fifty book jackets featuring a bright-eyed little girl done in pastels, I had that feeling you get when you see a face in a crowd you're sure is your eighth-grade biology teacher. (Except didn't he die in a skiing accident twenty years ago?) But the face is too far to reach and vanishes through a door, leaving a sense that time isn't what we think it is. That the past may move through the present in flickers, hinting at incomprehensible possibilities that are both intriguing and unnerving. I was sure I knew that little girl.

"What is it, Taylor?" Hallett asked. "You look strange."

I kept staring at the pictures. Martine on a horse. Martine in chef's garb, learning to cook. A sweet and wholly unrealistic little girl in whose brown eyes I saw an impish spark I recognized.

"I know who Martine is," I said, pointing to a cover in which the girl smiles from the basket of a striped hot-air balloon. "That's Martine, *our* Martine, as a child! The nose, the eyes, are the same. She dyes her hair now and dresses like the CEO of a pricey international escort service, but she has an accent. That's Martine."

"My God, you're right!" Anne said. "I see it. Those eyes..."

Everyone leaned over François' shoulders, close to the screen, nodding.

"So our guide is the once adorable, now sophisticated but always fictional heroine of a French children's series," Hallett said, looking at the back of her right hand a if it were a mirror. "Why do I not find this reassuring?"

"The books are actually Belgian, not French," François insisted.

My head was swarming with some proto-understanding that hadn't had time to coalesce, but I spoke anyway.

"She's an adult now; Martine is. And when I saw her she was anything but adorable. She was our age, maybe a little younger, which would be about right if the first of her books was published in the early fifties. At the Paper Doll Museum her hair was a gorgeous reddish gold and..."

"I've tried that color," Anne said. "I think it's called 'Cointreau.'"

"What I mean is that she looked great, well-dressed, accomplished and canny. There was that sparkle in her eyes. She knows what she's doing, whatever she is."

"Let's hope she does," Harry boomed, tugging on his amulet

earring. "Never thought my life would depend on a gift from a character in a book, but I agree, that kid is definitely Martine fifty years ago. Anyway, we've bought the domain name, 'Martine dot com,' and if we include 'Martine' a couple of times on each page, the website will appear high on the list of sites that come up even if you just type the name into Google or other search engines."

My several contusions were throbbing, my head hurt and the evening's insights had made me dizzy.

"I think I'll call it a night," I announced between dessert and coffee, causing a wholesale movement toward the door. François, Harry and Marlow insisted on escorting me and Anne the two blocks through a notoriously crime-free neighborhood to my place.

"Zank you, boys," Anne vamped at my door, striking a Zsa-Zsa Gabor pose. "But next time you vill bring more money, ya?"

We all laughed and François came in to walk Sadie so I wouldn't be left alone. In the afternoon I'd been drugged, unavailable to my ghoul if it showed up. Now I was awake, exhausted and probably fair game. Anne turned on her laptop as I fell in bed.

"Don't you think you should let your people back home know what's happened?" she asked.

I'd never thought of myself as having "people," although I guessed the Syndicate would fall in that folksy category, and my kids, and Tim O'Halloran now, and Miyoko, maybe even Molly Palmer, whose skill inside my trained body kept reminding me that everything may be a dance. But why upset them? I was three thousand miles away and out of their reach.

"No," I answered, "but I'll check my email later."

I was nearly asleep when François came back with Sadie, and I was glad to feel her warmth when she joined me on the bed. When I awoke hours later Anne was asleep on her cot, Sadie was snoring beside me and there were no footsteps on the gaslit street. I sat up and opened the shutters a crack, hoping to see something outside that would explain the bleak weight that seemed to have mushroomed in my chest while I slept. But there was nothing there, just a narrow street of pretty brick row houses you'd expect to see in a Dickens movie, or in miniature on a Christmas sideboard. The empty street felt like a blank slate on which I must write something, change something, *be* something.

François' endless apologies echoed in my mind, and Harry's stated belief that our job was to help others, to save the world. The idea was scarcely new, but carried an immediate urgency I couldn't grasp. Then I thought about the surly boy whose nose had snapped under the heel of my hand, and my strange power to animate stories. I had hit him to protect myself, a reasonable act respected by law, and I would do it again if I had to. I felt no guilt, no responsibility, yet I was now part of his story. And I knew what the rest of it would be. Courts, jails, prisons. Rape, degradation, hopelessness, the incremental ruin of an already weak and aimless character whose face would carry the mark of my hand forever. I knew the story, had become a paragraph in it. And I knew what I had to do.

The police called at 7:30 in the morning, asking me to come to the station for possible identification of my assailants in a lineup. They'd rounded up suspects the night before and said a police cruiser would pick me up at 9:00. I walked to a nearby drugstore, bought one of those bound, blank books meant to be used as journals, sent Sadie to Hallett's with Anne and was ready when a red-headed rookie cop rang the bell.

Fatso was easy to identify, as was the pale, scrawny boy with a bandaged nose even though there were others whose noses were covered in gauze and white tape. I was sure of one other, but no more. The police told me Fatso had previous convictions for robbery and assault and would be returning to prison for a lengthy stay even though he'd ratted out the others. They said the boy whose nose I'd broken was lucky because his eighteenth birthday was a month away. He'd go back to a juvenile facility, not to an adult prison. This time. They said his name was Kevin, which had no effect on me at all. My son's name is Kevin but this boy was not my son.

"I'd like to speak to Kevin, alone," I told the sergeant, a young

African American woman with beautiful, sad eyes and a service revolver at her hip.

"Not allowed," she said.

"I am accusing him of a crime," I said. "The law states that he has a right to face his accuser."

"That's in court."

"I won't be in court. I live in California. I insist on seeing him."

"Five minutes," she said, escorting me to a closet-sized room that smelled like an ashtray. There was a chipped, dirty Formica table and two metal folding chairs, one on each side of the table. Half the door was that security glass that has chicken wire in it. I sat facing the door and in minutes the boy was brought in in leg irons and a thick leather belt to which his handcuffed wrists were shackled. His eyes were brown, bloodshot and devoid of animation.

"Fuck you," he said, and sat, clanking, on the chair opposite mine.

"Five minutes," the sergeant reminded me. "I'll be right outside this door."

"Why don't you go to hell," he began, but shut up when I slammed the book I'd bought on the table.

"This is for you," I said, pushing the book toward him, its back facing up. "A gift."

The empty eyes looked across his padded nose, through me and into space. "Fuck off," he sighed.

"Open it," I demanded.

"It's upside down."

"It's supposed to be. Open it."

"I don't want no book."

"You want this one," I said. "It's about you."

It was an offer no adolescent can resist. His right index finger, restrained by the cuffs and chain, barely reached the corner of the book's cover as he flipped it open, stared and turned gray. An oily shame bloomed in his eyes and I watched as it spread into his mind and turned to a rage that could poison every move he made for the rest of his life.

"What're you, some kind of sex pervert old bitch? This is sick shit."

"It is sick shit," I agreed. "And it is your life if you're too cowardly to fight."

"Fight what?" he asked, all belligerence and drama, rattling his chains.

"That," I said, pointing to the book and the graphic comic scene I could barely stand to see even though I'd created it with my mind, figuring graphic comics would be familiar to him. "That will be your life unless you kill it and make another. I'm not talking about killing a person; I'm talking about killing the path to that picture. It's your life right now and it is your enemy. That life will destroy you. Is there anything you like?"

"What?"

"Like. Is there anything in the world that you like?"

He looked at the table. "Boats," he said. "I like boats."

In my mind boat images curled painfully, like pulled teeth, from forgotten moments in which I'd had little interest. I forced more comic book pictures against the blank white screen of a closed page and thought I might faint from the effort. Then I reached to turn the book over so it was right-side up.

"Open it," I said.

"No."

"You have to."

His grimy hand was trembling, but he did it, and stared again.

"That's you if you fight, if you kill that other life."

"Working on boats," he said. "That's me working on boats, on engines, except that Evinrude in the picture's so fuckin' old you could never find parts. And there's a chick…"

"A young woman," I corrected.

"She looks fine," he said.

"She's your wife, or someone like her is."

"No way."

"Way. But only if you kill for her. Only if you kill this stupid, pointless life you've begun and start another. So here's the lecture you've already heard a thousand times. Listen. You'll do your time in a juvenile facility even though technically you'll age out of it long before your sentence is up. With luck they'll keep you to avoid the paperwork involved in transferring you to an adult prison. It will be hard and it will be boring, but every weapon you need will be there – literacy classes, the GED, vocational programs. These are your knives, your guns, your fists. You can fight, or you can die inside until your real death won't even matter to you. It's your choice."

He flipped the book shut. "This is just shit," he said, then flipped it open again, front and back. "Hey! It's empty, it's blank. There's nothin' there!"

"You'll write it now," I said. "You'll write the story."

I stood, shaky from the effort, and signaled to the sergeant outside the door.

The boy named Kevin watched me, biting a furry lip. "You're a witch, right?" he whispered.

"Something like that," I replied, and left.

Chapter Twenty-Two

Suspicious Minds

Elvis Presley

Our farewell brunch was nearly over by the time I left the police station and got to Hallett's, and the group was at that awkward stage where there's nothing left to say. Even Sadie was glancing out the door as if she'd called a cab. We all had each other's contact information and promised to stay in touch. Hallett and Harry would provide regular, coded emails. In emergencies or in the event that we needed to speak to headquarters we were instructed to call using phone cards Harry gave us, a particular number with a Slovenia prefix that would be routed to Boston. Harry said we could just buy disposable cell phones and minute cards, disposing of them after one use.

François, Marlow and Anne would share a cab to Logan even though their flights were hours apart. Marlow wanted to shop for Red Sox sweatshirts for his grandkids and Anne said she just wanted to sit and read a novel amid swarms of strangers for a couple of hours before her flight. I suspected that we all looked forward to at least the illusion of a return to normalcy. Nothing feels less "normal" than an airport, yet the churning of ceaseless, anonymous transition in places where no one actually *is* can be comforting. And the safest places in the world for Revenants. It's impossible to be alone in an airport.

I hugged them all goodbye and then felt bereft, standing in Hallett's hallway with Sadie.

"You may not be quite ready to face things alone," Hallett said. "I'll be happy to stay with you tonight..."

"No, thank you though, but I'm fine," I told her. "Really. I can fight if I have to. I think the truth is that just getting pissed off, the mere willingness to fight is enough anyway. We *intend* to fight back, are determined to go after the thing. It's not physical strength that matters, but another kind."

"So it would seem," Hallett agreed. "And please, the apartment is yours for as long as you'd like. You said you'd be doing some research before you leave. I hope you'll let me know if there's any way I can help."

I hadn't discussed Pen's dollhouse with any of the group; to do so would have felt like a violation of her privacy even though it was a privacy she didn't know she had. But it felt okay to tell Hallett.

"My friend received a dollhouse in the mail," I began. "She knew nothing about it; it was just sent. And there's something terrible inside it, like a play running over and over - tiny dolls, blood on a floor. Of course nobody but I can see the dolls moving, or the blood. She intends to give it to her five-year-old granddaughter who writes poetry and is terrified of ceramic cookie jars."

Hallett Gardner nodded. "I see," she said. "But what does this dollhouse have to do with your research in Boston?"

"It's a replica of a Beacon Hill row house that was gutted by fire when my friend was three months old. Her father died in the fire. A historical society apparently owned the replica, could no longer store it and sent it to my friend."

"What historical society?"

"I don't know. The letter was signed 'George A. Hibbard,' and he just said "The Historical Society."

Hallett smiled. "George Albee Hibbard was a little-known

mayor of Boston for two years in the very early 1900's, Taylor. Some believe his is the ghost that haunts the old Majestic Theater. It's part of Emerson College now, restored to its *fin-de-siècle* glory, but that seat is never sold. By custom it's always empty. The signature on that letter was a ghost's."

"But the dollhouse is real," I insisted. "It was really mailed to my friend. Who would...?"

"The White Road is made of countless stories," she replied thoughtfully. "Your gift is to see them, even make them real for a time. I'm guessing, but perhaps when you became a Revenant you became a conduit for this story."

"The White Road? Conduit? I don't know, Hallett. The dollhouse is no myth like Marlow's tale about the wolf, François' Tarasque, even the alligator lunging at Anne that night. This is real, solid, not an illusion; it's from a real place and a real time and it arrived in the real U.S. Mail. Maybe I'm just imagining things."

Hallett arched one silver eyebrow.

"That's what we do," she said. "And the figures we see aren't all reflections of ancient myths. It would seem that this dollhouse holds a story that involves your friend. It's not your story but hers, except that of course only you can see it. I don't think it can hurt you since it belongs to someone else. Its purpose is to hurt your friend and her granddaughter."

"I don't intend to let that happen," I said

She toyed with a thin silver bracelet at her wrist. "I am a benefactor of the library. I'll call and make arrangements for you to access whatever materials you may need. Otherwise you'd have to prove residence and get a card."

"But I don't live here."

"My point. Be careful with this, Taylor. And let's get together before you leave. I'd like to tell you about the painting over the fireplace upstairs, and there's something else as well."

"Goody Hallett," I said. "Your ancestor?"

"Yes. Dinner tomorrow then?"

"I look forward to it. Thank you, Hallett. For everything."

I walked Sadie, left her to nap at the apartment and then hiked through the Public Gardens and past Trinity and Old South Churches to the huge Boston Public Library on Boylston. The afternoon held that autumnal aura I associate with the beginning of the school year, with books to read and a richness of cold nights ahead in which to read them. Boston's appeal to some inner Taylor was heady, and I wondered if there were such a thing as geographical infidelity. After all, I had family, friends, a house and a life three thousand miles away on a different ocean. Yet I'd fallen in love with a city whose charm seemed to have been waiting four hundred years, just for me. I'd never had an affair but thought it must have felt like this for my ex, Charlie, with the woman who'd replaced me - a delicious realization that your options aren't as limited as you thought they were. The understanding didn't stretch very far. I still resented his betrayal, when I thought about it.

At the library's main desk I introduced myself and found that Hallett had indeed made arrangements to facilitate my research. A library science intern was assigned to help me, and in minutes she located the same newspaper article Pen's mother had lovingly framed. There was infant Pen in July of 1945, in the arms of her mother, Beverly Warren, beamed upon by her handsome father, Garrett Warren. Mother and daughter, the article said, had just returned from England where Mrs. Warren had gone to the aid of her bereaved sister, a recent war widow. The baby, Penley Aurelia Warren, would be baptized the following Sunday at the Episcopal Church of the Advent on Brimmer Street on Beacon Hill. I hadn't been aware that Pen's middle name was Aurelia, but beyond that the article told me nothing of significance.

The intern clicked efficiently on a computer keyboard and brought up a single article about the fire that destroyed Pen's home and killed her father in late September of the same year, only three months after her mother's return from England.

"Fortunately," the reporter wrote in the style of the time, "Mrs. Warren had taken the couple's baby daughter to a doctor for shots when the cruel conflagration flamed up the home's wooden stairs, trapping Mr. Warren in a bedroom where he'd been resting. The family housekeeper, Margaret Godare of Chelsea, had taken a day off and so escaped possible death. Funeral rites for Garrett Warren will be held at the Church of the Advent with burial at Mount Auburn Cemetery."

There had been four dolls in Pen's dollhouse, three women and a man. Yet there were only two women in the Warren household then, according to newspaper coverage of the fire. I told myself the dolls had been placed in the house by a stranger, some long-dead Boston miniaturist, and were irrelevant. Then I wondered who the third woman was.

"Look at this!" the intern said, pointing to a list of many newspaper articles in which the name 'Margaret Godare' appeared.

I settled in to read and soon discovered that the Warren housekeeper had, in 1946, a year after the fire, founded a cosmetics company called "Lady Godare." Cosmetic production had ceased during the war and the market was eager. At first specializing in face creams, powders, lipsticks and rouge, the firm later expanded to offer shampoos and hair coloring, followed by diet products and plus-size clothing. Margaret Godare had made a fortune and received several awards from Boston area women's organizations honoring her contributions to orphanages and other children's programs. The company was purchased for an undisclosed sum by a giant corporation in 1989, and the "Lady Godare" name was retired.

There was no death notice for Margaret Godare, who according to the birth date mentioned in several of the articles, would now be ninety-seven if still alive. I thought it unlikely and assumed she'd retired to a warmer climate and died there. I also wondered how a housekeeper managed the large financial outlay necessary to start and build a business.

One of my students had written yet another tedious term

paper focused on his dream of selling a flexible seatpost clamp for racing bicycles. The paper was torturously boring, but well-researched, and I recalled that his estimate for production, marketing and distribution of this single item involved an initial investment of a hundred thousand dollars over a two-year period. Even prorating backward to account for inflation, wouldn't Margaret Godare have needed at least a fourth that amount to launch a multi-item business? Where did she get twenty-five thousand dollars, or even ten thousand?

The train of thought was interesting, but wasn't getting me anywhere near the story behind Pen's dollhouse. After reading miles of blurry newsprint from 1945, I had a headache and felt time-warped. My mother wore the shoulder-padded dresses I saw in the ads, and I felt drawn into my parents' world as if I were their contemporary instead of what I was at the time - an inchoate baby in a sundress who could never know the people they were then. Invading that lost world felt Disneyish, like a spy mission to a place where nothing can ever change. But those stories now frozen in newsprint had set in motion events that would form a future in which I now sat nursing a headache in a library. And in which Pen's little granddaughter might be hurt, although I still didn't know why.

After thanking the intern for her help I walked back, noticing that Brimmer Street was a block off Charles and on my path. The Church of the Advent, which I hadn't noticed before, was right there. Pen had been christened in this church, and less than three months later her father's casket had been carried through the arched wooden doors opening onto a brick sidewalk before me. Going inside, I was impressed by the Byzantine splendor of the place. Even empty and silent, it murmured odes to the power of ritual no matter what one does or doesn't believe. I didn't hear the footsteps behind me.

"I was about to lock up," said a smiling, white-haired man in a long black cassock with covered buttons all the way down the front. At his feet was a black and white cat that seemed part of the costume. "That's Jake. Could I help you with something? I'm Father Conroy by the way."

"Taylor Blake, visiting from San Diego," I said, shaking his proffered hand. "I'm just, um looking around. The church is gorgeous."

Father Conroy continued to smile and said nothing, his look that of one who, after years of experience, merely waits for the bullshit to end.

"It's a long story," I said.

"How fortunate that I have a few minutes before bell practice. Would you like to tell me?"

"Bell practice? I thought church bells were all programmed by computers."

His grin stopped just short of overt pride.

"Not here. Of course the band practices with a computer program and loose ropes to avoid driving all of Beacon Hill crazy with the racket, but you must hear our change ringing some time. Old English tradition, absolutely amazing. Now, what 'long story' has brought you here?"

"You don't happen to know another Anglican priest in San Diego, Father Tim O'Halloran, do you?" I asked, imagining for a second that Tim and the man were lifelong friends from seminary and Tim would have confided in him about being a Revenant, which would mean that I could.

"Don't think so," Father Conroy answered.

So I patched together a story about doing some lightweight genealogical research for a friend whose family had been connected to the church.

"The Warrens, 1945? I'm afraid that was before even my time, not that there won't be records. Perhaps you could return tomorrow and I'll have someone help you peruse them."

"The Warrens lived nearby and there was a fire in which the father died," I rambled. "My friend was a baby. She and her mother and the housekeeper, a woman named Margaret Godare, were out when it happened."

I don't know why I mentioned Godare, I was just rehashing the story, but the priest's eyebrows arched above his glasses.

"Margaret Godare? She's, well, I can only say that our church has been blessed by her interest over the years. She's quite supportive of our school, and the children's choir and... many facets of our ministry here."

"It can't be the same Margaret Godare," I said. "She'd be ninety-seven now. I'm sure she's, um, no longer with us."

"If you mean Margaret Godare of Lady Godare, Incorporated, she definitely is," he said. "Still sharp as a pin, too, although quite frail and no longer able to get around. I'm afraid... that is to say she's *very* frail, receiving hospice care now. Her death will end a long and warm friendship with this church."

"Do you mean you know her?" I asked, feeling like a spy again.

He looked at his watch.

"I do. In fact I saw her only last week at her place in Newton. If you give me your name and number I'll check to see if she'd enjoy a visit and then call you. You could ask her about the Warren family then, if she's up to talking."

Right. I'll just tell her all about tiny dolls who bleed on tiny floors. Still...

"Thank you so much, Father Conroy," I agreed and gave him my cell number. "I might have time to see her tomorrow. Is there a postcard of the church? I'd love to buy one for my friend so she can see where she was christened."

"Thousands," he said jovially, steering me to a heavy armoire near the doors. "Here, take one of the reredos and one of the altar decorated for Christmas. And here's one of the baptismal font, that's perfect, and hey, here's me in full regalia blessing the animals. That's always a fun Sunday, let me tell you. Once we actually had a pygmy hedgehog *and* a pair of Speckled Sussex chickens!"

I decided that if I ever really lived in Boston I'd go to this church, at least for the change-ringing and the chickens.

"I'd like to pay for the postcards," I began, but was dismissed by the wave of a priestly hand.

"Please give our best wishes to your friend," he said as he ushered me out the door. "Tell her she will be remembered in our prayers."

"Can't hurt," I said to the closed doors, and hiked up Beacon Hill.

It was getting dark by the time Sadie and I returned from a long walk, and I forced myself to walk by Pen's former home on Pinckney Street. I hadn't walked by it earlier and didn't want to then, fearing whatever ghosts might show themselves to my peculiar Revenant mind. But there were no ghosts. There was just a young guy in a business suit going in, and then the same guy in sweats with a young woman and a baby in a jogging stroller coming out a few minutes later.

"Pretty soon it'll be too cold to run along the river," she said.

"November," he answered. "It'll be okay until November unless it snows."

It was their house now, and they had nothing to do with its replica in my garage on the far side of the continent. As they jogged away I looked upward to the fourth floor and saw nothing but darkness reflected in black glass.

I'd grabbed a small pizza at a takeout place and heated it in the apartment oven while staring at the Boston area Yellow Pages on my laptop, determined to find Margaret Godare whether Father Conroy called or not. Then I wolfed down a doughy triangle of dripping, oregano-scented cheese while staring at a list of senior care facilities with addresses in the various villages that form the western suburb of Boston called Newton – Newton Centre, Newton Highlands, Newton Upper Falls and Lower Falls, Newton Corner,

West Newton, and Newtonville and six others. But no actual Newton.

There were seven senior facilities, five of which provided twenty-four-hour skilled nursing care. Then I eased another piece of pizza loose, acknowledging that a ninety-seven-year-old woman, even a wealthy one now receiving hospice care, would probably not live alone but in such a facility. Father Conroy said he'd seen Margaret Godare last week at "her place" in Newton. I was betting that place was one of the five names in front of me, residences providing skilled nursing care. By the third slab of pizza I knew I'd do it, not that I expected it to work. Even if Margaret Godare were able and willing to talk to a stranger, I was pretty sure she wouldn't be willing to tell me why dolls moved and bled and died in a dollhouse. Especially if she knew why.

When my cell rang I flipped it open with a greasy hand.

"Mrs. Blake? It's Jim Conroy from Advent. I called to check and Margaret would be happy to see you tomorrow if you have time."

He gave me the phone number and address for a facility called Newton Oaks, and explained how to get there on public transportation. The iniquity inherent in being less than forthcoming with a nice-guy priest made my hand shake as I wrote down the information, but didn't stop me.

"I appreciate your help," I said, wondering if I sounded like a spy.

Sated with pizza, I checked my email. Miyoko gave a glowing report of the work on my house and sent pictures of the finished kitchen. I loved it. Beth wrote that TJ seemed moodier than usual and attributed it to his missing his "Nanna," a grandmotherly endearment TJ has never, not once, used to address me. I assumed my daughter had been watching a DVD of "Peter Pan" with Hannah and fixated on the dog's name as a generic for kindliness or something. Tim sent greetings and said he'd pick me up at the airport so I could tell him all the news on the ride home. An additional email from Miyoko quoted a report from the senior

Delgado, stating that there had been no further intrusions on my property, and that a police canvass of the neighborhood had identified no similar break-ins. Delgado said that was unusual, as thieves commonly "worked" several neighboring houses. He concluded that my property was the sole interest of the intruder for unknown reasons, and recommended that I get an alarm system. Miyoko attached prices for several systems and said we could talk about it when I got home, adding that another client had given her an old Adirondack chair she thought would be perfect for my yard.

I was thrilled about the Adirondack chair, but didn't want an alarm system, knowing I'd routinely forget the code and be locked out of my own house. And the intruder seemed to have no interest in me, only in finding something that wasn't there. The interest was determined and made no sense. I wished he or she would just knock on the door and say, "Hey, I absolutely have to have that box of chickpea candy Kevin and Suzanna sent you from Egypt four years ago," and I'd just hand it over.

Meanwhile, I had to plan what I'd say to Margaret Godare.

Chapter Twenty-Three

The Old Lamplighter

Bing Crosby

The next morning I called Margaret Godare's residence, and panicked when I was quickly transferred to the nurse in charge of her area in the facility called Newton Oaks.

What could I say? "My name is Taylor Blake, I'm from San Diego and I'd like to chat with a dying woman about a malevolent dollhouse?" Still, in my limited experience with artifice, I've noticed that a partial truth is invariably more effective that a total lie. "I'm a friend of a woman whose mother knew Margaret long ago," I said. "Father Conroy has called and confirmed that it might be possible for me to visit her."

"She'd enjoy that," the nurse said. "I'm afraid all her friends have passed away and there's no family, so there aren't any visitors except Father Conroy, who comes every week. She's in hospice, you know. When would you like to visit?"

"I'm afraid I'm leaving tomorrow. Would this morning be all right?"

I was welcome to show up immediately, but then remembered Sadie. I had no idea how long this would take and couldn't leave her alone in the apartment indefinitely.

"My dog is with me," I began. "And I'm not driving but will take public transportation to Newton, so I can't leave her in a car. Would it be all right...?"

"No problem as long as she has her shots and is friendly with very sick old people," the nurse said. "We have therapy dogs in here several times a week and our guests just love it! What's your dog's name?"

"Sadie."

"Cute," the nurse said, ending any possibility that I might share the popular notion that Bostonians are rude and uptight. Everyone with whom I had any contact at all in Boston showed nothing but willingness to help and an easygoing tolerance for eccentricity.

Despite that, I dashed to Downtown Crossing one last time and bought a black knit beret to cover my Frankenstein stitches, which I was pretty sure looked more gross than eccentric. Then I loaded Sadie into her wheeled carrier and caught the green line T, as Boston subways (that also run above ground so aren't always "subway") are called, at Park Street Station. The oldest subway in America, Park Street's nineteenth century tunnels are spookily lit and festooned with curtains of grime. I felt as if I were being carried backward in time again, a pleasant sensation until I realized that I needed to tread carefully. Margaret Godare was the last living person who might explain why a doll bled and died endlessly in an exquisite dollhouse now shrouded in my garage. And yet how would I ever be able to frame the question?

After our stop, I took Sadie out of her carrier and we walked the twelve tree-lined blocks I'd mapped to the Newton Oaks Residential Facility. Its carpeted lobby bordered on elegant, but was empty. Clustered around gleaming coffee tables were conversational groupings of Queen Anne chairs upholstered in striped silk, looking as if no one ever sat in them. The lobby was a front, a staged oasis between the world outside and an interior world drifting and jittery at the vestibule of death. Sadie sniffed the air and looked at me with concern.

"It's okay," I said. "Do you think you can handle it?"

She moved closer to my leg and shook athletically, sending white dog hairs to fall through quiet sunlight on thick maroon carpet.

"I'll take that as a yes," I said, and tugged her toward a distressed cherry concierge desk in an alcove.

"I'm here to see Margaret Godare," I told a smiling young woman in a pale blue business suit, who gave me a stick-on name tag and pointed to an elevator. I had no idea what I was doing.

"Hello, Mrs. Godare," I said minutes later to an emaciated woman wearing pink fleece pajamas printed in floating teacups. I could see every bone, every vein in her spotted hands beneath a fragile drapery of skin, and her face was an animated skull despite skillfully applied makeup.

"It's Ms.," she answered in a brisk, if barely audible voice. "I never married. Well, I guess you could say I was married to my business. Lady Godare. Loved every minute of it, no regrets. Well, I really wanted to become a pharmacist, always loved mixing up chemicals, but they didn't allow women in those days, so I went into cosmetics instead. Same thing, in a lot of ways. I understand you know somebody whose mother I knew?"

With exquisite timing, Sadie chose that moment to stand with her forepaws against the bed, wagging her tail at Margaret Godare. I looked to the nurse's aide sitting in a chair near the window, who nodded and smiled.

"You can hold the puppy up so Miz Godare can see it, give it a pet. Our folks do enjoy a dog to pet."

So amid holding Sadie to be petted by a skeletal hand and murmuring doggy inanities, I said, "Yes, my friend Pen Barrows' mother."

Godare continued to talk to Sadie, mentioning to me that she was afraid she didn't know anyone named Barrows.

"Of course, I'm sorry, that's Pen's married name," I said. "Her mother was Beverly Warren."

The carpal bones hesitated in their brittle tracing of Sadie's fur, only for a breath. Then the milky eyes looked straight at me as if I'd threatened her. For a second I imagined a knife-flash of animosity in those eyes, as if Margaret Godare would kill me if she could. Then I told myself ninety-seven-year-old people lack the strength required for sudden, weaponless murder.

"And Beverly Warren's daughter - I do remember that her name was Penley - sent you to see me?" she said, her voice so neutral it sounded like a recording. The one that says, "Please hold for the next available representative."

"Oh, no." I shrugged, holding honesty between myself and the bed like an invisible shield. "Pen's never mentioned you. I stumbled over a number of articles about you while doing some research at the library, and then I went by the Church of the Advent to get a postcard for Pen since she was christened there, and when I mentioned your name from one of the newspaper articles to the priest..."

"Father Conroy. He called about your visit."

She seemed okay with that, and attempted a smile, but it wasn't the truth. I was clinging to the truth as if it led somewhere.

"He was so helpful. I wasn't sure I'd have time, but then this morning I realized I would..."

"Well, how nice that you and Sadie have come," she said, then leaned to sip water through a straw from a glass on a tray table at her shoulder. "Beverly Warren gave me my start, you know."

I was reaching to hold the glass for her, but she scowled beneath sparse, wiry white hair and I withdrew my hand.

"I've always taken care of myself," she explained. "Plan to keep it up until I die, which will be any minute now from what they keep telling me. Last time I saw Penley Warren she was a tiny baby; she'd be in her sixties by now. How is she?"

The old woman visibly relaxed as I rambled on about Pen's husband and family, the Spanish Colonial house in La Jolla, our long friendship. Casually, I said, "Pen's mother gave you your start? Pen would love to hear about that, I'll bet."

I haven't said "I'll bet" since leaving the heartland, but it seemed appropriate.

"You know about the fire, of course."

"Pen told us about it," I said, teetering at the edge of mentioning the dollhouse. This would be the moment. "She said her father died in the fire," I finished, shrinking back, the moment gone.

"Terrible thing," Margaret Godare replied as if defining some long-ago, impersonal event, like the Donner Expedition. "I was the Warren's housekeeper. Terrible, really. But Garrett Warren was in insurance, had a lot of it himself. Mrs. Warren, she loaned me the money to start Lady Godare out of the insurance."

Like mine, her syntax seemed to be regressing. A housekeeper might say, "Mrs. Warren, she…," but not the executive owner of a successful corporation. She was tiring and I still had no idea who the third woman was, the third doll, bleeding on a little bed.

"It must have been quite a job," I pushed on, "trying to manage a household during the war with rationing and all, and then a baby when things were still in such turmoil."

"Three people to feed, plus my dinners on days I worked, usually four days a week, eight to five," she mused, transparent eyelids fluttering. "I had to run all over Boston for meat, when I could get it. Rationing, you know."

"Mrs. Warren's mother must have come, to be there for the birth," I said even though 'the birth' supposedly happened in England. "So there were three people to feed."

"No, it was that maid, Bridget Flannagan, ate like a horse. I always said those Irish…"

She had fallen asleep. I gave my phone number and email address to the nurse's aide and asked if there were anything Margaret Godare needed.

"She need to die," the aide said softly. "Some of 'em hang on way past time. Maybe you comin' here, talkin' about the past, maybe it help her. I think it did."

I felt the need of a black cowl and a scythe.

"Thank you so much for your wonderful care," I said. "I know Pen will be glad to hear that her mother's friend is in good hands."

At an ice cream shop near the T I sat at a wrought-iron table on the sidewalk and savored a scoop of coffee ice cream, letting Sadie lick the cup.

"Barring sudden death in a plane crash or something like that, the last days of life are inescapably grim," I told her. "It's just the way it is. So I think the thing to do is enjoy every minute up to that point, don't you? And then just soldier through it."

She was pushing the empty ice cream cup around on the ground with her nose and didn't respond.

"Of course the Revenant thing complicates matters. I mean, it's *work*, dealing with stuff nobody else can see, fighting a ghoul, saving the world, if Harry's right."

She'd abandoned the cup, so I picked it up and threw it in a green trash container. It occurred to me that with the exception of the ghoul, what I was describing as "work" was a lot more fun than being confined inside a high school all day. I had mannequin shoppers, interesting new friends and a purpose at once more nebulous and more urgent than anything I'd ever done. Years lay between me and a bed like the one Margaret Godare inhabited so tenuously. There would be that bed; I was beyond the time in which it lies hidden, unthinkable. But before I slipped between those transitional sheets, I was going to enjoy a life of more intensity and meaning than anything I'd known before.

"Let's rock and roll," I told Sadie, loading her into her carrier for the T.

At home I heated the rest of the pizza for lunch while surfing the White Pages for Flannagans. There had been a maid in Pen's first home, named Bridget Flannagan. And hundreds of kinsmen still around, apparently, filling column after column of phone book text. I called an Aidan and got an answering machine playing Neil Diamond's "Sweet Caroline," two Alans who weren't home and an Ambrose who said Bridget was his little sister but she lived in Schenectady. Then I got an Amy who was happy to chat, but told me I was wasting my time since at least half of Southie has a relative somewhere named Bridget who's probably related to somebody named Flannagan.

"What's Southie?" I asked.

There was silence, then, "It's a *place*, like, to live, y'know? It's paht a Bahstahn."

I loved the accent and vaguely remembered something about Irish immigrants. Of course Bridget Flannagan would have been Irish.

"Sorry, I'm from California," I said.

"Wow, you evah see Brad Pitt?"

"Um, no. Do you have any idea how I might find any relatives of this Bridget Flannagan? She was a maid, during WWII."

"Her an' ever' other Irish girl back then. Back to the Hungah, y'know?"

"The Hungah?"

Amy Flannagan was growing impatient with my ignorance.

"Like, they was all *starvin'* and come here?"

"Hunger. The potato famine," I said, getting it. "But that was in the eighteen hundreds. This Bridget Flannagan lived here just sixty years ago."

"Y'know, I got a cousin, her husband, that's Jackie Rourke, his mother's in a club. They make, like, chahts of families goin' way back. Whyn'cha call her?"

I thanked Amy Flannagan profusely, then dialed Kate Rourke, mother of Jackie.

"Oh, Lord," she said after I explained that I was trying to find a woman who'd been a maid in the Warren home on Beacon Hill during WWII. "It's Evvie Doyle you'll be wantin' to talk to. Years now on Halloween Evvie's been tellin' a story 'bout her husband's aunt, who wore that name, you see – Bridget Flannagan."

"Is Bridget still alive?" I asked.

"Oh no, not alive," Kate Rourke said. "That's the story!"

I called and made an appointment to visit Evvie Doyle, who was eager to talk.

"I knew this day would come," she said.

"But this may not be the same person," I cautioned. "It's a common name."

"You just come on by," she urged. "Let me tell you what happened."

I fed and walked Sadie and grabbed a cab to Southie, Boston's Irish enclave. Evvie Doyle's house was half a brick-faced duplex with matching bow-front windows overlooking a street called Rogers. Gray paint had peeled from the cement steps revealing old-world maps of black underneath, but the lace curtains at the windows were blinding white. I pushed the bell and stood staring at a wreath of lavender silk flowers on the security door.

Evvie Doyle was about my age with buttery white hair she wore in a ponytail, big, red-framed glasses and a faded blue sweatshirt advertising "St. Brigid's Centennial -200 Years!"

"Sorry I didn't have time to change clothes, but I guessed you'd rather have some of these brownies I just made," she said, ushering me into a kitchen redolent of chocolate.

I sniffed appreciatively. "These brownies are not from a mix, I take it?"

"You take it right," she answered, laughing. "Belgian chocolate I order from San Francisco. Guittard, it's called, wicked expensive. But there's those around here who'd kill for a pan of Evvie Doyle's brownies, now wouldn't they?"

We were sitting at a table beside a wall of lace-covered windows overlooking a wooden deck and an alley. On the deck door was a shamrock made of green silk flowers. Evvie's coffee was rich, the brownies five-star and I didn't want to wreck the moment with talk of bleeding dolls.

"So you want to know about Bridget Flannagan, then?" she began. "Go on, eat your brownie now and I'll tell you. Murdered, she was. That's what Dan's ma, Bridget's sister, always said. Dan, that was my husband, God rest his soul, though he always told his ma to stop talking about it. Said it was history and probably just a tale anyway, better to let sleeping dogs lie."

"So your husband's aunt was named Bridget Flannagan and she was murdered?" I said, momentarily distracted by my brownie.

"And the child, too. Dan's ma Katie Doyle always said it was Garrett Warren that got Bridget pregnant and killed her when the baby was born. Killed the baby, too, so his wife wouldn't find out. Katie said Bridget told her Mr. Warren came to her room at night, over and over. Bridget said he was the one that got her in the family way."

"Oh dear," I said, thinking Pen would be heartbroken by this story.

"She wasn't home, the wife, when Bridget's time came," Evvie Doyle continued. "Expecting too, she was, and off to England with relatives, they say. Bridget lived in, had her own room up there on the Hill with the Warrens, but Katie would go see her sometimes until near the end, and Katie knew Bridget was pregnant but didn't tell the family."

"So what happened?" I asked in a cheery, chocolate-scented kitchen that seemed all wrong for the story I was hearing.

Evvie nodded and spoke more slowly. "Mr. Warren, he made Bridget stay inside the last three months, when she was showin' so bad, wouldn't let Katie see her neither. All alone was poor Bridget when her time came, y'see. Nobody to say if the babe was boy or girl, alive or dead when it was born, God have mercy on that little soul!"

I looked somberly into the table, then said, "If nobody was there, how do you know...?"

Evvie raised her eyebrows and tapped the remaining brownies with the flat of a knife. "Katie knew," she said. "She was there when Garrett Warren brought Bridget to the family one night late, all wrapped in blankets. Stone dead and stiff as a board was Bridget, blood all down her legs tellin' what happened, tellin' her shame. Said he brought her so they could bury her. But there was no baby."

"But surely somebody investigated," I said.

"No," Evvie replied. "They buried Bridget to hide her shame, put it out that she died of the Button Scurvy. 'Disposed of the baby like a dead cat, did Garret Warren,' is what Katie always said. And then my Dan would say, 'The man's dead, ma. Died right after Bridget, in a fire. Whatever happened, it's in God's hands, so let go of it with yours.' Men take these things easier, don't they?"

The story was ugly but not unusual. Pen's father would not be the first man in history to father a child with a servant girl, assuming that part of Kate Flannagan Doyle's story, here recounted by her daughter-in-law more than a half-century later, was even true. And I thought it probably was, remembering a doll bleeding and dying on a bed while another doll, a man in a plaid suit, merely watched. The doll on the bed was Bridget, hemorrhaging after the stillbirth of an illegitimate child. But had Garrett Warren just stood there until Bridget died, her blood pooling at his feet? I couldn't believe that of Pen's father. I couldn't believe that of anybody. Yet.

"So you're writing a book about people who used to live on the Hill, are you?" Evvie said, pouring more coffee. "Well now you've got a doozy of a story, don't you?"

I'd said something about researching little-known Beacon Hill history, especially stories of servants and tradespeople who're forgotten, as an excuse for interviewing Evvie Doyle. Now I wished I'd stayed home, except that wouldn't have solved the mystery of the dollhouse.

"Not a book, just some research," I hedged. "I'm just beginning, lots of work before…"

"Well, I'll show you some pictures anyway," Evvie interrupted, dashing upstairs and then back with an old photo album. She opened it on the table in front of me. "This was Bridget."

"Oh my God!" I said before I could stop myself. The black and white snapshots were of a coltish teenager whose eyes I recognized, whose mouth was only too familiar, whose hairline I saw every week, across a table from me at the Lotus Café. The photograph was Pen.

"What's wrong?" Evvie Doyle said.

"It's just that she was so attractive," I gulped. "What a terrible thing… her death… that way."

"Can't see it in the pictures, but Bridget and Katie both had the red hair, bright as new pennies, the both of 'em. But you're going to hear a lot of sad stories, what with your research, aren't you? Better not take it all to heart. They're all dead and gone. That's what my Dan would say, now wouldn't he? But here, take a look at this before you go."

She crossed the kitchen to reach into a cabinet over the sink, and pulled something down. When she set it on the table beside the brownie pan I could see that it was a wide ceramic clown, his bulbous, cream-colored sides a maze of lines where the glaze had cracked. The paint had worn off the big buttons down his front, but I could see from the remaining chips that they'd been red, green, purple, orange. The face paint had worn away as well, but the molded lips were smiling, and the pointed hat still bore chips of bright red. A toy meant to delight a child in another time.

"It's a..." I began, but Evvie Doyle finished the sentence for me.

"Cookie jar," she said. "Bridget bought it for her hope chest. Girls used to have those back then, didn't they? Pretty things for their homes when they got married? After Bridget died Katie kept it for her kids, and when Dan and I had our first, she gave it to me. All my kids loved it. Strange old thing, i'n'it?"

"How old was Bridget when she died?" I asked, my head swirling with images I didn't want to see.

"Oh, she'd have been about seventeen, wouldn't she? No more than eighteen. I guess you need that for your research?"

"I do," I said, standing. "Thank you so much, Evvie. I appreciate your sharing this story, and your brownies are out of this world!"

"You'll send a copy of your book, if it turns into a book, won't you? You've got the address."

"Of course," I said, thinking something more than a book might turn up on those peeling steps if I told Pen the story. Gentle, gracious Pen, whose mother was not Beverly Warren, but Bridget Flannagan. Pen, whose five-year-old granddaughter was terrified of ceramic cookie jars.

I walked to the Andrew's Square T Station, trying to make sense of the story. Pen was the baby Bridget's sister thought Garrett Warren had disposed of "like a dead cat." Except baby Pen had not died and was at that very moment, I thought, probably on her patio in gardener's gloves, happily trimming her bougainvillea. Pen believed she was born in England and that her American birth certificate had been "arranged" by her father when she and her mother returned from a trip they'd never taken. And Beverly Warren had raised Pen as her own, carefully teaching the little girl a story as pretty and as staged as the empty lobby of Margaret Godare's final home. I had a sickening suspicion about why Beverly

Warren had been willing to underwrite her housekeeper's business venture. And a worse suspicion about that fire.

When I got home I turned on the classical station for its calming effect, although it was Beethoven's Fifth Symphony, which isn't particularly calming, and then called the Newton Oaks Residential Facility. Sadie had apparently dragged something out of the trash and left it somewhere, because the apartment had a dank, fruity smell. I'd deal with it later. Right then I was going to ask Margaret Godare some hard questions, even if it killed her.

"I'm so sorry," a polished voice murmured over the music as my eyes watered from the sharp smell of autumn fruit, "but Ms. Godare passed away earlier this afternoon. Her aide was with her and said she went to sleep after a lovely visit from someone connected to her past. She died quietly without waking. Could I help you with anything regarding Ms. Godare? The priest has been here and will arrange the cremation. She asked that there be no service."

"No, thank you so much," I said, and snapped the phone shut, suddenly aware that the scent assailing me had nothing to do with an overturned kitchen wastebasket. It was the heady odor of persimmons!

In a corner of the apartment between the left-side window and the stairwell railing, something was chuckling. I heard it before it materialized, a seamed, bulbous shape like garlic, only shiny, cream-colored and swelling like a giant balloon. On its front were four bright circles, buttons in red, green, purple and orange, and above its slick, laughing face was a pointed red hat. Emptiness swirled in the colorless ceramic eyes. The footless thing was rolling toward me, its chuckle now the sound of planets laughing at the pathetic idiocy of hairless little monkeys who think their antics matter at all.

For a moment I was paralyzed with fear, sickened by the thing. I wanted to run and stumbled against the banister surrounding the steep stairway. The building was old, the ceilings eleven feet high. An eleven-foot fall over that banister would almost certainly break my neck, and a grotesquely obese ceramic clown was pushing,

pushing.

"Oh, but we do matter!" I yelled, grabbing for the music and feeling Beethoven's rage at his blindness grind inside my hands. "We matter to *us*, and nothing you can do will change that, you pathetic wad of cosmic sewage!"

I dived at it, Molly Palmer's practiced drills seaming to the music. I punched, kicked and punched again, my fists and feet sliding through brittle china that dissolved to slimy clay that pulled back, and back further. It was retreating, melting into the pottery slip from which it was made. I couldn't grasp it and felt my teeth snapping together like a dog's. I wanted to *chew* it, I realized. Chew it and spit it out. But it was gone, leaving only a terra-cotta discoloration under my nails and an echo in the darkening corner. The echo of a cookie jar, laughing.

Chapter Twenty-Four

The Answer Is Blowin' In the Wind

Peter, Paul and Mary

I was exhausted and still rattled when it was time to go to Hallett's for an early dinner, but I dressed carefully and walked down to a florist on Charles for a bouquet before arriving at her door. I knew Hallett as a friend and colleague in our strange new life, but she'd promised a discussion of her ancestor, Goody Hallett, whom I regard as an American icon. Royalty, in my view. Flowers were mandatory.

Hallett opened the door in a gray silk evening gown and pearls, explaining that Spalding was at a Red Sox practice and she planned to duck into a performance of "Don Giovanni" at intermission because she had to attend a later party given by a friend. "Tedious opera and I've seen it five times," she said. "And Taylor, how lovely! Let's head for the kitchen and a vase for these. You look a bit done in. Long day?" She stopped in the hall and looked at me over her shoulder. "Or shall I say you look as if you've seen a ghoul. Bad, was it?"

"No," I said. "I mean of course, it's always bad. I don't have to tell you it's like evil turned inside-out, Hallett. Like kicking over a rock and seeing something that isn't supposed to exist. Something meant to drain life into a sewer that goes nowhere. I swear I'll kill the damn thing one day!"

I pulled off my knit beret and stuffed it in my purse. The air felt cool against my stitches as I watched her arrange pale green roses and lotus pods in a white pitcher. I wasn't going to tell Hallett about Pen's real mother, the clown cookie jar, anything. The story felt like a long-buried bomb fallen into my hands, but it wasn't my story to tell. It belonged to Pen. And even though I hadn't pieced it together completely, I was afraid the ugly facts it contained would destroy her.

Hallett turned the pitcher to catch the glow of an overhead light. "These are exquisite. Thank you, Taylor. I thought we'd just have a bit of wine and some salad and quiche while I tell you about Goody."

"I'm eager to hear," I said, but she looked thoughtful.

"You won't kill the ghoul," she said as she donned oven mitts to pull a quiche from the oven. "Our task is to fight, but not to win. I was able to kill Philip's ghoul because it had already destroyed Philip. It would have died soon anyway; they die when we do. But as long as we live, our ghouls also live. Remember Marlow's story? When terrible forces restrained for millennia are unleashed, they cannot be conquered. In the old tales they always win, and whole civilizations vanish. The best we can hope for is a stand-off, but that will be enough."

I wanted to do better than "enough," but saw her point. Maggie McFadden had said the same thing.

Hallett said she was pleased that I'd recognized the strange red shoe painting over the fireplace in the third floor office, and wanted to explain her connection to the legendary Goody Hallett.

"The story was irrelevant to our work, so I didn't go into it when everyone was here, but since you seemed interested..."

"Very!" I agreed.

Over dinner she recounted various Cape Cod tales of this ancestor, a "witch" who supposedly made a pact with the devil, rode a whale and lured ships to their death with her lantern swinging from its tail.

"In reality her first name was Mary, Maria or Mariah," Hallett explained as Boston's sky grew dark and I leaned into the story. "'Goody' was just a title indicating a married woman. Men were called 'Goodman' so-and-so, and their wives were called 'Goodwife', shortened to 'Goody.'"

"But what about her love affair with the pirate Sam Bellamy, the illegitimate baby dead in her arms in a barn?" I asked. Another of my students, a bright young woman who went on to specialize in American folklore and was now the director of a crafts museum in North Carolina, had written her senior research paper on Goody Hallett. It's one of a handful I've kept.

Hallett grinned. "She may have had an affair with Bellamy, who knows? But if she did, the 'Goody' title suggests that she was already married to somebody else, most likely one of the Wampanoag Indians, so there's no record of the marriage. That would make sense, given the later story of her caring for the Wampanoag during the smallpox epidemic."

"And the red shoes?"

"I doubt that anyone had red shoes or red anything else in those days," Hallett lectured with enthusiasm, serving more spinach salad. "Red dye was painstakingly made from millions of dried insects shipped in secret from Mexico to Spain. Only European royalty could afford it, and the Puritans eschewed all bright colors. She might have concocted a temporary dye of beets or sumac berries just for the shock value, but whether she did or not, Goody's red shoes are code for 'witch.' She was different, Taylor. So different from her peers that they feared her and spun stories about her that endure to this day. There's a street in Eastham named Goody Hallet Drive, and a few years ago an osprey that hatched there was named for her and tagged with a GPS transmitter. Its last transmission was from a mountainous area of Brazil."

"Oh no!" I said, as crushed as a child at hearing that an osprey named Goody had died so far away.

"It may just be that the transmitter failed," Hallett said

hopefully. "But the real Mariah Hallett is probably my ancestor. Philip's as well. I can't be sure, but the name occurs consistently in both families, both with roots on the Cape. I find it difficult not to imagine a connection between her and this thing that Philip and I both became."

"I'm so sorry, Hallett," I said, "about Philip. Do you know how Goody died?"

"Only a date – 1751, and it may not be the right Goody Hallett anyway. But the spirit evident in all the countless stories about her suggests that she was something unusual, powerful. I think she was an embryonic Revenant, Taylor. I think there have been thousands over the ages, incomplete but frightening to their contemporaries. Let me show you something."

I hadn't noticed that Hallett wore an ankle bracelet until she took it off and laid it on the table beside my wine glass   A small oyster shell, rough and overlaid with the mysterious white alphabet left by marine worms, it was secured by gold wire to a slender gold band.

"From Martine," she said. "My amulet. I had a jeweler make it into an anklet. And a marine biologist confirmed my suspicion that it's a Wellfleet oyster shell, or at least the same species. Goody Hallett lived in Wellfleet, then called Billingsgate, and died there."

"The famous Billingsgate Sea Witch!"

"And the famous Wellfleet oysters!" she laughed, but I was remembering something.

"Didn't you say that Philip's amulet was a bit of driftwood?"

"Ah," she said. "Tim O'Halloran's assessment of your gift for linking stories was accurate, and I want to talk to you about that. I suspect that it may mean something. But yes, Philip's amulet was driftwood. Is that significant?"

"Maybe his bit of driftwood was from Sam Bellamy's sunken pirate ship," I said. "'Black Sam Bellamy,' Goody's pirate lover whose treasure-laden ship, the 'Whydah,' ran aground in a storm and sank on the shoals off Wellfleet in 1717, taking Sam down with it. Some versions of the story have Goody walking the dunes that night in the storm, waiting for him to return and take her away. They say she saw the ship break and sink in flashes of lightning. She saw her lover drown."

Hallett had leaned down to reattach the ankle bracelet with its oyster-shell amulet. When she rose again tears made her pale blue irises translucent.

"The parallelism does seem a little obvious, doesn't it?" she said softly. "Bits of that story in me and in Philip, repeating themselves."

"Bellamy's ship was hauled up from the ocean floor in 1984," I went on, thinking I was probably going too far and wishing I'd just shut up. "There's a museum in Provincetown... you could match Philip's amulet to wood from the ship..."

Hallett shook her head and smiled.

"I don't know what happened to Philip's amulet and it doesn't matter," she said. "It's gone and so is Philip. What matters to me is that Mariah Hallett lived for thirty-four years after Sam Bellamy's death. She risked her life to care for the same native people who rescued the first English settlers from starvation. As thanks they were treated like animals, quarantined and left to die when the smallpox virus brought by European invaders decimated their numbers. I commissioned the painting you saw upstairs six months after Philip's death. Goody's red shoes, the hallmark of her difference, are there to keep me on track. I have work to do. We all do. But there's something I need to discuss with you. What about your family tree, Taylor?"

I told her the story of Aislinn Taylor, my crazy maternal grandmother who in the minutes before her death warned me to hide inside life until something happened.

"And you'd never seen her before then?" Hallett asked.

"I didn't even know she *existed* before then. Apparently she'd lived... in an institution."

"And her husband, your grandfather?"

"Dead," I answered. "He died in a train crash long before I was born. At least that's what my parents told me."

"What 'institution' did your grandmother live in?" Hallett asked. "What was her diagnosis? And this grandfather, did you ever check up on the train crash in which he died?"

"It was, um, out west somewhere," I replied as a host of doors swung open inside my mind. "Hallett, I don't even know what his first name was. I'm not sure about any of it, never really cared. I just believed whatever I was told. But now that I look back, I wasn't really told much of anything, was I? Does it matter?"

"Your parents may have wanted to protect you from disturbing details of Aislinn's life, Taylor. Families tend to do that, to bury the frightening things. Sometimes it's best. But yes, it may matter. Your grandmother may be a telling factor."

She was watching me, both curiosity and assessment evident in her gaze.

"A telling factor in what?" I asked, feeling a shift in the conversation.

"In the role you are to play as a Revenant. It's possible that you are to be the Guide. That is why you were invited to come here, and I'm a bit embarrassed to admit that I did a bit of dabbling with the other requirements. I hope you won't think I'm a meddling incompetent."

"Hallett, I have no idea what you're talking about," I said. "What guide? What requirements? Meddling in what"

She smiled and folded her napkin, then sighed.

"We all walk the White Road now, a realm made of stories. Your particular gift is the understanding of stories, both their historical reality and their deeper meaning. This is your very *nature*, and so you may be the Guide. We know that the role is to be filled by someone who is 'the descendant of a dream." Do you know what 'Aislinn' means?"

"My grandmother's name? It's Gaelic, from *aisling*. And yes, it means 'dream,' but she was crazy, locked up for most of her life in a mental hospital."

"'Crazy' may be a kind of dream, Taylor. And what sort of hospital did you think I was talking about when I said I'd 'hospitalized' Philip? It's what we do with people who don't fit or can't survive in our reality, isn't it? But let me show you something else."

She stood and took a wrinkled origami dragon from a drawer in a sideboard. It was made of a child's wide-ruled notebook paper and I could see bits of crayoned words.

"Martine left this at my door nearly a year ago, about the time Harry and I began to organize things. It was very late, Spalding was asleep and I answered the door myself. She was halfway down the street by then, dressed as a chimney sweep. She tipped her top hat under one of the gaslights and then vanished, but I recognized her."

I stared at the origami dragon, remembering the little dragon on a vase at the Lotus when I had lunch with Jude. I'd dropped my fortune in the vase. The slip of paper that warned, "A new path appears. Beware."

"What does it say, the dragon?" I asked as she carefully unfolded it and lay it flat on the table.

"See for yourself."

The paper was brittle, like dried leaves, and smelled faintly of chrysanthemums. It twitched slightly beneath my fingers. "A guide will appear, the descendant of a dream," it said in a childish but elegant, crayoned script. "The guide will map stories, helped by a warrior and an antiquarian. Welcome the guide."

Hallett watched as I read the words, shaking my head. And

then the paper refolded itself on the table, again a dragon whose crisp wings rustled and stretched. It spread its wings against the table, trembled, rose and flew in arcs about my head. Then it climbed the shadows in a corner of the room and vanished.

"Well," Hallet said, wide-eyed, "I think that was clear. You're the guide!"

"That can't be," I said, still amazed and gaping. "I'm sorry, but I'm the last one to guide anybody. I really don't know what I'm doing, Hallett, and frankly I don't expect *ever* to know what I'm doing. I'm lost in all this. You and Harry – you're the guides. And I don't know any warriors or antiquarians."

She smiled again. "I'm afraid you *are* the Guide, Taylor. I'm the financial base and Harry's the communications expert, but neither of us possesses your facility with stories, a talent essential to the attainment of our goals. As to the warrior and the antiquarian, I admit to having tried to orchestrate that a bit."

She exuded chagrin. "François of course was here because he saw Frederic Langelin's mice perish under the power of the amulet. But I'm afraid I chose Marlow and Anne as your potential companions, trying to fulfill Martine's prediction. Marlow was career military before he retired, an obvious 'warrior,' and Anne chronicles the history of her region, so she's a sort of antiquarian. But while you all bonded wonderfully, my little plan to rush things was doomed. Marlow and Anne are not your warrior and antiquarian. Can you imagine who these figures are, the people in your life who fulfill these roles?"

For the first time I questioned Hallett's sanity. I was and am a retired high school teacher, ordinary as crabgrass despite being a Revenant. I didn't know a single warrior or antiquarian, and was certain Hallett had picked the wrong horse.

"No," I replied. "There are no such characters in my life, never have been. Really, Hallett, I'm not any kind of guide. I'm not the one Martine said would appear. It will be someone else, some other Revenant."

She was glancing at her watch. "I'm sorry I have to hurry off," she said, "but do give this some time to settle in, Taylor. If you are the Guide, the companions Martine described will appear. Perhaps they already have, and you just haven't seen them yet. You will let us know?"

"Of course," I said as we parted at the door. "And if no warriors or antiquarians turn up, you'll understand that I'm not the Guide, right?"

"Of course," she answered with a fond pedagogical look I recognized from having worn it myself a thousand times. It was the look of one who knows something you will also know, just as soon as you do your homework.

Chapter Twenty-Five

The Sounds of Silence

Simon and Garfunkel

I was unwilling to lend any credibility to Hallett's theory about my Revenant role as Guide, and so tired I just wadded everything in my suitcase. I walked Sadie and slept deeply until the next morning, when we caught a cab for Logan and then relaxed for the six-hour flight home. Sadie was in her unzipped carrier in my lap, her white forelegs again braced against the bulwark so she could watch clouds through the window. Occasionally her tail wagged in excitement, as if she saw something in the cottony vapor below the plane. A cat, a mouse, something to chase. I looked down at the same clouds and saw nothing. My attention was focused on a Beacon Hill scene that either did or didn't happen over sixty years in the past.

Pen said her parents had been unable to have children and were thrilled when her mother finally became pregnant. Except it wasn't Beverly Warren, but the seventeen-year-old maid, Bridget Flannagan, who became pregnant. Bridget told her sister, Katie, that Garrett Warren had been coming to her room at night, that he was the father of her child. But was it true? I thought about the newspaper photo of her family that Pen showed us, everybody saying Pen had her father's nose. People always say things like that when looking at old family pictures. Only a DNA test could prove Garrett Warren's paternity of Bridget Flannagan's child. And

Garrett Warren's DNA was buried somewhere in a Massachusetts graveyard.

The only thing of which I was sure was that Bridget Flannagan was Pen's mother. Evvie Doyle's dated snapshots were of a girl who might have been Pen as a teenager. The two were nearly identical, down to the flaming, coppery hair Pen has spent a lifetime in salons, muting with elegant golds. Pen was Bridget's daughter and probably Garret Warren's. The story unfolded in my mind.

Beverly Warren, eager for a child she cannot conceive. Garrett Warren, handsome profligate, seducing? raping? the Irish housemaid, who becomes pregnant. An agreement is struck. The Warrens will raise the child as their own. Perhaps Bridget is offered money. At the least she's offered a quiet, honorable way out of a ruinous situation, and the child will be well cared for. All that's necessary is a cover story and voilà! – Beverly Warren supposedly steams off to England only to return with a baby.

Except Beverly never goes to England. Instead, Garrett broadcasts the fiction while she hides in the narrow house with the pregnant maid and the housekeeper, Margaret Godare. I thought of how it must have been for Beverly and Bridget, imprisoned in those little rooms for weeks, perhaps months, by their own flaws, machinations, hungers. Beverly awaiting the longed-for child her predatory husband had sired on their maid. Bridget, young and terrified of both childbirth and a future in which she might be branded and ridiculed. And Margaret Godare, who knew all their secrets and wanted to start a business. I couldn't imagine a more dangerous confluence of pressures. Then something had gone wrong.

As I flew over Ohio, I knew that in my garage a doll in a plaid suit stood in blood as another doll lay dying on a bed. The dolls would play the scene endlessly, Bridget, Garrett, Beverly, and Margaret Godare. Bridget had given birth to Pen, probably attended by Margaret, but then she'd continued to bleed, to hemorrhage. Margaret had taken a squalling, newborn Pen to Beverly in another room. They could all hear Bridget's weakening screams over the baby's lusty ones, but did nothing. After a while

Bridget's screams faded, and Garrett Warren went into the room and stood by the bed, blood pooling at his feet. As he stood watching, Bridget Flannagan died.

I imagined Margaret helping Garrett carry what must have looked like a bundle of blankets to a pre-war car with running boards and a hood that opened from the side. It would have been late at night, the Beacon Hill streets empty and silent. He took the body to Bridget's family in South Boston. What did he tell them? That she fell down the stairs? There would be a death certificate. I wondered what was written under "cause of death."

By the time we were over Kansas, Sadie was asleep and I'd given up on the in-flight movie, which featured an adorably dysfunctional family of talking gerbils. What had happened after Bridget's death, I wondered. How did these people go on, knowing what they'd done? But they did go on. The fictive return of mother and baby from an England they'd never seen was staged and photographed. A false birth certificate was secured. An Irish Catholic baby named Flannagan became Penley Aurelia Warren at her Anglican christening. And they all lived happily ever after, or at least for three months after. Then a fire killed Garrett Warren and Beverly Warren loaned her housekeeper enough money from Garrett's life and property insurance to start a business, shrewdly investing the rest. Both women made fortunes. Pen was reared in affluence by a mother who loved her. I tried to take a nap.

But over some mountainous state, Colorado or Wyoming, I remembered that knife-blade flash in Margaret Godare's failing eyes. Even in her final moments, the woman had a savage edge. And hadn't she said she wanted to be a pharmacist? That she went into cosmetics because she liked "mixing chemicals"? I watched as far below a microscopic truck wound its way down a hair-fine mountain road toward a lake I could fit in my purse. I wondered why Garrett Warren, a healthy businessman in his twenties would be at home on a weekday morning, "resting" in bed. Had Godare seen her chance, laced his morning coffee with one of her "chemicals" and set the fire that would kill him in his drugged sleep, then slipped out for her day off? Why would a housekeeper who worked only four days a week need a day off? And how convenient that the fire occurred when Beverly and baby Pen were away getting Pen's inoculations. Had Beverly Warren and her housekeeper planned this together, or did Godare act alone, certain in the knowledge that Beverly would do anything, *pay* anything, to keep this baby she'd desperately wanted?

Over Arizona Sadie woke up and I realized nobody would ever know what really happened that day. Maybe the fire was an accident, maybe Garrett Warren had the flu or was sleeping off a hangover. Maybe Beverly Warren gave Margaret Godare a substantial amount of money out of kindness. What I did know was that Pen had been raised well and with much love.

When her mother died ten years ago the Syndicate sent a standing waterfall spray of white roses, orchids, snapdragons and lilies that Pen still mentions gratefully. She misses her mother deeply. They were close, good friends as adults. How could I tell Pen that Beverly Warren was not really her mother, but stole her fresh from the womb of a teenager who bled to death while her putative parents and a housekeeper did nothing?

Pen Barrows is, as I've said, a lovely person, kind and thoughtful. In over twenty years I've never heard her raise her voice. We joke that Pen in the White House would bring world peace in a matter of weeks. The sheer embarrassment of hostile generals at having failed to follow a protocol enforced by the arch of Pen's disapproving eyebrow would be sufficient.

But real life is not genteel, and Pen is not tough. The story of her life, I decided over the Arizona/California border, would destroy her. I couldn't tell her. I wouldn't.

What I had to do was obliterate the story, which meant obliterating the dollhouse.

Tim met us at the airport and I filled him in on our work in Boston and the new website, about which he was enthusiastic.

"I hope Hoagy Carmichael's 'Stardust' is on the music list," he said as I stared at the San Diego skyline and began to realize I was home. "And Kate Smith singing 'When the Moon Comes Over the

Mountain.' My mother loved that one. How about 'Wabash Cannonball'? And oh, my favorite when I was a boy, 'I'm an Old Cowhand from the Rio Grand.' I knew every word and sang it while I delivered papers. I pretended my bike was a horse."

He sang it for me as I accommodated that mental shift from distant adventure to the practical demands of return. I wanted to see my new kitchen floor and wondered if I should stop at a grocery after getting my car at Tim's. I could probably find coffee and dog food in the boxes of stuff from my cabinets still stacked in the hall, but the refrigerator would be empty. And had Miyoko told Chris Delgado's father that I'd be home tonight, or would there be an armed retired cop sleeping in my house? And what about the intruder? Bits of my real life floated like jigsaw pieces and snapped into place, the palm-framed picture familiar and navigable. Hallett's belief that I had some leadership function to fulfill among Revenants was forgotten.

I gave Tim the number Harry Laufer had provided, and suggested that he call about the songs he liked. We hadn't included any from the thirties, an oversight he was quick to point out.

"Not all Revenants will be *young*," he insisted, and we both laughed.

It was after eleven so I didn't stay to say hi to Angie, just opened the trunk of my car to toss in my suitcase, noticing a box of stuff I'd been carrying around since May. Gifts my students had given me at the retirement party they threw at the end of school. Coffee mugs, pens, a school t-shirt. I pushed the box aside, telling myself I'd go through it the next day, knowing perfectly well I wouldn't. I'd probably drive around with it back there until I sold the car.

After thanking Tim, I drove home and parked in the driveway. I knew the garage was clear, the pallets of limestone gone. I just didn't want to be anywhere near a dollhouse swathed in old beach towels in which a cruel drama was being enacted over and over. Delgado had taped a note to the front door saying there had been no disturbances since the night he scared the intruder into scaling the fence, but he'd stayed until 10:30 and had left the lights on for me. When I opened the door, Sadie dashed in and I pulled my suitcase to the kitchen, which looked like the centerfold of a decorating magazine. The floor was wonderful, with planks of stone cut like wide boards in muted, driftwood colors. The butter yellow walls made the freshly painted cabinets glow, and the new countertop matched everything. I couldn't wait to have the Syndicate over to show it off.

The living room was great, too. Miyoko had arranged for a carpet cleaner, and three walls were freshly painted in a warm sand color, the fourth in a deep, autumnal red, like maple leaves. I felt dramatic, just looking at it. I'd get a beaded shawl in the same color and start a reader's theater in my living room, I thought. Or something.

After sending emails to the Syndicate and Beth saying, "I'm home and still on East Coast time, so you can call early," I did laundry and sank into a steaming bubble bath that knocked me out. But I made sure the door from the kitchen to the garage was closed and locked before crawling into bed. The dolls couldn't reach the doorknob anyway, I told myself. But the thunk of the deadbolt I've never used felt good.

Chapter Twenty-Six

Lonely Boy

Paul Anka

In morning light the kitchen looked even better, prompting me to spend half an hour shopping for new china on the Internet, until Jude called.

"You just saved me two hundred dollars and that was only four place settings," I told her. "Not even the sugar bowl, salt and pepper or a serving dish. But you've got to see my new kitchen and the living room, too!"

"I get it," she said, "new kitchen, you're dying for new dishes. But don't do anything until I get there, okay? I have to see it and then later we can go to this discount place I know because you only need six for the Syndicate and if you buy sets you'll have to get eight. This place sells singles so you don't get stuck with those teensy appetizer dishes that hold one shrimp and a cherry tomato. Or the matching coffee cups that look like bud vases. So how was Boston?"

"Great, except I got mugged in an old fort and I've got a black eye, bruised ribs and eleven stitches in my scalp."

"You *what*?"

"I told you. But the police got them, did the line-up thing, and everything's fine. So tell me all the news."

I wanted to re-bond, and Jude rallied by telling me rehearsals for Isabel's production of "The Fantasticks" were going well and so far Jill's husband seemed to be sticking to AA. But her voice held an edgy undertone.

"What's wrong, Jude?" I asked. "You don't sound right."

"I'll tell you when I get there," she said. "It's nothing... new."

I called Miyoko and left a message raving about the house, then ran out to a convenience store for milk. When Jude showed up I offered her coffee and the cereal I keep around for TJ, lacking other edibles.

"Sure," she said. "It's been years since I've eaten Cheerios. And I can't believe this kitchen! It's fabulous, like a whole new house, Tay. And I love that kind of burnt-orangey red wall in the living room, except you need something there. Huge driftwood sculpture or one of those bare, twiggy trees. We could go out to the desert and get one..."

"Great idea, but not right now," I said.

"Oh yeah, your stitches. Not good to overheat your head."

"Right," I agreed, having no intention of discussing my next move, which was going to involve killing a dollhouse.

"So tell me," I insisted. "What's going on, Jude? I could tell from your voice on the phone..."

She looked pensively into her coffee cup, wisps of loose blonde hair framing sad eyes. "It's nothing," she began and then sighed. "Just that I have really bad luck with men. Not exactly news, huh? A chain of heartbreak since I dumped the real one. Since Luke."

"Luke," I pronounced, trying to remember who Luke was. "Ah, your soulmate who sent you the music box with a ballerina woodpecker a million years ago. You're upset about him?"

"I'm permanently upset about him," she said, pouring us both more coffee. "But that's ancient history. Right now what's happening is Joey's moving back to New York. Today."

"Oh, Jude, that's terrible! Why? He seemed perfectly happy…"

"Joey's always happy," she said. "But he says his sister's having surgery and he needs to be there."

"Well, sure. But he'll be back, right?"

Jude was glaring at the geraniums on my deck as if they'd just maligned her hairstyle.

"He won't be back," she said.

"Why not?"

"Because I just *happened* to listen in on a phone conversation with this 'sister,' Tay."

"And…?"

"And she's not his sister. She's his *wife.*"

"Oh, shit."

"No kidding," she agreed. "And the surgery sounds pretty serious. Joey's basically a good guy despite not telling me he was married and looking like a gangster. Hell, he probably *is* a gangster, but he's still nice. I mean it was nice of him to lie and tell me it's his sister, right?"

I wasn't up to the ethical complexity inherent in the question and just said, "Mmm," suggesting interest if nothing else.

"So I'm alone again," Jude said, more to the geraniums on the deck than to me. She sounded like a general conceding defeat. Lee at Appomattox. It wasn't like Jude.

"I'm so sorry," I said, and meant. "But we're all here for you and, you know, like you always say – there are a million guys out there."

She stood and flung her purse over a shoulder with finality.

"Yeah, and I'm tired of all million. I'm not going through this again, Tay. Gotta go to work. Give me a call later, okay? We'll go shopping for china."

"Sure," I answered, although my new-dish frenzy had passed. I had to think about methods for dollhouse destruction.

After Jude left I went to my dance class. I could always think there, the familiar moves requiring nothing but muscle memory, freeing my mind. Molly was doing stretches with a few early arrivals and I watched her, wondering if she had the slightest idea of the doors that might be kicked open by the music in that room.

"Hey, Taylor," she called. "Been away? And what's the hat about? You're going to cook in that thing!"

"Boston for a few days, got mugged, got stitches," I answered. "They're gross."

"So who cares? Lose the hat. Good to have you back."

She'd wandered over to the sound system and I followed her. "Molly, do you ever sort of think there might be more to all this than just exercise? I mean, you know, like…"

"Like other worlds at the edge of the music, waiting out there? I've always known that, since I was a kid. Did you know I used to sell cars? I was good at it, too, made money. But this? I dunno. It feels like what I'm supposed to be doing."

"Bringing light," I said. "You're a lightbearer. Pretty important."

She cocked her head. "Strange, my husband says that, too."

"What does your husband do?" I asked.

"He makes kites."

I wasn't surprised. Molly with an artist made sense.

"Kites, banners, all kinds of stuff," she went on. "Right now he's working on a forty-foot silk dragon wall hanging for a Buddhist temple in Los Angeles. It's gorgeous."

She was intent on the sound system, twigging dials as a Moroccan chant with flute and chimes filled the room. I took my place among the dancers, wishing silk dragons would materialize in my garage, breathing fire on that dollhouse.

I didn't know how I was going to get rid of the thing, only that it had to be destroyed before Pen could give it to her granddaughter. I'd never met the kid, but had a sense that she might be able to see the story repeating endlessly within those miniature walls. A kid who writes poetry at five? Sensitive soul. And one who's terrified of ceramic cookie jars? Like the one her great-grandmother bought for a "hope chest" before her life hemorrhaged onto a Beacon Hill floor? I told myself this was not rocket science. Any guest on a TV talk show could figure it out in minutes. That child could never see that dollhouse.

I danced gently, favoring my bruised ribs, and explored options with every move. Nothing I could concoct to tell Pen about a vanishing dollhouse would make any sense and she'd just think I'd lost my mind. Then I thought maybe I could just "accidentally" back the car over it, but what if the dolls survived? Would they keep enacting the play in my garage forever? The thought made me shiver. No, the thing and everything in it had to disappear, cease to exist. But how?

Near the end of class we did a long, meditative piece I love. It's like the slow, hypnotic movement in a tide pool and I imagined silk dragons rising from among anemones and starfish, their scales turning gold in the sun as they flew inland – toward my house. And somewhere in the elegant, repetitive dance of dragons, a single word settled in my mind – ash. I remembered a line from T.S. Eliot – "Ash on an old man's sleeve / Is all the ash the burnt roses leave, / Dust in the air suspended / Marks the place where a story ended." I bent to the floor as the music closed and knew what I'd do. House, dolls and story would burn; the story would end. I wondered how I'd ever function as a Revenant without the entire English literary canon pointing the way. Or without lightbearers like Molly.

In the gray shadows of the parking garage I sat in my car and thought about fire. Of course I could just take the thing out into the yard, douse it with charcoal lighter and burn it. But the smoke would bring questioning neighbors and what would I tell Pen? It would have to appear to be an accident. Fires could start accidentally. Faulty wiring, unsupervised candles, kids with matches. Except we had the wiring redone to code only ten years ago, nobody in their right mind would burn candles in that heat, and TJ was way too old for match play and I couldn't falsely blame him anyway. But then I remembered the thousands of student research papers stuck in my mind like bits of damp confetti. "The Argentinean Polo Saddle." "Corn, a Grass We Can Eat!" And one entitled, "Human Spontaneous Combustion: Is It Possible?" Bingo.

The student concluded that human spontaneous combustion *isn't* possible, but only after twenty pages of agonizing technical detail about the intricacies of spontaneous combustion involving grain dust, haystacks, some sort of ground nickel *and oily rags.*

On the way home I detoured to three different home supply warehouses, none of them in my neighborhood, and paid cash for two fire extinguishers and a quart of linseed oil. Once home, I hit the Internet for spontaneous combustion details and learned that under ideal circumstances it should occur in about three and a half hours, give or take. Then I turned the deadbolt on the door from the kitchen to the garage and walked into its baking hot gloom.

The dollhouse, still swaddled in Pen's old beach towels, was silent. I dragged it to the middle of the floor, then realized how obvious that looked and moved it to the side near the wall. The painters had left half-empty cans of butter yellow paint there, next to the cans of white the kids had used on the cabinets, plus a bunch of clean brushes and rollers. My can of oily rags would fit right in. I'd say I used the linseed oil to refinish the Adirondack chair. If only it would work.

Inside the dollhouse I thought I heard that miniature scream again, muffled by terrycloth, but I didn't look. Instead I went back into the house, sprayed the new red fire extinguishers with hair spray and then took them out in the yard and threw dirt from the vacuum cleaner bag on them. I wanted them to look as if they'd been sitting around for years.

After placing one under the sink and one in the garage, I walked by the hall mirror and stopped to check out what a criminal looked like. Because I felt like a criminal, carefully plotting a crime even though I wasn't sure who the victim was. Pen, technically, since the dollhouse was hers, but also me, especially if I managed to do some damage to my own house. For a minute I stared at myself, tentatively mouthing police-report terms like "dangerously senile white female" against the silvered glass. But the green eyes looking back were clear and uncompromising. I had to do it. I would do it, although it seemed that with all my supposed Revenant power I shouldn't have to go to the trouble. I should be able to make it vanish magically.

Dashing back to the garage, I stared venomously at the dollhouse inside its towels. I concentrated on its absence, on making it vaporize with the intensity of my will. But after ten minutes nothing happened except that I was hot and dizzy from the effort and oddly aware that I'd never actually spent ten minutes in my garage. I just parked the car there and went inside. The garage felt orphaned, neglected. I felt stupid and went back inside to make an iced coffee as Miyoko showed up at the door.

"I'm so glad you're pleased with it," she said, casting satisfied glances at the completed work. "Now all we have to do is find the right thing for that living room wall. I just dropped by to say hi and… what happened to your eye!"

My black eye had faded to a mottled yellowish green I thought I'd masked with concealer, but the stuff had apparently melted off while I danced.

"Got mugged in Boston, but I'm fine," I abridged the story. "Miyoko, the place looks fabulous! I can't thank you enough, and…"

A concerned look unrelated to my remarks rippled her forehead.

"What?" I said.

"Have you seen TJ since you've been back, talked to him?"

"No. Why?"

"Well, I'm a little worried," she answered. "He and Seiji had a fight and aren't speaking. I don't know all the details, but apparently the Indian kids did some sort of ritual, making Seiji an honorary Kumeyaay or something, a member of the tribe. I mean it's just kid stuff, and TJ was included, but he didn't want to be and left. When we went to pick the kids up, he was gone. He hitchhiked home, Taylor."

"From the reservation in Lakeside? That's thirty miles!"

"I know. We drove all over for hours looking for him. We were frantic until Seiji called him on his cell and we learned he'd made it back okay. I didn't know what to do, Taylor. Of course we should have talked to his parents right away, but I knew you'd be back and I was afraid the stepfather..."

"John," I said, shaking my head. "You were right to wait and talk to me first. John's hopeless with TJ and would have made matters worse. I'll talk to Beth, see what's going on. Thanks, Miyoko. I'm so sorry this happened."

"These are fragile kids," she said. "Both of them. Seiji's on a roll with the Indian stuff right now, but it doesn't seem to work for TJ. I think he feels left out even though Seiji always wants him to come along. And now they're not speaking."

I remembered six coins floating in Miyoko's car as we drove to Palm Springs, the coins vanishing into Seiji and what that might mean. I wanted to help and pulled Indians down from the sky at a closed miniature golf course. Now a Japanese kid was an Indian and my grandson was going off the rails. I thought I'd better get in gear.

"Let me see what's going on and get back to you," I told Miyoko at the door, then loaded Sadie into my car, drove to TJ's school and waited outside. It wasn't hard to spot him in the crowd erupting minutes after the exit bell rang. In an oversized tie-died green t-shirt decorated in stenciled skulls, he looked like a small, poisonous lizard amid a throng of happy-go-lucky wombats. I honked my horn and tried to look grandmotherly.

"Hey," I said when he came to the car, "wanna see my new dog?"

"Why are you here?" he asked. "Is mom okay?"

"She's fine. I just haven't seen you for a while. And you've never met Sadie."

"That's because you've been *gone*," he said irritably. "What do you want?"

"Just get in the car, TJ."

His sneer was new, an adolescent artifact not yet polished, but sufficient to its message.

"Now!" I said and leaned across to open the door. His slouchy entrance and stony fixation on the glove compartment did not bode well.

"Put on your seat belt," I insisted after a solid minute of seething silence.

"Why?"

I'd about had it. "What are you, three or something? Put the damn seat belt on or we sit here while every kid in your school wonders why you're immobilized in a Volvo with an old woman and a dog. Even I think there's a story in that."

"Yeah," he said, snapping the belt in place. "Fucking Hansel and Gretel and you're the fucking witch."

"I'm happy to be a witch; it's an ancient and honorable profession," I said. "But you're way in the hole with the two 'fuckings.'"

"I don't care."

"Well I do," I said, noticing that his jeans were so short I could see pale leg above his socks and he looked even skinnier than usual. Could he have *grown* in a week? Or had I not been looking.

At a drive-thru burger place I ordered a double cheeseburger and his favorite, a vanilla shake.

"I don't want it," he snarled.

"Fine. I'll give it to the dog as soon as we get to the park. She'll be thrilled."

"What park?"

"The park on the other side of town from which you'll have no idea how to get home, where we will sit at a cement picnic table until you tell me what's going on with you."

He unwrapped the cheeseburger and wolfed it down, followed by the vanilla shake.

"Feel better?" I asked.

"I'm too old for parks. And there's nothing going on. Everything just sucks."

He was petting Sadie, who was trying to get through the bucket seats into his lap from the back.

"Then we'll go to my place, but you've still got to talk to me," I said. "Your paint job on the cabinets looks terrific, incidentally.'

"Yeah," he agreed. "I think it was pretty good work."

His voice cracked and the sentence emerged in a man's bass register. Yet when we got home he ran around in the yard with Sadie like a child while I called Beth to tell her he was with me.

"I guess I haven't told you yet," my daughter admitted, "but

John and I are expecting again. I'm having a hard time with it this time, constantly sick, and TJ's being impossible. He curses at John and the other day we heard Hannah say 'fuck'. She's *two* and she's picking up everything TJ says and John's furious. TJ just stays in his room painting guns on everything when John's here, and the rest of the time he sneers at me like I'm a bag lady or something and eats everything in the refrigerator, then refuses to have dinner with the rest of us. John's looking into a pastoral counselor for him."

I watched TJ running in the yard, high-water pants, fuzzy upper lip and a looming Adam's apple in the late afternoon sun. A gangly, hay-haired kid who didn't look like anybody I'd ever seen.

"I'm sure John will make sure this counselor has adequate credentials," I said sweetly through clenched teeth. "You know, a Ph.D. or at least a Master's and a specialty with adolescents?"

"I don't know, mom. Look, Benjamin's screaming and I've gotta go. Thanks for keeping TJ for a while. It's a real help!"

TJ came in and consumed three bowls of Cheerios and the rest of the milk.

"Seiji's mom told me you hitchhiked all the way back from Alpine while I was in Boston," I began. "That was dangerous. Very. Do I have to tell you what might have happened to you?"

"No," he said in that deep new voice, "you don't."

"Then why did you do it?"

The freckled face looking at me from across the table was a little boy again.

"I don't know," he said, tears spilling. "Seiji's an *Indian* now and I'm *not*. He looks like an Indian and I don't, and I don't want to dig toilets on a reservation or dance around while some fat old man sings some language I can't understand. It's *stupid* and I hate Seiji! He's stupid for doing it and I just don't want to. So I took off."

"I want you to promise me you'll never do that again," I said. "You're at a time of life when sometimes you just can't stay someplace where you've wound up, but you're too young to have a car and you panic; that's okay. But if it happens again I want you to call me. I'll come and get you, no questions asked. Deal?"

"Are you going to tell mom and John?"

"Not right now," I said, "maybe later. Right now I need to know if you've heard a word I've said."

"I won't do it again, okay?"

He pushed away from the table, knocking over the chair.

"That's not what I asked," I said. "There will be other times when you don't want to stay someplace. I asked you if you'll call me so I can pick you up when that happens."

"Oh sure, cool dude has to have his granny drive him home."

"I'll come disguised as a hooker."

"In a *Volvo*?" he grinned and we both laughed. "Okay, deal, grandma. But no disguise."

"Deal," I said, wishing I could do some Revenant magic to make things easier for him, but I couldn't. There was nothing in my mind I could conjure, no story that would give him the necessary boost. It occurred to me that the mind he needed might be the one only his mother could name, the one buried in silence for fourteen years.

"The house looks really good," he said on his way out. "Especially that red wall, except it needs something on it."

"Miyoko's talking about a big wall hanging. I'm supposed to look at websites."

"What kind of wall hanging? Not one of those things with metal ducks flying over cattails like the dentist has."

"No metal ducks," I agreed. "I don't know. I have to look at

305

stuff."

"I'll look too," he said. "Give me something to do in my room."

"Do your homework in your room," I yelled out the door, falling back into character and wondering what to do next. Then I remembered what to do next and called the Syndicate.

"Lunch at my place tomorrow if you can make it," I announced. "I've got a new kitchen!"

Chapter Twenty-Seven

Silhouettes

Herman's Hermits

In the morning I got up early and took the space heater I use next to my desk during winter from the hall closet and turned it on in the garage, which was still cool from the night. Then I walked Sadie and drove to a 24-hour grocery ten miles away in order to heat up the engine. After getting several exotic salads and a pear torte for the Syndicate, I parked the car in my garage, hoping the combination of engine heat and space heater would jack up the ambient temperature enough for my plan. If it didn't work, maybe it would mean I was just supposed to tell Pen the truth, however painful.

But which "truth"? That Pen's biological mother was an Irish maid named Bridget Flannagan? There were ways to confirm that if Pen chose to do so. One kind of truth. Or that three-inch dolls were endlessly re-enacting Bridget's death inside the dollhouse, a bloody drama visible to no one but me? Another kind of truth, nonconsensual and dangerous. If I described it, Pen and the rest of the Syndicate would go into instant support mode, find me a therapist and go with me to appointments. They'd get tickets for concerts, arrange trips and take turns spending the night on my couch until I "got better." But not for one second would they believe me, not even Maggie. The dolls were too specific, too far from the hazier and more acceptable impulse of intuition. I wouldn't believe me, either. And Pen would give the dollhouse to Bridget Flannagan's five-year-old great-granddaughter. I couldn't let that happen. It was 8:00 and the Syndicate would arrive at 12:30. I had four and a half hours to murder a theater, and a play.

The day promised to be miserably hot and the garage was already an oven as I pulled the car out to the driveway after twenty minutes and watched the garage door rumble shut, but left the space heater blasting. Then I cut some cotton rags from a set of thirty-year-old pillowcases, grabbed seven or eight paper towels and headed out to the yard with the linseed oil. Miyoko's rescued Adirondack chair was attractively posed next to the fence where I'd nailed a plaster shell that had once been the hand of a ghoul. *My* ghoul, I reminded myself as I poured linseed oil onto rags and scrubbed the chair. The rags had to be dirty, the chair recently oiled, every element of the constructed story in place. It didn't take long, and soon I had the requisite pile of oily rags.

In the garage I set an empty economy-sized coffee can in front of the space heater for a few minutes to heat it, then crumpled the oily paper towels and cotton rags loosely in the can. I nudged it next to the dollhouse where a drape of towel hung loose, then took the space heater back to the hall closet inside. I didn't think my plan would work. The information I'd gleaned from the web indicated that spontaneous combustion is difficult to induce deliberately. It just happens by itself. Like becoming a Revenant, I thought. You couldn't choose it; it just happened.

While smearing more concealer over my now-yellow black eye, I decided that if the rags didn't ignite and burn the damn thing to a cinder I'd just stuff it with newspapers and burn it myself. Then I'd tell Pen the oily rags did it. But I wanted the rags to do the job, leaving a gap, however contrived, between me and responsibility for destroying both Pen's excitement over the dollhouse and a story that did not belong to me.

Oh, but it does *belong to you,* said my face in the bathroom mirror. *You alone.*

I knew if I showed the dollhouse to Tim, he'd see the doll-actors, see the grisly play. Tim was a Revenant. But Tim had no connection to Pen, and while he'd share the burden of decision with me if I asked, it would be wrong to involve him. Besides, the decision was already made.

I set the table and made iced coffee, sniffing nervously at the door to the garage, behind which silence reigned. I didn't smell smoke. I didn't even smell linseed oil. The door was solid, fit snugly and had rubber weather stripping on all four sides, facts I'd failed to consider.

"The best laid plans o' mice an' men/gang aft agley…" I quoted Robert Burns while hastily unsetting the table and moving everything outside to the deck, from which I could see the garage window directly above the dollhouse. Kevin had broken the glass years ago with a golf ball, and only the screen remained. If there were smoke in the garage, it would come through that window. I wondered if all arsonists had this much trouble.

"Hey, Taylor," Maggie McFadden called from my front door, "Isabel and I have arrived!"

"Come on in," I called, trying not to sound as Machiavellian as I felt. In twenty years of Syndicate lunches I'd never had a nefarious agenda.

"I saw Jill looking for a parking space," Isabel mentioned quietly. "You won't have heard yet, but Steve fell off the wagon again yesterday. Pretty bad this time, smashed his car through a fence and into a bougainvillea in somebody's yard and spent last night in the hospital. Don't say anything unless Jill does. She's really scared."

"Of course not," I said, noting that two of our number were suddenly hit with problems. Jude's boyfriend married and gone and now Jill's husband in trouble. For some reason I didn't think that would be the end of it, and I was right. Hand in hand on my walkway were Pen and a little girl in pink sneakers and a Kate Greenaway-style dress that made her look like a fairy. Her short, curly hair was dark, but the eyes approaching my door were small, intense versions of Pen's.

"Oh my God," I gasped.

"What?" Isabel asked, her back to the door. "You look like you've seen a ghost."

"No, I just, uh, realized I forgot to put ice in the coffee," I improvised. "And Pen, this must be your granddaughter!" I knew I was shrieking like a game show contestant but it was the best I could do.

"Darcy," Pen said, "I'd like to introduce you to my friend Ms. Blake, whose home this is, and to my other friends, Ms. McFadden and Ms. Rothman."

To us she said, "And this is my granddaughter, Darcy."

Midwesterners do not swoon or even falter in the face of cataclysmic events like tornados or somebody getting an arm ground up in a combine, so I just stood in my hall, smiling. But I'm an English teacher. I've read a lot and was thus not unaware that both Arthur Miller and Søren Kierkegaard would have loved to be there for lunch so they could carry on about irony. As it was, I got it without them.

"My son-in-law had to fly down from the Bay Area for a quick business meeting and brought Darcy along so I could spend the day with her," Pen explained, then whispered, "But I don't want her to see the dollhouse. It's going to be a Christmas gift!"

"It's in the garage," I said, trying to match Pen's elegant gleefulness. "She won't see it."

Jill showed up at the door followed quickly by Jude in the pink hospital scrubs she wears while cleaning private airplanes, saying the outfit creates an aura of operating room cleanliness that impresses her clients. She'd dressed the scrubs up with a six-inch-wide rhinestone bracelet and a red Indian shawl with hundreds of diamond-shaped mirrors glued to the fabric.

"Are you an actress?" Darcy asked after being introduced to Jude.

"Basically, yes," Jude answered after thinking about it. "But then, who isn't?"

Sadie was dancing around, demanding attention, and everyone had to spend time engaging with Darcy before spending even more time exclaiming over every facet of my redecorated digs. It was taking forever and I thought I'd never get them out onto the deck where I could watch the garage window for smoke. It had been three and a half hours. If my oily rags were going to do their thing, they should be doing it now.

"I'll just put everything out on the table now," I called cheerily from the kitchen. "And the iced coffee's already out there."

A swirl of muted mirror-flashes alerted me to Jude at my side, grabbing bowls of salad to carry.

"Taylor, it's hot," she said. "Why are we eating on the deck?"

"Oh, I thought, you know, it would be nice to be outside. But I'll put the umbrella up."

"I'll do it," she said. "But we're going to fry."

Just when everyone was finally moving toward the deck doors, my telephone rang. Everybody had cell phones, but still, it might be someone calling my land line to reach one of the Syndicate. Pen probably gave the number to her son-in-law. I had to answer it.

"Taylor," said Tim O'Halloran without preamble, "have you checked your email today?"

"No," I said. "Tim, I apologize but I can't talk right now. I'm in the middle of something and..."

"Sadie dog is a lady dog," Darcy was chanting a rhyme. "She can sniff her way in fog! We have fog where we live. I like it."

"You have guests," Tim said politely. "A poet, from the sound of it. But I'm afraid there's trouble. Do check on things and call me when you can?"

Unable to find a ball, Jude had grabbed an orange from the

bowl of fruit on the counter and given it to Darcy as a toy for Sadie. Darcy rolled the orange across my new kitchen floor, where it hit the garage door. Sadie dutifully chased it, clamped her teeth over it and then dropped it with a look indicating the general canine distaste for citrus.

"You're supposed to bring it back," Darcy told her, leaning to pick up the orange and then slowly straightening to regard the door.

"I think there's something scary on the other side," she told me, pointing at the door. "Do you know that?"

Everyone else was outside already.

"I do," I said quietly. "But you're quite safe. I won't let anything bad happen, okay?"

"Taylor?" Tim's voice on the phone betrayed concern. "Are you involved in something, um, *unusual*?"

"Yes," I said as Pen's granddaughter sized me up, nodded and dashed out the door to the deck. "But it's fine. No problem."

"Don't forget your amulet," Tim urged. "Use it if you need to."

"Roger," I replied. "Call you later."

Outside, the group was enjoying lunch and maintaining that bland conversational level required by the presence of children who aren't supposed to hear about alcoholism and adultery for at least five more years. Pen said that she and Darcy would have to leave early. They were going to a museum shop in the park to pick out a gift for Darcy's mom before the flight back up the coast. All the adults exchanged a look that said *then* we'd talk about alcoholism and adultery. I glanced at the garage window every fifteen seconds, a task made difficult by blinding flashes from the many little mirrors on Jude's shawl. I was getting a headache, but gamely nibbled on five different salads wilting in the heat. The garage window, its image embedded in my retinas by the effect of Jude's shawl, became a sort of purple rectangle on a white field, but exhaled no tendril of smoke. My dastardly plan had failed.

"We'll just see ourselves out," Pen announced before dessert. "Apologies, but we're on such a tight schedule. The house looks fantastic, Taylor, and we've had a wonderful time. Darcy, do you remember what we say to our hostess?"

The little girl with Pen's eyes, that were Bridget Flannagan's eyes, regarded me with a smile.

"Thank you for lunch, Ms. Blake," she recited. "I had a nice time and I hope the thing in your garage..."

"I'm so happy you came," I quickly interrupted. "And next time I promise there will be a real ball you can throw for Sadie."

"Okay," she said, and they were gone.

"What 'thing in your garage'?" Maggie asked. "What's she talking about?"

I hated the fact that nobody in the Syndicate misses anything.

"Oh, she threw an orange for Sadie and it banged into the door and there was an echo or something," I said. "She's so bright and imaginative! Did you hear the little poem she made up about Sadie?"

The ploy worked, but only because Jill wanted to talk about the advice her Al-Anon group had provided regarding Steve's latest crisis and Jude wanted to discuss her resolution to eschew men. I went into the house to get the pear torte from the fridge and ran into the counter. In the relative dark I couldn't see anything but a hazy purple rectangle, image of my smoke-free garage window. I'd wait until everyone left and then burn the dollhouse myself.

"There wasn't much damage to the car," Jill was saying when I returned, "but I've taken his keys and told him he can no longer drive. He didn't argue. I think he's more scared than I am. The doctor recommended a three-month rehab program and gave us a list, but I think we'll go with Betty Ford. It's out by Palm Springs somewhere. I can drive there to see him."

"We'll go with you," we all said in unison, Jude adding that we could shop the thrift stores in Palm Springs while Jill visited her husband.

"It's a Mecca for retired drag queens and the stuff they donate to the thrifts is a goldmine," she explained. "I got this bracelet there, two bucks."

The conversation careened between Jill and Jude, both needing support. The pear torte was excellent and Isabel insisted that we all spend every night helping out at rehearsals for *The Fantasticks*. Jill needed company once Steve was gone and it would take Jude's mind off Joey.

"Sounds good," Jude said, standing to leave. "I'll be there. But right now I've got a twin piston Piper Navajo to tidy up. The owner's flying a bunch of politicians back to Sacramento. Catered dinner flight, guaranteed crumbs on the floor. I'll have to clean it again tomorrow."

We all laughed and stood up, gathering dishes to carry inside.

"That shawl is fabulous," I kidded Jude, "but blinding in the sun. You could wear it on the beach to drive away men."

She didn't respond, but was looking curiously across the yard. I looked in the same directions but could see nothing, just my purple rectangle superimposed on the garage wall. I didn't know why I hadn't worn sunglasses. Everybody else did.

"Tay," she said, "isn't that smoke coming out of your garage window?"

"Oh shit, it is!" Maggie said, dumping plates back onto the table and sprinting for the deck doors.

Jude, Isabel and Jill ran after her, followed by me, squinting and shaking like an aspen. I hadn't even seen it. Maggie opened the door from the kitchen to the garage and clouds of dark gray smoke swarmed toward her face. The whole garage was full of smoke, but no flame.

"It's hard to see," I yelled, hitting the garage door opener and hoping the inward rush of oxygen would do the trick. And it did. As the door rumbled upward, the smoking rags burst into an intense flame that instantly caught the edge of towel hanging over the coffee can.

"What on earth is it?" Isabel said. "What's burning? And where's your fire extinguisher?"

Coughing, I shut the kitchen door. The dollhouse had to burn. It would take a few more minutes.

"I don't know what it is," I said, pretending panic. "Call the fire department! I know there's a fire extinguisher in the garage, but I think Charlie always kept one in the kitchen, too."

Jude was ripping open cabinets and eventually found the one I'd stashed under the sink.

"How do these things work?" she yelled, heading for the door.

I knew perfectly well how they worked, having memorized the directions the day before.

"I think it's written on the side," I said, grabbing the red cylinder from her hands. "I'll do this, Jude. You have to get to work."

The remark was absurd but nobody noticed as I opened the door again. The dollhouse was crackling, the towels burnt away and flames licking through its tiny windows like tongues. With a snap the clasps holding the façade broke loose and the narrow front of the little building fell burning to the cement floor, revealing the holocaust within.

The balsawood walls were nearly consumed, the floors collapsed, the stairs fallen and flaming in the entry hall like an Escher drawing in hell. On a bed hanging precariously from what remained of the fourth floor, a plastic doll melted in flaming drips that fell and splashed like slow-motion water drops. Another, the doll in the plaid suit, had lodged on its side under a balsa wood stair banister that lay charred across its body. Smoke seeped from the plaid cuffs and shirt front, but I thought I could see the face, the plastic mouth opening in a scream like a telephone wire moaning in wind. Then the doll exploded, the house collapsed and I pulled the pin on the fire extinguisher.

"Oh my God," that's Pen's dollhouse!" Isabel said from the door as I sprayed foam on the coffee can, the wall and finally on the ruined story.

"I think there's another extinguisher out here somewhere," I yelled as Maggie and Jude stepped into the garage. "Maybe over in that corner."

Jude found it and athletically sprayed the window, the wall and me as sirens roared to a halt on the street and four men in yellow hazard gear shouted, "Move the goddamn car out of the driveway!"

The side of the garage was waist-deep in foam, the can and rags and charred dollhouse invisible.

"I think we've got it," I told the firemen as my neighbors once again huddled in concerned groups at the edge of my lawn. "I'll just move the car."

After I did, they shoveled the foam onto the driveway and hosed it down, revealing ashes, tiny globs of melted plastic and the coffee can.

"What did you have in that can?" I was asked.

"Just some rags. I was refinishing an old Adirondack chair my decorator found," I babbled.

"Refinishing with what?"

"Linseed oil," I answered. "You're supposed to use linseed oil on wood."

"Lady, you're an idiot," one of them said, but was silenced by another one with chevrons on his sleeves.

"We'll check for hot spots and hose the wall, but there's not much damage," the second one said. "Just whatever that thing was, next to the can of rags."

"It was a dollhouse," Maggie said. "Very unusual."

"Well, it's gone now. I suggest you ladies go inside while we hose out here, and you…," he said to me, "need to get rid of the linseed oil. Don't ever use it again, just get rid of it. In fact, I'll be glad to take it off your hands if you don't mind. And never leave oily rags lying around anywhere again, ever, got it?"

"Got it," I said meekly and went to get what was left of the oil.

After Jill and Isabel and Jude left, I explained what had happened to the neighbors and dashed in to check my email. A neutral note from Harry Laufer said merely, "Hey, we miss you, give us a call when you get a chance." Code for "There's trouble."

I called Tim O'Halloran.

"I'll meet you for coffee in ten minutes," he said, naming a McDonald's in a shopping center.

He was already there when I arrived, and immediately said, "It's happened. Somebody's onto us. Somebody knows about Revenants."

Chapter Twenty-Eight

The Great Pretender

The Platters

"Somebody in Boston picked up a reference to magical 'old people' on a teen-oriented website called 'Incantation'," Tim said. "The site is devoted mainly to contemporary vampire lore. It would never have hit the radar but for one sentence – 'If your granny hangs with an old bitch named Martine, cover your ass, dude, 'cause gran's gone over to the dark side.'"

"Where did this come from?" I asked. "This website."

"Harry Laufer tracked the Incantation site to some high school kids in Tennessee, but how they heard about Martine is anybody's guess. It may be insignificant, just a local dig at somebody named Martine. Harry's sending an MIT student down there to interview the website kids, telling them it's a research project. We may know more soon. In the meantime we're advised to maintain contact with headquarters and have an escape plan."

By that time I was so tired I'd driven past the shopping center where I was supposed to meet Tim, and didn't even notice until I realized I was in a residential area several blocks on the other side. I couldn't have planned a competent, detailed route out of my own yard.

"Escape plan? You're kidding."

318

Tim looked frail in the harsh neon light, his violet eyes hooded.

"Nobody's kidding, Taylor," he said. "You need look no further than history for some idea of what may happen. We're different, unlike any of our own species. We have capacities they do not have. We're alien now and I don't have to tell you..."

"I don't feel alien," I broke in, "but I've read *The Painted Bird*; I know what can happen. So what's your escape plan?"

He smiled wearily.

"Angie and I talked it over and decided escape isn't an option for us," he said. "Where would we go? Oh, I suppose if they came for us, for *me*, we'd take Conan and seek sanctuary at the church, at St. Paul's. Of course the law no longer recognizes such sanctuary, but that's what I'd do. Let them storm the altar to get me!"

"That's the spirit, Tim," I said. "And if it comes to that, I'll join you. But I've never really understood what it is we're supposed to be afraid of. So what if people know about Revenants? I mean sure, the media would go crazy for a while, but..."

He snapped a plastic coffee spoon in two and nudged the pieces around on the table. "At the very least we would be the subject of intense academic scrutiny, Taylor. But more troubling than that are our gifts. Yours, for example, involve an ability to see stories nobody else can see. Have you not considered how valuable that gift might be to government agencies? Imagine yourself in a room with a person accused of terrorism, treason, murder. What if you could see the stories such people would hide?"

I envisioned myself in an underground bunker full of CIA agents and spies, but couldn't decide which ones were the spies. "I don't think... it doesn't work like that, Tim."

"We don't know how it works, Taylor. We know very little at the moment. But please don't be so naïve as to assume we would be protected from exploitation at best, and at worst, from irrational attacks by the ignorant. It can happen."

319

I shook my head. "I don't think it will. What you're saying just doesn't scan, at least not at the moment. The story doesn't feel right. It's too soon."

"Ah!" he said, the characteristic twinkle flashing again in his eyes, "Taylor and stories! What then do you anticipate?"

"I don't know," I answered, feeling the framework of every novel, every essay and newspaper article, every story I'd ever read, like a warm, muscular beast supporting us, the plastic table, California, everything. "But something will happen. Something will protect us, for a while."

He was laughing now, which made me feel better. "You're describing a messiah," he said.

"Why not? They're all over the place. You told me that the day you took me to the Paper Doll Museum. Only you called them lightbearers. The talented oddballs who never fit because the fit's too tight, but they illuminate the paths."

"So I did, Taylor," he agreed. "And I trust your faith in whatever story you're seeing. I'll sleep tonight. Thank you. But do keep in touch with Boston."

"I will," I agreed, and left to hit one more home supply place for the chemical sponge the firemen said I needed to clean the wall where I'd slaughtered a tale I didn't want told. I told myself again that the timing was wrong, that I had to do it. Darcy was too young and vulnerable to see it, and Pen too sweet to hear about it. But I'd save the story, or part of it. Only that Pen was probably the biological daughter of a young woman named Bridget Flannagan, who had been a maid in the Warren household when Pen was born. Nothing more. I'd write it and the document would be included in my will. I'd request that it be given to Pen or to her daughter at the time of my death. I would leave the story with those who really owned it, but only when its danger had diminished with time. A compromise of gnawing discomfort, but what compromise isn't?

Once home I stared at the phone on the kitchen wall, dreading the call I had to make. Then I went into the living room, still cluttered with boxes of books. To kill time I shelved two boxes – heavy, dated college texts I keep because there's something comforting about the presence of nine-pound anthologies with ponderous introductions by dead literary critics. I leaned against *England in Literature, The Complete Works of Shakespeare* and *The Victorian Age; Prose, Poetry and Drama*, and finally worked up sufficient nerve to dial Pen's number from my desk phone.

"Pen, I'm afraid something terrible has happened," I began.

"Isabel and Maggie both called. They told me," she said in the voice I'm sure she uses to address household vermin. "I can't believe you would be so careless, Taylor. I know it's silly, but that replica of a home I can't remember was... it was almost magical to me."

Not "almost," Pen.

"I'm unbelievably sorry," I plowed on, thinking of "unbelievably" as a term of art, true only in that cagey, diplomatic sense. "Nothing I can say will restore what's gone, and I know you're disappointed and angry. I don't blame you. But I hope someday..."

"Oh, Taylor, of course it was an accident and I'm so glad you weren't hurt. It's just that I wanted to give Darcy something special, a sort of heritage, you know?"

"'The hope and vigor of an earlier world,'" I offered, mangling a quote from William Morris along with the truth, but Pen liked it.

"Yes," she said, "something like that."

"But the hope and vigor are you, Pen, not some toy Darcy would only outgrow in a few years, and forget."

After a silence she said, "'An earlier world.' I hadn't thought of myself that way, but I guess I am old-fashioned."

"In the best way," I told her. "Darcy's heritage is *you*."

I'd been dead tired earlier but now I was completely drained. Talking to Pen had consumed quantities of nerve I didn't even know I had. It was almost time for dinner, but a nap was more attractive than leftover salad. I curled up on the couch with Sadie, was asleep in seconds and didn't wake up until the phone rang an hour later.

"Can I speak to Mrs. Taylor Blake?" an unfamiliar male voice asked.

"'May' I speak," I sleepily corrected his grammar, "and yes, this is she."

"Ma'am, this is Officer Rick Ballard, San Diego Police."

I assumed the call had something to do with the break-ins. "Oh good, you've found whoever broke into my house," I said.

"Beg your pardon, ma'am?"

"Two weeks ago? My house was broken into and my things thrown all over? Detective Delgado was here, they checked for fingerprints. Isn't that why you're calling?"

"I'm sorry, ma'am, I don't know anything about that. What I'm calling about is we've got a minor here, tried to lift a half-pint of vodka from a liquor store. Says he's your grandson, that he lives with you. That right?"

"TJ?" I said, my voice squeaking. "A liquor store?"

"Yes, ma'am. The owner's willing to let it go, not press no charges. Says the kid would get eaten alive in juvy, which is about right. Pretty nice guy, name's Ahmed. So whaddaya want us to do? Me and my partner, we can't just leave the kid here in the parking lot. We can take him down to juvy and book him for the night if you..."

"No! I'll be right there," I said. I'll come now. What's the address?"

I gulped some iced coffee, trying to wake up, and decided

against taking Sadie. I told myself I didn't want her to see TJ in handcuffs, neatly projecting my own distaste and fear onto a dog. I was embarrassed, ashamed and at a loss as to what I should do.

TJ, as far as I knew, didn't hang around with the kids who drank and did drugs. There are always those kids, even in grade schools now, but TJ was never friends with them. Then it dawned on me – TJ hadn't had any "friends" in years. He was a misfit loner until Seiji came along, and now he wasn't speaking to Seiji. He'd tried to steal vodka from a liquor store, not to gain acceptance with some gang of little thugs or to get some equally unhappy girl drunk so he could try his sexual moves, but *alone*. The enormity of it made me speed through the streets to a liquor store in a strip mall where two cops sat drinking coffee in a cruiser. In the back seat was a hunched figure that broke my heart.

"Thank you so much, officers," I said as one of them opened a rear door and watched as TJ sprinted to my car, got in and slammed the door.

"Thank Ahmed in there," the other one said. "He coulda pressed charges."

I went inside, where a man with deep-set black eyes was watching the news on a little TV. On the counter cluttered with racks of cigarette lighters and car deodorizers was a half-pint bottle of cheap vodka. TJ didn't even know enough to pick the good stuff.

"I want to thank you," I began, but he waved a hand to silence me.

"I did not call the police," he said. "They come in here for coffee, all the time. They came in the door when the boy, your grandson, tried to pay for a candy bar with the vodka stuck in the back of his pants. I knew it was there; I have cameras on every aisle and saw him do it. But when I told him to give me the vodka, he ran, right into the police."

"His family and I are grateful that you didn't press charges," I said. "He's never been in trouble and…"

The man sighed. "Tell his father to put a hard hand on him.

Some boys... I had a brother... some boys at this age must have the hard hand of a man for control."

I hadn't missed the past tense. "What happened to your brother?" I asked.

The man's black eyes grew darker, but his look wasn't angry or even sad. It was a look I'd seen in photographs of Abraham Lincoln, an expansive, somber pity.

"He was shot to death while robbing a liquor store," he said. "There was no father to control him. Our father died in the earthquake at Azad Kashmir."

The exotic place name thrummed in my ears like a song I'd never heard. I had no idea where Azad Kashmir was except that it must be far away, somewhere on the other side of the planet. And yet the father of this man who'd just saved my scrawny, helpless grandson from the dangers of a juvenile detention center, had died there.

"I'm so sorry," I said. "And again, thank you."

In the car I said nothing, aware that I'd promised to ask no questions and also that if I got started I'd verbally eviscerate the little idiot.

"Do you want to go home or to my house?" I finally asked.

"I don't want to go home. If I go home I'm going to kill John."

"You're not going to kill anybody," I said, chucking the rule. "John didn't tell you to rob a liquor store; you made that choice on your own. It's about time you started growing up, TJ. It's about time you started taking responsibility for the choices you make."

"I don't make any choices," he said, kicking the dashboard. "I don't *get* any fucking choices!"

"That's enough," I said, pulling into the garage. "Don't say anything else."

He rolled his eyes and got out of the car, then saw the charred wall where the dollhouse had stood. He pointed at it and mouthed, "Fire?"

"Yes," I answered. "And you may speak if you can be civil. It was an accident. A dollhouse burned."

"A dollhouse? Why would you have a dollhouse?"

"It was Pen's," I said, feeling woozy from exhaustion and hunger. I hadn't really eaten all day. "I'm going to eat. There's plenty of salad if you want some, but you have to call your mother first if you want to stay here tonight."

"Can't you call her?"

"No."

He went into the living room, presumably so I wouldn't be party to whatever story he concocted, but I could hear his voice, cracking and falling from boy-soprano to the rumbling bass in which he would speak for the rest of his life. What had Tim said about the processes of sexual maturity necessary to the continuation of life? That those processes obliterate the child each of us once was. The child TJ was dying in my living room, and the man he should become might atrophy and rot without help.

"What's the matter, grandma?" he said when he ambled back into the kitchen. "You look sick."

"Just tired," I said. "And very concerned that you've started on a path that only leads to misery and then more misery."

"John says liquor's a waterslide straight to sin," he said, devouring salad. "I just wanted to see what it feels like. It's no big deal, grandma. Chill. The guy didn't even press charges."

"That's because his brother was shot to death while doing exactly what you were doing – trying to rob a liquor store."

"No shit?" His eyes gleamed with respect beneath a forehead blooming in acne. "That's awesome!"

"What's awesome?"

"The brother. Going down like that, taking a bullet."

"You're insane," I said, meaning it. "What's awesome is that Ahmed cared enough to give you a break."

"I don't need any Ah-Med," he sneered, mocking the foreign name. "I can take care of myself."

I just stared at him, a ridiculous, self-destructive and possibly doomed creature I'd held in my arms only minutes after his birth. He'd been a cute kid, always a little strange, but I chalked that up to his intelligence, which is astronomically high on standardized tests the schools give. But in the last two years he'd changed, as if a dormant parasite had hatched in his bloodstream and was slowly transforming him into a monster from a Bosch painting. I hated to admit it, but I didn't particularly like my own grandson at that moment. Which would not keep me from trying to protect him. You just do, I guess.

"I'm really tired, going to take a hot bath and go to bed," I told him. "And tomorrow I'm going to have to talk to your mother about what happened tonight."

"Whatever, it's no big deal," he replied, "except John'll piss himself. Sorry."

In his eyes was a flash of delight so unwholesome I wanted to slap him.

"Hurting yourself to get at John is sick," I said. "In the end nobody will be hurt but you, and if you go too far you may not be able to get back." I might as well have been talking to a chair. He was chewing noisily and pointing toward the living room.

"Hey grandma, I've got some ideas about that wall thing you want. There's a really cool one I saw on a website, like with old barn boards in a pattern. They had it with brass strips, sort of, but I think bronze or even, like, black."

I felt as if I were swimming in a flat, dark lake with no shore in sight. I decided to swim away from TJ.

"Sounds interesting," I said. "Be sure all the doors are locked before you go to bed. Somebody tends to break in here once in a while."

"Not with me here," he said, polishing off the last shred of salad. "You need a man around."

Oh for God's sake.

"Don't know why I didn't think of that," I said. "I'll get one tomorrow. I think they're on sale at Walmart."

Soaking in a bath, I conceded a certain comfort that *somebody* was there, even TJ. Because I was too tired to fight a ghoul that might appear at any time if I were alone. In bed I gripped the little whistle on its silver chain around my neck, and fell asleep listening to my grandson stomping around. I hoped he wouldn't get into the only liquor in the house, a bottle of ninety-six proof plum brandy called "Slivovitz" that Kevin and Suzanna sent from a visit to Serbia four years ago. Much later I heard him vomiting in the hall bathroom and figured he had.

"Now you know," I called sweetly into the hall, and went back to sleep.

Chapter Twenty-Nine

Ruby Tuesday

The Rolling Stones

The day after TJ's failed liquor store robbery I dragged myself out of bed in time to force him go to school with his first hangover, then called Beth.

"TJ was in serious trouble last night," I began. "Whatever he told you will not have been the truth. The truth is that…"

"Oh mom, we just can't handle him anymore," she interrupted, crying. "John took him to see a counselor at church after school yesterday, but TJ called the guy a fucking asshole and ran away. We didn't know where he was until he called and said he was with you. Did he say why he did that, why he wouldn't even talk to the guy?"

"Beth, the police called me because TJ tried to steal a bottle of vodka from a liquor store. The owner was very understanding, really nice. He didn't press charges, or TJ would have been taken into custody. TJ gave the police my number and said he lives with me, probably to avoid John being involved. I went to get him, but Beth, I think it's time to get TJ professional help."

"What do you mean?" she wept. "We *got* him professional help and he was horrible. He doesn't *want* help. All he wants to do is be foul-mouthed and obnoxious and make us miserable. I can't even let him be around his brother and sister now because of his mouth, and I'm so sick all the time with this pregnancy I don't know what to do, and now this. Stealing! That's it, mom. John's been looking into places where we can send him. You know, places for troubled kids. I said no, but now..."

Her voice trailed away to a sniffle.

"You weren't exactly a poster child for flawless adolescence yourself," I reminded her. "But surely you recall that your dad and I didn't send you off at seventeen to some home for unwed mothers. We kept you right here with us. Nor did we ask you to give TJ up for adoption once you'd made up your mind that you wanted to keep him. We *helped* you. For *years*, Beth."

She was crying again.

"I know, mom," she sobbed. "But I'm so sick, I'm afraid I might lose the baby. The doctor says I need to rest, keep my feet up, not get upset all the time, but TJ couldn't care less. It's like he just wants to hurt us. I think he *wants* me to lose the baby, mom. Everything he does is so ugly and hateful, and John's tried, he really has, but TJ despises him and won't listen."

"Well," I said, trying to sound warm and empathic, "John's a fanatic. He may mean well – in his bizarre way I believe he does – but unfortunately that stuff just doesn't work with TJ."

There was a strained silence in which I took a deep breath and then asked brightly, as if the question were inconsequential, "Beth, who is TJ's father?"

Her voice was a mixture of hostility and despair, deep and cold as the quarries I dove into at night with other kids when I was in college. And as dangerous. "*John* is TJ's father," my daughter pronounced through ice. "He has no other father, there *is* no other father, John is the only father he's ever going to have, so just drop it, okay?"

"Sorry," I said. "I just thought..."

"Don't... *think*, mom. Do... not... think. I mean it. And I've got to go. Thanks for rescuing TJ. I'll talk to you later."

I walked Sadie, picked at breakfast and was late to my dance class. Backing out of my driveway I noticed a shiny black car pulling to the curb in front of my house, but assumed it was a realtor looking for clients and ignored it. It wasn't there when I got home, grabbed lunch, polished my notes for the talk on Poe at the community college that afternoon, got dressed and was ready to go. I took Sadie so I could go straight to the club afterward. But as we hurried out the front door, Sadie slowed on her leash, sniffing the bottom of the door.

We really have to go," I told her, bending to scoop her into my arms, when I noticed a business card stuck in the weather-stripping. "Merlin Fine Collectibles," it said beside a pen-and-ink drawing of an antique wooden Punch puppet, the strings curling off the edges of the card. There was only a website address — merlinfinecollectibles.com, but on the back somebody had written a phone number and the words, "Please call Mandy Geoffrey ASAP!!!" I remembered the black car in front of my house as I was leaving, and the name was familiar although I couldn't place it. Someone had the wrong address, I thought. It had to be a wrong address because the only things I've ever collected are foreign editions of "The Raven" that I can't read. I tossed the card in my bag and locked the door.

The talk for the community college kids was a great success, not the least because it was accompanied by a dog. The only thing I said about Poe's influence on Dostoyevsky was that Poe had, indeed, influenced Dostoyevsky. Both authors were interested in spiritualism, blahblah. I showed photos of Fort Independence and told the story of the duel between Massie and Drane, Drane's mythical death, bricked into a wall, and Poe's reported use of the tale in the creation of "The Cask of Amontillado." Encouraging discussion of the uses of contemporary myths in creating fiction, I asked the students to describe a few of the urban myths they'd heard.

They ran through the classics — the man with a hook on a lover's lane, tapeworm diet pills, breast implants exploding on planes and cell phone calls from dead boyfriends. Someone commented on the fact that the victim in urban myths, invariably dead or hopelessly deranged by the event, is always female. But then a guy in glasses and a Citadel t-shirt raised his hand.

"Not always," he said with a bit of a drawl. "My cousin sent me this new one on Facebook, says there's this creepy old chick named Martine, she latches onto other old people and makes them go crazy. Some kind of witch or something. In this one the perp is the female!"

"But the victims are still members of an oppressed group," a young woman insisted as I felt my hair stand up. How could the story have spread so far, so fast? The Web, of course. Half the kids in the room were texting on their gizmos even as I stood there.

"Like, the victims are always oppressed, like women. Old people are an oppressed group," the young woman said again, and I looked at my watch.

"I'm afraid I have another engagement," I said, "but thank you so much for your attention."

At the door the professor who'd invited me was generous with praise and asked me if I'd be interested in signing on as a substitute in the English department. I'd been out of the classroom for only a few months by then, and wasn't sure that I missed it. On the other hand, once in a while might be fun.

"Let me think about it," I said, grubbing for my keys at the bottom of my bag and finding instead the business card somebody named Mandy Geoffrey had stuck in my door. It was coming back to me.

Mandy Geoffrey. I tried to remember her and saw only an impression – a lanky, dark-haired African American girl who looked pretty much like all the girls look from sixth grade on – the long hair, the eyeliner, the push-up bras under skimpy tops suggesting a sexual sophistication they won't possess for another twenty years. She'd transferred into one of my senior English classes near the end of the semester when another teacher became ill and his students were farmed out to the rest of us. I barely remembered her. She didn't participate in class, but sat in the back texting on her cell phone. Similar activity on the part of the community college students had reminded me of her. But she must have done the work because I apparently gave her a decent grade and she graduated. I vaguely remembered that one of the other kids said she was an athlete of some kind. Swimming or track, I hadn't paid any attention. I dialed the number on the business card as I walked Sadie in the shade at the edge of the parking lot. A cultured female voice answered.

"May I speak to Mandy Geoffrey, please?" I said.

The woman drew a sharp breath. "Is this Mrs. Blake?"

"Yes. To whom am I speaking?"

"Vivienne Geoffrey. Amanda's aunt." She pronounced her name "Vivyahn." "I deeply apologize for this unfortunate situation and will of course compensate you for all damages. My niece's behavior was outrageous. But I must inquire. Do you still have it?"

"I'm sorry," I said. "Do I still have what?"

There was a three-second silence. "Amanda's gift. She finally told me she'd given it to you at a retirement party, but not until after breaking into your home in an attempt to find it. I simply had no idea she'd do such a thing and beg you not to bring charges. Amanda is... headstrong."

I glanced at my car. Whatever the woman was talking about was still in a box in my trunk amid coffee cups and ballpoint pens with multicolored ink. I barely remembered Mandy Geoffrey and had no idea what her gift had been. It was nice of the kids to throw me a party and I appreciated the gesture. But I didn't need any more coffee cups or pens, and would probably never get around to bringing the box inside.

Yet Mandy had been the one who crept in through the deck doors as I walked Sadie. She'd recognized another gift from that party, the little etching of an apple. She picked it up and then replaced it, two inches from its original position. And then later she'd broken a glass door and searched my house while I was at

Pen's. Why on earth hadn't she just called me and asked for the return of the gift if that were necessary? It made no sense. I pulled Sadie toward the car.

"Um, there were so many lovely things," I said while stuffing Sadie into the car and then opening the trunk. "Could you remind me about Mandy's gift?"

"The Inchbald flier," Vivienne Geoffrey pronounced softly. "I'm afraid Amanda was unaware of its value, which is in excess of thirty thousand dollars."

I had no idea what she was talking about. "I'm afraid I'm equally unaware," I told Vivienne Geoffrey, "but of course I'll return it, if I actually have such a thing. Let me check and call you back?"

The community college parking lot was a sea of baking glare as I stood pawing through the box in my trunk. There was a pep club t-shirt, six key chains and several miniature flashlights. A box of exotic teas, five coffee mugs and a framed 8X10 photograph of the high school. Then a jumble of pens and a refrigerator magnet shaped like an old-fashioned typewriter. And in a plastic sleeve at the bottom of the box was one of those fake old-fashioned fliers sold at Disneyland, historical parks, tourist attractions. Usually they say, "Wanted, Dead or Alive!" over your name and a computer photo. Or at least that's what I'd thought it was. I hadn't really inspected the gifts closely at the time, merely thanked the kids profusely for their kindness.

But it wasn't a tourist gimmick. It was a flier for a play called "Every One Has His Fault, A Comedy in Five Acts," by a playwright named Elizabeth Inchbald. I read the blurry, cheaply printed names of characters and cast from a play staged in Boston in 1809. Mr. Placid, it told me, had been played by Mr. David Poe.

Oh my God! This thing is real!

The fragile newsprint held me like music barely heard on a dark summer street. This was Poe's father! David Poe would abandon his family less than a year later, setting in motion a series

333

of events that would mold the heart and mind of a tortured, brilliant American writer. But on the night advertised by the flier, David Poe had acted in this play in a Washington Street theater. The place was only blocks from the Common where Anne Greenleigh's ghoul emerged like a muscular shadow from the Frog Pond. I was there! The theater was demolished in 1926, but I had walked over its ghost beneath the street. I had walked above the shadow of a baby named Edgar, born January 19th of that year, who almost certainly waited with his mother, another actor, in a dressing room, while David Poe strutted his hour upon the stage. In a hot California parking lot I could smell the smoking kerosene stage lights and sweaty costumes. I could hear the laughter of an audience not one of whom still breathed.

The slip of old newsprint was magic, and I envied the one who might purchase it from Mandy's aunt. For a moment I sat in the car as the world to which it had announced a now-forgotten play grew out of the asphalt. Horse-drawn carriages clattered on a lamplit street beyond my car, as outside a theater women in impossible-looking long dresses and coats clung to the arms of men in knee-length pants and white silk hose. In the shadows by a stage door stood a lean young man with dark curls, staring unhappily at the elegantly dressed theatergoers. I recognized the wild, deepset eyes. David Poe, saddled with a wife and newborn baby, his dreams slowly strangling in the clutch of responsibilities he didn't want. The scene vanished when I glanced again at the flier, nothing in the parking lot now but glare.

"Ms. Geoffrey," I said after dialing my cell again, "if you'll give me your address, I'll bring the flier immediately."

The Geoffrey home was in a typical San Diego neighborhood of ranch-style houses, only this one had obviously been altered. Expensively. A second story had been added, and all the unusual arched windows were new and equipped with scrolled iron security bars on the interior side. As I parked in front I saw two small cameras swivel from under the eaves at each side of the house, documenting my arrival. Mandy was standing on the walk in baggy satin basketball shorts and a tank top, tears wrecking her eyeliner.

"I didn't mean to break the glass in your door," she said as I got out of the car. "I thought I could, you know, just break the lock. I'm sorry, Mrs. Blake. I totally screwed up."

"That's putting it mildly," I said, holding the antique flier in one hand and Sadie's leash in the other. "Mandy, why didn't you just ask me to return your gift? It would have been so simple."

"You don't understand," she sobbed. "I'm not a child; I take care of myself. My aunt's crazy, she's a hoarder and a *hermit*, but I have to live with her until I'm eighteen. I didn't think that thing was worth all that money. I mean, it's just an old piece of paper, and she's got tons of that stuff and I thought you'd like it."

"I do like it, but I'm afraid nothing you've said explains your breaking into my house," I said, edging toward the door. "I'd like to speak with your aunt now."

"No! Just give it to me, okay? I didn't mean to hurt anything, just to take care of it, y'know? She told me I had to get it back, so I thought I could, you know, do it like a cat burglar. I was varsity in track, season conference best in pole vault. It was, like, a challenge. I don't want you to see my aunt. Could you just, like, give it to me?"

I pushed past her to the door, wondering if something in the water were responsible for an epidemic of stupidity in teenagers. Except everyone drinks the water, so it couldn't be that.

"Please accept my gratitude," Vivienne Geoffrey began as she opened the door, but trailed away as I stared at the ceiling and Mandy sulked behind me. There were fire sprinkler heads positioned every eight feet above the hall, in the living room and a large dining room to the left. The place felt like a bank, not the vermin-infested mess Mandy's "hoarder" comment had suggested. The senior Geoffrey was in her early fifties with clear hazel eyes currently clouded with chagrin. Her dark hair hung in dreadlocks over a white poet's shirt tucked into black palazzo pants. She was barefoot, her toenails painted purple with tiny silver stars.

"You have concerns about fire," I observed, feeling as if I'd gone to a set for "Scheherazade" to apply for a mortgage. The place even smelled like a bank, but Vivienne Geoffrey didn't look like a banker.

"I am a collector," she said, ushering me to a silk-upholstered Queen Ann chair in the living room. The chair reminded me of the lobby in Margaret Godare's final home.

"A fire or theft could be disastrous, hence the sprinklers and security. Merlin Fine Collectibles is my business and I've done quite well, but there are those who might call it a sickness, I'm afraid. My brother, Amanda's father, certainly did. He perished many years ago in a diving accident."

"It was a treasure hunt in the Caribbean," Mandy said proudly, wrapping a bare foot around a claw-and-ball chair leg. "He was fearless. I take after him. But my mom's sick, which is why I'm living with my aunt."

Sadie was squirming in my lap and I was anxious to get the whole thing over with. "I'm sorry to hear that your mother is ill, Mandy. But you may wish to reconsider those situations in which 'fearlessness' and the criminal code are in conflict," I lectured. "Breaking and entering is a crime. Your stunt could have had very serious consequences. *For you.* I want you to promise me that you'll accept the difference between real life, which is frequently boring, and fantasy. *Tomb Raider* is fantasy. You're not Angelina Jolie playing Laura Croft. Assuming you're into vintage movies."

She unwrapped her foot from the chair leg and inspected a painted toenail. "I totally am," she said, grinning. "But it's more like Michelle Yeoh. You know, 'Crouching Tiger'?"

I had to laugh and did a quick forearm block while holding Sadie with my other arm. "I do know," I said, and handed the flier to Vivienne Geoffrey.

"Thank you," she said. "If you'll send me a bill for the damage Amanda inflicted on your home, I'll send a check immediately."

I should have left then, but I remembered the Huck Finn mannequin pointing at a cardboard wizard and it hit me – Merlin! Vivienne Geoffrey's business was called "Merlin Fine Collectibles."

And hadn't Baba Yaga advised me to welcome the past? I had just relinquished a moment of the past, an ad for a play staged over two hundred years ago. Vivienne Geoffrey was watching me curiously.

"Is there something else?" she asked.

"Um, Merlin. Do you mind if I ask why you named your company Merlin?"

Mandy leaped up, rolling her eyes at the ceiling. "I can't hear this story again, but in case you don't think there are any Welsh black people, Ms. Blake, think Shirley Bassey. You know, she sang 'Goldfinger'?"

"You may thank Ms. Blake for saving you from your own incredibly poor judgment, and then you may be excused," her aunt said.

"Thank you Ms. Blake, I mean, seriously," Mandy pronounced and dashed into the hall. I wished I'd gotten to know her better. This kid who'd sat in my classroom for a month clearly had a story.

Vivienne truncated it to a genealogy beginning with a Welsh North Carolina slaveholder with family roots in ancient English history. He had freed his slave mistress, Vivienne's great-great-great grandmother, and their seven children before he died, leaving them adequate resources to escape the South and establish themselves in Illinois. I was fascinated.

"His surname was Geoffrey," she said, grinning and shaking her dreadlocks. "We kept the name, but I'm probably the only one who's taken it to extremes."

I cocked my head, not understanding, and she laughed. "Geoffrey of Monmouth?"

"Oh my God," I said, "he wrote the first version of the King Arthur tales! In the tenth century or something. He created the wizard, Merlin!"

"Not really," she told me, her eyes bright with enthusiasm for the tale. "The real Merlin lived five hundred years earlier, a pagan and a prophet. He was called insane and pushed off a cliff by a bunch of nasty shepherds, but you know what? All his prophecies came true."

I felt my ears lay back as a tremor of recognition reorganized patterns in my brain. Merlin's story, even more than Goody Hallett's, had been embellished and reified, had survived countless centuries. He was a wizard, a person with unusual abilities, and on any street in the western world a mention of his name will still be met with, "Oh yeah, Merlin the Magician!" Was he an early Revenant? The first, maybe?

"Ms. Geoffrey, I love this stuff, really want to hear more," I said. "But I have to go. I'm helping with a little theater group. They're doing *The Fantasticks* this weekend. Would you like to have lunch some time?"

Her body language was tentative, even furtive – that sudden attention to a wristwatch or remembered obligation. "Please, call me Viv, and I'm afraid I don't go out, but could you come here for lunch? I make a great curried tofu salad."

"Sure," I said, "but what do you mean, 'you don't go out'?"

She drew further into herself, looking past me. "Amanda describes me as a hermit, and the term is perhaps apt. I... find it difficult to leave my house, the past, the things I protect and store and sell to others, like the little flier that has brought you here. Let me show you. It will only take a minute."

I followed her up carpeted stairs, carrying Sadie and wondering why a woman who never left her house would be dressed like the hostess in a Moroccan restaurant. Under similar circumstances I'd still be in my pajamas. Then she unlocked a door, flipped a light switch and I gasped. The entire second story was a combination office/storeroom, but it was also a sort of museum. There were banks of filing cabinets and bookshelves and a myriad of illuminated glass cases holding strange old pistols, chess pieces, statuary, miniature carousels, trucks, tin soldiers, blocks, dolls. She pulled on a pair of white cotton gloves from a bowl near the door and reached for a wind-up toy, a cadaverous tin man with huge, painted teeth riding a green tin grasshopper.

"Made in Germany in the 1800's," she said as I imagined a little boy in *lederhosen* beneath a Christmas tree, playing with the toy when it was new. The room swarmed with images, stories, that eerie sense of delightful things hiding but accessible. Vivienne Geoffrey was watching me closely.

"You understand why I must stay with these things," she said.

I returned her look. "I do. But if you stay, you become a living ghost wandering through fragments of the past, like the negative image of a ghost from the past wandering through fragments of the present. You don't belong there. It's not good. There's even a self-help book about it."

She didn't reply, but merely replaced the tin toy on its shelf and turned to leave. "Who was it that said the one thing even the gods can't do is change the past?" she asked as she clicked off the light and re-locked the door.

I didn't know who said it and was trying to think of a quote-riposte when the weight of her remark, and her profession, fell like a shovel on my back. Vivienne Geoffrey was an antiquarian! A recluse buying and selling fragments of the past inside a suburban ranch house with more security than Chase Manhattan. The boy mannequin at the department store had pointed to "Merlin"; Baba Yaga had told me to welcome a past that was all around me in a dizzying collection of artifacts. And Martine's message in the origami dragon said the Guide would be helped by a warrior and an antiquarian. I still couldn't imagine myself guiding anything and definitely didn't know any warriors, but I liked the woman bounding down the stairs before me. She was interesting, and if Hallett's guess was correct, going to become a helpful companion.

"Viv," I said at the door, "I'll take you up on the curried tofu lunch. I want to talk about Geoffrey of Monmouth and Merlin, and I want to spend hours looking at all your treasures. But the time after that we go *out* for lunch, okay?"

"Tall order," she replied, "but I hear you. And thanks again for your understanding about Amanda."

"I have a grandson a few years younger," I said. "I understand."

Chapter Thirty

Earth Angel

The Penguins

Isabel's community theater group had rented the auditorium of the San Diego Women's Club for the *Fantasticks* production, but despite the fact that I'd been there countless times, the place felt slightly odd as I walked in. I thought maybe I was still shaky from meeting an antiquarian whose friendship might mean I had to be "the Guide" for a collection of clueless people trying to save the world. Still, the club's Gothic wainscoting in the entry hall felt like a flimsy barrier behind which something observed my movements with sinister intent.

Heavily embossed oak leaves in the Lincrusta walls above the wainscoting seemed to rustle even though I knew they'd been motionless since their creation in 1885. The Women's Club paid handsomely for their restoration only ten years ago, and Jill had given a well-attended lecture on Victorian décor to celebrate completion of the project. The oak leaves were shaped of dried and painted oil affixed to heavy canvas backing. They had never moved. Yet I heard the unmistakable murmur of leaves.

You're tired, Taylor. You need to slow down.

The dance at the Women's Club at which I'd found a gray vellum envelope beneath my plate, inviting me to the Paper Doll Museum, felt eons past. Nothing had changed then. Nothing was expected to change. We'd reached a comfortable plateau in which we'd replicate days, months, years, until one by one we as comfortably vanished. I tried to remember if it had been pleasant, and thought it was. Although hadn't it made me uneasy as well? That well-trod rut of sameness? I was deep in thought as I pushed open the stenciled doors to the house's former refectory, sometime dance hall, now theater.

On stage a man who looked like the ruined ghost of a prize fighter was singing "Try to Remember" in a haunting baritone that sounded like wind before a storm. He was muscular, *sturdy* in the sense of Elizabethan brigands, bo'sun's mates and coachmen, with a Dickensian nose that appeared to have been broken more than once. He could be cast realistically in anything from Chaucer to Dylan Thomas, I thought. The Monk, Falstaff, The Prisoner of Chillon. Worldly characters, beleaguered characters. Yet his voice was trained and sufficiently rich for a Verdi opera.

"That's great, Nick," Isabel called from offstage, and apparently hit a button, because the accompanying music stopped. "You've got it down; you're glorious. Now please go to your costume fitting."

Pen and Maggie were near the stage, coaching two actors from scripts. They saw me come in and waved. They might have been characters in a play themselves, I thought. Everything was feeling like a play.

Sadie and I walked along the wall of the old building and climbed the four stairs at the side of the stage apron. Behind a threadbare velvet curtain Isabel in a beaded caftan was urging a couple of teenage actors, a boy and girl, to loathe each other.

"You've been had!" she yelled. "Your parents won, they control you, you'll never see what life's about now. Get it?"

The kids practiced snarling as Isabel noticed me.

"Taylor, thank God you're finally here! There's so much to do, I've got a million things for you, but first you've got to see these costumes."

She pulled me to a plastic-draped rack and pulled off the plastic. There were the beaked leather masks, the peculiar white, birdlike mask of the plague doctor, wigs like horned hats made of hair, and rows of quaint costumes no one not born in fourteenth century Italy could possibly recognize. The costumes shimmered, like ripples of heat on a desert road.

"This one's mine," she said, showing me a sparkling black dress appliquéd in white satin diamonds, and an elegant white half-mask. "I'm playing Bellamy, the girl's father, only it's Mrs. Bellamy, the mother. I just can't get down to a tenor. So where have you been?"

I told her about TJ, Beth's threatened pregnancy, plus my gig at the community college. I left out Vivienne Geoffrey, needing time to think about what she might mean.

"If only Beth had asked the Syndicate," she said, "we could have found something better than John. As soon as the play is over maybe we should hire somebody to shoot him and then we can start looking for Mr. Right. At the moment the seamstress beckons. Dress rehearsal's tonight and I can't zip my costume!"

"Isabel," I called after her as Sadie pulled hard on her leash, "who's the El Gallo, the guy singing 'Try to Remember' when we came in just now?"

"Oh, you've seen him before, that's Nick Mautner, the baritone," she called back. "Best voice in the show but a little touchy. Vietnam. Never got over it."

Sadie had managed to pull her leash out of my hand and was wagging her tail at something under the costume rack. A mouse, probably. But then a large, muscular dachshund emerged from beneath a harlequin stocking and calmly sniffed my dog's rear. His rust-colored coat gleamed in the stage lights, and I grinned, happy that Sadie's reproductive days were over. She was clearly impressed.

"Your dog have his shots?" a gruff baritone voice behind me asked.

"'Her' shots, and no, I'm using her as an experiment in the spread of rabies as germ warfare," I snapped. I was, I realized, too tired to be around people.

"Not funny," Nick Mautner growled and grabbed the dachshund up in one huge arm.

"You're rude, but you've got a terrific voice," I said as dog and man walked away, but only the dog seemed to hear, and wagged his tail against Nick Mautner's back.

"He's gorgeous," I told Sadie. "But his owner's a jerk."

Isabel assigned me tasks involving ticket sales at the door and trash management at intermission. During performances I would work backstage, bringing Cokes to the actors (meaning, make sure nobody's drinking anything stronger), but my important job involved keeping track of wardrobe.

"The costumes are on loan from the Dell'Arte School up in Blue Lake and have to be shipped to a mime troupe in San Francisco early next week, so this is crucial," she explained. "Every wig, mask and stocking has an inventory code and has to be accounted for after every performance. We're talking thousands of dollars worth of costumes here, Taylor. Anything goes missing and I'm liable for it, since the little theater group doesn't have insurance. Think you can handle it?"

"No," I said. I hate responsibility.

"Great," Isabel replied, ignoring my response while gesturing to a stagehand. "Fantastic. Just keep an eye on the shoe clips. They tend to fall off."

"What's a shoe clip?"

"You know, the buckles, ribbon rosettes, the decorations on the shoes."

"Oh," I said, as she was swept away by the two kids, who were actually fighting over how to appear to be fighting.

Jude showed up and we spent the rest of the evening learning the wardrobe codes. At eleven we left, and Sadie curled up in her bed the minute we got home. I checked email for news from Boston. Nothing. But Miyoko had sent a note.

"TJ and Seiji seem to have settled down," she said. "They showed up here after school, TJ saying he wanted to go up to the reservation to get some old barn boards. He said he's making a wall hanging for you, so I took them up there to get the wood. Wound up with a carload of Indian kids at McDonald's for dinner. TJ didn't say much, was mostly interested in the barn boards, which are in my garage. I think this is supposed to be a surprise, so don't say anything."

I was glad TJ was hanging out with Seiji again, but didn't delude myself that he was out of the woods. My grandson was a mess and I knew it. What I didn't know was what to do about it. He'd be fourteen in a few months. Not an age at which boys respond well to grandmothers, or to women in general. They need to be around men at that age, insatiably crave role-models. But his Grandpa Charlie was in Europe somewhere with his girlfriend, Kevin was in Sweden and TJ barely knew his uncle anyway. The only man around for TJ was John, who wanted to send him away to a school for troubled kids. I tried to stop worrying about it and went to bed early, which was fortunate since Hallett called at eight-thirty the next morning.

"I know I'm violating protocol, but you didn't answer your cell," she said. "There's some news about the website situation. A student researcher went to Tennessee and had no trouble learning the source of the tale on the kids' website. They showed her another website by a man, a journalist, who has quite a reputation as a researcher in contemporary folklore. He's written several books, lectures all over. He's a heavy, Taylor, well-respected in academic circles despite his lifelong fascination with witchcraft and the occult. It would seem that he heard a story about somebody meeting Martine, getting an amulet. He doesn't know much, only that older people are involved and may be 'stricken by apparent madness' as a result. But he included the story in his blog, asking for more information. By now he may have discovered *our* website and will keep digging."

I was barely awake and couldn't begin to match Hallett's concern. "What are we going to do?" I said, thinking there really wasn't much we could do. Once something's out on the Net, it's there forever.

"Harry may fly down there to talk to this man, try to lead him off the track. His name is Lucien Salnier and he lives somewhere in Louisiana."

I woke up fast. *Lucien Salnier? Oh my God!*

"We're going to call Anne Greenleigh to see if she's heard of him or can find out where he lives. The name sounds French, doesn't it? I thought perhaps François..."

"It's Cajun," I said, barely breathing. It couldn't be the same man, but somehow I knew it was.

"What?"

"The name," I said. "It's Cajun. Luke Salnier is a Cajun."

"Luke? Do you know this man, Taylor?"

"No. But I know someone who does. Or did. Hallett, don't let Harry do anything until I get back to you. Don't contact Luke Salnier until I've talked to my friend, okay?"

"Agreed," she replied. "But exercise great caution, Taylor. This man could be dangerous to us."

"I will," I said, and called Jude.

"Tay, what's up?" She answered, practically yelling. "Oh, wait a minute. Forgot about the earplugs. I'm at work."

"I have to talk to you," I said.

"Sure. I'll go straight to the club with Isabel once I'm through here. Couple of hours. I'll see you there, okay?"

I could hear a helicopter taking off in the background.

"No," I insisted. "I really need to talk to you right away. As in immediately. Where are you? I'll come there."

There are ten small airports in San Diego City and County, and since Jude cleans planes in all of them, nobody ever knows where she is.

"Montgomery Field," she said, naming an airport in the heart of town. "But what's wrong?"

"It's... an emergency. Too complicated to explain on the phone. I can be there in twenty minutes. Where can I find you?"

"Restaurant," she said, going straight to typical Jude-mode, totally focused. "There's a little Mexican restaurant at the airport. I'll meet you there in twenty."

I got there in fifteen, and dashed into the restaurant as orange windsocks snapped over four runways. I could see Jude's car heading in from a nearby lot where small airplanes rocked in the breeze, secured by tie-downs fastened to wings and tails and clamped to eyehooks set in the tarmac. An orange and white checkered flag flapped from a pole stuck in her rear window, creating a festive mood I didn't feel.

"What's the emergency?" she asked, throwing herself into the booth across from me in the restaurant while signaling the barman for coffee. She was wearing a lime green mesh vest with wide reflective tape over her pink hospital scrubs, and looked efficient. Also happy. I wondered what I was about to do to her.

"I have to talk to you about Luke," I said, then watched as a wary sadness crept into her eyes.

"Luke? Is this some kind of joke, Taylor? Why would you...?"

"Look, I'm sorry, Jude, but he's found out about us. He's *writing* about us on his website, and people are picking up on it."
"What people?" she said. Who's 'us'? Luke has a website? How do you know that? Taylor, what *are* you talking about?"

I could have screamed when the barman brought coffees and grinned at Jude.

"Taquitos?" he said, then turned to me. "She always gets the taquitos."
"Yes, fine," I said while dumping sugar into my coffee with

shaking hands. "Two." When he finally ambled away I tried to condense the story.

"'Us' is Revenants," I whispered despite the fact that we were the only people in the place. "Lucien Salnier has stumbled over a story somewhere. He knows about Martine, he knows about the amulet, and he knows the experience can be dangerous, horrible. I have friends, Jude, other Revenants. There's a sort of headquarters, in Boston. An MIT professor named Harry Laufer..."

"Boston? You were just there, Taylor. Is that why? You were there with these other people? These other... Revenants?"

"Yes. I know it all sounds crazy," I said. "But it isn't. It's real. What happened to me that day when I called you? It's happened to others. I can't explain it, but we all see Martine and then we're different."

"Different?"

I was so nervous I couldn't look her in the eye.

"Yeah," I said quickly. "It's like things we knew when we were children come back, and we can do things – sort of magical things – but we each have a ghoul, and believe me, it's no picnic. But if people find out about us we're in trouble, Jude. And Luke has. One of the Boston people wants to go to Louisiana, try to talk to him, urge him to keep silent. I said wait until I can talk to you."

She stared into her coffee and didn't look up when the taquitos came. Their scent was inviting and I picked one up, shredded cheese raining into my lap.

"Jude?" I said. "Say something."

"I'm scared," she said. "What if he doesn't even remember me? He was special, Tay. But I was too young to know that. I wanted him to be my twenty-year-old's version of 'normal', whatever that was. This Revenant thing? It's so up his alley, just the sort of thing he'd love. It's like the ivory billed woodpeckers, y'know?"

"This is beyond woodpeckers," I said. "According to Hallett Gardner – she's the head of the organization – Lucien Salnier is a major figure in what I guess would be called 'folklore', only trust me on this, Jude, we're not talking Disneyland here. If this Salnier reveals what we are, *who* we are…"

She was looking out the window, her eyes wide but converging on nothing.

"What do you want me to do?" she asked, still staring into space. "I don't know what it is you think I can do."

I'd come up with a plan on my way to the little airport.

"You could talk to him, Jude," I said. "He knows you; he'll listen to you. Just ask him to pull Martine and everything connected to her off his website until we can get together with him. Tell him your best friend's life depends on it."

She turned from the window to regard me over two plates of taquitos. Jude Shapiro, my friend of more years than I could count, fake blonde hair blazing in the sun.

"*Does* your life depend on it, Tay?" she asked.

"Possibly," I told her.

She straightened her shoulders and pulled her cell phone from her bag. "Okay then. What's the number?"

Miraculously the restaurant still had a pay phone. I grabbed my address book and all the change in my wallet, and called Anne Greenleigh.

"It's Taylor Blake. Did you find a number for Salnier?" I asked, breathless.

"You mean that hunk of an author y'all wanted to autograph some books for a charity auction?" she countered, giving nothing away in case… in case what? I still didn't really understand why we had to engage all the cloak-and-dagger. Who would have any interest in Anne's phone calls?

Only the government, the right, the left, multi-national corporations and wacko religious fundamentalists, you idiot!

"That's the one," I replied, leaping into character. "Our women's club auction is always such a hit, and autographed books are so popular. Could you give me his number?"

"He lives in Baton Rouge," she said, reciting a number with a 225 area code, "but he travels a lot. Good luck!"

Jude was pale but determined when I returned to the table.

"Use your cell," I told her. "Here's his number."

"Luke?" she said after punching the numbers, the knuckles of her free hand white as she clutched her coffee spoon, "it's Jude Shapiro."

She was silent for several minutes in which I could hear deep-voiced syllables. The syllables were tentative. Jude was crying.

"I still have it," she whispered. "The music box with the dancing woodpecker. I've always kept it."

I waved a hand across her face, mouthing, "His website? Ask him."

"Yes, but I'm calling to ask a favor," she said. "I'm in San Diego and yes, it would be great to talk, but not now. Luke, you have to pull everything about 'Martine' and this story you've found about her off your website right away. It's really important. I have a friend. Her life could depend on it, Luke."

More baritone syllables, questions.

"I can't answer you, Luke. I don't really know. Just please do it? I think they'll... I mean you'll be contacted."

I nodded violently. He would definitely be contacted.

"Here?" Jude gasped. "When? Well... yes."

Then she flipped the phone closed, looking radiant and

terrified at the same time.

"He'll take down the stuff on his website and blogs right away," she told me. "And he'll be here day after tomorrow."

"Here? Why?"

"He said he wants to see me, to hear what I've been doing for forty years. Oh, Tay, he remembers me!"

"That's because you're memorable, Jude," I told her, biting into another taquito as a shadow crossed her face.

"What he remembers is a kid barely out of her teens," she said. "I weighed a hundred and five back then, wore a size six and could stay up all night and still get to work the next day."

"And you were too naïve to see the value in him," I reminded her. "I think he's coming here to see if that's changed, not to check out your jeans size."

"He's probably married and has grandkids."

"Could be. But he's flying across half a continent and most of a lifetime to see you, Jude. Obviously something about you matters to him. And not to belabor the point, but something about *him* matters to *us*, to Revenants. Will it be okay with you if I call Boston, tell them he's going to be here? Harry Laufer and Hallett will want to talk to him. They'll probably fly out as well."

"Sure," she said, although I could tell she wasn't really listening.

I called Hallett from the restaurant pay phone and heard what I'd expected. She and Harry would be here in two days. I left Jude to finish cleaning airplanes and drove home. I was tired and thought I'd skip my dance class to take a nap. Fat chance. TJ was sitting on the deck when I got there. At eleven o'clock on a school day.

Chapter Thirty-One

Dead Man's Curve

Jan and Dean

"Will you give me a ride to the art museum?" he said when I opened the deck doors and let him in. He was already grubbing around in the refrigerator by the time I could say, "Art museum? Why aren't you in school?"

"I cut out before lunch. I really need to go to the museum. I have to look at something. I'm working on a thing for your wall, grandma. It's for you. I wasn't going to tell you, but I have to check out this artist."

He had new jeans and a haircut. He looked taller, older, more teenager than child. And his huge blue eyes were sparkling with intent. At first I went to my default setting and started to launch into a lecture about truancy, but stopped myself. His grades were good and he rarely missed school. And I'd done the same thing one day in seventh grade when I wanted to finish reading *Jane Eyre*. I told my history teacher, Mrs. Gelb, I was sick and had to go home. Then I climbed a tree where nobody could find me and read my book. I *had* to read it, couldn't wait. My grandson seemed similarly driven.

"Who's the artist?" I asked as he made a turkey and cheese sandwich with artery-clogging quantities of mayonnaise.

"Spanish dude. I wanna see how he does it. I have to look…"

"Okay," I agreed, calling his school to say I'd made arrangements to take him somewhere and he'd failed to inform the office. "But this is a one-shot, get it?"

"Got it. Thanks, grandma."

He finished the sandwich in the car and took the museum steps three at a time on his way in. Later I would tell Beth he was fine that afternoon, because he was. There was nothing wrong.

In the car he told me about the wall decoration he was making and asked if he could work on it in my garage since there really wasn't room in the Foxwell's. I said sure, but he'd have to help me clean stuff out to make room. Within minutes he was referring to my garage as his "studio." I hadn't seen TJ as engaged with anything in years. He said he'd catch a bus home, and I drove away looking at the organ pavilion across from the museum. The organ was silent in the clear afternoon air, but I heard an echo of Angie O'Halloran's Bach, hidden in the light. The echo felt apprehensive, restless.

At home I walked Sadie and then tried to take a nap, knowing we'd have another late night with the dress rehearsal. But I couldn't sleep. Questions about TJ, Vivienne Geoffrey, Pen and the ill-defined threat hanging over Revenants flipped across my mind like a slide show. Eventually I dozed off, barely noticing a faint scent of persimmons drifting through the open windows. A threat, but diffuse.

The rehearsal that night went well even though Isabel had insisted that the cast wear the masks and more uncomfortable bits of costume in order to get used to them before the following night's full dress rehearsal, and everyone was missing their marks. She looked great in her white half-mask, like the tooth fairy grown ripe and vaguely menacing. But the real transformation was in the baritone El Gallo character, Nick Mautner.

If the night before he'd looked like a ruined prize fighter, that night he was a medieval Zorro. His was a Scaramouche costume, all flashing black, that gave him an eerie gravitas. And his voice filled the space in the way an aged wine expands an evening. Many-masted sailing ships could ride that voice, with a thousand geese behind.

"I apologize for being sarcastic last night," I told him during a break, as Sadie and his handsome dachshund played with an empty Coke can backstage. "Of course Sadie has her shots, and she's getting a kick out of playing with, um, your dog. What's his name?"

"Rommel," he said, the word booming deep across the stage. "You a friend of Isabel's?"

"Yes, one of them. I'm Taylor Blake. We're here to help out. Why did you name your dog after, well, I mean, a Nazi?"

With a thick thumb he pushed the black mask over his forehead and into a graying crewcut that had once been the color of sand. His nostrils flared and I could smell Old Spice wafting from his flushed jaw.

Wüstenfuchs, he pronounced, "the Desert Fox. Rom and I live in the desert near Borrego. He loves it out there, so I gave him Rommel's name, who since you obviously don't know anything about it, was one of the greatest field generals of all time. Troops under his command committed no war crimes. Not only that, but he defied Hitler's orders and refused to authorize any killing of captured Jews. A lot of German officers opposed Hitler and were executed because of it. A few, including Rommel, tried to assassinate the bastard. They were all killed, but because of his military record, Rommel was allowed to commit suicide. Not all Nazis were Nazis. You should know what you're talking about before you talk."

Having less than no interest in military history, I *didn't* know what I was talking about and recognized the flaw for what it was – a deplorable, chosen ignorance. Nick Mautner had called me on the very thing I can't stand in other people. I liked him.

"You're right," I told Mautner and would have said more but the cell phone in the pocket of my blouse was vibrating. It was

Beth and I could barely understand her.

"Mom," she sobbed. "TJ's been hit. An accident, I'm sure it was an accident even though the man who hit him said... He's in the hospital, they're setting his leg but he may have a concussion and... can you come? I can't let John near him and I can't stay. I'm having some bleeding. I've got to go home and lie down. The baby..."

"What do you mean you can't let John near him?" I asked, feeling my chest constrict.

"He found porn on TJ's computer," she said, the words sounding metallic. "John just flipped out, told TJ he was too evil and sick to be around the little kids. He told TJ he'd have to go away to a 'school for scum' until he learned right from wrong. TJ tried to hit him and John threw him against the sink and TJ just ran out. I thought he'd go to you, but..."

"What happened?"

"He was running across a street, major street, two lanes on each side, down in Tecolote Canyon where there aren't any lights, and a car hit him. The driver said he never saw TJ until he... until he was in front of the car."
"Which hospital?"

"Mercy."

"I'll be there as soon as I can."

The two kids were singing "Soon It's Gonna Rain" as I stood, stunned, amid masked actors.

"Something wrong?" asked Nick Mautner.

"My grandson has been hit by a car and I have to go to the hospital," I told him. I don't know why I told him. He was a stranger and all my friends were nearby, but I wasn't thinking. He shrugged as if I'd mentioned a need to replace a taillight on my car.

"I'll drive you," he said. "You'll probably be there all night.

Got anybody to stay with the dog?"

"No, I don't know." I couldn't plan that far.

"She'll stay with me and Rommel," he said. "I'll have one of your friends drive your car home. When you can leave the hospital you'll call me, I'll come and get you, bring the dog back, drive you home." He hung his cape and mask on the costume rack, scratched a phone number on a paper cup and handed it to me. "What's her name again?"

"Sadie," I said, lost in images of TJ flung across a dark road by a speeding car. "Originally it was Zadok, but..."

"Handel, the Coronation Anthem, right?"

"Yeah, that."

"Good name. Let's go."

Nick drove me to the hospital in a pick-up truck that smelled like coffee and dachshund, that faint, Frito-ish scent their paws have. He said nothing but occasionally rested a big hand on the dogs, crammed together in the seat between us. I was surprised when he parked in the hospital lot and got out.

"Be right back," he said, locking the doors but leaving both windows open two inches.

"Thanks, but you really don't need to go in," I said. He just stared straight ahead and kept walking. I felt like I had a military escort, which was oddly comforting.

At the desk I said, "Blake, Taggart Jared," using TJ's full name. Of course I'd surreptitiously looked for any "Taggarts" in Beth's life after she selected TJ's name, but there was nobody. Then one day while cleaning her room I noticed a little paperback art text called *Watercolour Painting* amid her forgotten high school stuff. The author was somebody named Paul Taggart, but he was in Scotland and thus hardly suspect. I only noticed the book because of the British spelling; we don't use foreign texts in the public schools. Too expensive. When I showed her the book, she looked funny for a minute and then said, "Yeah, I just liked that name – Taggart."

"Pediatrics, Room 207," the Pink Lady at the hospital desk told me, and Nick Mautner followed me on the elevator to a ward decorated with Winnie-the-Pooh images I was certain TJ found humiliating. Beth was at the nurse's station talking to a doctor, so I just ducked into the room.

"Hey," I said to the sullen, bandaged form on the bed. He has badly scraped up and his left leg under the white blanket was in a cast. A stocky woman in Winnie-the-Pooh scrubs was sitting beside him, but stood when we entered.

"I'll step out while you visit for a few minutes," she said. "Just don't let him go to sleep. He's on concussion watch. He can't sleep for another four hours and push this button right away if he vomits."

"Who's that?" TJ muttered, looking at Mautner standing behind me in black, looking like Johnny Cash.

"This is Nick Mautner," I said. "He's El Gallo, the narrator in Isabel's play. He gave me a ride over here. Nick, this is my grandson, TJ."

"Why's he here?" TJ snarled as Nick just stood there, filling space.

"Stand up, boy," Nick said quietly.

TJ looked surprised. "You crazy? I've got a broken leg!"

"Seen guys with *no* leg stand when they had to. You stand when somebody introduces you."

"You don't belong here so fuck off," TJ mumbled, and Nick's lip curled in a dramatic contour of disgust as he turned to leave.

"Wait," TJ growled at Nick's back, ripped the blanket off and struggled to stand on one leg, the hospital gown twisted around his stomach, revealing the white Jockey underpants he's worn since he was out of diapers. The image brought tears to my eyes. His other leg was in a plaster cast, foot to knee, and he winced with pain. Nick turned around and gave an infinitesimal nod.

"More like it," he said. "Now sit down."

The exchange took less than a minute and struck me as insane. I was about to throw Mautner out, figuring he was some kind of sadist, which was why he'd come to TJ's room in the first place, but the look on my grandson's face suggested that I stay out of it. He blinked back tears and stuck out his lower lip.

"I can stand," he told Nick. "Thank you for giving my grandmother a ride." Then he jammed a pale, freckled arm into the medicinal air between them, and Nick shook his hand.

"No problem," Nick said, throwing his bulk into the chair the nurse's aide had vacated. "Now, what the hell happened to you?"

TJ glanced at me in that way dogs look when they've overturned the trash, only you haven't seen it yet. Guilt writ large. I gestured to the hall where Beth was, and left, aware that I'd just witnessed some arcane masculine ritual that seemed ridiculous only to me. TJ *liked* it. Fine. I didn't see how it could hurt.

"Who's that man with you?" Beth asked, paler than TJ as she leaned against the counter surrounding the nurse's station. "He looks like a hired killer."

My daughter doesn't look like me, more like her dad. His nose and ears and wispy hair. But she's not Charlie, I reminded myself. She's a woman and pregnant one time too many. Not the life I would have chosen for her, but the one she chose for herself. My job was to pick up the pieces. Popular images of cheerful, aproned grandmothers baking cookies mask a reality nobody discusses. I entertained a brief fantasy of moving back to Boston under an assumed name. It felt good.

"Friend from the cast of Isabel's play," I explained. He'll take care of Sadie. I'll stay with TJ. You need to go home."

"I do have to go, mom," she said. "The baby, there's some bleeding, and…"

"Yes, go!" I urged. "We'll talk about this tomorrow."

She looked at the floor. "There isn't much to talk about. Pornography, mom! He's not even fourteen yet. And John's fed up. TJ's going to have to go to..."

"A 'school for scum'?" I completed the statement. "Over some dirty pictures? Beth, your brother went through the same stage; they all do. It's disgusting but to some extent they outgrow it, or most of them do. The way to handle it is to get TJ involved in other things. He's really jazzed about an art project right now, wants to make a 'studio' in my garage. Get him in some art classes after school or weekends. Play up his strengths and don't make a big deal about the porn. Take away his computer until he gets the message, and..."

"It's too late for all that," she said, looking down the hall toward the elevators. "We've tried, but nothing works and he's wrecking everything – the little kids, our home, our marriage. He's like poison, mom. I don't know why he's so horrible, but maybe sending him to this school will straighten him out. John already made the arrangements. He's taking him as soon as possible. It's a place in Colorado. I don't know how we're going to pay for it, but..."

"Colorado?" I said, mentally estimating mileage. "So he won't be able to come home on weekends?"

"No," she said. "He won't be coming home... at all."

I wanted to shake her. I'd had it. "Beth," I pronounced with every shred of authority that accrues to the term, "mother," and that authority is, frankly, more than any human being should have to shoulder, "I want to know who TJ's biological father is. I want to know *now*."

"Oh, you do?" she snapped back, crying. "Why? Because you think he'll ride in on a white horse and rescue his son? Well, he won't, mom. He doesn't even know he *has* a son, okay? So stay out of it!"

She turned to leave but I grabbed her arm and whispered, "If

you wanted me to stay out of it, you might have mentioned that
fourteen years ago, Beth. But you didn't. No, you were only too
happy to live at home then and sporadically for the next ten years,
you and TJ, in and out until you finally decided to marry that idiot
John and become a walking incubator. Your choices leave me
dumbfounded, Beth, but they're yours and I haven't said a word.
But I'm saying one now. *Who*?"

We were moving toward the elevators, a mother and
daughter seeming merely deep in conversation. It wouldn't do to
make a scene. We don't make scenes.

"All right, I'll tell you," she said, jabbing the button that said
"Lobby." "I hate you for this, mom. I'll never forgive you. It's none
of your business, never was, but maybe it'll knock you off your high
horse."

She turned to look me straight in the face, anger flushing her
cheeks. "When you go home, look up 'ML!' on the Web. Just the
initials and an exclamation point. You'll figure it out. We all know
how damn smart you are!" Then the elevator doors whooshed
open, she didn't look back and I felt like Alice down the rabbit hole.
Nothing was making sense; nothing I knew applied.

Chapter Thirty-Two

The House of the Rising Sun

The Animals

When I went back to TJ's room, Nick Mautner stood, said, "Call me when you want to go home," and left. TJ was subdued, toying with a book lying beside him on the white blanket.

"What's that?" I asked, still reeling from my confrontation with Beth.

"A lady came by with a cart of books. All kids' books. I picked this one." He held up a facsimile edition of *The Wonderful Wizard of Oz*, its cover illustrations charming and dated. "The pictures look weird."

I sat in the chair. "That's because this is a reproduction of the original book the way it looked when it was first published. Over a hundred years ago," I said, wondering why my voice sounded wistful. I wasn't alive in 1900, but the pen-and-ink drawings drew me there anyway. To a time before Internet porn and two-ton cars that obliterate human bodies like insects under a shoe. Exhausted, I thought of Vivienne Geoffrey, locked in the flotsam of the past, and envied her the escape. "Do you want me to read it to you?"

"I'm practically fourteen," TJ said. "It's a kids' book." But his eyes were eager.

"Well, it's all we've got," I began, "but there are some things you don't know about this book. Things kids don't know."

"About *The Wizard of Oz*? What things?"

After thirty years at this, I knew what I was doing. "The Emerald City, for starters," I said. "Some scholars think the author, L. Frank Baum, modeled the Emerald City on the Hotel Del Coronado, right here in San Diego."

"No way."

"Way. Baum spent a lot of time at the Hotel Del, writing. He lived in Michigan, but he came here often and that's where he always stayed."

"I can see him doing that," TJ said, copying the old-fashioned drawing of the scarecrow on the book cover onto his cast with a ballpoint pen. "That place is sort of magic, it's so old and... fancy. Can we go out there? I wanna compare these old pictures to the way it looks now. What else?"

So I read him the story, inserting bits of whatever literary criticism I could remember. "Some people think it's about politics in Baum's time."

"They're stupid," TJ countered. "It's about life. It's even got drugs, the poppies. I guess he wanted to warn kids, even back then."

"Drugs are pretty scary."

"Yeah, they f..., they mess up your brain."

"Things can mess up your brain in other ways, too," I said, seizing the moment. "Like pornography."

Silence, then he scowled. "Mom told you?"

"Of course, and it's not the end of the world. You're growing up. We just want you to get it that real girls and women aren't ever like porn. It's a kind of lie, like the dealer who tells you drugs are just fun and won't hurt you." He looked blank; I was over my head.

TJ stared at the scarecrow on his cast. "Nick says guys just like to look at girls that way sometimes, but some of it's totally sick. He said when he was a cop one time he completely trashed this place where they were, you know, taking those pictures. He said he beat the shit out of the guy that was doing it."

Okay, there are two worlds. I wasn't going to make a dent in TJ's blossoming male world with oblique references to the humanity of real girls. But apparently he'd talked to Nick and liked the idea of beating up pornographers. I guessed it was a step in the right direction. And Nick as a singing cop was food for thought.

I abandoned the lecture, managed to keep him awake for four hours, and when the nurse came in again at three a.m. we were both asleep.

"You look beat," she noted. "And Taggart here will be fine. Why don't you go on home?"

I nudged him. "TJ, I'm wiped out. Will you be okay if I go home?"

"I'm fine," he muttered. "What can happen in a hospital? But you'll come back tomorrow?"

"I'll be here."

"Thanks, grandma."

"No problem."

I wasn't about to call Nick Mautner at that hour. I'd call him later and make arrangements to pick up Sadie. So I grabbed a cab and was glad to see my car in the driveway and a note from Jude stuck in the screen door.

"Call as soon as you can," it said. "We're all here for you."

The house felt wrong without Sadie, but I told myself she was okay, sleeping somewhere with another dog. In my living room/office I moved the mouse and awakened my computer. Still standing, I typed "ML!" into Google. The first hit was Merrill-Lynch, but after that I could make no sense of what appeared.

On my screen was a staged photo of a heavily made up woman in a long, stringy, sable brown wig parted in the middle. The dark bodice of her dress had tiny pleats, and over her shoulders was a dark cape. In the background, a white road snaked into a fanciful landscape of mountains spiked like frost on a window. Her smile was still mysterious although I'd seen it a thousand times. The real smile, that is. I was looking at a model posing as the subject of the most famous painting in the world. ML! Mona Lisa.

But the model's face wasn't Mona Lisa's, and the deliberately hooded eyes weren't dark, but bright blue. And strangely familiar. I scrolled down through more shots of the same model costumed as popular paintings – Vermeer's *Girl with a Pearl Earring,* Manet's *Berthe Morisot with a Bouquet of Violets,* an Alphonse Mucha fantasy figure in gorgeous wig and diaphanous costume. A French song I couldn't understand accompanied the page, and at the bottom in Art Deco letters was an announcement, also in French. I could read enough to learn that "ML!" would be playing at a club in Paris the following Friday and Saturday nights. "ML!" was a show of some kind. Interesting, but what did it have to do with TJ's father?

Then I scrolled back through the photos. I was bleary from lack of sleep and had trouble focusing my eyes, but something in the model's face demanded close scrutiny. In Manet's portrait of the artist Berthe Morisot, she faces the viewer directly in ambient daylight. And the model's face regarding me from Morisot's fashionable nineteenth century hat and jacket was TJ's! TJ grown angular, the jaw more defined, but I'd know those enormous blue eyes anywhere. The model's skin was obscured by heavy makeup, but near the hairline of her wig a few telltale freckles were visible. She was unquestionably related to my grandson. An aunt, I thought. Maybe a cousin. Then I typed the French text into a translating program and quickly became more confused.

ML! was not TJ's aunt, but a man. His show, involving exquisitely costumed recreations of famous artworks, had been extended indefinitely. There were rave reviews from *Télérama* and *Pariscope* calling ML! "... a feast for mind and eye, ...provocative, upscale drag that redefines the genre..." and "At last - drag goes highbrow!"

So was Beth telling me TJ's father was a French drag performer? She'd taken a class trip to Europe her junior year, the usual two-week whirl of major cities. But TJ was conceived a year later, during the summer after she graduated. Where had she met this guy? And why would a gay man be interested in her? Beth assumed I'd figure it out, but I wasn't figuring it out. I needed help. Then I remembered where I could get it.

Three a.m. in California is noon in Paris, I learned after typing "Paris time" into Google. François Loreau would be in his shop, unless he were out having lunch at a sidewalk café. I imagined an artichoke casserole and glass of opalescent wine, the melded scents drifting across a tiny white tablecloth. I could actually smell it. Or I could smell *something* as I searched my address book for the number.

His "Allo," on the phone was cheerful.

"François," I began, "it's Taylor Blake and I have a very strange favor to ask. Would you be willing to go to a drag show tonight?"

The scent of hot artichokes and wine is somewhat similar to the scent of persimmons. I was smelling persimmons, I realized. Not a French casserole. Against the freshly-painted, rock-red wall of my living room a density was forming.

Oh, shit!

"I can't talk," I told him quickly, 'it's *here*! But please, if you can, go to a club called *L'Orange Bleue*, on *rue de Seine*. Check out the performer; he's called 'ML!' Don't mention me, okay? Just see what you can find out about him, his real name, anything."

"I do not know what is 'drag,' but I will go; it is nearby," François agreed as a sickening figure emerged in billows of persimmon scent from my wall. "Fight, Taylor! Go! Now!" Then there was only the dial tone and a high-pitched mewling from my ghoul.

It was classic now, a medieval nightmare called up from the dregs of time. A grotesquely hunched and armless semi-human figure whose scabrous, insect-like legs emerged from its neck, it stood only two feet tall, but seethed with menace. Its head was as wide as its height, with bulging, solid black eyes that could see nothing and in which nothing could be seen. The thing staggered toward me, snapping teeth like black nails erupting from its wide, lipless gums. Filthy hair hung in tangled shocks from patches on its head. The smell of persimmons was so strong I was gagging, but I grabbed the French dictionary and threw it, hitting the thing's mouth. A lumpy fluid gushed from the wound and writhed on my carpet.

"Pathetic!" I yelled, reaching for more big books. "A third-grade kid could do better than this!" It lurched into furniture but kept moving, robotlike and mindless. Its teeth sounded electrical, like the crackling of empty tracks in a subway station late at night. The third rail. Deadly. I threw *The Complete Works of Shakepeare* into its head, practically falling over myself with the effort. I was too tired. I was weak, and reached for the chain at my neck. The thing kept moving. Then there was a sound, and it stopped.

It was half-transparent now, a hideous, frozen monster on the carpet near my desk. And the sound was my doorbell. The ghoul, half-dissolved, didn't move, but I walked backward into the hall, trembling as I watched it.

"I called the hospital after four hours, figured you might need a ride then," Nick Mautner announced from the dark beyond my door. "They said you got a cab. Thought I'd bring Sadie. You all right?"

He held my groggy dog in his arms while the faint outline of a medieval ghoul stayed right where it was. Nick couldn't see it, but Sadie squirmed and growled, sniffing the air.

"Not exactly," I said, watching the thing, which didn't move. "But thanks for bringing Sadie. Please come in."

He was humming "Celeste Aida" an octave lower than its usual key, and I saw the ghoul recoil, as if the sound were acid on its skin.

"Nick, sing it," I urged, "the words, loud." A peculiar request in the middle of the night, but he just shrugged and shut the door, then took a deep breath and sang. Italian words filled my living room like explosions of silk– *Celeste Aida, forma divina*... – as the armless horror shuddered and vanished with a shriek only I could hear.

He set Sadie down and looked at me, puzzled. "What's going on?"

"Complicated night, family stuff," I sidestepped much but stayed within the loose boundaries of truth, amazed that this man I barely knew could banish a ghoul with his voice.

"Why did you ask me to sing?"

"Just love that aria, I guess. Nick, I'm so tired I can't stand up. Thanks for bringing Sadie, but you shouldn't have driven all the way back from... from wherever you live. It's so late and opening night is tomorrow..."

"Oh, I just sleep in the truck down here," he said. "Easier than driving back and forth from the desert."

He'd said he lived near Borrego Springs, a desert town that's a two-hour drive over the mountains. And it was nearly four a.m.

"The couch is yours if you want it," I told him. "I'll get you a blanket and pillow."

"Great," he answered. "I'll get Rom."

I threw the necessities on the couch while he was out, and fell into bed with Sadie. Sometime later I felt another weight jar the mattress and root under the sheet. In the split second before experience reminded me that *people* generally do not root and dig enthusiastically in bedclothes, although dachshunds do, it crossed my mind that my visitor might be Nick. The idea was not as shocking as it should have been, an amusing curiosity I filed for later consideration. There wasn't room on the couch with Nick, I figured, so the hefty dachshund had come to join his pal. I was trapped between two sleeping dogs but too tired to move anyway, and was again asleep in seconds. I knew the next day was going to be a zoo.

Chapter Thirty-Three

A Whiter Shade of Pale

Procol Harum

I didn't hear the phone ring, but shrewdly recognized the arrival of morning in the fuzzy light blasting the edges of my venetian blinds. There was also a scent of coffee and a deep voice in the hall, bellowing "Phone." Sadie and Rommel had vacated my bed, so I could move.

"Hello," I said after fumbling for the bedside phone and then sinking back into pillows.

"Mom, who answered? What's that guy doing there?"

It was Beth, and I couldn't quite remember what he was doing there.

"Sadie," I remembered. "He brought Sadie."

She seemed mollified. "Oh. Well, I don't want to talk about... last night, except for one thing. He didn't know I was seventeen, okay? I'd graduated so he thought I was eighteen. He was so unhappy and I was trying to help him. And that's all, the end of it. But what I'm calling about is I need your help. It's serious, mom. I talked to my obstetrician this morning and he said I have to have complete bed rest for at least three weeks, maybe more. John's left already, he's taking Hannah and Benjamin up to Los Angeles to stay with his mother, but they're discharging TJ from the hospital today. I can't take care of him, mom. And John is... I just can't have TJ here even until he goes to Colorado."

I entertained a momentary fantasy of three women in Greco-Roman robes, spinning, measuring and finally cutting the thread of every life. The Fates. I sighed, realizing this moment, or its possibility, had been spun long ago in choices made blindly. Of course I would get married, have children. That was what you *did*. But I wasn't blind now. I could refuse and go on a hiking tour of the Hebrides instead. Yeah, right.

"Of course," I told my daughter, "you have to do whatever is necessary to protect the new baby. I'll take TJ."

"Oh, thanks, mom," she began, but I went on implacably.

"What I mean is that I'll bring TJ here from the hospital, Beth, and he'll *stay* here. There will be no 'school for scum.' He'll stay here; he'll go to his own school. And if I can't handle him, *I'll* choose what to do next."

"Forget it, mom," she said, "I told you John's already made the arrangements. It's a school called 'Academy Ten' for the Ten Commandments, and the kids take care of cows before and after classes. They make cheese and stuff. It's very disciplined."

I didn't point out that golden and fatted calves notwithstanding, cows do not figure significantly in either Testament. And I had already considered my response. TJ might require a controlled environment if he didn't shape up, but not now and not one based on the Ten Commandments and cows.

"John is irrelevant in this discussion," I said. "He never adopted TJ and has no legal standing in regard to him. You are TJ's only parent and can make decisions for him until he's eighteen, but I advise you not to fight me on this, Beth. It could get very ugly."

She was crying again, and I was tired of it. "It's because you know who his father is, isn't it?" she sobbed. "You think you can hold that over me. You can threaten to tell John and..."

"You mean John doesn't know?" I interrupted. I didn't know, either, but apparently it was a shelling point.

"Are you kidding? John? No, he doesn't know; he can't; you *can't* tell him. And he does want what's best for TJ no matter what you think. I agree with him, too. TJ's pushed us too far. This school will be good for him, so stop meddling and just accept it. I have to go, mom. Thanks for keeping him until he can leave."

"TJ will be here until he leaves for college if I can manage it," I said. "Take care of yourself."

Nick was in the living room folding blankets when I stumbled into the kitchen.

"Trouble?" he asked.

"You could say that," I answered. "Thanks for making coffee."

"Least I could do. Dress rehearsal's tonight. Be there?"

"Afraid not, but tell Isabel I'll be there tomorrow night for the opening if I can make it."

"Roger," he said, then scooped Rommel over his shoulder and left.

The coffee was five times stronger than I make it, but drinkable with a lot of milk and sugar. I carried my cup out onto the deck and watched Sadie bury a rawhide chew toy in a shallow grave she'd dig up five minutes later. The activity seemed less irrational than the mess I'd just gotten myself into. For a moment I was actually tempted to bury my coffee cup in the yard, just to see what it felt like, but the phone rang.

"Allo, Taylor?" It was François. "My wife and I go to the show, ML!, last night and it is wonderful!" he said. "Colombe, my wife, is in love with the costumes and say she will go back with her friends. I have not seen this kind of show, where a man dress up like these beautiful women and pretend to sing, but it was so good and interesting. The man tells the story of the famous paintings and..."

"Who is he, François?" I interrupted. "Did you learn anything about the man?"

"Oh yes. He is American, an art historian from a university in California, teaching courses at the Sorbonne. He is a visiting professor in Paris for the autumn. The name on the program is 'Thomas Jalland, Ph.D.' I talk to him about making some postcards of scenes in his show, to sell in my shop. We will meet to discuss this."

"François, you're *formidable!*" I said, pronouncing the word the French way – "for-mee-DAAHBluh - as a compliment. "Did you get a phone number for Jalland?"

I had no intention of phoning Thomas Jalland, but wanted to know I *could*.

Oui, François laughed, and recited ten numbers I carefully wrote on a paper towel in my kitchen. "When will you come to visit?" he concluded. "Now that you have interest in someone here?"

"Some day," I promised, "but don't mention me to Jalland. It's... rather personal."

"Ah," he said in that tone invariably accompanied by a knowing Gallic shrug. "Please call again if you need my help."

"Thank you, François," I said. "And check your emails. We must stay in touch."

Code for "trouble."

"I know. *Au revoir,* Taylor."

I typed the Paris phone number into my computer's address book under "Jalland, Thomas," and stared at the name. The initials were T.J. Beth had been efficiently symbolic in naming her fatherless baby Taggart Jared. Clues to a mystery I told myself did not need to be solved. Then why leave clues at all?

I knew why she'd chosen "Jared." When the kids were little, every night I read them poems by a heartland poet named Jared Carter. I wanted to give them my past, I guess, the farms and barns and lightning rods and narrow, dusty roads. I wanted them to see a fictional little town called Mississinewa that was like my own little town. And Beth had chosen the poet's name for her son because she wanted the initial "J." But why "Taggart?" A name from a high school art class text. Then my brain made the bridges. Art. Thomas Jalland was an art historian as well as a performer. I headed for the garage in bare feet and bathrobe.

And after fifteen minutes in swirling dust that still smelled burnt, I found it in a crumbling box of Beth's old things. A British paperback textbook I'd only noticed because of the spelling of "watercolour" in the title. By a Scottish artist named Paul Taggart who was older than I am and probably never set foot in California, much less seduced my daughter. But on the inside cover was an inscription – "This book was my introduction to the making of beauty. I hope it will show you the way as well. Congratulations on your graduation. Mr. Jalland."

Mr. Jalland, the traditional teacher's honorific.

It came back to me then. Beth and Kevin both attended the high school where I taught. They were never in my classes, but of course I knew their teachers, was close friends with some of them. And a high school teacher's lounge rivals the most incendiary tabloid for gossip. In Beth's senior year an art teacher left abruptly near the end of spring term due to a family crisis. A substitute was brought in to finish out the year. His name was Jalland, he was only there for a month and I never actually met him, but I remembered the talk.

"Guy's a faggot," a male math teacher groused over coffee every morning, just to stir up trouble. To which pejorative all four guidance counselors and most of the English Department, including me, predictably objected. It wasn't really a big deal, more a conversational thread. The openly gay head of the history department always parried with comments like, "Yeah, and I'd kill to know where he got that tie with Renoir's 'The Umbrellas' printed on it." It was the end of the year when everybody's tired and irritable, and it offered an avenue through which we could feel a part of trendy social issues, I guess. Jalland-the-gay-art-sub was occasional fodder for conversation in the teacher's lounge, but it went no further. Certainly nobody stopped to consider the feelings of a young kid fresh out of college and still struggling to find his way through the often homophobic minefield that is American culture, especially in schools. Nobody except, apparently, Beth.

She was in Jalland's class but didn't say anything about him, although she and her friends went through a phase of watercolor scarf painting he must have taught them. They all wore those painted scarves at graduation. And then what? I poured another cup of coffee and sat on the deck.

I could see it, imagine how it happened. Even as a child, Beth *liked* boys, worried about them, was eager to help them. In kindergarten she struggled to help her brother Kevin with his Cub Scout projects and later baked cookies for his track team. She was one of those girls who dig earthworms for the boys' fishing trips and sit cheering in blazing sun at Little League games instead of joining the team. I knew girls like that as a child, but after about fourth grade they weren't my close friends. Later I'd hear that one or another of them had cooked a hundred pounds of spaghetti for a Lion's Club fundraiser, stood smiling at the side of a philandering politician husband or was found buried with seven others under the chicken coop of a serial killer. I guess the outcome depends on the sort of man to whom they devote themselves, but that *is* what they do. And although I hadn't exactly wanted to acknowledge it, Beth was one of them.

She both admired and felt sorry for a teacher only a few years older than she was, an unhappy boy still coming to terms with being gay. He thought she was eighteen that summer after she graduated from high school, and she didn't disabuse him of the idea. They must have become close, spent time together. She had a summer job at a mall boutique and spent the rest of her time with her friends. She never told me Tom Jalland was one of them. She never told anybody how she'd decided to "help" him. But the endeavor must have been a success, at least once, because halfway through October she came home from her freshman year at Mills College, telling us she was nearly three months pregnant. TJ arrived the following March, slightly early at five pounds, eleven ounces. The subject of his paternity was verboten. Until now.

I ate some toast to absorb the caffeine in Nick's idea of coffee, and typed "Thomas Jalland" into my computer. What came up were his degrees – Master of Fine Arts from the School of the Art Institute of Chicago and a Ph.D. from Yale – his class schedule at U.C. Berkeley for the coming spring semester, his scholarly publications and the picture required for faculty websites. Again, I shook my head in disbelief. It was TJ aged to late thirties in a professor's button-down shirt, wool tie and tweed jacket. The hay-like red-blond hair was close-cropped, the freckles abundant and the familiar blue eyes sparkling with mischievous intelligence. I felt a glow of pride, as if he were really my son-in-law. I liked him. It was weird.

Next I called TJ at the hospital and told him he'd be coming to my place.

"Your mom's having problems with her pregnancy and has to stay in bed for several weeks," I told him. "John has taken the little kids to his mother."

"The baby's not going to, like, die, is it?" he asked, to his credit.

"Things will probably be all right as long as Beth can rest and have some peace."

"Is that why they want to send me away, because mom's having problems with being pregnant?"

I hadn't prepared a speech yet, so winged it. "No, TJ, although she definitely can't take care of you right now. The reason for the school idea is that your behavior is so atrocious that it's affecting everybody in really bad ways. Hannah is picking up your awful language, you hide in your room, snarl at your mother and deliberately drive John crazy. To that add hitchhiking, trying to rob a liquor store, downloading porn on your computer and running away only to get hit by a car. The driver suspects that you may have jumped in front of him on purpose, which is scaring all of us. You're out of control, TJ. It has to stop one way or another."

"It wasn't on purpose; I was running away from something chasing me. A coyote, I think. Do *you* think I should go away?" he asked in that cracking voice.

There are coyotes in San Diego's canyons, also foxes and the rare wildcat as well as rattlers. But if anything was really chasing TJ apart from his own misery, it was likely to have been one of the marginal homeless people who also inhabit the canyons. Either way, he must have been terrified.

"That will be up to you. What's going to happen right now is that you're coming here to live with me. There will be rules and I'll probably arrange for you to see a counselor. If things go well, you might stay indefinitely or you might go back to live with your mom and John at some point. I don't agree that you should be sent away to a school in Colorado where we can never see you. It's just not going to happen."

"I *hate* John," he whispered, fighting tears.

"And that's the first rule," I decided as I said it. "Forget John. He's out of the picture. He doesn't matter, he has nothing to do with you. In a few months you'll be fourteen; you're no longer a child but becoming a man. It's a rough time, but I *know* you can get through it. Understand?"

"How do you know I can?"

"Because you're too smart to fuck up your entire life just to get even with John."

"Grandma! Zero points!"

"Sorry, this is hardball, TJ. Are you in or out?"

"In," he said after a pause. "I'm in. But grandma, tell me the truth. Do you know who my father is?"

Don't lie, Taylor. Not now.

"That's something to talk about later. It's interesting but not relevant. You're on your own, TJ. Don't make up some fantasy father. I'm here to help you, and Grandpa Charlie will help, too, but you've got to take charge of your own life now. I know that's a pretty tall order and I'm not sure I could have done it at your age, but let's give it a try. What time will you be discharged?"

"Ten-thirty," he said. "And this is so cool! I got a thing like a scooter where I prop my leg with the cast on a seat and push with the other leg. It's got hand brakes and a basket for my books and goes really fast. The physical therapist said crutches are totally retro. The scooter's orange, too. I can probably go to school this afternoon, huh? I want to show Seiji."

He was back to being a little boy and the transitions were making me dizzy.

"We'll need a doctor's permission for you to go to school," I noted. See you at ten-thirty."

Only after hanging up the phone did it occur to me that I was dragging a troubled child into a world much stranger than the mess in his head. A grandmother with magical powers who's routinely threatened by a soul-eating ghoul. Scarcely optimal, but still better than a school for scum, with cows. And adolescence would protect him from seeing much of anything beyond himself. I hoped.

I needed to talk and called Jude, who arrived fifteen minutes later to help me get TJ's room ready.

"He changed plans and will be here *tonight*," she said over the vacuum cleaner.

"Who will be here tonight?"

"Luke. I'm picking him up at the airport at seven-fifteen. Where do you think I should take him for dinner, Tay? I mean, it's not like it's a date. I don't know what it is. Oh, Tay, I'm so nervous!"

I pulled myself back from the overwhelming realization of what I'd just done, and tried to empathize. This guy was the axis of Jude's personal mythology, the soulmate lost forever to an error in judgment but eternally present as an ideal. What if he'd gained a hundred pounds, had bad teeth and a wife in tow? When possible, myths are best left mythical.

"Is he, um, coming alone?" I asked, regarding TJ's rickety half bunk bed with a fresh eye. If TJ were to stay for long, he'd need a new bed. I'd talk to Charlie about finances once he got home from wherever he was. I was going to need help.

"You mean is he bringing a wife. He just sent an email with the airline, flight number and time, Tay. What if there's a wife? What should I do?"

"Same thing," I said, trying to exude a contagious, Buddha-like calm. "Invite them to dinner, ask what they'd like to see, offer suggestions about things to do. You're southern, Jude. You know how to do the gracious hostess thing."

"I'll just *die* if he gets off that plane with a woman."

"Southern hostesses don't die," I pointed out. "They carry on."

"They can carry on all they want, but *I'll* die," she insisted. "Still, I'm going to wear something businessy – you know, the tailored suit and crisp white blouse look - just in case. Do you really think you can take care of TJ at this stage, Tay? Teenage boys are difficult."

"So are teenage girls," I answered from experience, "but I'm not going to have TJ sent off to some fundamentalist farm. If it doesn't work I'll find a school for him myself."

Jude was thoughtful. "The Syndicate always worried about John and we were right. Do you think I should wear sparkly earrings, or stick with pearls?"

"Pearls," I said. "Take the high road until you have a clue about what's going on."

"I'm just SO nervous," she said again.

I was, too, but pearl earrings weren't going to help.

Chapter Thirty-Four

Running Scared

Roy Orbison

The rest of that morning went swimmingly, although I knew better than to assume it would last. TJ and I finally left the hospital at noon after spending fifteen minutes trying to load his scooter into the trunk. It was heavy and cumbersome, but he quickly figured the dimensions for a ramp and stayed in the car while I ran in to a home supply store for boards. Then we went by Seiji's to get the materials for TJ's wall hanging from the Foxwell's garage. Miyoko made us sandwiches and while TJ was in the bathroom whispered, "Let us know the minute you need help. This isn't going to be easy."

"I raised two," I whispered back. "What's one more? But thanks, I know I'm going to need all the help I can get."

She shook her head. "Things are different now, Taylor. Drugs, sex... by the time they're out of grade school kids are buried in stuff they can't handle, but they think they can."

"My plan is to keep him busy."

She grinned. "Don't forget that means keeping *you* busy."

I was already busy battling a ghoul, ostensibly with a goal of saving the world, but I couldn't tell Miyoko that. After loading barn boards in the back seat, I drove to Beth's to pick up some clothes for TJ, assuming John wouldn't be back from Los Angeles. I didn't want to see John.

Beth was in bed and burst into tears when she saw TJ.

"It's all right, mom," he told her, rocking his scooter back and forth on her bedroom carpet. "You have to take care of your baby. And I'll just be at grandma's. I won't be far away."

"You did well," I told him. "I'm proud of you. Now, leave your laptop here and let's go."

He bristled, the bad old TJ surfacing. "What? I need it for my homework. And games. I play *games*, grandma!"

"I told you there would be rules. You'll use my computer, in the living room, in plain view until you get a grip on what's okay and what's not."

I didn't like the nasty look growing in his eyes. "I can look at whatever I want," he snarled.

"Yes, you can," I told him. "There's enough diseased garbage out there to fill a medium-sized ocean, and if that's what you want to put in your mind, nobody can stop you. But...not...in...my...house."

He sulked. "Games aren't garbage."

"We're not talking about games and you know it."

His nasty look faded to sulky chagrin. "Are you going to put kiddy controls on your computer?"

"If I have to."

"Well, you don't have to."

"That remains to be seen."

The conversation transpired over mere minutes as we loaded his scooter into the trunk again, but I felt as if I'd been juggling water balloons packed with nitroglycerin, for hours. TJ, on the other hand, seemed relieved and cheerfully drew the Tinman from Oz in the dust on my dashboard.

"Cute," I said. I was already tired and it was only two in the afternoon. And only the beginning.

When we got home TJ consumed most of a tub of grocery guacamole with corn chips and asked for a Coke.

"There's fruit juice," I said, then watched half a quart disappear. He went to rest in bed while I walked Sadie, and he was, fortunately, still asleep when I got back. The phone was ringing. It was John.

"Taylor, I don't want to argue with you," he said.

"Good. TJ's fine. Thank you for calling."

"Look, Beth and I appreciate you letting him stay with you for a few days, but..."

"Your."

"What?"

"*Your* letting him stay. 'Letting' in the way you used the word is a gerund, a verb used as a noun, and so requires a noun modifier." Pain-in-the-ass is my fallback position. It gives me time to think.

John was, as usual, uninterested in grammar, and merely bellowed. "I've had it with your meddling, Taylor! You're a mother-in-law joke, you know that? Prissy little old fart of a schoolteacher who thinks she knows everything. If you cared about Beth at all like a normal mother..."

"I'm not the one who's yelling and upsetting Beth," I pointed out. "You need to calm down, John."

"What *we* need is for you to back off and let us take care of our children as *we* see fit. Beth told me what you're up to, keeping TJ with you and all that, and I'm here to tell you you're not going to get away with it. That boy is out of control and needs discipline. We've chosen a good, Bible-based school where..."

"No, *you* chose the Ten Commandment Dairy or whatever it is," I interrupted. But you are not TJ's father. You cannot make decisions about his welfare."

"I've spoken with a lawyer," he said, showing his ace. "Beth agrees with my decision and I was told that no judge would give a troubled teenage boy to a crazy old woman when his family is willing to pay for him to be retrained at a good institution."

"Retrained! What is this place, a center for brainwashing? Over my dead body, John."

His laugh was unpleasant. "That will be the happiest day of my life, Taylor. Now, when did the doctor say TJ would be ready to leave for Academy Ten?"

"TJ will not be going to Academy Ten, John," I said quietly. "Good-bye."

Shaken, I called Maggie McFadden. I needed a social worker and Maggie's connections in that field are unparalleled. She called back within fifteen minutes.

"Academy Ten is an uncredited, fundy-religious camp-school for 'bad' kids in the middle of nowhere in Colorado," she began. The staff are uncredentialed, the educational program is a joke and two years ago a fifteen-year-old girl who'd been sent there by her parents ran away into the hills and died of exposure. The official line was that search teams were dispatched immediately, but an insider later admitted that an all-night 'prayer vigil for her return' preceded any attempt to find her. The temperature was fifteen degrees that night. We cannot permit your grandson to be sent there, Taylor. You need a lawyer, but I've got to tell you it will be a mess. The best option is a long, dragged-out case in family court. Maybe long enough for things to settle down, for John to come to his senses, and in the end a judge might allow TJ to choose his domicile. And then again maybe not, in which case the mother's wishes would prevail."

I took the phone into the garage in case TJ was awake, my breath shallow. "Maggie, what if his real father stepped in? What if his biological father refused to allow him to be sent to this place?"

"That would complicate things even more, definitely buy more time. But what are you talking about? What biological father?"

I told her the whole story.

"Wow," she said. "Too bad Beth didn't stick with him!"

"He's gay, Mag."

"So?"

"Beth isn't."

"Oh, yeah."

"So what do I do now?"

She made that sound horses do with their lips. An inconclusive sound. "Nothing right now. You'll have TJ for a few days. Let me make some calls, check on a few things. I guess you won't be at the dress rehearsal tonight?"

"No, but I'll be there tomorrow for opening night."

"You knew Steve went up to Betty Ford today, didn't you?"

I didn't know. I hadn't called Jill and had no idea how things were going for Jude and the mysterious Luke Salnier. I missed the Syndicate. "That's good," I said, and hung up.

I made a tuna casserole and fruit salad, TJ got up, Seiji came by to try out the scooter and stayed for dinner. After that they went out to the garage to work on TJ's project, requiring that I move the car out to make room. I wandered around feeling what is popularly deemed "conflict." I didn't want to stay home; I wanted to be at the dress rehearsal. The boys were having a great time sawing and drilling, and I was bored and depressed by the prospect of many more nights, an endless river of nights, just like that one. I'd cook, do laundry and sit around supervising TJ until he finally grew up and I dropped dead from the effort. Where was my ghoul when I needed it, I thought. I wanted to punch something to a pulp.

It was only eight o'clock when the doorbell rang, but it was unnerving. Nobody ever comes to my door at that hour except kids on Halloween. A man in polyester slacks and a Hawaiian shirt was holding a manila envelope that glowed green under my porchlight. "Are you Mrs. Taylor Blake?" he asked.

"Ms." I said. "But yes."

He nodded, looked at his watch and handed me the envelope. Then he walked to his car at the curb, wrote something on a clipboard and drove away while I stood there. In the envelope was a letter from an attorney informing me that I was to "release" Taggart Jared Blake to the care and custody of his mother, Elizabeth Aislinn Blake Montgomery, in the person of her duly selected "agent," John Howard Montgomery, the following morning at seven o'clock. In the event that I refused to do so, a charge of kidnapping would be brought against me, resulting in my arrest and possible conviction, blahblah.

I regretted having named Beth for my crazy, proto-Revenant grandmother who, I thought, would not be happy about it. Panicky, I headed inside to call Maggie on her cell at the dress rehearsal, but TJ was scooting gleefully into the hall.

"It's ready!" he announced. "You have to hide your eyes, grandma. Seiji's bringing it in because I can't lift it. You're not gonna believe this!"

I sat in the kitchen with my hands over my face, wondering if Beth knew what John had done. And wondering what I was going to do. In the living room TJ was whispering. "There, right there. That's where it goes." Then, "Okay, grandma, you can see it now!"

Against my red-leaf colored wall Seiji was straining to hold a large geometric sculpture of weathered boards, cut and arranged with delightful balance and rhythm. It was perfect for the room, and for me.

"TJ, it's absolutely wonderful!" I said, hugging him across his scooter's handlebars. "I can't believe you made this. I mean, it's just right, it's just what I'd choose except there's nothing like it. What a talent you have!"

"You think so? Really?"

"No question. Let me get my camera and take a picture before Seiji's arms give out. We'll have to figure out how to hang it tomorrow."

"Yeah, it'll need molly bolts and a couple of guys to fasten it to the wall," TJ said, mugging after I came back with the camera and took shots of the two of them with his creation. "Maybe that guy Nick can help."

"Maybe, after the play is over. What do you think about focus lights on it, like they have in museums?"

"Way cool!" Seiji agreed, sighing as he carefully set it down. "Dude, you're an artist."

"Yeah," TJ said, glowing beneath his freckles. "Like Picasso!"

Closer than that, TJ.

I took Seiji home and tried to call Maggie from the car, but she wasn't picking up. It wasn't really the last straw. Vivienne Geoffrey's remark about even the gods being unable to change the past stuck in my mind. The gods couldn't do it and neither could Beth. I already knew what I was going to do. At ten I gave TJ his antibiotic and a Tylenol, and he was asleep in minutes. At eleven I carried the phone to the garage and dialed a ten-digit number nearly six thousand miles away. It would be eight o'clock in the morning there. I was shaking so hard I had to brace my arm against the car.

"May I speak to Thomas Jalland?" I said in a creaking voice I didn't recognize, like a footstep in wet snow.

"One moment," the answering male voice told me politely. "I'll get him."

"My name is Taylor Blake and before I say anything else, I want you to know that I have no intention of harming or exploiting you in any way," I told Jalland when he came to the phone. "But I need your help."

"Blake," he pronounced as if trying to remember where he'd heard the name. "I'm sorry, but I'm afraid you've reached an incorrect number."

"I'm Beth Blake's mother, Mr. Jalland. I believe the two of you were friends many years ago. Fourteen years ago. And please don't hang up. I'm not calling about Beth, but someone else."

After a few seconds he said, "Of course I remember Beth," trying for a courteous bonhomie that didn't quite work. "What is it, Mrs. Blake?"

"An intrusion for which I apologize. This is very awkward and I'm so sorry. Beth never wanted anyone to know, but I'm afraid there's an emergency. Please hear me out and then if you wish, terminate this call and I give you my word that I will never bother you again."

"Sounds very dramatic," he said uneasily as his companion whispered, "Dramatic? Tom, you're turning green! What's going on?"

"There's no way to ease into this," I plowed forward, perspiration running down my sides. "You have a son, Mr. Jalland. Your relationship with Beth resulted in a fine baby boy. He's now thirteen."

There was a long silence in which I could hear the other guy saying, "My God, Tom, what's wrong? Should I call the police? I'll get the phone book. What's the word for 'police' in French?"

"She says I have a son," Jalland finally said, his voice faint. "It's Beth's mother, the girl I told you about. That summer before I went to grad school."

"Oh, my God!" the other one said. "Sit down. Maybe it's a joke. Maybe she's trying to blackmail you. Do you think... it's true?" He actually sounded hopeful.

"Your friend is wise to be suspicious," I told Jalland. "But it is true and you may be able to help the boy. If you'll give me your email address I'll send you a photograph that I think will allay your misgivings."

"Uh, okay," he said and recited an address. The querulous voice was TJ's.

"I'll put the phone down, send the photo and come back. Then you may dismiss this call as fraudulent if you want."

In the living room I copied TJ's most recent school picture from my files and then added one from earlier that night. Both were gone in seconds. "Mail sent." I took a deep breath and tried to walk with great calm back to the garage, where I closed the door and picked up the phone.

"Here it is, here it is," the other man whispered eagerly in the background. Then, "Oh...my...God, Tom, it's *you!*"

"Um, hello?" I repeated several times. "Mr. Jalland?"

"Why... why didn't Beth tell me?" he asked, obviously upset. "I didn't know. I would have been there, sent money, taken care of him somehow. All this time, I just didn't know. I'm so sorry, Mrs. Blake. My God, he looks just *like* me!"

"Ask her about that thing they're holding on the wall," the other guy urged. "And how did he break his leg? 'He?' What's his name?"

But Thomas Jalland couldn't talk.

"I'm afraid the new dad is a bit emotional," the friend said, having grabbed the phone. "Hell, so am I. We've been trying to adopt, and... I apologize. My name is Pete Salerno. I'm Tom's partner. We're married. I hope you're not... I mean I hope this doesn't come as a shock."

"No," I said. "That's wonderful. My grandson's name is TJ –

Taggart Jared. He just made the wall piece in the photo for me."

"It's really good," Pete Salerno said. "Tom, his name's TJ and he *made* that! Your kid's an artist, too!"

There was more fumbling with the phone and Tom Jalland spoke again. "I'm sorry, this is just an unbelievable shock. You have no idea how much we've wanted... I don't mean..., that's impossible and unthinkable, but could I... maybe not right away but at some point if he felt okay about having a gay dad, maybe I could talk to him, do something for him?"

"You can do something right now," I said. "But first, thanks for... for not hanging up. I was so afraid..."

The remaining conversation took place over several hours and at one point I woke Maggie McFadden for a conference link. I needed a pro at handling messy family crises.

"Damn, if we were only there!" Pete kept muttering. "We just live up the coast in Berkeley. It's an hour and a half flight. We could *be* there!"

"But you're in France so we'll rely on other measures," Maggie insisted.

Tom was somber. "Just tell me what I can do to protect TJ. I'll do it. I will *not* allow my son to be harmed if there's any way I can stop it."

"No problem," Maggie chimed in.

And so the plan was laid.

Chapter Thirty-Five

You Don't Own Me

Leslie Gore

I called Tim at an indecent hour, then called Miyoko, told her everything and arranged for her to take TJ to her place for breakfast at six. He couldn't be present for the scene that was about to transpire, and I couldn't stop humming the theme from "Gunfight at OK Corral" as I woke him up.

"Why are you not asleep?" he asked groggily. "You never get up this early and you're already dressed!"

I'd planned to make up some excuse for getting him out of the house, but when the time came, I couldn't do it. It was his life we were all manipulating; excluding him from it was a contradiction in terms. And that meant telling him the truth at five-thirty in the morning the day after he'd been hit by a car.

"Go brush your teeth and then I need to tell you some things," I said. "Go now, okay?"

He didn't argue and hopped away, his orange scooter glowing in the dim light like an effigy from a forgotten religion. I sat at the end of his bed and leaned my head on the handlebar until he hopped back. "Okay, what?" he asked, sitting beside me.

"This is going to be rough, but before I begin I want you to know that it's going to turn out okay."

His huge blue eyes narrowed. "Grandma, *what*? Is it mom? The baby?"

I shook my head, fighting an emotional tsunami that would obliterate coherence. He was such a good kid beneath the adolescent nastiness. He loved his mother. I wanted to throttle her. "It's not your mother. You have to go to Seiji's now because John will be here in a little while. He has a lawyer. He wants to take you to a school in Colorado. It's not going to happen, but I don't want you to be here when he shows up, okay?"

I could see his scrawny chest heaving beneath his t-shirt, hear his shallow breathing. "Mom wants me to go, too, doesn't she?" he said.

"Your mom is sick and frightened right now, and your behavior is so bad that it's clear you need help," I hedged. "She's too weak to think clearly and John has convinced her that this place will help you. I've looked into it and do not agree that you should go there. You're *not* going there; you're going to stay right here, get help here. But this morning is going to be a mess I don't want you to see."

He'd tried, but couldn't hold back tears. "You said 'lawyer,'" he sobbed. "Is he bringing the police to get me, to take me away?"

"Possibly," I said, "but they aren't going to touch you and neither is John."

"You can't stop them," he wept, wrapping his arms around me. "Mom and John get to decide what happens to me. Parents get to decide, not grandmothers."

I held him close, hoping I was doing the right thing, not that there were alternative options at that point. "You're right about parents," I told him, tipping his face up and forcing myself to smile. "Which is why you need to listen carefully and don't have a heart attack on me, okay? There's some surprising news. At the hospital your mom told me enough that I could figure out who your biological father is. I called him last night and told him about what's happening to you. He didn't know you existed until last night, understand? It was a shock, but he was happy to know, TJ. And he's going to help. He will not permit you to be sent away."

"My *father*?" he said slowly as if the word were suddenly foreign. "Who is he? Is he coming here?"

"His name is Thomas Jalland and no, he's in France teaching art history. There's a lot more to tell, but not right now. Okay so far?"

The doorbell rang. "Better get dressed," I told him.

He looked stricken. "Is that the police?"

"No, it's the Syndicate," I said, grinning for real.

"Your friends? They're here?"

"Yep. And Seiji's mom is on her way to get you".

"I'd better get dressed."

In the half lit morning his eyes were enormous as he stared at me. "You found my father," he pronounced as I memorized his face. My life as a Revenant was going to be a roller-coaster and so was TJ's as a teenager. I didn't imagine a warm, fuzzy relationship in the next five years with this strange boy who was my grandson. He would need guiding hands other than mine, and I would see to it that he had them. But I would not forget this moment, ever.

"Yes," I said, and went to answer the door. The Syndicate were all there, dressed in funereal perfection, silent and fierce. Maggie had called everyone at four-thirty in the morning, and by five forty-five they were at my door.

"I'll make coffee," Pen said, and turned on the kitchen light. "Don't worry, Taylor, we're here."

TJ rolled out on his scooter in jeans and his blue frog t-shirt, and went straight for Jude, whom he knew better than the others. "I have a dad," he told her, watching with those wide, shocky eyes for her reaction. And she was stellar.

"I heard," she told him without bursting into tears, "that he's a pretty neat guy, and a college professor! No wonder you're a little smart, huh?"

I beamed at her as TJ beamed generally. "Art," he said. "He teaches about art."

I was about to point to TJ's wall decoration leaning against the living room wall when the doorbell rang again. It was Miyoko and I made the introductions quickly, everyone understanding the need for alacrity in getting TJ out. Jude helped with the scooter and as Miyoko pulled away from the curb another car slid quietly into the space. Tim emerged in priestly black, his violet eyes somber.

"Thank you," I told him, then introduced him to the Syndicate.

No one said much, and at six-fifteen we all went to stand outside. Maggie had explained that in such situations the "official move" is usually made at least forty-five minutes before the stated time in order to derail escape attempts. Pen and Tim stood at the head of our little group, and didn't flinch when minutes later John's car pulled to the curb, followed by a black and white patrol car. The cops didn't get out, merely blocked the driveway and sat there, watching. I held Sadie in one shaking hand as John approached, my other hand gripping the portable phone in my jacket pocket.

Cleancut in a suit and tie, my son-in-law looked "nice," and I was glad for Beth's happiness with him. Their life together was none of my business and I was sickened by the need to interfere. But the nice man on my walk could only be nice to people who thought exactly as he did, a category excluding everyone else on my walk, not to mention my grandson.

"Who are you?" he asked Tim as Pen smiled graciously.

"John," she said, "this is Father Timothy O'Halloran, a close friend of the family. Father, this is John Montgomery."

Tim extended his hand and after awkward seconds John shook it, frowning.

"I pray we can resolve this painful situation in a way conducive to the boy's well-being," Tim began. "Surely now is not the time to..."

"I don't know who you are, but Taylor's put you up to this and even if you're really a man of God, which I doubt, it's not going to work," John interrupted. "Taylor's not religious, so don't think you're fooling me. What a stupid joke. Now get out of my way."

Pen and Tim didn't budge, but Maggie and Isabel moved closer. Isabel was wearing stage makeup and a dramatic shawl that moved in the breeze. She glared in silence at John, Salome regarding John the Baptist seconds before the beheading. John scowled at her and I longed for a camera.

"I'm Dr. Margaret McFadden," Maggie said, reeking of nunhood even more than usual because she was wearing black, "long a close friend of your mother-in-law. I head the Interfaith Consortium and would like to offer professional counseling services for you and your family. Our staff are well-trained and credentialed and can help. Please..."

"I've had enough of this," John said, gesturing to the patrol car. "I'm here to get my stepson." He looked at me. "Taylor, bring TJ out here, *now*."

The two young cops got out of their car and moved across the grass, looking grim. No doubt their training had included mention of the fact that domestic disputes are frequently deadly.

"He's not your stepson," Jude pronounced from my side. "You didn't want to adopt another man's son, remember? He isn't yours and you have no legal right to do anything with him." Under her breath she whispered, "Don't let me kill the son of a bitch, okay?"

"I am acting as his mother's agent," John said, pulling a sheaf of papers from his jacket and shoving them at the cops as the phone rang. The phone clenched in my hand, set on speaker, the volume all the way up.

"Hello," I said, after which everyone heard Beth saying, "Let me talk to John, mom. And I don't *ever* want to talk to *you* again!"

"It's going to be all right," I told her softly and then Jill took the phone to my son-in-law.

"Bethy?"

"I've changed my mind," my daughter told him, perfectly audible through the phone's speaker function. "I want TJ to stay with my mother. I don't want you to take him to that school in Colorado."

"What do you mean? I've decided, Beth. It's the best place..."

"No. Just leave him there, John. Just come home."

The cops had moved between John and the group. "Was that your wife, the boy's mother?" one of them asked, and John nodded.

"How about you go on home, then, talk this over?" the other one suggested amiably, his thumb tucked in his duty belt, fingers grazing a holstered gun. "Things'll work out. Lotta nice folks here, willing to help. Kids'll drive ya crazy, but things can work out."

John seemed momentarily confused, then angry, and strode to this car without saying more. For a moment I felt a twinge of something – not sympathy but a kind of sad curiosity. What would it be like to be deaf and blind to everyone's story but your own? I noticed Tim on his cell and minutes later Angie arrived in her car, bearing a box of ham and cheese croissants.

"I was parked around the corner," she told me. "Tim and I talked it over and agreed that I'd probably lose it and do a full-body tackle on your son-in-law if I were here."

Pen ushered everyone inside and I went to get TJ.

"Everything's fine," I told them all as Seiji and Miyoko loaded the scooter. In the car I explained to TJ what had happened. "Your father, Tom, phoned your mother from Paris this morning. As your father he has the legal right to participate in decisions about your welfare. He does not agree that you should go to the school John selected, and explained his wishes to your mother. She then called my house, I gave the phone to John and she told him she'd changed her mind, that she wanted you to stay with me. John left, and that was that."

He was drawing in the dashboard dust again, not looking at me. "So did the police come?"

"They came, and they left after your mom called. It's fine, TJ."

"John is such a fuck!" he told the dashboard. "I hope my real dad comes back and beats the shit out of him!"

I pulled the car into the parking lot of a restaurant that wasn't open, and turned off the ignition. "I told you this was going to be rough," I said. "*Really* rough. It's natural for you to be angry at John; I have to fight those feelings, too. But this isn't about John, it's about you. If you let your anger at him take over your life, then all you are is anger at John. That's not much of a life, but you get to choose."

"But I *am* mad at John," he said, pounding a fist on his good knee. "He tried to get rid of me! You can't just stop being pissed off when somebody does that."

"No, but you can put the anger someplace where it doesn't get in the way of all the other things you are."

He was scowling, a thirteen-year-old mind trying to understand an idea most adults never quite get. "Put it someplace? Like where?"

"For now, how about the back seat?" I said, making him laugh. Then he pantomimed violently throwing stuff back there with both arms until he was breathless.

"I'm never getting in the back seat," he said.

"Okay, but later can we move the anger to the garage or something? I'd hate to drive around with it back there all the time, y'know?"

He grinned. "Grandma, you're crazy!"

I started the car and grinned back. "You think so?"

He watched me intently for several minutes before answering. "No."

So far, so good, Taylor.

"So when are you gonna tell me about Tom Jalland, this guy who's my father?"

I wasn't ready for that one yet. I had a house full of people waiting. But he was frantic to know something, anything, so when I pulled into the driveway I didn't get out of the car.

"It's complicated," I began, and he just stared at me.

"Tom Jalland and your mother were friends during one summer fourteen years ago."

He shook his head and grimaced the way you do at politicians trying to lie their way out of sleazy sex scandals. "Grandma, come on, they had to be more than *friends*."

"TJ, Tom is gay, and..."

"If he's gay why would he get a girl pregnant?"

"My guess is that he was still young and pretty confused."

"Was mom in love with him? Did she know he was gay?"

"At some point I think you can ask her about it. Not now, she's too upset, but later. I think they were very close and she wanted to help him, but that's just my idea of what happened. It may not be quite right."

"She wanted to help him not be gay?"

"Maybe. Later the two of them can tell you about these things. I can't."

"I don't think that works," he said thoughtfully. "We had a unit on it in Sex Education last year. Gay people are okay the way they are."

Thank God for sex ed!

"But mom would try to help, wouldn't she?" He was nodding as if at an idea that might just work. "She has a big heart."

And there it was in a nutshell. Beth had a big heart. It was true.

"Guess I'm lucky she does," he said, looking impish and wise. "I wouldn't be here if she didn't. So what else?"

"He's a college professor, he has a partner named Pete Salerno and he does these incredible arty drag shows. He dresses up like famous paintings and sort of teaches people about them."

"That is so cool!"

"It doesn't upset you that he does drag shows?"

"Well, I guess it's pretty gross for a *father*, but then he didn't know he *was* a father. But Grandma, a lot of gay guys do drag, and rock stars who aren't even gay. They wear makeup. It's for fun, to be dramatic. And you know... I like art. I'll bet I get it from him."

He got out and I popped the trunk for him, thinking it had gone pretty well. Maggie would pick a good counselor for him at her agency, and it would take months, even years, for him to come to terms with the complexity dumped on him that morning. But it hadn't been traumatic, so far. He wasn't going under. I allowed myself a vast, shuddering sigh and was glad to see Jude and Tim coming to help with the scooter.

"He looks so happy," Jude whispered. "How much did you tell him?'

"Everything, the short version," I told her. "I think he understands Beth better than I do. He said she has a big heart. And he's storing his rage at John in the back seat of the car."

"Can I put mine there, too?" Jude joked, looking different somehow. Thoughtful and *merry* in a way I'd never seen.

As Tim walked to the house with TJ, I asked her, "How did it go with Luke last night? I'm sorry I forgot, amid all this. What happened? What's he like, now?"

"Tay, it's like no time has gone by," she said. "We just... started talking like it was all yesterday."

"And...?"

"And he's not married, never got married, but he has a daughter who's thirty-something and works with him. He adores her. Anyway, we're going to take it slow, see what happens. But Tay..." she whispered, "I feel like he's still my soul mate. That hasn't changed."

"Wow," I said. "I can't wait to meet him."

"Oh yeah, I forgot. I'm supposed to tell you to go to the Hotel Del for a meeting. Luke's there talking with your friends from Boston about, you know, that thing, and you're supposed to be there. He said somebody else is supposed to go, too, and you'd know who it was. He'll be there all day, but we'll be together tonight for the show. You're going, right?"

"I think so, if TJ can make it. I'm really glad about Luke, Jude. How many people get the chance to reconnect like this? No matter what happens, right now is wonderful!"

In the house everybody was congratulating TJ on getting through an ugly crisis like a champ, and letting him talk about Tom Jalland. Much was made of the wall decoration, and Tim was eager to hang it until I took him aside.

"Hallett and Harry Laufer are meeting with Lucien Salnier, the folklorist who's onto us, right now at the Hotel Del. We're supposed to join them as soon as possible, but I don't see how I can leave TJ. You'd better go on."

"I knew they were here and that something was happening," he said. "I expected that we'd be involved. Angie and I discussed it and she'd like to stay with TJ while you're gone, if you think it appropriate."

TJ was flushed with excitement, but obviously shaky and worn out. I brought his antibiotic and Tylenol with a glass of water, and thanked everyone while urging him to lie down for a while to protect his broken leg. He'd be asleep in minutes.

"Father Tim and I have some things to attend to," I told him. "But Mrs. O'Halloran will stay here until I get back." I figured he'd assume the "things" we had to attend to involved his situation, and he didn't question it.

"Just call me Angie," she told him before Tim and I left. "And expect some killer French toast when you wake up. Can't let the rest of those croissants go to waste!"

The Syndicate all hugged me and left quietly. To Jill I said, "I'm sorry I haven't asked about Steve. I know he went to Betty Ford. Is he doing okay?"

"I think so," she said, smiling a little wistfully. "Taylor, who'd have thought we'd have to deal with... all this... at this time in our lives?"

"I think it's because this is the time when we *can*," I told her and then remembered Jude's remark. "We've been around the block so many times we can do it blindfolded backward in beach thongs during a terrorist attack while singing every word of 'Lollipop' in perfect four-part harmony, right?"

It was good to hear her laugh.

Chapter Thirty-Six

Eve of Destruction

Barry McGuire

The Hotel Del Coronado opened in 1888 and sits on a sandy isthmus connected to San Diego by an elegant bridge spanning the bay. The Del has hosted sixteen presidents, countless movie stars, Edward, the Duke of Wales, and the woman for whom he would abdicate the throne of England, the divorcee Wallis Simpson, a Coronado resident. The Hotel Del is haunted by the ghost of Kate Morgan, a young woman who checked in on November 25th, 1892, waited four days for a lover who never showed up, and early on November 29th was found dead of a self-inflicted gunshot wound on the hotel steps. But its alluring past paled beside that morning's meeting beneath the grand old Victorian's peg-and-glue beams.

"Revenants are a threat to consensual reality," Luke Salnier was saying as Tim and I entered Hallett's suite. Salnier was stretched on the carpeted floor with Hallett and Harry Laufer, watching an electric train move around an oval track. I could smell the chemical steam emerging from the black Lionel engine, but was more drawn to the miniature train station. There was a water tower, a livery stable and a shop with a cigar store. Nobody touched the train, and as they all stood to greet us, it vanished.

Hallett introduced Harry to Tim, and then Luke Salnier introduced himself.

"That train was in the window of Doucet's Hardware Store every year at Christmas," he told me and Tim, grinning. "Harry… *brought* it for me. When I was a kid I'd stand outside for hours watching it. God, how I wanted a train like that! I'm Luke Salnier and I'll do anything I can to help y'all."

Tim and I had been stuck in rush-hour traffic getting to Coronado and I was already exhausted from having been up all night, but the room was charged with a zingy energy that woke me up. "I've heard so much about you," I told Luke.

"Ah, you're my Judy's friend," he answered with a warmth suggesting mutuality in Jude's soul mate thing. But *Judy*? He had a bit of an accent, a deep, weathered tan and was dressed in a three-piece suit complete with cuff links and a collar pin. The dark curls that had captured Jude's attention forty years ago were shot with gray, but he moved with the lanky, awkward grace of a kid.

"Luke may have a better understanding of us than *we* do," Hallett said. "We haven't spent whole lifetimes studying inexplicable things, but he has."

Tim was smiling at the carpet. "Maybe one more look at that train," he said, and out of nowhere it was back! Only this time the steam locomotive pulled cattle cars and a red caboose past an adobe station with a hitching post, horses, cowboys and Indians. The cigar store was now an office under a sign announcing "U.S. Marshall."

Everybody dropped to the floor to admire the now-westernized toy as Luke whistled in admiration. "You did that!" he addressed Tim, who nodded gleefully before the little train again dissolved into thin air. Harry had begun the game in summoning Luke's childhood memory, Tim had altered it. I caught a spirit of childlike glee dancing in hotel-room air. A wish to show off for Luke Salnier, who was not a Revenant but got a kick out of our antics.

"I heard about Martine from the family of a woman who vanished from her home up in Natchez," he told us after we'd abandoned the floor for chairs. "The story was that somebody named Martine gave her a piece of lace and told her to fight something horrible."

A lop-eared rabbit in lace collar and cuffs hopped across the carpet and evaporated as Hallett smiled. Luke watched it, delighted.

"Her grandson's wife is a friend of my daughter, and Solly, that's my daughter, Solange, told me about it. Solly works with me on the website, we co-author books, she does a lot of the speaking tours now, a real chip off the old block. I drove up to Natchez to investigate and knew right away the story was different, so I put it up on my website and blogged it, asking for information, similar stories. The next thing I know I get a phone call from a woman who broke my heart forty years ago, asking me to pull the story, which I did.

On the marble coffee table a pink princess telephone appeared, rang once and disappeared. I thought Jude would have had exactly that phone, and made it appear. It was fun.

"But culling my material won't do much good," Luke went on, shaking his head and grinning at the coffee table. "Once something is on the Web it spreads, takes on a life of its own. And now that I understand what's happening I urge you to take a more aggressive approach. Any protection afforded by secrecy is short-lived. And I'm afraid you really do need protection. The Natchez woman hasn't been found."

The rest of us exchanged a look he didn't miss. "You know something," he said, suddenly acute. "What is it? Where is she?"

Harry glanced at Hallett, who whispered, "I can't," walked from the room to an adjacent bedroom and closed the door. Harry told Luke of Phillip's fate, bleakly conjecturing that others who didn't fight almost certainly perished.

"The ghoul is the magnetic opposite of each Revenant," he explained. "But rather than repel, it consumes. For no reason except that it can. That's the horror of it – it's dreary, absolute pointlessness."

Luke shook his head, not comprehending.

"If there is any message in the anadrome, 'live/evil,'" Harry said, "the ghoul is its negative illustration. The Natchez woman will have perished in ways we cannot imagine."

Luke was pale beneath his leathery tan. "I didn't realize…"

"Do you think you can help us?" Tim asked as Hallett rejoined the group.

We stopped showing off then, and answered Luke's questions for hours, sparing no detail. After lunch he answered Tim.

"We must consider," he explained, "what it means that this entity *only* attacks people who are beyond the normal age for reproduction. That this cohort is its *only* conduit to the heart of human life."

"And children," Tim said. "They sense it, always have."

"But they are protected by innocence," Luke insisted. "No Revenant retains that quality, or should. Now this force gains access through wisdom, not innocence, and wisdom affords no protection."

Harry tugged at his earring. "We have another sort of protection against the ghoul. Remember Frederic Langelin and his nightmare mice. I think our greatest threat lies in possible exploitation by agents of power – governments, corporations."

Luke stood and strode to observe the Pacific Ocean beyond the window. "I will publish information defining the Martine tale as an elaborate hoax," he said. "I am regarded as a reliable expert on contemporary folklore and will be taken seriously, but the ploy will only buy time. However, there's something you're unable to see."

Hallett joined him at the window, where the afternoon light cast them both in silhouette. "What?" she asked.

"That when the truth is known – that something is draining

the very soul of life itself through Revenants who do not fight it — the only way to preserve life will be to eliminate the conduits, who are Revenants."

"But it is we who stand between those who've come after us, and ruin." Tim answered. "We're the barrier!"

"Tim is correct," Hallet said quietly, "but the wisdom of his vision may not be as obvious to those around us. The scenario Luke presents must be taken seriously. If we are seen as bearers of a psychic plague rather than the only hope for fighting it, we will be quarantined, perhaps exterminated."

I couldn't really grasp the idea. It felt apocalyptic, fictional. I was too tired; I had too much to do. But a heavy darkness had fallen across the room like a shadow.

"There's time to build a defense, "Luke said. "Rational people won't take any of this seriously even when confronted with concrete evidence. You have that on your side. I'll use every means at my disposal to divert inquiry, and your organization can further that agenda through your website by reinforcing the idea that you're just a bunch of delusional old kooks playing computer games. Nothing will happen right away."

Everyone nodded somberly except Harry, who was grinning and rubbing his hands together. "We're fighters or we'd be gone by now, Luke. What you're describing, human intervention against us, is nothing compared to the ghoul. We can handle whatever happens, and your help will be invaluable. Thank you."

We left on that note, Harry and Hallett for the airport, Luke to join Jude, and Tim and I to return to the upheaval at my house. Harry had been inspiring, but after leaving the group I felt as if I were moving through gray Jello.

"Your friend Isabel was so kind as to give us tickets to 'The Fantasticks' tonight," Tim told me as I collapsed in his car. "Will you be there?"

"Wouldn't miss it," I said even though I was so tired I was dizzy. Maybe I'd take a nap. But TJ had slept most of the morning and was in high gear after Tim and Angie left.

"Does Tom Jalland want to, you know, talk to me or anything?" he asked before Tim had pulled away from the curb.

Maggie and Tom had discussed this during the night's long conversations; a protocol was in place. "I think he's going to call you this afternoon," I said. "Pretty soon, in fact." Then I lurched away to walk Sadie. TJ would need privacy for this call. When I got back he was waiting at the door.

"He did call, grandma! He said the 'piece' I made for your wall is really good and he thinks I've got talent. He said he was sorry he didn't know about me until last night and we're both in shock and need to take it slow so we can get to know each other when we're not shocked. He said he talked to Maggie last night and he thinks I should go to some counselor she knows because he had a really hard time when he was my age and he wishes somebody found a counselor for him. I told him I didn't need any counselor and he said everybody does sometimes and I should at least give it a try. He sounds pretty smart. He said we could email once a week but only in my spare time after homework and everything. He's going to send me an art book and some pictures of him and his partner Pete. And then..."

The barrage of words was like a fine rain as I stood, exhausted, in the hall holding Sadie. I felt like a statue, words falling and bouncing gently upon an empty bronze head in a garden. It was pleasant, but I knew I was going to have to rally and say something.

"He's seems to be a fine man, smart and interesting and funny, and the two of you may become friends over time. But remember, you're no longer a little child. He can't rescue you now, TJ; only you can do that by making good choices about the things you do."

TJ rocked his scooter thoughtfully. "He said it was okay for me to call him dad," he said. "Do you think I'm too old for that?" Insecurity swimming in those blue eyes.

"Nobody's ever too old for that," I said.

He nodded. "Cool. Okay if Seiji comes over? Then he can go with us to the play."

"Sure." I was going to bed.

But despite being exhausted, I couldn't sleep. The kids were moving stuff around in the garage, fairly quietly, and weren't the problem. The problem was that each time sleep tried to knit up my "ravelled sleave of care," a stitch got dropped and I had to start all over again. Had I handled TJ's situation the right way? Would my daughter ever speak to me again? What if John left her when he learned about Tom? It would be my fault; Beth and the children would have to be cared for. *By me*, and how could I afford it? Why on earth had she married that pathetic fool in the first place? But he wasn't a total nightmare; he didn't drink, didn't beat her. What did I want? And as TJ said, Beth has a big heart. But things would get worse for all of us if Luke's prediction came to pass. Except we had time to avert that, he'd said, and Harry was so confident. But what if it happened? How long did we have?

I drifted into that queasy late afternoon sleep that isn't really sleep because the light's wrong, the sounds and scents of daytime too pressing. You know you're asleep, but the awareness signals that you're not. I could hear the kids messing around in the kitchen, making sandwiches, as a dream struggled at the edges of my mind. A dream ripe with the smell of persimmons.

I was a child again. I'd come home from my half-day kindergarten where we'd colored pictures of traffic lights – red at the top, yellow in the middle and green at the bottom. The traffic lights weren't interesting like my coloring books at home, offered no story except that you were supposed to obey the colors when crossing the street, which I thought surely everyone already knew. I handed my mother my traffic light picture, changed to play clothes and wandered outside, but none of the neighbor kids were around. The older ones were still in school, the younger ones probably napping. The tree-lined residential street was eerily quiet beneath an autumn sun.

I traveled the sidewalk, tracking fallen golden rain tree pods, which made a satisfactory popping sound if you stepped on them just right. When I looked up I was at the corner where an old, two-story house built of local limestone sat on a raised lot. The owner lived on a farm and rented out this "city" property, and my dad said nobody stayed there very long because it was impossible to heat. When it was empty we kids would play castle on its stone-walled porch. But it wasn't empty then, because another family had recently moved into it, including a pale boy named Eddie who sat at a table in front of me in kindergarten. Eddie wasn't very clean and cried all the time, but I thought maybe he'd come out and play.

There were two big persimmon trees in the sloping yard of the stone house, overgrown and thick with fruit. Crushed and rotting persimmons littered the sidewalk amid jumbled yellow-orange leaves. Scuffing my Buster Brown shoes through the mess sent cascades of peach-pumpkiny scent to ride the still air as I climbed the steps toward the house. There was somebody there, half-hidden behind one of the limestone porch columns. It was a man and something was wrong with him. I thought it must be Eddie's father because his hair was the same oily tan color as Eddie's, and his clothes weren't clean.

He was rubbing his stomach down low by his legs, and his eyes looked funny, like he was praying and laughing at the same time, only the prayer and the laugh were inside out. They were bad.

"Hey, girlie," he whispered, beckoning toward his stomach and a purple thing sticking out like the insides of an animal that got run over by a car, "come on over here. Just for a minute, girlie. I won't hurt ya."

I thought he'd been run over by a car and his insides were falling out, but that didn't seem right, and a sick feeling roiled around me like the scary, cold stink of toilets in gas stations. Except all I was really smelling was persimmons, their scent making a picture in the air. The picture said this man wanted to tear apart the street and the trees and the sky. He wanted to tear apart my house and my little table by the window where my crayons and my coloring books were. The picture said I couldn't color anymore at my table because it would be gone. The window, too. And my parents would go far away and I would be all alone. It said I could *never* be a little girl again, but would be a bad thing, like the man.

And I ran. I ran home sobbing and stumbling and choking and it was a long time before I could tell my mother about the man. When I did, I could feel her change into something crackly like lightening. She gave me a Popsicle and told me to color at my coloring table, but I could hear her unlock the chest in their bedroom where I was never allowed to go because there were guns in the chest. I heard the snick of metal and watched her stand motionless at the front screen door, staring up the street at the stone house. She just stood there with a revolver in both hands, the barrel pushing against the screen. She stood there for a long time, like she was deciding what to do. Then she put the gun in her apron pocket and called my father on the phone. In the dream I heard her voice, but then I was awake and the voice was mine, keening softly in a California dusk my mother never saw.

The dream was no dream, but a memory. Or part of it was. The events happened, but how could a five-year-old see the ruin of childhood inherent in the diseased soul of a man? But I had seen that ruin, hadn't I? And the vision was back, riding a scent of persimmons to threaten now the ruin of adulthood, the literal spine of ongoing life.

Eddie's father was a pestilence that, unchecked, would mutilate the nature of innocence. But he was only a caricature of the threat now looming – a beast determined to mutilate the nature of wisdom.

The dream was revelatory, at least about why my ghoul bore the remembered scent of persimmons, but it was also draining. I wanted to get back in bed, but remembered that I had to be at the Women's Club an hour early to sell tickets at the door, and dragged myself to a standing position. In the shower I ignored the "Donna Deanna Overture" humming in the tiles and tried to remember what happened after that day, but there were only images.

My father and some other men talking on our front porch before I went to sleep. My mother beside me in a rocking chair, reading "The Four Little Puppies" out loud and showing me the pictures even though I knew the pictures and could read the book by myself, even the fourth puppy's name, "Obadiah". Later I woke up a little when my father came home and I could hear him and my mother talking. The next day Eddie's chair at the table in front of me in kindergarten was empty, and no one was living in the stone house. Its front door was open and persimmon leaves had blown over the wooden floors. My father and I walked to the stone house and looked at the leaves on the floor.

"A very, very bad man was here but he's gone now and he will not be back," he told me. "You were smart to be afraid of him. You were very smart to run away. But you don't have to be afraid and run any more. The bad man is gone."

Of course as a teenager later I was old enough to understand what had happened. I'd been accosted by a "pervert," as everyone defined such things back then. My father and a number of other men, many of them fathers of my schoolmates, had tramped through slick persimmons and orange leaves to the stone house that night, and threatened the man. "Be out of town by morning." It would not have been necessary to say anything more, although I suspect that the demand was reinforced by some physical violence. Small towns then and probably now have efficient methods of justice that operate quickly and in silence. When I understood, I wondered what happened to Eddie. I still wonder.

After the shower I called Miyoko and filled her in on the morning's events. We agreed that she'd pick us all up for the play. I didn't trust my bleary-eyed self to drive. Dressed in my new outfit I felt marginally better and decided to relax and enjoy the evening despite the fact that I couldn't keep my eyes open.

Chapter Thirty-seven

Stay

Jackson Browne

Everything felt normal in Miyoko's car, a sensation I'd nearly forgotten. The kids were wearing their blue frog t-shirts and TJ said he wanted to make another one for Tom Jalland. Seiji had taken the gay father news in stride, but then Miyoko and her husband were terrific people. I'd mentioned to TJ that other kids might have stupid, hateful attitudes learned from their parents. He just looked at me in disbelief.

"Grandma," he pointed out, "I *have* a stupid hateful parent. John, remember? I *know*."

"Cool," Seiji said regarding the t-shirt idea, "except does this guy like guns?"

"Nah, he likes art," TJ said. "Think I'll put an Indian design on his instead of guns."

"Hey, can I have one like that, too?" Seiji asked.

"Sure," TJ said. "Guns are way juvenile."

Miyoko kept looking straight ahead, but grinned and gave me a thumbs-up in the darkened front seat. Progress, definitely.

But something felt strange as we parked and walked to the Women's Club. I couldn't pin it down, it was something in the air. A scent, overly sweet and foul, like... rotting persimmons.

Oh, shit!

Except I wasn't alone. The thing couldn't come after me in the middle of a crowd. I chalked the smell up to something drifting up from the ocean below. Somebody burning trash on the beach, a dirty fishing boat anchored close to shore. I chose not to acknowledge that the scent was neither fire nor spoiled fish, and focused instead on faking a springy, athletic walk to mask my exhaustion.

Once inside I was caught up in a whirl of activity. Still, I noticed that the Lincrusta leaves on the wall, elaborately ruffled acanthus, now resembled the droopy, oval leaves of the persimmon tree. And they were moving slightly, as if the walls of the old building were breathing. I told myself sleep deprivation was distorting my vision, but the leaves still moved and I felt an enervating chill.

Isabel and the cast were in costume and makeup, roaming around nervously and giving contradictory orders. "Put the ticket table there, and the refreshments against the wall. No, that wall's too close to the restrooms; put it on the other side." Seiji and I were struggling to set up a heavy table with collapsible legs when Nick Mautner appeared and accomplished the task easily.

"How's it going?" he asked. "You look a little beat."

"Up all night, but disaster has been averted, for the moment," I told him. "By the way, you look terrific in black!" I felt strange, as if the room were two things at once. One, a pleasant but fast-moving reality in which I seemed to be chatting with an attractive man in a Zorro costume. The other a shifting, queasy space of leafed walls behind which something breathed, and waited. It made me dizzy.

Nick did a brisk military bow, doffing his velvet cap and swirling a voluminous black cape. "M'lady," he pronounced and then went to help Isabel with the sound system.

"I think Nick likes you," TJ observed from his scooter.

I was busy writing numbers for the raffle on the backs of tickets with a felt-tip pen. "Don't be silly," I said, feeling an uncharacteristic glow at the idea.

He grinned. "I'm not."

Tim and Angie arrived, the priest in full cowboy costume, followed by Pen and her husband, and after that a sell-out crowd that thrilled Isabel.

"We need more chairs," she yelled. "Does anybody know what the fire code says? How many people can we pack in here?"

It was standing room only, and as the lights dimmed I stood in the wings checking out the crowd although I was so tired I had to squint to focus my eyes. TJ and Seiji waved from the front row, the Syndicate were all there, and only when I saw Molly Palmer with a pony-tailed man in a black t-shirt, jeans and a tuxedo jacket did I remember I'd given her a couple of tickets. I caught her eye, waved and then drew a sharp breath as a familiar figure appeared in the darkened aisle beside Molly.

The figure's red-gold hair and coffee-brown eyes were the same, but instead of lacy peach silk she was wearing an iridescent fox-brown Pierrette costume with gauntlet sleeves and a huge black bow. It was Martine! Of course that's where she would show up. Beside Molly, whose gift for dance had opened a door in my mind and shed light on a path I didn't even know was there.

As the overture began, Martine nodded slowly to me, her eyes phosphorescent in the dark. Then she vanished, and Nick's voice draped the room in velvet. "Try to remember," he sang, and I thought of Tim in the park that morning, Angie playing Bach, a journey to a museum that didn't exist. Except it did. And so did Martine, a grown-up character from a children's book. But why was she there?

After that I was busy with Jude, supervising costume changes and buoying the actors backstage. I was running on fumes, so tired I could feel the backs of my eyes moving against bone, but the momentum of the event seemed to keep me functioning. The entire world has seen *The Fantasticks* at least five times, but in the ancient costumes the story assumed the atmosphere of a medieval carnival in which profundities leapt and fell like pins in the sparkling hands of jugglers. At intermission people were raving, and Isabel was delighted. A reporter from a local paper wanted to do a story on Nick, and interviewed the kids who played Louisa and Matt.

The second act was flawless, and in celebration the performers decided to wear their makeup to the cast party at a nearby restaurant. The Syndicate were all going, Miyoko and the boys, Tim and Angie, even Molly and her husband, who didn't know anybody but me and didn't seem to care. Everybody was coasting on the music, the fun, the success of the show. I was running on nothing but adrenalin but wasn't about to miss the party.

"You and the kids go on," I told Miyoko in the warm afterglow of the empty theater. "I have to close out the costume inventory. I'll catch a ride in a few minutes."

Jude and I worked backstage, making sure all the masks, capes, shawls and shoes were accounted for. She exuded a sort of bewildered calm I'd never seen before, unquestionably a reaction to finding Luke again and wondering what it meant. When she left with Luke for the party I felt like throwing rice at them just to reinforce the possibility, but their sudden absence left an emptiness that hummed I my ears. I shook my head to dispel the feeling and headed down the apron steps toward the hall outside. I could hear Isabel holding forth in the lobby. I'd get a ride with her.

The taped accompaniment was still playing from speakers on the stage, the music eerie without the sung melodies. Empty now, the big room was filling with shadows as I glanced back at the stage and noticed a small black shape on the boards. One of the shoe rosettes, I thought, and dragged myself back up the steps to the stage. Isabel had been adamant about accounting for every shred of the expensive costumes, and had made me responsible.

I was sick of being responsible for the whole damn world, sick of my daughter's weakness, sick at the prospect of trying to raise TJ at this stage of my life. One more little piece of an elaborate costume from a time five hundred years in the past was meaningless, irrelevant. I was so tired I felt nauseated and fell into that default setting in which you just blank out and automatically do what you always do. In this case that meant following through on my promise to Isabel. I'd rescue the damn shoe decoration and put it back, carefully documented, with whatever costume it belonged to. Everybody would be gone by the time I located the right costume and I'd have to call a cab to get to the party. Whatever, I was too exhausted to care and sighed as I bent to retrieve the rosette.

But when I touched it, my hand froze. The black satin rose was no longer lying on the stage floor, but attached to a pointed black shoe below a leg in striped stockings and harlequin pantaloons. And the stench of rotting persimmons billowed from it like smoke. I knew what it was.

"You!" I whispered, struggling to stand upright. Before me was a harlequin in the traditional bright patchwork and the plague doctor's mask, its hooked beak only inches from my face. I was gagging on its smell and terrified of the unfathomable emptiness I saw behind the mask. There was nothing there, only a magnetic emptiness that swirled and mocked every thought to silence.

On its head three bells on a jester's cap made a sound like Pachelbel's Canon played on a music box. The wistful melancholy of the tune brought tears to my eyes as it impossibly melded with the taped music still coming from the speakers. I had always loved the Canon, but now each note fell flat and somehow profane, the music of boredom, stupidity, the cruelty of the mindless. The sound spilled throughout the million threads of my nervous system like vapor. I *was* the music, and its message was simply the truth – that life is ephemeral, empty and wracked with pain.

Beneath the mask a hollow presence reeked of autumn fruit, its scent hurled across time from my first experience of evil. I had run then, to those whose task was to protect me. A woman at a screen door with a gun. A man who stomped through leaves at night and drove evil away. They played their roles well, and I grew up unscathed. But they were gone, and the evil at its fetal stage in an obscenity was now grown to a maturity commensurate with my own. It reflected every cruelty, every ignorance, every hopeless horror I had seen in a lifetime. I heard its mirth echo behind my eyes, tasted its petulant contempt.

I was ugly; I was old; I was a distasteful joke at the end of a meaningless life. I saw myself in diapers and patchy hair, holding a dead dog and drooling vacantly over a cruciform table to which TJ lay strapped. He wore a prisoner's blue denim shirt, an i.v. line still hanging from his arm. His eyes were vacant, and a chemical haze seeped from his ears, the cuffs of his shirt. The haze smelled like burnt persimmons, and I saw that everything I had done in my life was useless, led nowhere, had no effect on anything.

But deep inside me something coiled and writhed and then leaped into the music mapping my body, colonizing every nerve. Sad, repetitive, chromatic music that I loved, its message unerring through each key change. But it *was* a message. Even sadness was a message; feeling *anything* was a message. The music had meaning, and in that quality I knew that it defied the ghoul. It always had: it always would.

"You lie!" I yelled and with all the strength I had, I grabbed at the beaked mask, but the ghoul jerked away like a fish, lithe and mocking. "There cannot be *nothing*; it's impossible." I kicked, pulling dregs of strength from bone marrow, toes, teeth. I kicked and punched at an empty costume reeking with a stench that didn't fade but seemed to be moving into the veins of my hands, my arms and neck. It felt like a painful anesthesia distilled from rot, from every failed endeavor and idea since the first. It was a paralysis; I gasped and fought, willing muscle and tendon to move, but my body was a lifeless cage.

My arms and legs turned to glass, thick and cold, and I fell as the ghoul leaned close as if for a kiss, a rape, an annihilation. But Martine had been there, and in that moment I knew why. I remembered what I was, and forced one brittle hand to pull an old

Crackerjack whistle from its silver chain at my neck and shove it clumsily to my lips. The movement was glacially slow and burdened with despair, but I felt metal hit my teeth, dredged a last breath and forced air into a barely remembered toy.

The sound it made was faint, like a single, clear bell heard in an immense silence. Its murmuring resonance didn't stop when the whistle fell useless to my chest as I lay on the floor. The murmurs swelled to a chorus of bells, and from the darkness behind the stage I watched, paralyzed and struggling to breathe, as Barbara Stanwyck strolled majestically to the ghoul and ground her cigarette in its jeweled holder through an eye of the beaked mask.

The thing screamed, a sound like a thousand violins, untuned and bowed by demons. Clark Gable, still staring into the distance, twisted its motley arm until it broke with an unwholesome crunching sound. The thing's shrieks filled the old hall like tearing metal as Queen Holden babies in pastel snowsuits chewed its ankles to bloody stumps and the Mouse King noisily devoured its fingers. Harry Truman clasped its shoulders in pinstriped arms and crushed them together with a sound like wooden ships breaking apart on jagged reefs. John Wayne aimed his paper pistol at its heart, calmly pulled the trigger and merely nodded as torrents of iridescent black nothingness spilled from the wound. Kim Novak and William Holden, still in their fifties swimsuits, ground bare knees into its jester's cap, crushing its head with a sound like popping rain tree pods as the thing screamed and screamed. Then Buster Brown giggled, Tige barked, and suddenly the bells fell silent. The Kabuki dancer executed an elegant paper bow over the hollow mask and mound of bright fabric on the floor, then vanished. I was alone.

The paper dolls were gone, the mask, the belled hat, the striped stockings and motley pantaloons dissolved like mist. The music stopped, somebody in the foyer turned off the lights over the exit doors and I breathed clean darkness like oxygen. Then I stood, unfurling up and up as I did in a Yucatan horse barn long ago. I was alone; nothing stopped the fernlike uncurling of my spine in a dark that held me up, tall and unyielding.

I knew the horror would be back. As long as I lived it would follow me, muttering a desolate, hypnotic litany of death-in-life. I also knew I would fight it until I died, an army of symbols that comprised my life forever ready to defend me if I fell. I would do whatever necessary, become the guide Hallett Gardner described, do *anything* to thwart this thing that swallowed meaning. What had the origami dragon said? That the guide would be accompanied by an antiquarian and a warrior? Vivienne Geoffrey was an antiquarian, fallen into my life through circumstances sufficiently strange to feel destined. Okay. All I needed was the warrior.

A stripe of light sliced the blackness as one of the foyer doors opened.

"Taylor, what're you doing in the dark?" Nick Mautner yelled, turning the house lights on. "We're heading out to the party. I thought maybe you'd like a ride."

Ah.

"I'd love it," I said to an ex-cop Vietnam vet who named his dachshund for a military hero. A man whose baritone voice could frighten ghouls.

It seemed obvious.

ABOUT THE AUTHOR

Abigail Padgett is the award-winning author of the Bo Bradley mysteries –
Child of Silence, Strawgirl, Turtle Baby, Moonbird Boy, The Dollmaker's Daughters –
the Blue McCarron mysteries – *Blue, The Last Blue Plate Special* – *Bone Blind*
and the Taylor Blake paranormal mysteries of which *The Paper Doll Museum*
is Book One.

Made in the USA
Columbia, SC
10 October 2020